I0761607

ROAR of the LAMBS

ALSO BY JAMISON SHEA

I Am the Dark That Answers When You Call
I Feed Her to the Beast and the Beast Is Me

JAMISON SHEA

HENRY HOLT AND COMPANY
New York

To JXJ, the Bones to my Kirk,
for our adventures in Buffalo and beyond

Content warning: *This book contains body horror and gore, classism, racism and misogyny (specifically misogynoir), kidnapping, and a greedy tech bro trying to destroy the world. There are also allusions to transphobic bullying and the death of a parent.*

Henry Holt and Company, *Publishers since 1866*
Henry Holt® is a registered trademark of Macmillan Publishing Group, LLC
120 Broadway, New York, NY 10271 • fiercereads.com

Library of Congress Cataloging-in-Publication Data is available.

First edition, 2025
Book design by Aurora Parlagreco
Printed in the United States of America

ISBN 978-1-250-38173-6
1 3 5 7 9 10 8 6 4 2

Chorus of Dreams from the Gate of Horn

Yes, the moment shall decide!
It already hath decided;
And the secret once confided
To the keeping of the Titan
Now is flying far and wide,
Whispered, told on every side,
To disquiet and to frighten.

Fever of the heart and brain,
Sorrow, pestilence, and pain,
Moans of anguish, maniac laughter,
All the evils that hereafter
Shall afflict and vex mankind,
All into the air have risen
From the chambers of their prison;
Only Hope remains behind.

—Henry Wadsworth Longfellow,
"The Masque of Pandora"

December 1899

The young girl sat on a cardboard box, her short legs swinging absently, threadbare sandals dangling from her dust-caked feet, and she was half asleep. Not fully, though her mouth was slack, and her head kept drifting downward before she realized and snapped it back to attention. A sore spot ached on her scalp where it struck *hard* against the uneven cave wall behind her.

It was dangerous to sleep in the mines, she knew, in part because of the collapses and noxious smells and the way miners sometimes forgot she was even there and swung their tools too close. Once, she'd even been burned on her leg when a lamp was knocked over where she sat. However, the biggest danger came in the form of the foreman.

The man who gave orders in the mines, Mr. Beit, had a temper and a sadistic streak. Like many of his kind, he liked to see the discomfort of everyone who worked under him mining for gold, and he didn't change his position when it came to children. The last time she'd fallen asleep, she'd been yanked up painfully by her hair and struck with the wooden handle of a pickax. And because Mr. Beit was Mr. Beit, no one did anything, and she'd managed not to cry until she was out of sight.

She considered herself lucky still, to some degree—others who drew his ire were sometimes hit so hard they had to be carried out half dead. More than once she saw skulls opened, bits of brain swaying in the elevator shaft. The shards of bone and thick spatters of blood they left behind were quickly covered with dirt and gravel. And better this than fighting wild dogs for scraps outside the camps.

"Sofia!"

A voice bellowed from deep inside the mine, and that was her cue to move. She leapt from the box with considerable grace and darted down the row.

Sofia was the name she responded to, not because it was *hers* exactly, but because that was what Mr. Beit and the miners called her. She was orphaned young and didn't remember her parents, what they looked like, how they talked; whatever name she'd been given was long lost when they vanished, and the pioneers who found her in what was formerly territory occupied by the Portuguese deemed *Sofia* suitable. The young girl wasn't sure any name suited her, really.

And the only reason Mr. Beit kept her around, he'd made clear more than once, was because she was small and nimble. She didn't take up too much space darting through the misshapen halls and never stumbled over rock or made a mess. She was his runner, who took messages to camp, or to the Afrikaner soldiers, or to the leading laborers in charge of keeping everyone on track.

"*Sofia!* Someone bring me the girl!" Mr. Beit's voice was agitated, louder than usual, which meant that he was either very angry or very excited.

She swung herself around a tight corner and wiped the tiredness from her eyes. "I'm here, sir!"

The ceiling hung low and dangerously sharp, and the vestibule carved out before her had yet to be fitted with lights. Nonetheless it was bright. Perhaps *too* bright.

Mr. Beit, along with a couple of miners, gathered around a narrow crevice from where the light seemed to be shining, and none of them looked at her approach. The glow was stronger than any flame, any lamp, despite their depth within and below.

The girl had never seen *gold* shine like that.

It felt wrong, somehow.

As she took one small step closer, she caught a whiff of a sour smell. Like eggs, or meat gone bad and rotting in the sun. Even from afar, it made her nose wrinkle, not that she'd get any closer—her job was to stay out of the way. Also the laborers sometimes told fanciful stories of strange odors and glowing rocks, signs that told them to head back and stop digging. She thought immediately of gases they said could dissolve a person from the inside before they ever had a chance to run, or gleaming stones that burned skin off of bone.

Then why are they standing so close?

"Sir?" she asked softly, curious, craning her neck from her safe distance to glimpse inside.

The truth was that she preferred being a runner over the other use Mr. Beit had for children, even if it meant early mornings, long days, and very late nights, always at the ready. It meant that she didn't have to be like John, the boy who was even smaller than her and currently wedged between jagged rocks ahead. He moved slowly, carefully, contorting himself to avoid getting stuck or losing his find. Even from her place, she noticed his bare torso covered in scratches.

Her breath went shallow just watching.

"I have something for you to take to the site manager," said Mr. Beit finally, addressing her without looking at her. His gaze, like the others', was focused only on John, on whatever they'd found. The light made him look ghostly white, like sand. "Don't stop for a snack, to look at the blue skies, *nothing*. Straight there, and straight back, you hear?"

She nodded eagerly. "Yes, sir."

Sometimes, when the discovery was really good, he asked her to bring it directly to the American businessman who never came to the mines. He rarely left his rooms, according to some of his younger servants, and spent most of his time staring at papers. It had been weeks since the last discovery, however, a chunk of gold the size of her head, and though she'd struggled to carry it, she'd expected him to be excited. To look up from the letters before him. Instead, he'd simply ignored her *and* it.

Now she rolled her shoulders and schooled her expression, readying herself again.

"Well done, John!"

A skeletal boy emerged from what was no more than a thin slit in rock. He handed off the lantern he'd been carrying in one frail, brown hand and turned to carefully extract his shoulder and a sizable *something* that he held with the other. The vestibule grew brighter still, light crashing against craggy walls, honing their angles.

The young girl flinched at the same time as the others when it was freed, all turning away to shield their eyes.

A harsh, clean light flooded the vestibule. It felt like she'd risen out of the shafts into midday, her eyes taking a long time to adjust and make out Mr. Beit's shape. Sweat beaded his forehead, stained his dusty shirt. The other miners and John stepped back, revealing what the foreman now held between his big, worn hands.

A box.

Smaller than the chunks of ore that they hauled from the mine every day. Perhaps carved, its edges were too sharp, too perfectly straight to have broken off naturally from whatever luminous stone it was made of. The girl wasn't close enough to see any detailing besides a small gold clasp, but it glowed too brightly anyway for her to be sure of anything. So brightly, she shuffled on her feet in unease.

A wordless voice tickled against the back of her neck, and she whirled around to find only air.

"This is a bad idea," one of the miners muttered.

Another only shook his head.

"You people are always so superstitious," countered Mr. Beit, before swiping the sweat from his forehead with the back of his hand. "That's why you don't get anywhere. Let's see what we have here."

The moment he flipped the latch and swung the lid back, the walls shook. Stalactites speared the ground around them, felling a miner in the process. The young girl herself pitched back, smacking her temple against the cavern wall, and slid to the ground as a loud rumble tore through the mine. Her vision blurred from the pain spiraling through her head and also the light.

It swelled brighter than the sun.

So hot, her skin stung and her breaths burned.

Mr. Beit's shout filled the vestibule, rippling down the mining corridors, and the girl exchanged a glance with John that lasted only a second. A long second where she wondered if they were better off on the edge of camp with the dogs, if perhaps they weren't so lucky to be in the mines after all, scraped and bruised and dirty in exchange for stale bread and thin soup.

She decided to leave.

Then the ceiling caved on them all with a deafening crash.

CHAPTER 1

The Great Cassandra Is a Fraud

"*Am I gonna die here?*"

Winona Bray charged extra for death predictions. Every time someone fixed their mouth to ask whether they'd die young, in this place, and when, she insisted on a death fee to ensure at least *she'd* have enough to get out alive.

Fortune seekers drawn to the Red Hourglass were predictable with their questions, the nervous way they tried to skirt around what preoccupied and scared them most. It always started with love or money—whether to go on the date or play the lotto, take the new job or finally break up—but then, with their whistles wet, the people of Buffalo loved to end with, *Will I die here? Young? Please, oh great Cassandra, will you tell me if I see the world?*

Truthfully, all of it bored her, but it was good for business.

And right after she charged them their death fee, when they sat across the table from her, begging, she'd do what she always did: take their palms in hers, peer right past the depths of their souls, into the web of their futures, and then lie.

Winona Bray was psychic, but she was also a liar.

She dropped the customer's sweaty palms and wiped hers on the underside of the thick, velvet tablecloth. Draped in a haphazard way, it felt a little too expensive for this, and she couldn't believe Hortense would spend so much for such a price-gouging gimmick—an *illegal* one at that—but the Red Hourglass wasn't

Winnie's shop. Expensive cloth covered in hand sweat wasn't her problem.

Despite the setting September sun peeking through a slit in the heavy curtains, it was hard to see the young man. He was obscured by the thick haze of incense burning in each corner of the room, the plumes of black opium smelling musky and sweet, but still Winnie looked dead at him—at his greasy hair shoved under a faded beanie, the silver ring through his lip that was red, inflamed, obviously infected—and smiled.

"Yes, I saw your fate," she admitted, speaking slowly with a rasp in her voice and hoping the effect made her seem wise and mysterious. "It brings you to Cincinnati—have you ever been?"

At the mention of the city, his eyes gleamed.

She knew his answer already, the same way she knew other things he hadn't asked or said. Like his hair was overgrown because he was afraid of haircuts ever since his aunt clipped his ear trying to make him look like a member of BTS. He was a barista at a Starbucks downtown, which he hated, but only because the local spots wouldn't hire him. She knew that he would remain here for another seventeen years, driving down every day from that poor Irish corner of Tonawanda up north, until his dad got sick from all the drinking—*because what else was there to do here?*—and then he'd head over to the car parts plant out in Lockport and take over the shifts. The only reason he even wandered into this shop was because he choked on an ice cube last night at a barbecue, which made him think about death, and he'd parked so close to a fire hydrant just to ask his inane question that he'd have a ticket waiting for him when he was done.

Not that she said any of this.

He nodded stiffly, mystified. "No, I've never been, but my sister moved there a couple years ago! I keep meaning to visit. *Wow.*"

Winnie knew that he was going to die in Buffalo exactly the way he was born, crying in a dark car on the side of the road. Except this time, he'd be alone, wrapped around a telephone pole at age sixty-seven, and only his ashes would make it out—sitting in his niece's trunk as she drove all the way back home. To Cincinnati.

She was best at knowing the little things, all the secrets and bad details no one ever wanted to hear.

"Don't worry—you'll make it out of here one day," promised Winnie, giving him a bland, watery smile that made all her clients smile back. And tip.

This was why people came to her: to be lied to, to be reassured about the unknowable.

With just a touch, Winnie could slip deep into someone's past, present, and future. It wasn't the most pleasant sensation in the world, but it allowed her to see all the little filaments of fate that comprised a person. And while she figured it probably wasn't nice to charge people for fake fortunes, in her defense, getting out of Buffalo was expensive. The University of Cambridge, calling her name with their archeology program, a chance to touch history and tell truths people wanted to hear, was expensive. *Life* was expensive—she didn't make the rules or set the prices.

Most importantly, if Winnie couldn't see any future for herself at all, if her power never told her if she'd make it out, why should anyone else get to pay for that privilege?

The young man swayed in his seat on the floor, like he'd been holding his breath, waiting for a verdict. He puffed out his cheeks in a long exhale before finally grinning at her, and said, "You really had me going for a sec."

"People are like spiderwebs," explained Winnie as she climbed to her knees. "There's a lot of strands to sort through, so many points branching off, threads diverging."

Her clients believed what they wanted; they heard what they wanted. Winnie could go on the news right now and predict the weather perfectly, saying it was going to blizzard, and people would still head out in flip-flops and summer dresses and act surprised. That wasn't her fault, just like it wasn't on her to shake someone's shoulders and tell them they would die if they rushed to make that ten o'clock appointment—she'd already tried that before. Her family wouldn't ever let her forget.

"And what if you're making it all up?" the young man asked, chuckling as he stood. The tension melted from his shoulders. "Is there, like, a life warranty? Money-back guarantee?"

And though he laughed, he reached for her tip jar. Winnie seized his wrist to stop him, squeezing tight, and it started again.

In a slow creep, heat moved up Winnie's arm. It was as if she'd placed her hand on an old radiator, the fire reaching and reaching into her shoulder and sprawling across her collarbones. It coiled around her neck and inched up until it filled her mouth. Until it spilled from her nostrils. And then finally, the heat claimed her sight.

Let go, she told herself, though she couldn't pry her fingers away so easily.

Seeing into people was like being burned alive, and her reflex to grab the man was so sudden, Winnie didn't have a chance to fight it or pull back. With no warning, she couldn't do anything but look, and wait for it to settle.

In her mind's eye, she had to watch him leave the shop, curse at the ticket tucked under his windshield wipers, and climb into his beat-up truck with old takeout cartons and greasy napkins on the floor. A simple engagement ring had been sitting in the glove compartment for ages, filaments reaching out from there to connect on a worrisome blond named Lindsey, who—

Snapping back into herself, Winnie snatched her hand away

and tried to stop herself from glaring. Her face schooled to perfect calm as she pointed to the label on the jar. NO REFUNDS. "I'll toss you a bone. Lindsey knows you pawned your dad's war medals six months ago. You might want to give her the ring soon, she's planning to leave you."

Even through the incense, she saw him flush and rear back fearfully. It was easy for him to think of her as just another fraud stroking egos, but, like the rest, he certainly didn't appreciate the truth. After all, a seventeen-year-old Black girl from the wrong side of Main Street charging for under-the-table fortune readings in a neighborhood like Elmwood—who'd be expecting the real deal?

His fist tightened as if he was about to retaliate, before Winnie gestured coolly to the beaded curtains and the shop beyond. Through the windows, he'd just missed a parking cop's retreat.

"I can show you the pricing again if you'd like to ask more questions." Her voice was sweet, and she fluttered her lashes. This always worked to clear them out; people didn't like being squeezed for *more*. Herself included.

Anger fizzled out of the man, and he whispered his apologies and tottered for the door. And Winnie lingered there, kneeling by the table, soothing the flesh of her fingers until his touch faded. Contact always lingered after looking, like the sting of a sun rash, so painful it should have been visible. So she worked at the skin and slowly drifted back through the beaded curtains. She didn't watch him go, only listening to the bell jingle as the door opened and clattered shut behind him, his muffled curse that followed.

The stack of bug necklaces in resin sat exactly as she'd left them when he'd come in. This was the real reason Hortense hired her: The old woman's fingers weren't as dexterous with the rotating jewelry stand, and it was a pain to hang up scorpion-in-resin after scorpion-in-resin, thick spiders in glassy blocks that all had to be neatly arranged and facing front. The display was positioned right between the cash register and the little candy trays full of crystals meant to entice visitors. Sometimes, she liked to make up stories about how the scorpion served as an amulet to ward against Scorpios, how beetles enhanced hard work and endurance, because people loved deep shit without ever really *getting* deep. It impressed them enough that they were more likely to ask her for readings about love and death, and then she'd spin even more outrageous lies from a kernel of truth. As long as everything was on shelves and Winnie locked up at the end of the day, Hortense didn't seem to care.

The Red Hourglass felt more like a collection of curios than a shop to Winnie. In the display window, beneath the custom neon sign that glowed bloodred on the sidewalk like an omen, there was a little taxidermy scene of a fox chasing a menagerie of mice and rabbits through a field. On a table near the entrance, beneath a large bell jar, was a fully rearticulated python skeleton with a whopping price tag of $1,100. A giant tortoise hung on the wall beside a mounted stag's head whose eyes followed her around the shop. A rat in a red satin jacket smoked a tiny cigar right behind the cashier desk.

All fools in death.

There weren't only animals but also little bags full of rose petals and dried berries and shredded leaves. Tiny bottles of oil blends boasted creativity boosts or love spells, enhancing psychic vision or drawing in money. An entire wall of candles was arranged by color, including decorated saints, and the expensive ones were "predressed" with plants and herbs and spices and oils all around the top. More shelves and tables were covered in brass and gold idols Winnie couldn't identify, heavy sculptures of gods from all over the world at your service. She stacked cauldrons in a corner, polished giant crystals carved in the shapes of skulls and obelisks and cats in a locked case, and stared at the real, dead squids in yellow preserving fluid in another. Reference books and tarot decks were alphabetized in a coffin-shaped bookcase. A jar full of fake bird feathers always seemed to need replenishing.

It surprised Winnie at first how many people actually came in to buy things; every few days, there was always something new to stock. She wouldn't complain though—between the minimum wage Hortense paid and the readings she took off the top, Winnie would be on a plane out of here by graduation next spring.

She was squinting at an earthworm encased in resin that she'd unpacked from a box and held up to the spotlight, when the bell rang again.

"Welcome." Winnie didn't glance back and instead focused on tilting the resin, trying to find little blood vessels in the light. It was mostly indistinguishable brown, the bulb overhead spreading too much. "Let me know if you need anything."

Her phone light didn't do any better a job, so she hung up the necklace, chucked the empty box aside, and cut into the next. It was filled with dozens of bags of rocks, organized by color: blue veined with gold, green, obsidian, and gray, stones she didn't know the meaning of.

A shadow fell over her as she topped up a candy dish with little hearts made of rose quartz. The customer cleared their throat.

"You do psychic readings, right? Or am I too late?"

"Yes, I'm . . . ," Winnie started, but then froze.

When someone came asking for a reading, she knew what to expect: usually older, and either into New Age stuff, wearing something bright and flowy, or down on their luck, looking lost and full of doubt. Her customers often avoided eye contact, as if coming to the Red Hourglass, to see her, was something to be ashamed of.

But standing here was someone about *her* age, looking right at her.

"I . . . ," she tried again to no avail.

First, her gaze locked onto gentle hazel eyes decorated by a violent smear of black eyeliner. Light-skinned, probably mixed, their face was open and pretty, graced with long lashes, an upturned nose, and a cupid's bow. Such a striking face that made her mouth run dry. Her heartbeat climbed to a roar.

But then came the mullet, which she'd seen once at a distance, wavy hair dyed a repugnant shade of vomit green and trimmed on the sides. Several hoops and studs decorated their earlobes. A transfer student with the same look had survived only a week at her school before getting kicked out, and no one knew why. They'd looked like trouble then . . .

And they stared expectantly at her now. A dark brow raised, waiting for her to remember that they'd spoken. For her to pick her jaw up off the floor and stop staring back.

Winnie blinked and stepped away, unable to hide the scowl that overcame her as she moved around to the other side of the register. "I'm—I'm available."

She felt relief the instant her back was turned—she didn't like appearing out of sorts. Psychics weren't supposed to be surprised.

"Cool, I'm Apollo," the stranger started, offering a hand over the desk for her to shake. When she didn't take it, they curled a fist and gave a nervous laugh.

The motion caused the lime-green sweater hanging on their frame to shift, exposing jutting collarbones and delicate skin. Winnie tried to focus on the fabric instead, to tell if it had stretched out over time or was just bought this way. Probably the latter, considering all the shiny silver rings on their fingers, a pampered kid who could afford getting kicked out of private school, just trying to look edgy and buy a Ouija board they'd only use once.

"And you are?" they prodded.

"Cassandra," she lied. Her fake name was the only thing standing between Cambridge and her family finding out she was here.

She slid the box of crystals aside to reveal the pricing sheet and let Apollo scan the tiers. There were three: one question for $15.95, two questions for $29.95, and a full consultation lasting thirty minutes for $49.95, not that anyone was ever desperate enough to pick it. She didn't know anyone who'd pay that much for a girl like her to give them life advice.

"So, Apollo, what do you need a psychic for?"

"I'm actually here for my cousin—do you know him? His name's Cyrus Rathbun."

I knew it.

"Tall, skinny white guy with dark hair? He seems to know you."

"Don't know him," replied Winnie curtly.

She didn't make a habit of remembering her clients, but she did recognize the name from freshman year English. Her teacher used Alexander Rathbun's picture as the definition of *old money* when they read *The Great Gatsby*—the Rathbuns were Buffalo history, sinking their money into every nice building around, from City Hall to the Albright-Rathbun Art Gallery, and half the schools bore faded plaques with their name etched in gold.

So while she really didn't know *Cyrus* Rathbun, if Apollo was related to someone like that, she certainly could help them out of some of that money weighing down their pockets.

"And it doesn't always work, reading other people, but I can certainly read you." She smiled sweetly and looked at them. "I recommend the full consultation—everyone always has follow-up questions, and the charges add up. And for an extra fee of $59.95, I will lift the restriction on how many and what kinds of questions you can ask."

Winnie expected Apollo to bristle, to wrinkle their nose

the way rich people did before trying to haggle. Instead Apollo mirrored her smile, their eyes dazzling in the light, making her dizzy, making her imagine a razor-sharp wolf's grin. Then their chipped-black-nail-polished finger tapped on the full consultation anyway. Once, twice.

It felt like a challenge.

"One of these too," they added, casually plucking a crystal—a rose quartz heart—from the nearest tray and pocketing it.

With a swallow, she rang them up, keenly aware that Apollo watched her every move. Their gaze burned through the faded black university hoodie that she stole from her brother.

It unnerved her—Apollo watched her like they were waiting for something to happen, as if this was all a formality for something *else*. In the summers, her cousin Yas used to catch flies and pick the wings off, and she'd look at them exactly like this. Winnie's back itched where her wings would have been.

"Please follow me," she said calmly, nonetheless.

Back through the hanging beads, she led them to the reading room where the floor was covered in cushions of purples and reds and mauves, with purple lights and a humidifier behind every plant emanating a soft, esoteric fog. The low table at the center held only an amethyst ball on a stand, which was purely for decoration, and her tip jar full of folded bills.

Winnie sat on one side and tucked her feet beneath her. "So, tell me about yourself."

Apollo dropped quickly, ungracefully, and laid a small backpack at their side. They glanced around at the walls of weird paintings, the shelves of ritual things like drums and cymbals Winnie didn't know what to do with, and even the shadows, as if something might rise from them. Too suspicious for someone actually getting their fortune read.

"Shouldn't it be *you* telling *me* about myself?" they quipped.

She didn't laugh.

Apollo cleared their throat. "As I said, I'm Apollo Rathbun. My cousin is back in town, and he mentioned you, so I'm here to try this out. And you're . . ."

"The only psychic in the area?" supplied Winnie.

"Well, yes."

It sounded like an accusation.

Winnie clasped her hands on the table. "And what's up with your cousin exactly?"

Apollo brightened, straightening in their seat. "I've known Cyrus my whole life, I used to look up to him, and I love him, don't get me wrong. He's just not exactly . . . easy to know. You know the type: ambitious, always trying to stand out, only looking out for himself."

"What's wrong with that?"

They tilted their head like she should've known. "He wants my help. Like an unofficial research assistant for his PhD. I'm not in school, and so he offered to pay me and then split it fifty-fifty if we get rich quick, but I want to know what that thing says." They jutted their pointed chin to the crystal ball. "Should I? What if he picks a fight, and I get stuck with nothing? Or what if this idea is the next big thing that will change the world?"

Doubt it.

Winnie got these kinds of questions occasionally, people asking about their business dreams and genius inventions that they couldn't make work. Almost all that came to her failed. Maybe a Rathbun making it was more likely, but *she'd* yet to see a good project getting pitched at the Red Hourglass. People with good business plans didn't seek out psychics. If Cyrus had ever come to her, then the project was probably doomed.

Still, she held out her hand. "I'll need to see your palm."

"So you don't use the ball?" they teased, and leaned forward with a grin. "Or the cards—won't they say something?"

Why are they baiting me?

"Not for me."

She didn't actually know how to read palms either; it was just a cover to let her focus in peace, tracing the lines of Apollo's soft hand in hers. They were warmer than the last guy, very alive. *Bright* was the word that came to mind. The fire when she touched them jumped and spat as it barreled up her arm. It dashed into the crook of her neck, caressing skin and leaving her to choke on the taste of smoke, leaving the heat to warm her lips.

Then it stung her eyes, and when she blinked it away, Winnie saw Apollo. Standing over a white couch, scowling down at a flyer for the Red Hourglass in their hand. *Winnie's* flyer, advertising her psychic readings, that she'd warned Hortense against in case her family ever found out.

Why do they have it?

She caught the tail end of a conversation on the phone tucked under Apollo's ear, where their father warned, "You're going down the wrong path, and I won't tolerate it."

They only snapped coldly, "Good thing you don't have to anymore."

Then they hung up and went back to staring at the promise of a psychic consultant surrounded by photoshopped smoke, searching for something Winnie couldn't lock on. A door shut nearby. And spurred on by the sound of approaching footsteps, Apollo folded the flyer hurriedly, shoved it into a pants pocket, and rearranged their features to aloof.

Winnie shifted her gaze and followed a thread toward the future.

In it stood a house spotted in black. Ash and the scorch of old burns. The front door, along with all the windows, was boarded up by flimsy plywood. The stairs creaked as Apollo climbed the porch, following an older guy carrying a crowbar. He was just as they'd described—white, long-limbed and lanky, with the same hazel eyes narrowed to scan the area. He was at least a few years older, attractive in a disarming way, and wore pressed chinos and a watch that could easily get Winnie to Cambridge overnight.

"Are you sure it's safe?" asked Apollo, and though there was plenty more in their future to pick through, Winnie decided to stay here. There was something familiar about this. Something she didn't want to miss.

Cyrus pried the plywood away and shoved the front door open. In a chipper voice, he called over his shoulder, "Positive!"

He stepped into the entrance, over the charred, gummy remains of children's shoes littering the floor. Debris scattered with every footstep. The silence was dense, heavy.

"We just need to see what's inside. Look for anything worth something, in good condition, to sell before we chuck it all. And with your track record, what do you have to be afraid of?"

Apollo grimaced as they stood on the threshold, rapping their knuckles on the exterior. They pursed their lips at the comment, not that Winnie could see why.

The black-kissed brass numbers over the mailbox shuddered with their taps. *483.*

Stairs rose on the left, and a hall led all the way back to a kitchen on the right. Peeling, burnt wallpaper that Winnie knew had once been white felt brittle under their fingertips. The living room was covered in decrepit bookshelves, and the books once loved and well-worn were now little more than cinder.

Winnie ripped her hands away from Apollo. The connection

broke. In her sudden jerk, the crystal ball went flying and rolled across the pillows. She knew that house, those shelves, that wallpaper that used to be embossed. She returned to it often in her dreams.

It was *her* house. The old one.

"Did you see something?"

From the other side of the table, Apollo looked amused, brows arched and mouth lifted in a smirk, waiting for an explanation Winnie wouldn't give.

What could she possibly say? Their question had nothing to do with what she saw, and she didn't care about their cousin, whether Apollo would succeed or fail, if this project was any good.

What are they doing in my old house?

She grabbed the crystal ball to steady her trembling hands. The unease refused to settle, even as she told herself that it was fine. That it meant nothing.

That none of it was her problem.

"Yeah, I . . . I saw a lot, actually." Winnie's skin still smarted from where Apollo's palm touched hers, where the fire had started, but the cool of the amethyst relieved her. It helped get rid of Apollo, pry her back from under their skin. Give them distance. "Deep down, your cousin really does care about the family. Really motivated to take care of people. A kind heart, well-liked, and philanthropic too, even if he has a strange way of showing it. He's trying to make this work, make real change, and he needs people like you to help get him where he's meant to be. Loyalty will benefit you in the long run."

There, Winnie told herself. It wasn't her best work, but it was still a nice, neat lie, vague enough not to foment too much doubt.

"'Loyalty'?" Apollo repeated as they sank back, nodding. Then they broke into another grin. Harsh and sharp, like they knew she was full of shit. Their look was one Winnie feared but almost never got, so cold and confident, and the audacity of it from someone with her flyer folded in their pocket made her want to lie even more. Worse.

"Yes, loyalty," she gritted out.

For a moment, the pair glared at each other in distrust, neither willing to break. She didn't know what Apollo had come for, and quite frankly, she didn't care if they didn't believe her either. No one important ever did, even back when she used to tell the truth. Right now, all she wanted was for them to get out.

They climbed slowly to their feet. "You're such a fraud."

Winnie flinched. This wasn't the response she'd expected somehow. "No, I'm not—"

She tried to argue, but Apollo was already heading for the door. The chains on their wide pants jingled with every step, and over the din, they gave a calloused wave and shouted behind them, "Keep the change."

Clutching the ball tight, Winnie expected it to crack. Her indignation was mounting, but alone with her thoughts, it quickly gave way to something else—namely confusion. Why would anyone go poking around a house little more than ash with nothing left behind? Why did Apollo come here at all?

"*Fraud*," she muttered under her breath as she returned the amethyst ball to its stand. Then it was her turn to smile. "We'll see about that."

If anything of value still remained at the house, it would be *hilarious* to show just how much of a fraud she was by getting there first and cleaning it out.

CHAPTER 2

Not Even Fun Enough to Be Haunted

The Great Cassandra is a fraud.

Apollo hauled their luggage over the threshold like a body bag and tried to erase the psychic's face from their mind. *Heart-shaped face and clever brown eyes.* Like a gravedigger, hard but honest work, they dropped one bag and then another into the grand foyer of old Rathbun Manor and laid the lies from her full, pretty mouth to rest. No one worth their salt would say Cyrus cared about his family. That he was well-liked. He kept his distance from the Rathbun clan as much as he could, his parents included, which was why Apollo didn't understand his reason for transferring from Berkeley to here of all places while a term was already underway. For voluntarily staying in this house. When they'd found the psychic's flyer sitting at the top of his things, Apollo couldn't help but go poking around.

The girl was certainly pretty in a disarming, harmless kind of way, but also a dead end. The only things Apollo knew for certain were that Cyrus was here to chase some new idea, he wanted their help, and Apollo, freshly on their own, couldn't refuse.

They sighed, arms sore from carrying bags up the long driveway. From officially moving *out* and now moving in.

"Home, sweet . . ." They didn't finish.

Apollo called it Rathbun Manor because that was what their grandfather called the big, redbrick house scaled by ivy, a once-imposing estate locked right in the middle of a once-bustling city. Now though, Upper Bryant was quiet, a ghost of a neighborhood comprising the mostly empty houses that managed to escape demolition, now converted to offices or foundations bearing the great names of families.

If they squinted hard enough, they could see themself, their two siblings, and Cyrus running through the hall, chasing each other, screaming, *belonging* to a once-great family. Grandma Jean would yell at Apollo to mind the expensive vase, and Grandpa Ted would only laugh and pat Cyrus's head, advising him to mind the young ones.

However, when the memory cleared, there was only dust. It coated the lip of the door, the little stand where they set their keys, and the rug on which two bags lay. There was no noise, none of the laughter or squeals, none of Grandpa Ted's music in the study, their dad and uncle arguing from the kitchen. The lights were off, and the air was stale, and little Apollo had nowhere else to go.

They flipped the switch to the crystal chandelier, but nothing happened.

"Thanks, Cy."

Their cousin clearly hadn't gotten around to fixing the lights like he said he would. They were the only one he called when he'd landed, and they'd driven him in their run-down van from the airport to the manor none of them had set foot in in ten years. Not since Grandpa Ted's sudden death, and since Cyrus's parents whisked Grandma Jean off to California.

Apollo didn't know what went into setting up a house anyway, what else this place needed. They'd only glimpsed the living room last week, seen him spreading out on the couch with printed documents he'd called research—*what does a fake psychic in Elmwood have to do with physics?*—while they caught up and ordered pizza.

Or rather, *Apollo* talked, and Cyrus pretended to listen. They complained about their dad, the tight grip he tried to hold and how hard it was to know who they were when Apollo's parents were always *there*, encircling them . . . And something in that last sentence caught Cyrus's attention for real.

Their cousin had looked up from his papers for one human moment, nodded thoughtfully, and said, "You should move out. Stay here."

All Apollo could think to do was scoff then.

This place was a museum of their childhood, preserved and covered in musty cloths to prove it. Could they even just *move in*? But then Apollo considered that they'd just turned eighteen, that this house belonged in the family, and every day with their parents was hell ever since they'd been kicked out of school. Again.

Why couldn't they?

As if reading their thoughts, Cyrus had grinned. Lounged back on the couch, his sneakered feet propped on the coffee table and too damn close to the candles. "We could live here together! Housemates! Hell yeah."

"Hell yeah," Apollo echoed now, their voice a whisper, afraid to wake the dead as they stepped over their bags and got to work. Moving in with the cousin six years their senior *seemed* great when Cyrus offered, but now it just felt . . . drab.

Lonely.

Without any power, and unsure when Cyrus would return, Apollo was resigned to darkness unless they did something. So armed with their phone, they jerked open the cellar door in the hall and took one slow, careful step after another, light aimed at their feet to avoid tripping over their heavy boots. And as they weaved through shelves of lawn tools and cans of oil, they couldn't help but return to the psychic.

Specifically, how her eyes had rolled back into her head the moment they put their palm in hers, a cute trick they would have applauded if she hadn't called for "good faith." That wasn't what they'd asked, and it wasn't what they wanted to hear either—since when did good faith help anybody?

Apollo wanted to know if they were trading one prison for another. Good faith certainly never kept them out of trouble before.

They skimmed the wall of old wine, grabbed a bottle, and blew dust off the faded label. "Merlot," they read luxuriously, voice filling the cellar, before tucking it under their arm.

Then, continuing on their way through the basement, Apollo waved the phone light around for a circuit breaker. Power box. Whatever it was called. They stepped around old, broken furniture, chairs with missing legs, a discarded dresser, a table littered with broken glass that their twin Artemisia once dropped a toy on.

In the corner, behind a low dresser, was an arched door painted black. A large padlock sealed it shut, rusted but firm enough that Apollo's sharp tug couldn't undo it. They didn't remember this room, but filed it away to come back later with a key.

And after almost a full circle, Apollo found the circuit breaker nestled under the stairs.

Flipping all the switches did nothing. No clicking, humming, zapping sounds. So they flipped them all again, sighed, and settled on candles.

Apollo had tried to make it work at home, for what it was worth. They tried not to fight with their dad, tried to be there for their siblings, to get good grades and stay out of trouble, *blah blah blah*. But trouble always seemed to find them, single them out in a roomful of people. Things unfolded quickly, one instance after another of write-ups and suspensions while their parents and friends and siblings pulled them in every direction until Apollo finally snapped. Everything blew up, and when the dust settled, Apollo found their parents and themself on opposite sides of a war they didn't even want to fight.

Long ago, they'd thought coming out as genderqueer would be the problem, but that turned out to be far from it. Getting expelled back-to-back was.

This is not who you are, what you stand for.

Apollo's dad never considered that maybe it was.

Back upstairs, in the little room with the pool table, Apollo swept open mildew-spotted and moth-eaten curtains for the last rays of dying light. Then the lounge area that fed into the dining room. They circled back to liberate what Grandma Jean always called the reception room, the pantries and the kitchen. A solarium full of dusty cushions and cobwebs that nobody ever used. Yet no matter how many windows were uncovered, the house still felt dark. Dank. *Dead.*

And in all of them, furniture was draped in white cloths like misshapen ghosts that they also ripped off.

The alcohol stand in their grandfather's study was untouched. Collecting dust. Some of it smelled sour but still potent. Cigars seemed rancid and crumbly. The cracked leather chair squeaked and peeled when they sat, but it was still comfortable, nice-feeling. On top of the desk sat a badly tarnished brass paperweight in the shape of an apple. When Apollo pulled at the drawer, it didn't lurch. They tugged again, sure that the bending wood would buckle with enough force, only for the same result: Nothing budged. Upon closer inspection, they found little gold locks and scanned the room for a key. Dug through cups of dried-out pens and checked under musty rugs. They only managed to dredge up a piece of scrap paper behind a chair that read:

Co zeci uh Qsiyjybi, jy oya azjibhqezj?

"Gibberish," Apollo grumbled, tossing it aside.

Everything in this place was locked.

So they reached back, pulled a bobby pin from their wolfish cut, and inserted it into the desk lock.

Despite all their father's accusations, Apollo didn't actually know how to be a delinquent. They could throw a punch, clearly, but didn't know how to pick locks, though it didn't seem particularly hard—there were tutorials online. So they fiddled with the pin while they watched, feeling the ends catch . . .

To no avail.

The first video they pulled up was for beginners with a pair of thin metal sticks. Another recommended an eviscerated can of Coke, not that Apollo had either on hand right now. Frustrated and with nothing else to do, they ordered a hobby picklock kit to the house with the fastest shipping available and ventured on to the next thing. Their phone rang in a video call as they headed to the second floor.

"If you're calling to say you miss me this soon, that's kind of pathetic," they started, a wry smile on their mouth. They collected dust on the warped banister and rubbed it between their fingertips.

Artemisia, nearly identical and younger by two minutes, snorted on the other line. "I literally claimed your bed the moment your van left the driveway."

"Ouch."

Listening to their sister talk about her classes, Apollo opened one door after another in the long hall, scouting a bedroom they might like. Some had mold-ridden wallpaper and others canopy beds. It was a big house always intended for a big family, but their dad balked at the upkeep, and how little remained of the Rathbun inheritance to cover it. Grandpa had no money or trusts, it turned out . . . Just the house with its unsealed windows and sagging, cracked floors. So it sat empty, left to rot in an unvisited part of the city.

No wonder Cyrus didn't bother to lock the front door.

Coming here was just another thing Apollo's parents couldn't understand.

Artemisia read their silence on the other end and sighed. "You know you don't have to stay there. You can just apologize about Kavanaugh and explain the principal's ultimatum was cutting your hair. Maybe they'll understand."

Apollo huffed. The parents they knew weren't *understanding*. They didn't even stay in the room long enough to give understanding a chance.

"Maybe they won't."

They pulled back red curtains on a room with flower-patterned maroon wallpaper, a bronze four-poster bed, and the least amount of mold on the ceiling. No walk-in closet, but a private bathroom to cover in green hair dye seemed like a good deal. A standing mirror, horribly dusty and hauntingly opaque despite the cloth that had been thrown over it, was shoved in a corner.

All theirs.

"I can come with you; I'm sure there's room—"

"You know you can't." They left the curtains open, hoping sunrays would kill the musty stench, and scanned the hall for linen closets. "This is where the family rejects live. I need somebody talking me up on the inside."

She laughed because it was true—she was their parents' golden child in a way Apollo and their brother weren't. Artemisia could do no wrong, ever. She was sweet and kind and smart, while Apollo only knew how to bite, and ironically Orion wasn't very bright. The "understanding" parents she thought of hadn't even *spoken* to Apollo in days, not since they said they were moving out.

"Besides," Apollo added with a grimace, "this place sucks."

"Oh yeah?" she asked, shuffling on her end so that all Apollo saw was the kitchen ceiling and the wavy end of her ponytail as she fetched a snack. "How's Cyrus?"

They shrugged, their fingers trailing down the hall as they perused. "Not here. And the house is moldy, dusty, dark—none of the lights are on yet." They climbed for the attic and shivered. Maybe they'd find some spare blankets, candles, anything to make this place hospitable. "And it smells funky. No Wi-Fi, obviously."

Even with summer warmth leaving the city, Rathbun Manor was unreasonably chilly. Did this place even have central heating? Still, it was better than home.

Down below, the front door opened. Cyrus shouted a curse as he stumbled on the bags they'd left lying in the entrance.

"You're right, it does suck. Have you seen any ghosts?" Artemisia probed.

At the top of the stairs, Apollo pulled on a dangling string of lights to no avail. Not that they expected better. There were no blankets here either, only boxes and boxes and boxes. All of them coated in a thick layer of dust, but worth a try. Maybe Grandma Jean packed a stray candle or two.

"Nah, not even fun enough to be haunted."

Toggling on the flashlight again, they propped their phone on a stack and flipped off a lid. Curiosity soared at the box's contents—they'd all grown up so far removed from anything Rathbun, Grandma Jean so far away, Grandpa Ted dying when they were still so young. What was the old family like? What did they do?

Apollo frowned.

Leave it to the rotting house to layer on yet another disappointment: The papers up top were just deeds, contracts. *Boring.*

The next was filled with leather-bound notebooks, *TAR* embossed on the covers in gold. Their grandfather's initials. As they moved them aside, wondering why these were here and not downstairs in his study, they decided to add *keys to the desk* and *padlock* to the search list.

Only, in the other boxes were more of them. Dozens, maybe even a hundred notebooks.

Suddenly the light switched on.

"Found Grandpa's diary," Apollo muttered, flicking through yellowed and coffee-stained pages. Inside was neat looping script they didn't expect and could barely read, doodles and diagrams, the same arrangement of letters as that scrap of paper downstairs, and worse—mathematic equations.

Also boring.

Artemisia let rip a loud, demonstrably false snore and frowned. "Fine, I won't move in. Bye!"

Footsteps neared as she ended the call, the wood groaning underneath. Cyrus's head of disturbingly neat hair crested the railing.

Apollo angled to wave.

"Let there be light, finally!" Cyrus exclaimed magnanimously, spreading his arms wide. His grin was as proud as a child's. He nodded toward the boxes. "What's that?"

Apollo tossed the notebook down and shrugged. "Grandpa's journals. By the way, all the sheets in this place smell like old people—do you know where the extra ones are?"

As if transfixed, Cyrus drifted closer. His eyes trained on the boxes, on the journals inside, his hands outstretched. His fingers traced over the gold initials as if he hadn't heard anything Apollo said. Up close, he resembled Apollo's father, not just pale white, but even the particular loose wave of his hair, thick and black. He had the same square jaw, though he was much leaner. Taller. Their dads were also twins, so Cyrus could've been mistaken for Apollo's brother. And a better heir to Richard Rathbun than Apollo would ever be.

The look in his eyes wasn't like their dad's though. For all Richard's severity, his weakness was in his eyes, soft, fearful. Cyrus's gaze was sharp and incisive. Bold. The way Apollo wished more people could be, the way Apollo *strove* to be if they could help it, which was the whole reason they packed all their things in the first place.

Cyrus was so focused on the notebooks, lost somewhere in the promise of those pages, that he seemed to forget altogether Apollo was standing next to him. Vanished. Gone.

"Uh, dude?"

His head snapped up to look at them, blinking as if he'd awakened from a dream.

Apollo pointed to the stairs. "Linen closet?"

Cyrus nodded, giving the notebook a second, parting glance, before he brushed the dust from his hands and started for the second floor. "Right! Follow me."

November 1900

Scientia vincere tenebras.

Alexander Rathbun ran his thumb over the engraving on his gold pocket watch for the third time that afternoon and shuffled impatiently on his feet. His eldest son, Joseph, was due to arrive a week ago, but the boat to New York City and the rail thereafter were delayed, always delayed. In his impatience, he forgot to be angry with his impetuous heir for abandoning the mines in their sorry state and insisting on coming home early. He left the electric hansom waiting just outside the station entrance to prepare for their immediate departure.

Father, we found something, Joseph had written in a letter some months ago, alongside news of a collapse that killed thirteen. *Something that might change the world.*

Joseph was hardly experienced enough to even know the kinds of things that could change a world, but Alexander found himself curious nonetheless. It also didn't hurt that Joseph was his favorite of all his children, and Alexander had missed him so much. He didn't regret sending Joseph off to manage the mines they leased from the British South Africa Company, since it was critical that the boy learn the new family trade, and it did well enough for now. His son, and whatever was so important Joseph couldn't wait to tell him, was Alexander's greatest investment on their future.

So to quell his nerves, he turned his attention to the railway station where he paced, which was a poor excuse for a station if anyone asked his opinion. It could have been a beautiful building, a *feat* even among beautiful buildings, but instead it was squat, little more than a desperate wood awning entirely exposed to the elements. That was why he'd proposed a new Central Terminal—despite his own father's questionable dealings, people still looked to the Rathbun family for things like this. Alexander envisioned large windows to rival Grand Central, one that let in light to scatter over expensive marble. People would clamber here to see the massive crystal chandelier he'd commission to hang above the rows of seats—*real seating!*—and trickle heavenly rays down upon them.

The city deserved beautiful things to admire, and all Alexander needed to give it to them was a little more guarantee of *funds*.

Alexander had first proposed the idea with his father's support when he was not even a man yet, and it had taken him time to secure the perfect architect and draw together the plans. He reviewed everything, even though he didn't understand the details of architecture. Soon, he envisioned walking the grounds and overseeing the laborers. The Central Terminal would be his great accomplishment, his monument, one of the last visible contributions of their family to the city, and just as his father encouraged him, so he would now aid Joseph in his own endeavor to carry on the Rathbun legacy.

If the locomotive ever arrived.

All around him, the station bustled with activity, people scuttling to neighboring trains for their departures, to say goodbye to their loved ones. On account of the awning's low ceiling, voices and the sound of movement carried everywhere, tangled in the thick, dark smoke of the engines, creating the effect that it was busier than it was, though this was no small city.

Then the ground shook, and commotion stirred as a train

rolled into the station. Its great horn blared. Alexander considered making his way closer to the platform, to greet his son the way he wanted to greet him, with a hug and a kiss, but the crowd was off-putting. Lowly. A barrage of smells and noise. From the overpass, he watched people spill from the cars and onto the platform, a stream fighting against those shoving to make their way on. The rail would continue south along the lake to Pennsylvania, but like many, Joseph's final destination was here.

Buffalo.

Alexander barely recognized his boy stepping off the train—no longer a boy at all but a *man*, he stood tall and straight above the rest. He was handsome, though his dark hair was long and unruly, curling at the ends, and his complexion had bronzed from the southern African sun. He spotted Alexander eagerly and waved, pushing his way through the crowd and up the stairs to the overpass. The footman carrying his luggage fell behind.

But sticking close to Alexander's side was a girl.

A little Black girl, no more than eight years old and wearing a plain gray dress, following deftly except for a slight limp, while she stared wide-eyed around the terminal.

"Mr. Rathbun, sir," said Joseph in a mask of severity.

It took everything in Alexander to pull his gaze away from the girl and onto his son's face. Joseph held a stiff posture for only a moment before a wide grin overtook his unshaven mouth, and he seized Alexander in an embrace.

"It's about time," Alexander replied thickly, with mock scorn in his voice. "It's rude to keep your father waiting. I hope your travels weren't too cumbersome."

His son continued to beam. "The ship was rocked by heavy waves and storms the whole way, and I was sick for most of it, but I didn't care. In fact, we should open more mines in Africa and send me back to ensure they're functioning. I am an expert now." His blue eyes were brilliant with mischief.

"Is that so?" Alexander glanced around himself, around Joseph, to the two carts of luggage being pushed behind him, and finally to the girl. "And who is this?"

Joseph stumbled for only a moment before planting a hand on the girl's shoulder. "This is Sofia. She was one of the survivors from the mine collapse. We found her along with the discovery with her leg broken, covered in burns. No parents to speak of, and I was feeling charitable—figured she can learn to be a maid. A gift for Isabelle."

Under Alexander's scrutiny, the girl did not react. He figured either she didn't understand a word of English, or she was good at holding her tongue, but he wasn't interested enough to care which.

The discovery.

He smiled. "So where is this discovery, then, that you couldn't explain or even name in your letter?"

Joseph seemed to leap with each step, light on his feet and eager. "For reasons that will imminently become clear, I cannot show you here."

So they hurried to the waiting electric hansom. They took their places in the back, the girl situated beside the driver, while luggage was loaded onto the rear, and soon they were off. For all of its defects, the railway station was at least a short distance from the great manors that lined Buffalo's Main Street. On the drive, they passed the Kelloggs—to whom they were distantly connected through marriage, by the way—the Endicotts who worked in banking, the Darts in engineering, and of course, Isaac Hawley, whose great-great-great-grandfather developed the Erie Canal. And there, right on the corner of Bursey Street and Ashton Place was Rathbun Manor.

Alexander was told his own great-great-grandfather procured a high-in-demand architect, *the* Richard Upjohn, to design the home in the style of Gothic Revival. It had beautiful white detailing on the arches that framed the south-facing porch and even an oriel window overlooking the front. Their gabled roof was the highest and most striking on the block.

He and his son carried themselves inside, where Joseph was immediately ambushed by his youngest sister, Isabelle, who seized him the moment he cleared the doorway.

"You're supposed to be getting ready for the Hawleys' event, Isabelle," Alexander warned. The sharpness of his tone was enough to send the girl vaulting away, so that he and Joseph could help themselves to his finest bottle of scotch. As he poured, Joseph sent Sofia with the butler and instructed the journeyman to leave one of his suitcases in the study, and Alexander couldn't help but raise his brows.

The young man's energy was frenetic as he walked the length of the room, and Alexander's interest and apprehension grew. He had always known Joseph to keep a level head—even when he came up with some rash idea, he had a calmness to him. Yet he could not keep still long enough to sip his drink until the journeymen left and Isabelle was long out of earshot. He moved quickly to close the curtains and both study doors, one after the other. And when they were engulfed in darkness, finally he lit the gas lamps.

Alexander had yet to invest in electric lighting; just like the Central Terminal, he was waiting for the mines to flourish.

"When the mine in southern Rhodesia collapsed, the rescue unearthed something," began Joseph as he opened his luggage and sifted through his shirts. He left them unfolded and in a heap as he searched for what Alexander was sure was a precious jewel.

Then again, what else could there be in a mine? He hardly understood the secrecy.

"But the locals wouldn't go near it. They're superstitious—they say it's an omen."

Retrieved from among his clothes was a sizable object covered in a silk scarf. Joseph unwrapped it gently. Alexander's mouth watered as he pictured his Central Terminal finally coming to life.

"Now, the manager is of mixed heritage; his father was a Brit, his mother a local woman, so he was not as superstitious as the rest and brought it to me. And would you believe me, Father—I considered that maybe the locals weren't entirely wrong."

"*What?*" Alexander finished his drink in a rush. "What are you talking about?"

The item Joseph unwrapped was not at all a jewel. It was a box. It seemed to be made of antler or bone, too brittle to be any kind of stained wood, too off-color to be stone. It was carved on all sides with intricate tribal drawings that Alexander would have loved an anthropologist's interpretation of.

But still, it was merely a box and not a diamond or an emerald or any other jewel that the other mining families were finding their wealth in, like Cecil Rhodes. And for that, he couldn't hide his disappointment.

"Is this it, then?" he asked flatly.

Joseph's excitement should have been enough to make him enthused too, but Alexander had expected more from a son who spent a year there, overseeing their mining company in search of precious *gems*. Yes, the expeditionists came back with artifacts all the time, that was fine, but was this all?

His son shook his head, undeterred. "Watch."

Very gently, Joseph set the box on the edge of Alexander's oak desk, came around to the other side so that it was facing away from them, and unlatched the gold front. The metal was unusually shiny for something that had been nearly lost in a cave for who knew how long, though it was always possible that the locals were only lying to Joseph, to trick him with their wiles. He didn't expect his son to be so naïve, but he also didn't expect his son to come home so soon over a *box* and with a little girl in tow either.

However, the moment Joseph cracked open the lid, a harsh white light flooded the room. Alexander had to shield his eyes and step back.

It was like staring into the sun. So luminous that day had returned to the room from behind the heavy curtains. The gas lamps' flames flared brighter. Wind whipped through the space, ruffling Alexander's hair and the lapels of his jacket. Heat warmed his cheeks, his lungs. The walls of the manor shook.

And through it all, with dark circles under his eyes, Joseph was grinning.

It was only a crack, and he closed the box quickly and straightened. His smile, his restlessness, seemed more appropriate and contagious now.

"What was that?" Alexander blinked and watched the box. It was a curiosity, of course, and he understood his son's reaction, though he wasn't quite sure *what* he experienced. How such a small thing could produce such a monumental feeling.

But he'd get an idea.

The gas lamps dimmed slowly, returning to their original strength, and in the low light, Alexander saw his son shrug haplessly. Joseph took on a bashful coloring as he latched the box shut and undid the top button of his shirt.

"I don't know what this means, but I thought you'd want to see immediately."

Alexander clapped a hand on his son's shoulder, still warm from the thrilling heat. "You did a fine job bringing this here. It could mean a fortune."

CHAPTER 3

Not a Raccoon or a Mouse or a Ghost

The end of Heritage Street was a ghost town. Run-down houses sat across from a park that was vacant, and people avoided the area as a whole as if death was contagious, starting at house number 483.

Winnie frowned as she strolled through the field she used to play in. The massive fir trees had been cut down and uprooted, leaving no shade from the sun and only unkempt yellow grass lining the sidewalk. On the playground, the swings had been cleaved from their frames like meat picked clean from bone, and the plastic slides that once were vibrant shades of red and blue and green were painted the muted gray-brown of a corpse.

A cop car patrolled on the other side like they wanted to keep it this way.

"This is depressing," her cousin Yasmine remarked, adjusting the straps of her backpack. She was tagging along as the lookout, because Winnie wasn't sure she could be here, much less go inside.

Even if it was technically her house.

Yas had been waiting for her when school let out as usual; she attended Beaufort Academy, which released a half hour before Kavanaugh School, so there she was in her silly green uniform, parked right at the gates, asking where Winnie was going. Why Winnie couldn't hang out, when she already had Winnie's work schedule memorized.

Winnie was too excited to come up with an excuse.

"Let's hurry up and get out of here," she said now, picking up her pace through the park.

The other houses around 483 were also vacant. One's windows were boarded up, another's porch in disrepair, and all the front lawns were sunburnt and overgrown. Only one of them experienced a fire. Scorch marks framed the windows covered by plywood. Water and time ate at the stairs and roof. With the yellow grass and robin's-egg-blue paint, it resembled a corpse gilded with a very dirty patina. Ash, rust, and dust settled in the cracks.

"So what are you looking for exactly?" Yas asked, trailing along the side to the yard.

The gate creaked when Winnie pushed it open. She didn't glance back. "Mama's ring. We can't find it, and I think it might've been left behind."

Evoking the name of their dead grandmother was enough for Yas to not question further. She didn't really understand that Winnie was psychic; she seemed to believe that Winnie was simply *perceptive* with a side of anxiety and liked to weave stories. But it was just that—anxiety and lies.

So Winnie didn't bother mentioning the premonition of Apollo and their cousin, just like Winnie never told anyone the truth about her job. Yas thought she worked at a small co-op grocery store some days after school, and completely unrelated, now she was sneaking around her old house gutted by flame in search of a lost family heirloom.

In the backyard, Winnie drifted toward the garden shed and rosebushes. Or, what once were rosebushes. They were desiccated, spindly bushes now, long dead and not a blossom in sight. There was a dip in the soil where someone had once dug a hole and never filled it.

When their grandmother Catherine grew too sick to tend to her roses, the câre had fallen to her eldest daughter, Winnie's mother, though Winnie had taken over . . . But now, there was nothing left but brittle bones. Only the memory of soft pink petals and curious little Winnie giving extra care to one patch more vibrant than the others, Catherine with her sun hat and shears, seventy years old and tearing at weeds. That was a long time ago, scant images instead of rich memories.

There were old toy trucks and figurines still scattered in the dirt, bleached from the sun and ruined by the elements. Plastic enduring where the roses did not.

Yas picked up the truck. "You think Marcel wants this back?"

Winnie couldn't help but meet her gaze and snort at the thought of her brother's reaction if she brought it home. Surprise, and then annoyance when he realized where she got it.

She opened her backpack. "Throw it in."

The back door was hardly boarded save for a thin sheet of plywood across the front. With a rock in hand, Winnie nodded to show Yas to her post on the sidewalk, where she whistled and sang to cover the groan of plywood and nails being ripped away. The smash of glass and the trickle of shards falling thereafter.

The door ground on its hinges as Winnie pushed it open and looked inside. The house opened black before them.

Perfectly safe.

"In and out?" Yas asked, ready to keep an eye from the inside as they'd discussed.

She nodded.

It was an organized operation for such a nebulous reason: a vision of two strangers breaking into Winnie's old house, looking for something to sell. What, Apollo hadn't seemed to know.

But Winnie got here first, judging by the still-sealed front door.

The fire on Heritage Street had broken out in the early afternoon after Winnie, her brother, and their mother left for Mama's wake. She didn't remember why, but her father had stayed behind, promising to follow soon after—so he was inside when a sudden blaze tore through. From what little Winnie was told, there wasn't much to save: a few photo albums and birth certificates, some jewelry, and a singed blanket. All she had was destroyed, her father gone, and she'd tried to warn them.

She'd never seen the aftermath before, but ten years later, she understood why.

"Oh my god." Yas took the words from her mouth as her fingers pulled at the remains of blackened wallpaper.

They climbed to the main landing in silence, looking through gaps where the drywall had been eaten away. The railing and stairs were cracked and groaning with every step. Part of the ceiling had caved, charred wood planks dangling in front of them like a chandelier. Or rib bones.

The house was frozen in a scream. Melted toys and twisted garbage bins nestled in an alcove beside piles of ashes that once were carpets and laundry. In the kitchen, the drapes were etched away, and the dining table was cracked and broken. Her grandmother used to make them stay until they finished all their okra or pork and beans, even though Winnie had insisted ever since she was three that she was vegetarian.

"You should . . . ," Winnie began, gesturing to the front.

Yas extracted herself from the room. "Good call."

Winnie stared at the scatter of mixing bowls and appliances strewn about, the ruined remains of whatever her father was last up to. Was this where it happened, or did he try to flee? Was the smoke or heat worse in the end?

Her pulse hammered in her ears.

The report had been inconclusive, stating only that the fire began in the basement, and she saw the spot in the hall where it had gouged its way through the wood from below. Maybe Apollo's cousin restored and sold furniture? What would they think, knowing someone had perished here?

She didn't know why—she certainly hadn't seen anything—but her gut insisted that she start downstairs. "I'm gonna check out the basement!"

In the corner of her eye, she caught Yas waving, and then she doubled back through the stairwell and descended a level farther.

The basement was where the bogeyman had lived. Sometimes Marcel would call out to Winnie and grab at her ankles while he hid beneath the stairs. Once a light bulb died when she was down there, fetching fertilizer for her grandmother, and she swore she saw something move in the corner.

Today, with daylight trickling in from the soot-stained windows, there was only ash. No bogeyman, no moving shadows. Wire racks that once held extra food and water, heaters and blankets for the snowstorms were all overturned, folding over a steel table her father had used to prep his meats and fish when he went hunting. The skins he'd saved probably burned with the rest.

"Vseq . . ."

Winnie froze at the sound. *What is that?*

She ventured closer, stepping over beams, careful not to get ash on her Kavanaugh jacket or her mom would flip. It sounded like . . . scratching.

"Find it?" Yas shouted from above.

"Just a sec," Winnie lied, crawling over the tangle of racks.

The noise was the shuffle of something small, like a little rodent trapped in a vent or under debris and trying to get out.

Skittering, scratching, or . . . *whispering*. Something vying for her attention, demanding to be found.

"Vseq ebi oya qseq uh guwi ci?"

She froze.

It could be her father's ghost. Maybe he was trapped down here, maybe he'd died down here trying to put the fire out, waiting all this time for them to come and find him. To be reunited with his family. To shake his daughter and ask, *Why didn't you save me?* Because surely, he'd be angry to have this little psychic who'd failed to adequately warn them about the fire.

No one listened to six-year-olds. And back then especially, Winnie hadn't understood what she saw or how little anyone cared what she had to say. She didn't know how much fighting it took to be heard.

The scratching grew louder. Skittering, gnawing, screeching, it was the scrape of metal against metal. Of nails drawn long down a chalkboard.

"Vseq ebi oya qseq uh guwi ci!"

With a wince, Winnie stepped around a support beam, inching closer. Practically expecting to find a body abandoned ten years ago, or her father alive by spite alone. Yet there was no one behind the table or on the floor, and sitting on top, there wasn't a raccoon or a mouse or a ghost. No movement at all, in fact. It was only . . . a box.

And the moment Winnie laid her eyes upon it, the noise stopped.

Whatever was scratching, skittering, gnawing, fleeing went dormant, until it was just her breath and her, staring at this beautifully pristine, white jewelry box. It was unmarred by ash, though the table surface around it was coated. Not charred or damaged, not even by time or moisture, mold or mildew, rats or ants or raccoons or whatever else could be hiding down there.

"Hey, Win . . . ," called Yas, her voice close to the hole above.

"Just a second!" she piped back up, not taking her eyes from the box.

It looked precious, so important that she didn't understand why it'd been left behind. Was this what Apollo and their cousin were after? How could they know it was here? With every step, Winnie questioned more why Apollo came to see her of all people. Why they even needed a psychic, why her flyer was in their pocket. Was it for this?

The box seemed to hum as she neared, and glowed white as if there was some light triggered from within. The basement felt a hundred times brighter, quieter, since she'd noticed it. And it looked so *familiar* too. Winnie didn't remember anyone in her family ever having it—otherwise she would've coveted it—and yet she knew she'd seen it before.

Yet it lured her closer, like a dream.

"Winona! *Get up here!*" Yas's voice was insistent. A warning.

Footsteps and broken glass shuffled overhead.

So Winnie unzipped her bag and threw the box inside. Chucked right over Marcel's dirty toy truck and her already battered copy of *The Canterbury Tales*. Its material felt strange, harder and heavier than wood, both rough and smooth at the same time. And on the table, it left a perfect, rectangle imprint, as if the ash had fallen *around* it, but somehow not on it.

But she'd have to ponder it another time.

She fetched her grandmother's "lost" sapphire wedding ring from the pocket of her coat, jogged up the stairs, and rounded the corner.

"Winnie!"

Ever the liar, Winnie raised the ring and said, "I found it! What's the rush—?"

Yas wasn't alone.

Winnie had underestimated her vision, and now Apollo Rathbun was here.

CHAPTER 4

The Perfect Victim

Apollo drove in silence, shifting in their seat as Cyrus called out instructions. They watched the city transform the moment they crossed Main Street and headed east, how the buildings grew squatter, square and flat. Paint faded and brick chipped. Windows were boarded up or covered in bars or filled with spiderweb cracks. Vacant lots piled high with old, rusted cars claimed street corners. The sidewalks sprouted weeds here, and the trees receded.

"As I was saying," muttered Cyrus as he pointed for Apollo to turn down a side street. Here the porches drooped, the fields where torn-down houses lay in rubble overgrown. "Did you know Grandpa Ted left us properties around the city and outer towns? I need your help going through them all."

The moment Apollo's van struck a massive, unavoidable pothole, Cyrus accented it with a grin.

The streets here were full of them. Telephone poles were eaten away by weather and age, all tilted and full of gaps and ready to fall. And it was only their imagination, but even the sky seemed to turn gray with smog here, dull and neglected, as if it too had been quit on.

"I guess I can help," they told Cyrus, even though they didn't like not having a choice. No plan of getting on their feet just yet, not when all their summer job savings were in this van.

Cyrus was offering a lifeline before they resorted to sleeping in their van, living off of pickles and ramen noodles.

"Is this project just becoming a landlord, then? Is that why you're so secretive?"

Cyrus giggled. "No. I'm still working out the details."

He'd seemed delighted with Apollo's find yesterday, slipping back up into the attic when he thought Apollo was distracted. There was something about the journals and papers that piqued his interest.

At the dead-end sat three houses, each in deplorable shape. One had been eaten away by fire, charred along all its boarded-up windows. The wood bowed too, and the grass was a sickly shade of yellow. There was a large field across the street that might have once been a park, only there was no maintenance anymore. Nothing even to maintain.

It all felt like a sore spot to be forgotten; the city would wait until the problem sorted itself out, until the fields and houses disappeared or gave an excuse to be torn down and replaced with something else, *someone* else. Like a Whole Foods or a tech company.

Apollo felt like they were staring at themself. They were a place falling apart and abandoned, and their parents thought they could wait it out, let the world keep bearing down and choking out Apollo's life until nothing else grew and they finally became docile. It was easy to pretend Apollo was a problem, that they didn't exist, until all the nasty things that comprised them went away.

So Apollo did them a favor, and they still hadn't said a word.

It was a peculiar kind of loneliness, to have parents still alive in the world and feel their absence nonetheless.

Cyrus tossed open the door as soon as Apollo parked the van, before they could even kill the engine. "Ready?"

He was impatient, had always been too hungry, even now, when he was about to pick through a house that probably shouldn't have been left standing. It was suspicious. Cyrus wasn't a prankster at least; he had been exceedingly serious for as long as Apollo could remember, so they figured they'd find out soon what was so interesting about a condemned building.

They nodded once, climbed out, and eyed the house. It looked cemetery-like, sparse and quiet, with shattered glass coated in dust. Cyrus sprinted up the steps, a crowbar in hand.

"Are you sure this is safe?"

Without looking back, Cyrus nodded and began yanking at plywood. "Positive!"

They conceded and followed him, feeling the wood give a little with each step. The porch creaked dangerously.

"I wouldn't bring you here if it wasn't."

The plywood splintered away with Cyrus's sigh, and he nudged the front door open. The dark of the insides seemed to extend far beyond what Apollo knew the house to be. It was waiting for them to enter so it could swallow them up. And the fire that licked its insides was lying in wait for however long to devour.

They smelled the stale, acrid smoke.

Cyrus stepped in, hands on his hips, and looked around. "We just need to see what's inside. Look for anything worth something, in good condition, to sell before we chuck it all. And with your track record, what do you have to be afraid of?"

That felt pointed.

One school fight and a minor dress code disagreement didn't exactly numb Apollo to the inner workings of the criminal justice system.

They couldn't hide their wince as their cousin trekked in, leaving them to drum their fingers on the outside to work up the courage. Was that really what Cyrus thought of them?

That Apollo liked trouble and danger and whatever this was?

"Do we really own this?"

"Yeah," he replied as he moved around debris with his shoes. "Grandpa bought it, like, a decade ago, right before he died. He probably wanted to fix it up, but the tenants who used to live here caused a fire, and then he had his heart attack, so I guess everyone just forgot about it. The records are back at the house, I can show you."

Apollo tapped their fingernails on the bronze house numbers and nodded again. It all *sounded* aboveboard, perfectly logical, and Cyrus had no reason to lie, yet . . .

The story was incomplete. They knew that much.

Cyrus probably found something about the house, plans or details, in the journals. If it was exciting enough, it made sense he'd come rushing to bring those plans to fruition, cash in on the easy money that came with a flip rather than languish as a doctoral student forever. Apollo's mom loved shows about this kind of stuff, and they used to watch together before all the trouble started.

"You better not lie to me, dude," Apollo warned, even as they crossed the threshold. "You know I hate liars."

If Cyrus really thought Apollo was bad, then they didn't have to finish the threat. Which was good because they didn't *have* much of a threat anyway.

"I promise!"

Apollo tried not to let their eyes linger for too long over the shoes on the floor, the toys and framed photographs eaten to shit amid the debris. They tried not to think about how there was a family who had lived here, who probably lost everything and couldn't come back. Was anyone hurt? Cyrus hadn't said; it hadn't even crossed his mind.

"Uh-oh."

They turned their head toward the high voice in the other room. *Who is that?*

"Who are you?" Cyrus's tenor did not echo through this house like it did Rathbun Manor. It fell flat but was still sharp as a spear.

Apollo rushed to follow the sound.

A girl in a green school uniform stood in the center of the decrepit living room, eyes wide, *caught*. Her hair was slicked back into a curly ponytail, the dangling gold hoops in her ears swaying as she backed away. Her sneakers were pristine, the laces the most perfect shade of white, the toes uncreased—they looked brand-new except for the speck of ash. She adjusted the straps on her backpack, as if she'd come here after school to loot the place, and angled her head toward the hall.

"Winnie—"

And then *she* walked in.

Cassandra. Or Winnie, as this girl knew her.

With an easy stride, the psychic from the Red Hourglass arrived from the hall, and Apollo could feel the anger rolling from Cyrus's shoulders amid their own confusion. He studied the two girls with a wrinkle in his brow, his hands curling into fists.

The psychic didn't even give Apollo so much as a passing glance as she took her place beside her friend. As if she didn't recognize them.

Or was putting on a façade.

She was a better actress than they gave her credit for.

"What are you doing here?" Cyrus ground out.

"How did you—" Apollo started to say at the same time, but they couldn't find the words to finish.

The psychic wore a school uniform too, her red-and-gray plaid skirt hiked high over her knees, a light gray tweed jacket over a plain white shirt, the school's coat of arms embroidered on the pocket. Kavanaugh, of course. The two girls looked related, had the same round cheeks.

Suddenly the burned-out house and Cyrus's secrets were getting interesting.

"Who's this?" asked Winnie innocently, blinking her doe eyes in show. Her clear-rimmed glasses made them look even bigger and *more* fawn-like. She knew she was pretty, even among the wreckage, and was milking it. There was something in her coat pocket, and her hand fidgeted inside for a moment. Then she looked Cyrus in the eye—avoiding Apollo in a way that felt intentional—and said, "What are you doing here?"

Cyrus took a step toward her and bared his teeth. A shadow crossed his face, something in his pinched brow making Winnie step back in kind. Even to Apollo, who'd grown up with him, he suddenly seemed dangerous.

But *why*?

"I should be asking *you* that question. Why are you here? Are you familiar with breaking and entering, because I could call the police—"

The girl in green shook her head. "That's really not necessary—"

"Breaking and entering?!" Winnie's voice pitched higher as she balked. "I used to live here. This was my house; you can ask anyone on this street. Who are *you*?"

Apollo's brows rose, and they measured Cyrus's reaction. Was this house why he'd been looking into her, had her flyer among his things? His eagerness took on a strange color, and they had to wonder if Cyrus *knew* she'd be here. If he was looking for her.

Maybe they used to be a thing, judging by Cyrus's seething.

He scoffed and took out his phone. "No, actually, this is *our* house." He gestured to Apollo, who shrank back and preferred not to be seen at all. They had nothing to do with this. "I'm Cyrus Rathbun, and thanks to our late grandfather, we own this place."

Winnie stiffened.

Apollo cleared their throat, not that anyone paid attention to them. This exchange was growing serious, and it felt like someone should at least try to defuse it, even if they didn't know how. Historically, they always did the opposite.

"Hey, maybe we should—"

Cyrus wasn't done twisting the knife. "Want to tell me what you're doing on our property? In our house, that's been condemned and unoccupied for a decade?"

A chill ran through the room, but Winnie didn't answer. Neither did her friend. The girl in green only shifted closer to the psychic, who finally let her gaze drift to Apollo. As if to put the shame on them too.

They flinched, even though it didn't make sense why these two were arguing over a house that was a strong wind away from collapsing, the walls thoroughly eaten through by flame. It hardly mattered who it belonged to on paper or in practice. There was something neither was saying aloud.

Winnie shoved her hands into her pockets and took another step back. In a softer voice, she told Cyrus, "Like I said, I used to live here, no matter what your papers say. I came looking for something."

Silence passed between them all as Cyrus studied her and Apollo studied him. It should have been a straightforward solution, then, to let them go on their way as Apollo and Cyrus went about looking at the place. If this was her home, weren't they the trespassers, then?

Instead Cyrus charged at her. "All right, you little thief, hand it over. Whatever you took—"

He lunged. Apollo gaped.

"No!" Winnie reeled back from his reach. "It's mine!"

"Let go of her!" the girl in green shouted.

Just as Winnie turned to bolt, Cyrus seized onto her backpack. She threw an elbow in his direction.

Apollo unfroze from their place, from being a spectator in a show that was no longer entertaining, and stumbled forward. They took Cyrus's shoulder to tear him away from the girl. He only shrugged out of their touch and tightened his grip.

His only focus was on snatching Winnie's hand free, to reveal whatever she'd found. If she was a con woman, Apollo knew it stood to reason that she was also likely a thief, and Cyrus probably determined that whatever she held was rightfully his. *Theirs*, Apollo corrected, since they owned this place too.

But they didn't want anything from here—she could have it.

"Just let it go, Cy," Apollo tried to reason, tugging at their cousin's lanky arm.

Winnie jerked hard to break away at the same time Cyrus gave her an aggravated shove. Apollo held their breath as they watched in slow motion: She pitched forward, feet tangling over a broken coffee table. The arm she threw out to catch herself wasn't strong enough, or she crashed to the floor too quickly. A deep *snap* reverberated through the room as she landed on it, at an angle, with all her weight.

Winnie's screams filled the silence afterward. Her pain was sharp and jagged, her eyes limned with tears, her face twisted, her arm clutched to her chest.

"I . . ." Cyrus's mouth went slack. He hovered close, cheeks flushed with anger, still holding Winnie's backpack in his uneasy grip.

Apollo raked a hand through their hair and snatched the bag from him. A dozen accusations bubbled up on their tongue, but nothing came out because everyone stared at the silver ring sitting amid the ash; that hadn't been there before.

"It's my grandmother's wedding ring, you serial killer," Winnie hissed through gritted teeth, her fingers closing around it. "We lost it in the fire."

Guilt panged in Apollo's chest. They should have grabbed Cyrus sooner, harder, told him no louder. They shouldn't have even driven him here. Now a girl was hurt and all they knew to do was stand around awkwardly, looking just as much a brute as their cousin, while the girl in green helped Winnie climb to her feet. Ash, dust, and dirt soiled her coat and knees.

Everywhere I go, trouble follows.

Apollo cleared their throat and extended her backpack. "I'm sorry about him. Look, my van's out front, I can drive you to urgent care—"

Winnie's friend yanked the bag away and sneered. "We'd rather Uber."

What if Winnie told? What if they were sued, Apollo charged with assault *again*? In that prep school jacket, Winnie probably had angry attorney parents who'd be out for blood.

Apollo couldn't help but picture the look on their father's face that day, when he'd rounded the corner and seen the black eye and bruised cheek. From fear to disappointment in a heartbeat. How quickly their mother had leapt into action, ready to summon hellfire until she saw the other kid. Then she'd turned distant. Their parents hadn't reacted at all when the second expulsion came only a couple weeks into the new school year. Apollo didn't want to experience that again.

Winnie hadn't left a mark on Cyrus; she was the perfect victim, unlike Apollo.

They froze in place, watching her go, feeling sick, and beside them, Cyrus ground his teeth. Not saying any of the things Apollo thought he should have, long after the chance had passed.

September 1901

The Pan-American Exposition was deep underway when Alexander Rathbun arrived. He moved among the travelers who blocked sidewalks to marvel at the new buildings made of little more than paper and electrical wiring. They were beautiful architectural things, just like the beautiful architectural buildings developed by his family, and the city would soon demolish them all the same.

But he didn't want to dwell on the ways the city had wronged his family, for he had other intentions today. Intentions that would give him *more*, like his Central Terminal.

The suitcase in his hand swung with comfortable weight in every step toward the Machinery & Transportation Building. This was where the famous X-ray was held, according to the brochures. It had even made it into local news that Thomas Edison had one and was offering to bring it for the Exposition. And if he was here, then he would have an interest in the Rhodesian box.

Alexander had penned several letters to Edison already without any luck. It seemed that they were being shuffled in with all of his fan mail, or else the address he had found was incorrect. Some of his letters returned unopened while others never returned at all. None of it hindered his desire to have eyes on the box, *distinguished* eyes in particular, because Rathbuns were a distinguished people with acumen.

Scientia vincere tenebras and all that.

Even in September, the air inside the Machinery Building was thick and humid and smelled of sweat. His nicest linen suit wasn't enough to regulate his temperature as Alexander wended around the tight corners in search of the X-ray machine. It was only when he noticed a growing crowd cordoned off from a display by rope, and the tangle of cables and wires on a table, that he slowed. It looked so small and unimpressive, but then again, what Alexander held was also small and unassuming.

And anyway, he wasn't really interested in the X-ray. He was here for its inventor.

"Excuse me," he said, catching an operator's attention. Their white coat looked so very official, and it filled him with esteem. "I'm looking for Mr. Thomas Edison. My name is Alexander Rathbun, and he should be expecting me. We exchanged correspondence on a new scientific discovery of mine."

It was an exaggeration of the truth, of course, but he was sure that some of his letters did get through and Mr. Edison's were just lost in the return. All his staff must recognize the name.

Yet the operator only blinked at him.

Alexander supposed that despite their white coats, they could have been lowly assistants who knew nothing at all. Perhaps even this man was slow, or couldn't understand him over the incessant chatter of onlookers.

So Alexander raised his briefcase and said more slowly, loudly, to cover his bases, "Where is Mr. Edison? I have something to show him."

The operator shook his head. "Why would I know where Thomas Edison is?"

"That's his machine."

And then the operator chuckled for a long time. Alexander

stood watching him, baffled by his audacity, while the operator gathered himself again.

"No, this was built by Dr. Henry Odell," he explained, offering a pamphlet that Alexander refused to take, "based on some experiments by Nikola Tesla."

The operator spoke slowly, as if it was *Alexander* who was confused, which he supposed he was. He'd come all the way here through this throng of people to see someone that the papers had mistakenly predicted would be here, but now he had nothing to show for it and no idea what to do next. Would he have to travel all the way to Edison's address in Florida?

Embarrassed, Alexander cleared his throat and fished out his pocket watch, pretending to check the time. He weighed the alternative of staying for a demonstration anyway, with the hopes that the creator of this machine, even if he wasn't Edison, would surely care to see something of the box's magnitude. It defied Alexander's schooling and understanding of how the world worked, the laws that governed it, and there had to be other scientists he could gather into his employ to expose its mysteries. To deliver on the motto engraved on the underside of the watch, which Alexander's own father gave him, that he would then pass on to Joseph when he'd fulfilled his destiny.

A man of his station surely couldn't just turn away, sulking.

He nodded stiffly. "Well, I suppose I have a spare moment, then—I keep a busy schedule, you know. Where is Dr. Odell? Perhaps I can speak with him?"

"He's unavailable today. Haven't you heard? The president's in town for the fair." The operator triggered the machine, which flashed briefly, and then shrugged.

Yes, Alexander had seen the news, heard reports and gossip on President William McKinley's speech and the little mishap that preceded it. Somehow, a welcome cannon struck the train car upon his arrival. It all sounded interesting, of course, but he hardly understood the appeal of shaking hands with the president when one could be making *history*.

Alexander nodded. "Obviously I heard the cannons myself, I *live* in the Bryant area, after all."

When the operator made no effort to acknowledge this, to say anything more about the scientist's return, he frowned and turned away without another word. He felt scorned and foolish.

The day was heading in an awful direction, and no attempts to correct course had worked. First, the president had come to town, disrupting all of Main Street with his fanfare and dramatics. Then, there was no Thomas Edison for this invention that he was sure would be here. And finally, even the inventor who *wasn't* Edison was unavailable, leaving only his incompetent operators to run demonstrations for a gawking and ignorant crowd. Now Alexander was sweating in this stifling building with his box no one had a clue they wanted to see.

It was almost uncanny the way this world seemed hell-bent on driving Alexander toward becoming an inventor himself, just to do what needed to be done. If the greatest minds had no interest in comprehending what this magnificent device could do, then it was on Alexander to do so. His duty to bring *Scientia vincere tenebras* to life. And since shaking a president's hand was so appealing to the common scientist, he'd do it with the president's patronage too.

"Farewell, then."

Alexander took his leave and did his best to do it with dignity, instead of storming out the way he would have liked. People still recognized him, and they would talk, let the Hawleys know that little Isabelle Rathbun was not to be associated with. The sun's glare down on him felt aggressively personal.

The queue for the president was easy to find, with the wailing trumpets and waving flags. He inserted himself quickly and fetched the box from his briefcase. It would be quick and easy, he figured, to greet McKinley while he explained the box's origins and then open it for a wondrous display.

While the line shuffled along, he rehearsed his pitch: *My name is Alexander Rathbun, and this was discovered in my family's mine in southern Rhodesia. I believe it can change the world and become a hallmark of your presidency—*

"Next!"

Alexander was nudged impatiently from behind. Feeling warm and a little faint, he took a step and was ready to throw a scowl over his shoulder when the president met his gaze. McKinley, clean-shaven, with shrewd eyes and a dimpled chin, was shorter than Alexander expected.

They shook hands quickly.

"Hello, sir, my name is Alexander Rathbun and—"

"Thanks for coming," McKinley chimed in as he pivoted to the next person who came up beside him.

"*Hsyv suc.*" A gentle breeze, or perhaps a fly, tickled Alexander's ear, making him shiver.

Event organizers motioned for Alexander to follow the exit from stage like all the others, but he *wasn't* like all the others. He and what he held were *important.* He flipped the latch and dug in his heels.

"This was discovered in my family's mine," said Alexander, raising his voice and refusing to move. If he could just finish what he was trying to say, just a few seconds, he was sure he'd capture the president's genuine interest. "And if you'll permit me a moment of your time—"

The instant he pulled the lid back, the ground trembled. Perhaps too close, light filled the air, passing *through* McKinley and making him glow, and the president stumbled back from the impact and then doubled over. The wall behind him, made of paper, inexplicably caught fire.

Someone screamed.

It was only a quick flash before Alexander shut the box, but panic erupted nonetheless. The earth was still quaking. The president's aides swarmed forward as he gaped and took a step back, but not in time to avoid the blood trickling from McKinley's mouth, splashing on the pant leg of Alexander's neat, linen suit.

In the commotion, the man who'd jabbed Alexander from behind was then tackled to the ground, leaving the Rathbun patriarch to back away still, to melt into the crowd, and to flee the spreading blaze.

He knew then that he was on his own, that this was something he couldn't share. With anyone.

CHAPTER 5

No Stench, No Reply

Apollo stormed into Rathbun Manor with their skin buzzing. The longer they thought about it, the more something felt *off*, unsettling, seeing Cyrus and the sudden rashness of his actions. How easily he'd snapped Winnie's arm had set Apollo on edge.

The sound of her bone breaking, how fragile she'd looked then on the floor, had engraved itself on the inside of their skull.

They didn't know what to do, or how, but something had to be done. That frustration had to go somewhere.

Like a gift, on the doorstep lay a package with Apollo's name on it, a padded little square they'd enjoy ripping into. They carried it inside, dropped into their grandfather's cracked leather chair, and pressed the heels of their palms to their eyes.

It didn't feel like Cyrus was there just to evaluate a house and see what could be salvaged. He'd thought the psychic was a petty thief, that she was stealing something he wanted, perhaps, but he didn't tell Apollo that he was looking for something in the first place. In fact, he did a great job of convincing Apollo that they were sifting through garbage.

As they watched the two girls leave, Apollo felt like they were being controlled again, shoved into a neat box for someone else's benefit. *Managed.* How were they supposed to become their own person, see what they were made of, if Cyrus was next in line trying to curate them? If everything Apollo did was guided by someone else's calculations?

"Find your own way home," they'd snapped at Cyrus as they stormed out and climbed into their van.

They'd had enough of wearing their parents' collar, they wouldn't trade it for another now. Cyrus was their cousin; older, sure, but they would be his equal or nothing at all. And whenever he got home, Apollo planned to set him straight.

"But for now . . ."

With a sigh, Apollo turned to the package.

Rather than make a clean incision with the gold letter opener, they pried at it with their bare hands. Tearing piece by piece, shredding parcel paper, digging in with their nails and then teeth, the way they wished they could dig into Cyrus. See what was underneath, what he was hiding.

The package was a polyester pouch. Black, unmarked, and bulky. It was zipped shut, no brand names, no instructions, and from inside, a collection of thin metal tools and transparent practice locks fell into their lap.

Right. They'd ordered these to break into the desk.

The lack of instructions didn't matter. Apollo immediately pulled up those videos again, step-by-step tutorials on how to use the picklocks with all their various shapes, to break into their grandfather's desk and the big padlock downstairs.

It seemed easy enough—a tension wrench anchored in the lock, some flimsy metal piece wiggling around inside. There were a dozen techniques, but they went for one with the least coordination required: Bouncing the picklock up and down, undulating like a seesaw, was child's play. It would only take a moment.

Just like how it didn't matter if you played the part of the perfect, obedient progeny for most of your life, it only took a moment for everything to fall out of place. One moment of independence for your life to come undone.

Click.

And it worked.

The drawer popped open, even at the behest of Apollo's incompetently criminal hands. They pulled it wide and tossed the picks aside to sort through the contents: a thick, iron key, which probably went to the lock downstairs, and letters abandoned halfway through in their grandfather's same neat script that they could hardly read. Some were even older, judging by the yellow pages and faded ink, and signed by the initials A.C. A couple old invoices stained by a ring of coffee crinkled as Apollo pushed them aside. A scrap of paper fell from the bunch with the letters arranged strangely in a table:

T	U	V	W	X	Y
Q	A	K	V	R	O

It didn't make any sense. Apollo's translator app couldn't even detect the language, and there was no indicator to even guess at the meaning anyway.

A password, coordinates to a map—who knows?

Last was another paper, folded up and shoved to the back. Inside was a doodle, a drawing, of a rectangular box. It was shaded dark, and there were markings all around the exterior, drawings of wind and what Apollo could only guess was a medieval rendition of a dragon or something. The flyer read *Morning Star: Revolution in the Palm of Your Hand.*

It also meant nothing to Apollo. None of it meant anything to them, in fact. There was no money, no secret deeds to more burned-out houses with eclectic, pretty con women lurking in their depths, no apparent reason for Cyrus to transfer to the University at Buffalo, to be in this decrepit manor, asking for Apollo's help, at all.

Nonetheless, they stared at it for a long time, hoping for some direction, some inspiration, before finally grabbing the iron key and heading downstairs.

The lone black door in the cellar seemed even more ominous when Apollo turned on the lights. The rusted padlock, peeling away in sheets, came across as a warning. What was the saying? *Abandon hope, all ye who enter here*? That was all they got from their first week at Kavanaugh before they got chased away from there too.

With their ear pressed to the wood, they waited and listened for the telltale signs of someone inside, some imaginary prisoner trapped in their grandfather's basement like in Artemisia's favorite horror movies. After all this time, would they even be alive?

They couldn't fathom what else was so important, or dangerous, to make their grandparents, or even great-grandparents, seal it behind such a heavy padlock. Were it a war bunker, the door might have been metal and not sealed at all. A secret room was betrayed by the indication of the door altogether. A prisoner, however . . .

It probably had nothing to do with Cyrus though. If Apollo knew their cousin, he would have taken a battering ram to the lock days ago if he wanted inside.

Then again, Apollo wasn't so sure they knew him at all. The cousin they grew up with was abrasive, but not enough to brawl with a girl half his size. But even as they twisted the key in the lock, as it popped open and fell heavily into their hand, they felt guilty for lingering on this.

Cyrus hadn't done nearly as much damage to Winnie as Apollo had done to Patrick Barnes. Was the measure of a person just the sum of their worst moments?

Leaving the key and padlock on a nearby shelf, Apollo opened the door and waited for something to come running out. For the stench of death from a prisoner long forgotten to repel them.

"Hello?" they called, even though they desperately didn't want an answer.

No stench, no reply.

They groped the wall by the door in search of a light switch, but when it flipped, nothing happened. If the room had been shuttered as long as Apollo suspected, the bulb had probably burned out long ago.

Enabling their phone light, they looked around and slowed. The hairs on their arms, on the back of their neck, stood on end.

The room appeared to be quite large, larger even than the bedrooms on the second floor, and it connected to a dark hall. Along the perimeter, someone had placed dozens of thick, white candles.

They flashed their light into the hall, but it reflected nothing back. Ate the light completely.

"Fuck no," said Apollo, turning away.

It was mostly empty, and in the center, what stopped them from taking another step forward were scribblings in chalk on the floor. Exceedingly creepy and unintelligible, just like what Apollo had found in their grandfather's office upstairs.

"*Jesus Christ*," they muttered under their breath as they sidestepped around it.

The only furniture in the room seemed to be a cabinet with a partially melted white candle on top, surrounded by sheets of yellowed paper. Each page was the same size and, Apollo assumed, torn from the same book, judging by the uneven edge, the same print.

They held one up to the light and grimaced.

It was poetry.

Their grandfather kept *poetry* in his creepy cellar dungeon. Some of it was annotated, with faded notes that were hardly legible, and other parts underlined, such as:

"From gloomy Tartarus
The Fates have summoned us
To whisper in her ear, who lies asleep,
A tale to fan the fire
Of her insane desire
To know a secret that the Gods would keep."

And scribbled in the margin was,

"Lbyc pgyyco Qebqebah
Qsi Leqih seki haccyzij ah."

Reading through it once, twice, didn't help Apollo understand why it was here, didn't ease the dread that was inching up their spine. All of it felt *weird*, and if their parents were still talking to them, Apollo might have considered packing up and moving back home today.

From above came a shudder at the front door. Then Cyrus called their name.

"Down here!" Apollo shouted, though they expected their voice to reverberate around the room, and the dark hallway swallowed that too.

They continued flipping through the pages, waiting for their cousin to descend but unsure what to say when he got here, how to explain this room. It was too weird to keep to themself, they knew that much. Weirder than Cyrus, even.

"*To know a secret that the Gods would keep.*" They mouthed those last words again, listening to Cyrus's steps creaking down the staircase.

When he rounded the corner, his footsteps stopped.

Apollo looked up and found Cyrus *grinning*, of all things.

"You found the key? Where was it?"

It took a moment for Apollo to stop gaping. To go from slack-jawed to angry, their grip so tight on the papers that the edges were starting to bend. They folded the stack, shoved it into their back pocket, and charged out before their cousin could waltz right in.

Cyrus wasn't paying any attention to them. He was peering into the room, mouth cracked wide, wonder on his insufferable face, and Apollo had to stop themself from throttling him in the doorway. He didn't look like someone who'd just found a weird dungeon in his grandfather's cellar. He didn't look afraid or even surprised.

He looked excited. Always so damn excited.

Apollo slammed the black door shut and whipped around. "What aren't you telling me?"

"What?" Cyrus asked with a hint of affront. His eyes twinkled as he finally, *finally* took in Apollo. Their rage. Rage that was directed at him.

"You need to spill."

A long silence drew out between them as Cyrus's gaze flicked from them to the door. Apollo refused to yield so easily, refused to let him get away with lying again, keeping secrets, treating them like a child to guide and care for. Either they'd do this together, as partners, or not at all. And judging by the contents of this little room, Apollo was fast deciding they wanted no part in whatever it was shaping up to be.

"You hungry?" was Cyrus's reply instead, his voice measured and calm. Cavalier, even. He turned his back on Apollo—*brave* of him—and climbed the stairs. "I brought pizza."

Apollo was sick of pizza.

They ran up the stairs after him. "Cyrus, I'm not playing."

"I know you're not. Come, sit down."

The smell of pizza, spicy, charred pepperoni and too much cheese, filled the back hallway when Apollo stepped onto the landing. It should have made them hungry, but instead their stomach roiled. Neither of them could cook well, so they'd been ordering takeout from local joints—and it was Buffalo, so every other local joint had pizza and wings—and now the thought of a single bite made Apollo sick. That room, Cyrus's evasiveness, the sound of Winnie's arm breaking, all of it made them sick.

"I don't want to sit down. I want you to tell me what you're up to," Apollo insisted, piercing their cousin with their gaze. Though their voice didn't waver, the agitation made them tremble. They spun the spiked rings on both middle fingers, trying to focus on the feel of the metal. "I know you're looking for something."

Cyrus opened a cabinet in search of plates and paused to look back at them. "What makes you think I'm looking for anything?" He cast Apollo only a cursory glance as he pulled down dishware and a roll of paper towels. When he removed a knife from the rack, Apollo took an involuntary step back.

He frowned. "Seriously?"

Apollo just crossed their arms. "Grandpa's freak dungeon aside—and we'll talk about that later—you didn't break that girl's arm over some trash in a house you don't want. You don't even want to *be* here."

He tilted his head in consideration and then served himself a slice of pizza. He was doing his best to disarm and confuse Apollo, to pretend they were only paranoid. "I was born here, and UB has one of the best physics departments in the country. Of *course* I want to be here."

Apollo saw red and took a charged step.

Something in their expression must have said what they couldn't, because Cyrus raised a hand in surrender and marched over to the couch still covered in papers. Thick reference books lay open on the coffee table, sheets of printed studies with charts and equations Apollo didn't understand covered every surface of the cushions and armrests. Their cousin grabbed one bulky manila folder and held it out to them.

An offering.

No, in Cyrus's eyes, he was handing Apollo an *opportunity*. And if they still wanted to be bold like he was, decisive, then they had to seize it.

CHAPTER 6

Better Than Dissecting Cats or Scamming the Elderly

"I don't even wanna know what you were *thinking*, going into that house."

Winnie's mother pulled the car into the driveway and glared. She hadn't stopped ranting since they dropped Yas off, and the sheer volume of it for four straight blocks made Winnie's ears ring. Their porch light was already on, and Winnie could see flickering from the TV through the front window.

Yet another person to witness her screwup.

"It's condemned for a reason, Winona. Do they not teach you how to read at Kavanaugh? What are we paying for?"

Technically they weren't paying anything, because she was a scholarship student, but Winnie didn't say that. Instead, she slouched in her seat and took it all.

She'd hated the staff at urgent care calling her mom to deliver the news, and part of her died inside to see the panic on her mother's face when she rounded the corner. The notch currently in Daniella Bray's brow hadn't eased when Winnie explained how she broke her arm. And where.

Sort of.

She couldn't mention the Rathbuns, or the box she'd found in the basement, or Mama's ring, because the first two were psychic nonsense, and the last was a death sentence. Yas had enough self-preservation to keep her mouth shut, because their moms—*sisters*—talked, and she didn't need to be in more trouble.

Rather, Winnie had stared at the hospital linoleum floor, and said, "I went to the old house and—" Just this was enough to light a fuse in her mother's eyes, so she stayed quiet until they got home. Until now.

"I'm sorry," she mumbled, doing her best to sound like she meant it. She *was* sorry to have scared her mother, but not sorry that she went inside the house. "I've been thinking about it lately, and I was bored."

It was an easy lie that people always believed—bored high schoolers got into trouble.

"So join a club!" her mother retorted, grimacing when her eyes fell on the bright pink cast. She hadn't been able to watch the doctor wrap Winnie's swollen, purple forearm again and again. Her squeamishness had swelled above the panic for just a moment.

Still, it didn't escape Winnie's notice how much calmer her mom seemed, knowing that it was just a forearm. In the place of fear, now she could be annoyed and scold her.

When the silence had filled the car to the brim, and Winnie was looking sufficiently admonished, her mom asked, "Well? Did you see anything? Is your curiosity satisfied?"

Not at all.

Winnie didn't know what answer she was supposed to give, what would make her mother feel better. She didn't want to be a headache; that was Marcel's job. "Yes."

Her mother put the car in park and framed Winnie's face, cupped her cheeks like she used to when Winnie was little. They didn't look that much alike, maybe in complexion, their cherubic cheeks; Winnie's button nose and round eyes took after her dad. A long quiet passed between them, with Winnie hoping her mother wouldn't press for more details.

But worse, she just turned around and climbed out with a sad smile. As if she could tell Winnie was lying but didn't know what to do. Couldn't take knowing the truth. It was a look Winnie knew well and wished she didn't. If she lingered on it, it made her feel wooden and small.

"You know, I could have been doing something really bad," Winnie quipped brightly instead as she followed, trying to lift the mood. Hoping to push her mom back toward annoyed instead of shuttered.

Annoyed meant she cared.

Her backpack weighed heavier on her shoulders when she hopped out, like the white box inside was a potent secret. She was dying to open it, see what it was worth, see what she'd broken her first bone for. Maybe she could pawn it.

"Imagine if I was, like, dissecting cats or scamming the elderly."

Her mom didn't laugh. She gave a sidelong glance that was even better in some ways, the kind that said it *was* funny, but she wouldn't give Winnie the satisfaction of laughing. To that, Winnie beamed.

Through the front door, Winnie's gaze fell immediately to the boy draped across the couch. The TV remote lay in Marcel's lap, some medical drama playing on low though he hardly looked up from his phone.

"Shouldn't you be on campus?"

He bobbed his head. "I live here, don't I?" When she waved her arm cast dramatically for him to see, his brows shot up, and he asked, "What'd you do? Get into a fight? Did you win?"

Their mother sighed loudly, pointedly, and walked quickly past them.

Winnie pushed up her sleeve to show it off. "So boom—I was

in the parking lot, right? And some guy's van hit black ice, so I had to jump in and stop it from crushing this girl from my biology class—"

"Ohhhh my god," her older brother groaned, running a hand over the smooth, shiny waves in his low-cut hair. He rose to get away from her.

Her grin returned as she shuffled to her room, even though she was still sore from her fall. Urgent care had only given her ibuprofen when she came in, and though her arm was feeling better now, there were still the bumps and bruises on her hip and shoulder. A dull ache pervaded her entire body. Nonetheless, her plane ticket out of here might be secured in her backpack, she had escaped Cyrus, *and* she made Marcel cringe.

She'd had worse days.

With the soft *click* of the door, Winnie shut herself inside and flipped the switch. At once, the pink light strip surrounding her desk and the string lights framing her bed flickered on. It took some effort, but she yanked off her jacket and began to empty her backpack.

First were the books, the piles of homework because seniors at Kavanaugh had it the worst. Marcel's toy truck. And then the box—

Winnie hissed.

Something had nicked her.

She shoved her finger into her mouth and scanned the inside of her bag. There wasn't anything sharp she could see: a pen, a rogue pine needle, a sheathed X-Acto knife accidentally taken from the art studio, a broken zipper. Nothing.

Yet right there, a gash ran down the pad of her index finger, the sting of split skin she couldn't miss. A fat bead of red collecting at the seam.

Brow furrowing, Winnie retrieved the box more carefully and set it on her desk, next to the clock blinking 6:37, the nearby lamp aimed like a spotlight in an interrogation.

It was small, the size of a jewelry or card box, hardly long and wide enough to fit her phone although there was some depth. It was a washed-out shade of white, not pure like eggshell but more off-white like antler. An antique carved from *bone.*

When she gently raised and lowered it, it was considerably heavy.

Diamonds and gold-plated jewelry didn't weigh anything at all, but full platinum jewelry, maybe? Actual gold bars? She shook it, hoping for the telltale jingle of metal, but heard nothing at all.

The surface of the box was covered by intricate carvings: violent, crossing patterns and sharp swirls on top, and all the sides bearing strange pictures. A cracked egg, a thick snake, rays of light, and seas of flame. Text among the swirls read: *Lbii qsi Hqeb, Haccyz qsi Hibfizq. Uz qsi exohh U xigyzp, qy qsi exohh U biqabz.* Hell if Winnie knew what it all meant, where it came from.

She traced the letters with her middle finger and—

Again, she sucked in a breath. On what appeared to be a smooth surface no less, carved from bone, she'd cut herself again.

"How are you doing this?" she asked.

Then she pivoted to the internet, snapping a photo and doing an image search. Maybe she'd find the manufacturer, maybe see what the box was made of, how much it was worth. Winnie had never handled real bone before. She didn't know if it was supposed to be this rough to the touch.

Maybe it happened with time—the box *did* look old. Dirt and dust collected in the crevices.

However, the search yielded nothing. No matches anywhere, nothing even close to this size or color, with or without these markings. But she knew there were other ways to learn about objects, ways to find secrets buried. Ways her family would kill her for trying if they knew.

"Hviiq lecugueb pubg . . ."

As if to encourage her, the scratching returned. Winnie glanced up from her phone to that same noise right in front of her, coming from the box.

"Jyzq oya vezq qy hii vseqh vuqsuz?"

The skittering was low at first, but the longer Winnie stared at it, weighed her idea, the louder it grew. Less a suggestion and more of a demand. Gnawing and pleading until the noise of scraping nails was inside her skull, scratching against her nerves.

She winced. "Fine!"

And then she licked her lips and planted her hand flat against the lid.

The heat that seized her was instantaneous and all-consuming. The moment Winnie touched bone, the muscles of her palm stiffened, and she couldn't let go. Worse than the sweaty guy from the shop, worse than reading Apollo, worse than the pain of her broken arm or anything she'd ever felt before. It made her heart stumble in her chest and burned her tongue.

"*Gyyw eq vseqh qy dyci, ezj oya vugg sigf lbii ci!*" the thing yelled right in her ear.

Immediately she saw herself, standing somewhere in darkness. Immediately, she felt *wrong*.

"But I can't . . . ," she started to say.

In the vision, Apollo Rathbun leaned close, curling around her. Their hand pressed against her ribs, hers flat against their sternum—*skin to skin*, eyes locked on each other. They held each other so near that the two of them shared a breath, and the air around them stilled like something was about to happen.

Winnie had never read herself in something before.

Then burning hands seemed to grab her face, turning her sharply away from herself and toward a storm raging over Lake Erie. The sweet scent of petrichor and the sour stink of water filled her nostrils as the sky darkened. Wind whipped massive waves from the surface, crashing against rock, as something shifted in the clouds.

A solar eclipse glowed above.

"*Jy oya hii?*" The same scratching, whispering, skittering curled in the crook of her ear, and she shuddered, tried to fight it to no avail.

A shadow flickered by the moon, undulating through the sky. Something large, resembling a maw stretched wide, serpentine and racing for the sun—

This vision didn't behave like all the others. It blurred around the edges, like a nightmare. Winnie didn't want to read the box anymore, but she also couldn't pull her hand away, and it wouldn't let her go. Like her skin had fused to the lid, like sharp claws were pinning her in place. When she closed her eyes to resist seeing, her lids were pried back open for another vision.

The filaments of fate she was used to transformed to chains that jerked her here and there.

Eyes watering, Winnie found herself peering into a room next, one filled with dark wood furniture that she'd never seen before. There stood a version of herself in its doorway, her arm still in its pink cast. Her glasses were missing, exposing a red and tender cheek beginning to swell. She held her breath while the walls shook hard enough to crack.

A flash of light, and then a tremor cleaved the wood flooring apart, crackling loud like the smashing of children's toys, harsh like child's play. Loud enough to make Winnie feel as if her own body was splitting too, rippling up through the walls and ceiling.

Like a camera, another flash, and she saw her grandmother's desiccated rosebush, and then the vision cut to a pale, white hand with an expensive silver timepiece holding the antique box. It wanted her to watch as the lid was pulled back. As light poured out, overflowed, reaching past her, past the chasm, filling the room until . . .

A final flash, and blood was pouring from Winnie's mouth in a torrent. It streamed from her nose, her ears, her eyes, down her front in a dark, lethal dose. Faster than she could plug or swallow it back down, she bled and bled and managed to release one panicked breath before her eyes fluttered shut and her body dropped to the ground.

Someone screamed.

She didn't want to see any more. She was fighting it—

In the present, there was a knock on the door.

The box let her go, and Winnie wrenched away from her desk and out of her chair. She crashed to the floor, coughing, scrambling back, *shaking*. Her lungs gasped for one breath after another. Her throat felt raw as if she had been the one screaming. The heat from the vision lingered all through her like a full-body fever, one that left her pulling off her uniform shirt, her socks, already starting to soak in the sweat.

Shoulders heaving, bleary-eyed, she looked around.

She was still in her bedroom. The lights were on. The strange box sat on her desk unopened, clasp firmly latched. A fresh pink cast was on her arm, and two of her fingertips were smeared with blood.

The knocking continued.

"Yo, Win!" Marcel's voice boomed. "Dinner's ready."

Dinner?

Winnie grabbed her phone and looked at the time. Somehow

an hour had gone by in the seconds she'd touched it. In the seconds the box *did* something to her, hijacked her ability when she tried to read it.

"I'm coming!" she shouted back, voice hoarse, though her body sagged to the floor in protest. She had to wait for her pulse to slow first, for every single disjointed image to make sense or fade away. For a moment, she opened her mouth to tell her brother but quickly stopped herself and clamped it shut.

The visions weren't real.

"It was a dream," she told herself instead.

It could only ever be a dream, because Winnie never saw her own fate. She couldn't, despite all her years of trying. It made no sense that this box, this strange, whispering thing that she found in a basement, had suddenly become the mirror she'd spent years wishing for.

Apollo Rathbun wasn't someone she ever planned to see again, and anyway, she couldn't *touch* people like that. Giant creatures didn't materialize behind storm clouds. Winnie didn't die a gruesome, bloody death in Buffalo at age seventeen.

But Winnie was a liar, and sometimes that meant lying to herself until she believed it.

CHAPTER 7

Not One but Two Death Certificates

Apollo took the folder but didn't look away from Cyrus's face. They didn't want to appear too eager, too easily satisfied with nonanswers in case this folder was *all* their cousin offered. Accepting this had to feel like their own choice, instead of another concession.

"Everything I know is in there," said Cyrus, still with an irritating degree of calm. "I didn't want to say more until I found it. Until I was sure."

They had no idea what *it* was, but let him keep talking until he revealed it. Their cousin was so close to showing his hand.

Rather than eat, Cyrus slumped in an island bar chair and sighed. "I just got back from meeting my adviser at the university. I wanted to ask about getting some equipment that might help us."

Apollo's brow furrowed, their fingers itching to open the folder, but they remained still, agonizingly so. They were almost there.

"If this all comes together," said Cy, "we could blow up. It could be *big*."

"'We'?"

Apollo had been an adequate student back when they were in school. No real chance of valedictorian or honor list, but they got decent scores and now were on the path to securing their GED, since no school would take them. Still, they weren't remarkable enough to have any role to play in Cyrus's university research. In *particle physics*.

They didn't even really know what that meant.

"The Rathbun family," Cyrus supplied, reading Apollo's mind. "See, there's an old heirloom that Grandpa Ted thought could make some money. A *lot* of money. Houses like this take a lot of upkeep, and I guess, we're not what we once were."

Apollo didn't need Cyrus to explain this much. It wasn't something their own father talked about, but Grandpa Ted had recounted it like a cautionary tale during barbecues in the summer. The Rathbuns built the city, owned the real estate, and were responsible for developing some of the most beautiful buildings downtown. Once they'd owned a mining company, and then a steel mill, but everything failed or came to an end eventually, and Grandpa Ted hated it. Even as a kid, Apollo could read his shame for what the family had come to, how everything they owned continued to dwindle to nothing.

If there was any chance to reverse it, Grandpa Ted would have seized the chance. So why didn't he?

"One night, Grandma Jean said something that got me thinking."

The anger that coursed through Apollo like lightning earlier had ebbed, and they found themself sinking into the chair opposite Cyrus, setting the folder of papers on the counter between them, lured by his story. They wouldn't have been able to pry themself away even if they wanted to.

"She drinks now, by the way, she's not like how you probably remember. Anyway, she said that I was just like Grandpa, and not in a nice way."

"Like him how?"

Glassy-eyed, Cyrus grimaced. "Self-centered. Obsessed with money and prestige. Apparently 'studying that fucking antique' was more important to him than his own family, and I was a bastard just like him because I'd rather spend my time furthering mankind than cleaning up after her. Am I wrong?"

It had been a few years since Apollo saw their grandmother, but they couldn't remember if she'd been sober. If she seemed any different. And they certainly didn't recall mention of any special antiques.

They only shrugged.

Cyrus gestured to the folder, and finally Apollo opened it, painfully slowly to make it seem like they were in control. At the top was a copy of the same flyer they'd found folded up in the desk. An ornately carved box. *Morning Star: Revolution in the Palm of Your Hand.*

Was this what he thought Winnie took? An old jewelry box?

"She also let slip that my dad pulled some strings to change how Grandpa died on paper so that it wouldn't embarrass us. He didn't die of a heart attack, he died looking for that." He nodded to the flyer.

Apollo couldn't help but scoff. An antique box that could change a family's fortune and a conspiracy to cover up a patriarch's death—it all sounded ludicrous. They may have been kicked out of two schools, but they weren't gullible.

"So what's the real story?" they asked glibly, moving the flyer aside. "With the girl? Are we related or something? A secret Rathbun baby?"

This made Cyrus laugh, and he rose from his seat to pour himself a drink. "Why? Saw something you liked?"

Warmth rushed to Apollo's cheeks. A dozen rebuttals were on

the tip of their tongue, ready to defend themself against even the *thought* of liking someone like her, but Cyrus had already moved on.

"Definitely not related, I checked." He wriggled his brows before turning away. "But look at the death certificates and fire marshal report I got down at City Hall."

"'Fire marshal'?"

Inside the folder were two official-looking documents printed on heavy stock, sealed with the State of New York, stamped by the County of Erie. They both certified the death of Theodore J. Rathbun. However, one was signed March 9, 2013, and the other March 11. *Two* death certificates for the same man.

The first: *Cause of death: Fire. Dead on arrival. Location: Found at 483 Heritage Street.*

And the next: *Cause of death: Myocardial infarction. Dead on arrival. Location: Discovered outside of Rathbun Manor, 2289 Ashton Place.*

Two very different truths from the same very official source.

Apollo flipped to the next papers in the stack, a stapled report bearing the letterhead of the county medical examiner's office.

Re: Two-alarm blaze at 483 Heritage Street on March 9. Two bodies were found inside. The first belonged to Jacob Bray, 38, resident. Cause of death is asphyxiation due to smoke inhalation. A second body was discovered below, in the basement near the source of the blaze, belonging to an older man, unknown to the family. Dental records identified him as Theodore Rathbun, 67.

And after was another memo, this time from the Buffalo Fire Department.

The source of the fire remains inconclusive. All explorations into arson and electrical failure have been exhausted. There were no candles, space heater, or discernible faults in wiring near the point of origin.

Apollo's head was throbbing. They'd expected Cyrus to come

up with some crazy scheme to keep them from storming out, to keep them as a low-paid lab assistant who didn't ask questions, but they didn't expect signed and stamped documents from the city. Chasing these down—*both* copies—must have been how he spent his days, why it took so long just to have electricity.

Yet the tangled web only seemed to be getting *more* tangled the longer Apollo looked, the more they flipped through the pages. Next came a stack of newspaper clippings: PRESIDENT SHOT AT BUFFALO FAIR, 1901; REAL ESTATE PATRIARCH SUDDEN DEATH, 1907; GRUESOME DEATHS DISCOVERED IN CONNECTION TO BOOTLEGGER TUNNELS, 1923.

Then followed photos of strangers, some old and others recent, all labeled by name—Catherine Casey; Jacob Bray; his wife, Daniella; son Marcel; and daughter Winona. *The psychic.*

That was why her flyer was among Cyrus's things: He was looking into her. Into them all. In connection to a fire.

A house, a girl, a handful of deaths, and a box called Morning Star. This was what Cyrus had given them, but Apollo didn't see how they fit into it, why he cared, why he needed *equipment*—

"That family used to work for Grandpa Ted a long time ago." Cyrus pointed to the photos before downing the last of his dark drink. Then he poured himself another. "He suspected them of stealing the antique; it went missing around the same time they quit. I think he went to retrieve it, and they killed him and set the fire to cover their tracks."

Sourness slicked Apollo's stomach and threatened to climb its way up their throat. They swallowed it back down and angled away from the pizza. "And the rest? All over a pretty box?"

He nodded eagerly and helped himself to the fast-cooling food. Stale grease saturated the air. The sound of his bites, the slurp of cheese, of sauce, made the room swim in Apollo's vision.

"That's what I thought until you found those boxes in the attic." He chewed as he talked, the wet dough visible in his long California vowels. "But it's not just a box. It's . . . it's . . . the *future.* My kind of future, in fact. All we have to do is find it, and I'll prove it to you."

His eyes gleamed, unsettling Apollo. Gleaming the same way they'd suddenly flashed when he attacked Winnie.

"Okay," said Apollo slowly, "but none of this explains why you broke the girl's arm. She didn't deserve that."

Cyrus froze midbite, and for a moment, he had a look of genuine remorse. Only for a moment. "*Fine,* you're right. I'll try to find her tomorrow and apologize."

That soothed Apollo's stomach a little, if he meant it. The sound of her bone breaking, her shrill scream, kept playing over and over again in the quiet lulls.

"Oh, and speaking of apologies—I took care of that trouble you got yourself into. You don't have to worry anymore."

Apollo closed their eyes to stop the room from spinning further. The past few days were disorienting, and now they felt like they were drowning. With all this information coming down on them, it was hard to tell which way was up. "What trouble? Took care of it how?"

"The Barnes boy? I gave what people like them are always after: *money*. Guess we're more alike than I thought."

A cold sweat rolled over Apollo's body. They darted up from the chair and into the hall, crashing into the doorframe of the nearest bathroom before it all came up. At their back, they could've sworn they heard Cyrus shouting, "You're welcome!"

They dropped to their knees, folded over the toilet bowl, and retched.

September 1901

Joseph Rathbun tossed his newspaper aside when he heard his father storm through the door.

All of town was talking about William McKinley's death and the subsequent funeral, how his body was carried back to his home in Ohio, the supposed murderer's trial in the coming days, and the new President Roosevelt's fortitude. He kept his mouth shut when neighbors remarked at the shame that it happened in Buffalo, and by an anarchist no less, because he wouldn't dare hint that he suspected otherwise. They didn't know about his father rushing inside, looking haunted and with blood speckling his pants, or understand that the earthquake that preceded it was connected.

They didn't know about the Rhodesian box.

It was better to let the anarchist hang than sully the family's name, and they needed this. Although, judging by the slam of the doors, the banging of his suitcase on his desk in the study, the elder Rathbun's pitches today had not been well-received.

It would seem that the scientific community was not interested in the wonders of the box. They were not wooed by its *potential* alone. Perhaps they didn't understand just what Alexander was offering, or they simply couldn't believe it. His father was hesitant to put on a show again, which didn't help either. And it was no secret around the Rathbun household that Alexander was growing impatient. All the family had to show for the mines so far were a small pile of gold nuggets and a few diamonds, amounting to just enough to remain invited to events, to pay the bills, to keep afloat but not prosper. Isabelle had enough for a wedding when the time came, but little else.

However his father had dreamed of this box as their new fortune, and science was yet to yield even the slightest return.

That was why Joseph found an alternative.

When the commotion settled, he climbed to his feet and grabbed the bundle of letters that he'd put together. It was his own personal correspondences from the past several months, as he tried another approach for the box in case his father's in science had failed.

It occurred to him that perhaps the box, with the superstition surrounding it and rumors of omens, wasn't based in science at all. Maybe it was something *divine*.

When Joseph was at Cambridge, he'd come across an electric student of philosophy named Crowley. It was years ago that they'd studied literature together, crossed paths at the occasional party or salon, but now Crowley was known in European circles for his belief in *magic*. He was deep in the occult, busy traveling the world not to plunder mines like Joseph had but to further his knowledge of alchemy and the esoteric.

It wasn't that Joseph even believed in these things exactly, but Crowley himself had spent years in Egypt, studying the ancient religion. He'd hoped that Crowley might have some recommendations of folk rituals to consider, reference texts to consult, or even connections to the esoteric lodges that might lend some assistance.

Where there were lodges, Joseph understood, there was *money* to be found. Powerful people that his father failed to reach.

He knocked on the doors to the study and was immediately greeted by his father's gruff resignation.

"Come in."

Joseph hesitated.

In his hand were letters where Aleister Crowley also expressed interest in seeing the box himself, in exploring that particular mine in southern Rhodesia for what else might be buried inside. It would remind his father that the company's operations had yet to find anything else quite like this.

And Joseph wasn't so foolish as to not inquire with his other English classmates about the state of Crowley's finances and libertine predilections, not that he'd mention such things to his father. Certainly not when he was in a temper already. But maybe *now* wasn't the best time to talk about the occult, about magic and alchemy at all, even if Crowley was a well-connected classmate with some interest and in the process of founding his *own* order to study things exactly like this.

"Joe, I know it's you."

He swallowed, pushed through anyway, and closed the doors behind him. The lights were low, and his father already had a drink in one hand and a pipe burning in the other. It was definitely a bad sign. He cleared his throat and did his best to swagger forward, confident. "I take it the meeting didn't fare exactly as we hoped?"

Alexander hung his head. "All the way to New York City to see Edison, and I was turned away at the door! By an assistant no less! Disrespectful that they don't recognize the name anymore."

Though he was only half listening, wondering how to segue to the letters, Joseph nodded.

"And what is it you need?" asked his father before bringing the pipe to his lips.

Joseph gently rested the stack of envelopes bound in twine on his father's desk. His hands quivered despite himself. "I've been exchanging letters with an old friend of mine from Cambridge . . ."

His father's eyes were beginning to glaze over. Joseph recognized that it wasn't simple tobacco his father smoked at all; and the longer he stood in the office, the more he could smell the sweet scent of opium and knew he had to talk fast.

"His name is Aleister Crowley, and he's known in Europe as an expert of the occult. I thought that perhaps we could—"

"'Occult'?" Alexander stirred.

Joseph nodded. "I thought that—that perhaps we could consider alternate means to evaluate the Rhodesian box. Perhaps there isn't much science can tell us at all, and it is magic."

"'Magic'?" Alexander roared before he broke into a fit of laughter. Giggles, actually, just as that operator had done to him. He gestured to the box, sitting on the fireplace mantel. "You think that's magic and not a feat of nature?"

It conjures earthquakes, Joseph wanted to point out.

Instead, trying to salvage the conversation, he pivoted. "I simply want to invite Aleister to Buffalo and have him take a look. You see, there is an organization called the Order of the Golden Dawn, full of distinguished European gentry in search of a particular stone, and Crowley might introduce me to one or two of them who will—"

"We're not interested," his father said plainly.

We, he said. Not *I*.

Without even looking at the letters before him, Alexander shoved them away and sent them tumbling off the desk and onto the floor. "If the scientists don't show their interest, then I will become like them and study it myself. *Scientia vincere tenebras.*"

Joseph didn't know what that meant, or why his father kept

saying it. The old man *knew* he wasn't good at Latin. Instead he stuttered out, "Study it yourself?"

They had a business to run, a household to care for. Isabelle was due to get married soon, and Joseph had his own young family to care for. He was temporarily taking care of things here instead of returning to Rhodesia, but he couldn't very well leave his father to chase the folly of being his own inventor forever. The idea was ludicrous, and they didn't have money to waste.

A breeze flickered through the room. "*Si luzjh oya fuqulag, ucceqabi. Si vugg zyq guhqiz.*" It was just their luck that the house now needed insulation work against the drafts.

Gritting his teeth, Joseph retrieved the letters at his feet and tried again. "Maybe I just meet with the Order myself. Show them—"

"No." Alexander's voice took on an edge. "My answer is no, and that's final, Joseph. Now get out."

His jaw worked at some other angle, at some rebuttal, at words he wanted to say but couldn't. The old man was being unreasonable, both stubborn and arrogant, while Joseph was the one to actually discover the thing. It was *his* find, *his* feat, swept out from under him by his own greedy father.

Joseph turned around.

"And fire that girl, Sofia, immediately," Alexander called at his back. "I don't want her making any connections between us, the box, and the late president."

He nodded stiffly, his grip on the letters so tight that he smudged the top page, as if Joseph and his discovery were always destined to fade from history.

CHAPTER 8

Stranger Danger

"*Jy oya azjibhqezj zyv, guqqgi hiib? Jy oya azjibhqezj?*"

The scratching didn't stop. All night long, something in the box atop Winnie's desk gnawed and scratched and skittered. Even without understanding its words, she knew it begged for her to open and set it free, and it wouldn't stop until she did. Not that she slept at all anyway—how could she, considering what she saw? Considering how unfair it was that she'd finally caught a glimpse of herself in the filaments only to see her death.

And it could only be death to bleed so much, so fast.

She raised and dropped the heavy casted limb in her lap.

Dying *soon.*

She had about six weeks of the cast on her arm, which meant that if she understood what she'd seen—and she hoped she didn't, that she'd misinterpreted or lacked context, which happened on occasion—she had even *less* than that to stop it. A countdown to get out of town, otherwise the box would get its wish, and Winnie would pay the price somehow.

What an awful gamble.

She sat up in bed and glared at the bone-carved box. Moonlight from the window seemed to make it glow opalescent. It looked innocent. Just a fine box for jewelry or treasures, just a girl watching it in a quiet house on a quiet street in a quiet city, where nobody else was watching themselves die in slow motion.

Was that why she'd never seen her own future before? Because she didn't *have* one?

"Are you going to kill me?" she whispered, though she didn't want an answer. She wanted quiet. Peace. A better fate than the one she'd seen. "Am I gonna die here? Soon?"

The skittering, hissing, scratching paused for only a fraction before continuing. "*Syv dez oya yl egg dbieqabih lieb jieqs?*"

Winnie tossed her sheets aside and stripped the case from her pillow. She grabbed the box from the inside and wrapped the case around it, the same way people bagged dog shit on the sidewalk, and with it raised in her fist and swinging like a thurible in church service, she marched down the hall and descended to the basement. She shoved it all the way in the back, behind the Easter decorations and broken vacuum cleaner, no longer afraid of what might be hiding in the shadows.

How could anything beat what was coming?

"As soon as I get a chance, you're going to a pawnshop."

And she meant it. Soon, she'd be free of it. She'd cash it in for enough to get to the other side of the ocean and let it be someone else's problem.

In Winnie's future, the one she made for herself, she'd be fondling old cooking pots and telling the world about all the forgotten and ignored people who came before. Alive and loud and needed, someplace else.

A weight seemed to lift from her shoulders at the idea, the determination in it, as she climbed the stairs and headed back to bed. There was no way such a thing could be real, a box so full of foreboding that it was basically bursting at the seams. Storms and chasms and light so severe they felled a body. A monster so massive that it could barrel toward the sun like a game of fetch.

Life simply couldn't be that unfair.

Back in her room, she crawled into bed and squeezed her eyes shut. The box was lying, or her curse of sight broken, and she willed her body to forget everything she'd seen.

"It was a dream," Winnie reminded herself, over and over again, as she tried to sleep but failed. It went on long after the red sun crested the horizon, light filling the sky like a threat.

In the kitchen, Winnie felt Marcel eyeing her as he filled his thermos with coffee and milk and jingled his keys to drop her off at school on his way to class. His sidelong glances followed her when she pulled on her blazer and sneakers and headed for the door. All the way down the short walk of the driveway, as she climbed into the passenger seat of his surprisingly new-looking used sedan, he held his tongue and watched her with the extrasensory perception only an elder sibling could have.

"What's wrong with you?" asked Marcel finally, when she'd buckled her seat belt. His usual snark had been stripped from his tone. It was still bullish and deep, but he had enough concern to bypass the ridicule. "Are you sick or something?"

She shrugged.

She didn't know how to explain, even if she wanted to. Though he knew about her ability, it wasn't something she was supposed to talk about anyway. She wasn't even supposed to use it, so if she said that she'd planted her hand square on the lid to read the box, Marcel wouldn't listen. Or believe her. Or understand. In some ways, it felt like she was on her own. He was afraid of Winnie and her gift, even if he'd never admit it—she'd seen it in his eyes, her mother's, the day she'd tried to warn them of their father's death. It'd taken months for Marcel to just look at her the way he used to.

And now there was another death on the table—*hers.*

However, if Winnie said nothing, it felt like the equivalent of just letting herself die. Not seeing the world, doing something that mattered, finding her place—all the things she'd made fun of her clients for.

She squeezed the seat belt between her fingertips and asked softly, "You know that thing I can do?"

"What thing?"

With her pointed silence, Marcel immediately understood. He sat up straight in his seat and adjusted his grip on the steering wheel. His expression hardened. "Oh."

Winnie pursed her lips. "What if I . . . What if I saw something really bad again—"

"I thought we decided you wouldn't see anything anymore."

She bristled. "Well, I'm not a lamp. I can't just unplug it—"

"Then don't look it in the eye," he offered instead, far more forceful than necessary. Like he was trying to convince himself instead of actually helping her. Instead of listening. "If something scares you, you don't look it in the eye, and it can't hurt you. You know that . . . that 'thing' you do only brings trouble."

Trouble.

At her core, without even trying, Winnie was a problem.

There was finality to his words that she didn't fight. Because what was the trouble she'd brought so far exactly? The fire—was that her fault? Or was it being such a bother that everyone spent more time trying to shut her up than saving her dad? How horrifying it must have been to have a six-year-old predicting another death on the day of her grandmother's funeral.

She only nodded absently, feeling worse. Each breath was a knife in her chest.

Maybe Marcel was right, and she could ignore what she saw,

avoid it if she just . . . what? Did nothing? Stayed away from Apollo? Well, they did just fine finding *her*. Maybe pawning the box and brushing the visions off as an ibuprofen high would make it all go away. A misunderstanding. An overactive imagination.

Anxiety.

Marcel nudged her. "I'm serious. You know your nerves are bad. Just ignore it, and you'll be okay."

He punctuated it with a smile because he really believed it to be true.

That only looking at your wounds made them real. That bad things only happened to people who spoke up. If Winnie had never said anything, if she'd known her place as a lamb, meek and quiet and gentle, would her father still be alive?

No.

But she could pretend, because it made her family feel better. Even if it made her feel more alone. Lying was what she did best, what people wanted from her, and she was too much of a coward to do anything else.

So Winnie returned her best smile, feigning relief even as it all ate her up inside, and let her world keep on spinning. The red gates of Kavanaugh School came into view, as if to remind her that if she wanted to get away, on her own, then there was work that wouldn't wait.

The moment Winnie heard chimes playing over the speakers of Baker Hall, she darted out of her seat and Mr. Rodriguez's AP Physics classroom. She wasn't the kind of student to skip class, to skip *a whole day*—not that Kavanaugh would let her get away with it without her mother knowing—but this Tuesday, she wished she was.

Her shift at the Red Hourglass didn't start for another hour, but it was the whole day that felt wasted. All this pent-up energy would be better spent doing something with her life in case it was cut short.

Which it wouldn't be, of course.

Everything she saw when she touched the box had been a dream and perhaps even a warning. Sure, her premonitions always came true, but these weren't normal premonitions—they were disjointed, incoherent, starring *herself.* The first of them, Apollo pressing up against her in the dark, was proof.

There wasn't any other rational explanation for that alien look on her face, the breath held between them. Apollo wasn't her type, all mullet and spoiled rich kid abrasiveness, and Winnie couldn't even touch anyone like that without her eyes rolling into the back of her head. Everything else had to be discounted, *ignored* like Marcel said.

Weaving between students slowly trickling into the halls, she untucked the pencil from behind her ear and shoved it into the gap between the cast and her arm. Thinking of Apollo made her think of Cyrus, and thinking of Cyrus made her arm itch. He was a variable of the equation she had yet to consider, but she'd also factored him into the to-be-avoided category based on his unsavory vibe alone.

With slight wiggling motions, she used the tip of her pencil to scratch at her arm, scraping and scraping for a shred of relief. It was unfair that she walked away with a broken arm and a doomed prophecy while the Rathbuns left the altercation still owning her house.

"You're gonna get lead poisoning," muttered a voice at her side.

Kristina, one of the only other Black girls at Kavanaugh School, kept Winnie's pace. She gave the arm only a cursory glance as she applied fresh gloss to her lips, and when they stepped out into the sun, her gaze immediately scanned the perimeter for a green uniform in a sea of red. For Yas Coleman.

They weren't close friends—Winnie was limited in the friend department—so much as the next best thing, where Kristina had a thing for Yas, and Yas had a thing for her, but they both pretended it was only a matter of coincidence, lingering around the gates of Kavanaugh for anyone else. Plus Kristina shared AP Physics for last period, which meant they walked out together, rather than Winnie walking alone.

Winnie snorted. "No, you can't."

"You don't think there's *lead* in *lead pencils*?"

Whatever Winnie might have rebutted got lost in the moment she saw *him*. They stepped through the thick gates that guarded Kavanaugh's campus, and her attention snagged on the figure straight ahead. The streets around their school were lined with cars when classes let out, parents just off of work or the parents' drivers for a special few. Yellow school buses parked in a row for all the kids who lived in the outer towns, far beyond where city buses reached, and weren't lucky enough to have a car. *Yet.* A senior wouldn't be caught dead riding one.

And in the middle of this all was a tall guy with a head of dark hair parted neatly down the middle, leaning against the side of a shiny new truck.

Cyrus.

His ankles were crossed casually, the press of his slacks and leather shoes pristine and expensive, and among the rich parents standing around and talking to each other, he fit right in. Even with the sunglasses low on his straight nose, staring at his phone. He looked like the kind of money Kavanaugh bred, his silver necklace twinkling in the sun, his good looks attracting the attention of the pack of moms chatting nearby.

"You know him?" Kristina raised her eyebrows.

Winnie scowled and turned away, catching a glimpse of Yas's green hoodie pushing against the stream of red-and-gray coats. Beaufort was far laxer in their uniform than Kavanaugh's tailored jackets. "Hell no."

It hadn't occurred to her that others might also find Cyrus attractive, that his thick hair and strong brow and *money* might be appealing. But between Kristina's impressed nod and the passing glances from other students around them, it seemed all too possible. All Winnie was willing to see was the entitled bastard who broke her arm, the kind of person who could get away with it but still show up at her school to rub it in.

As if he could sense her glaring, Cyrus glanced up and locked on Winnie. Pulled his sunglasses away and *waved* at her.

"What the fuck is he doing here?" Yas sneered.

"Who is it?" Kristina prodded again, more excited this time.

Yas answered, "The dude who broke Winnie's arm," at the same time Winnie quipped, "He owes me money."

The skin beneath her cast itched worse as Winnie marched forward and stepped into the street, though the sensation was quickly replaced by annoyance. Rage. *Ick* slithering down her spine. She didn't know what Cyrus was doing here, or how he found her, but she was getting sick of seeing his pretty, well-carved face. First in Apollo's future, hovering over them like a dark cloud, like a predator sinking its claws into their shoulder, and then at *her* house with the audacity to accuse her of being a thief.

She was the one who had to sit in urgent care, hardly able to even hear the doctor and nurses over the pain.

There was something so smug about the way he carried himself despite this fact, how he could just show up like he owned the whole damn world. With the way he had acted, he probably wanted the infernal box, and if that was the case, he couldn't have it.

Even if Winnie didn't want it, even if it turned out to be worthless, she wouldn't give it to him on principle.

"What are you doing here?" Winnie stopped just far enough away so that he couldn't lunge for her again and crossed her arms. "If you're stalking me, I *will* scream 'stranger danger' and tell the soccer moms that you're offering me drugs."

She should have, regardless. Just to make him squirm.

He turned sheepish when he glimpsed the pink cast sticking out of her sleeve, a stark blush of scarlet flooding his cheeks. His shoulders crawled up to his ears as he tossed up his hands. "Relax, I came to apologize."

Winnie arched a brow but didn't move. Didn't unclench. "Is that so?"

Bullshit.

"Yeah, I shouldn't have grabbed you," Cyrus replied quickly, rubbing his chin. Contrition didn't look good on him, though she found she liked it better. "I shouldn't have put my hands on you, and I . . . I wasn't thinking."

She continued to watch him and blink, wondering how far she could press this guy and his guilt if she said nothing. He had yet to actually utter the words *I'm sorry*, and even so, she had no use for explanations or false apologies; she couldn't spend that, and it didn't glue her ulna back together either.

"I didn't know where you went to get treated, so I came here."

"You tracked down where I went to school . . . ," Winnie stated slowly, considering his words. "To explain yourself? And that's not supposed to be creepy?"

Cyrus scoffed and pointed toward her blazer, to the coat of

arms embroidered on the breast pocket. "I went here for primary school, smart-ass. I recognized the crest. Next time you break into someone's house, maybe don't wear your uniform—"

"I wasn't *breaking*—" She ground her teeth and took a deep breath. None of this was going how she'd expected. "This is a shit apology, by the way. You're only here because you want to make sure I won't tell anybody."

His eyes sharpened like daggers on her, and Winnie had to steel herself against the urge to step back. Run away. As he loomed over her, her bones suddenly felt bird-thin, far more breakable than they did last week. But she went to private school; she was an expert at reading rich people, especially white yacht boys, far better than they could read her.

Rather than tremble, she adjusted her nice Kavanaugh coat, the collar of her white shirt underneath, and straightened. She put her cast on display. Then her voice softened. "I'm a straight-A student at the Kavanaugh School, a senior destined for Cambridge, and just how do you think people will react if I reveal a strange older man came into my house and grabbed me while I was working on a history assignment and then followed me to school?"

Though he wasn't *that* much older, just barely into his twenties, he still stiffened.

"The *Buffalo News* loves an underdog, Cyrus; I tried to pull myself up by my bootstraps, and you, a descendant of a rich and powerful family, attacked me and tried to steal my grandmother's wedding ring. And I even have a witness."

Cyrus blanched. "Look, I'm sorry. Really—"

"Apologies don't cover room and board," Winnie replied sweetly, pointedly, letting her eyes go round. "However, you can always buy my silence."

She enjoyed the look of shock on his face then, watching

Cyrus startle and stumble back. He didn't expect her to strike, to look so soft but also be a serpent, so fast with fangs so sharp. But Winnie was good at what she did—when it came to lying, she considered herself the very best. In truth, the world couldn't have cared less what she had to say before, and it certainly wouldn't care now, but people like Cyrus didn't know that. He couldn't understand anything at all when he was on the defensive; their brains stopped working the moment you even implied the word *racist*.

He spent a long time studying her, a glint in his eye as he recognized her game. As he saw her in a new light. And then he nodded and shoved a hand into his pocket. Even his wallet was nice, embossed with his initials, probably crafted from Italian leather. "Clever. Very clever of you."

"I *did* say I was destined for Cambridge."

He grabbed all the bills inside and folded them up in a wad. Winnie tried her hardest not to count. She didn't want him to call her bluff, to break her other arm when she walked away, and she could tell he was waiting for her to lapse into gratitude she'd never give.

Winnie snatched the money from his hand and slipped it quickly into her breast pocket. Any longer and someone would think it was actually a drug deal. "Thank you, Cyrus, for being so reasonable. Apology accepted."

He only continued to look her up and down but didn't reply.

Unsure of what else to say, she pivoted on her heels and darted back across the street. Yas and Kristina had been watching the exchange with interest, and she could feel the moms throwing eyes their way.

Once the trio started down the block, Yas threw an arm in Cyrus's direction. "What the hell was that?"

"Told you he owed me money," Winnie quipped as she finally

counted the cash. It was a good chunk of what she needed for school, but bills for X-rays and casts meant it wasn't everything. It wasn't enough.

In truth, she wasn't so upset about having her arm in a cast, but she wanted more. For the trauma of touching that box, for what it showed her.

"Wait!"

Cyrus's shout rang out behind them, and when Winnie turned, she caught him jogging toward them, on their side of the street, a hand raised in the air. They slowed and watched his approach, watched him unfold and hold up a piece of paper with a photocopied sketch on it. The contrast was dialed high, rendering all the text excluding the phone number scrawled at the bottom illegible, but at the very center of it was a drawing of a carved box. *The* box.

"If you're looking for a job, I'm looking for help."

Winnie inclined her head. "For what?"

"I'm looking for a family heirloom," Cyrus explained. "It's been in the family for ages, and it's gone missing. We think it's been stolen. It's an old box, lot of carvings on it."

Stiff, all she could do was blink.

"I'm offering a reward for anyone who finds it."

"How much . . ." Winnie swallowed and tried to steady her voice without giving anything away. Without making it obvious that she knew exactly where it was. "How much is it worth?"

"It's actually worthless," Cyrus stated grandly, "but I'm offering five thousand dollars. Sentimental value."

And in the corner of her vision, Winnie caught Kristina's and Yas's brows both shooting up, caught them exchanging glances before they peered closer at the drawing. But she merely nodded and reached for the paper, her smile wooden.

The moment Cyrus pressed it into her hand, his fingertips brushing hers, Winnie's skin burned. It rippled through her chest, flame licking the back of her eyes, until she saw herself in the Red Hourglass.

It was quiet, still and dark, and she was standing alone with Cyrus. Not like how she'd stood with Apollo, in an embrace, touching each other, *tender*. No, Cyrus was rigid, his hands by his sides, his breathing tense, and Winnie was holding a knife.

The lavender pocket knife Marcel had gotten her for her sixteenth birthday. The blade was drawn.

"Do it," he whispered, his hazel eyes piercing and intense, before he closed the gap between them. Though the blade pressed into his soft knit shirt a little, he didn't look away from her face as he urged again, "*Do it.*"

It sounded like a dare—*Why was he daring her? And why was he there in the first place?*—but, instead of sinking the blade into his side, Winnie raised her face to his, lips parted, and—

"You okay?" asked Cyrus of the present, standing on the sidewalk in front of Kavanaugh's gates. He extended his hand to touch her shoulder, flashing his familiar silver watch, and Winnie reeled away. "Your eyes just . . ."

She had to force the air back into her lungs. Her fingers trembled while folding the flyer and shoving it into her breast pocket next to the money. "Yeah, I'll keep an eye out."

And then she rushed away without another word, looping her arm with Yas's, feeling Cyrus staring into her back.

CHAPTER 9

Beside the Cemetery Dirt

I am losing my mind.

The moment Yas and Kristina disappeared around the corner, Winnie darted across the street and headed south through Elmwood Village toward the smaller shops. They'd left her outside the co-op grocery where she pretended to work, but her true destination emitted a bloodred glow that marred the pristine sidewalk. The Red Hourglass only had two employees: Winnie and Hortense, who owned the store and operated it whenever Winnie was in school.

Now she pushed herself to walk faster, to run, breaking into a full sprint as if she could leave the premonition from Cyrus behind.

The knife, his stare, *the watch*—it was Cyrus who would open the box that killed Winnie. So why would she ever try to kiss him? *Him?* Cyrus?

Because I'm losing my mind.

She whipped open the door to the shop, relieved by the jingle over her head. "Hi, Miss Hortense!"

At the register, the small woman with skin the color of walnut peered up from behind a thick book. Her dark, curly hair was swept back in a clip as always, a deep purple shawl thrown around her shoulders. Her brows wrinkled. "What's the matter, Winnie?"

Winnie's smile went rigid. "'The matter'? Nothing!"

"Then why are you acting like you're being chased?" said Hortense as she set her book down and rose from her chair.

It was easy to think Hortense younger than she was, and sometimes the reality of watching her move struck Winnie. Her skin had the beginnings of lines, but was still quite smooth. Her smile was wide and warm, and the personality she exuded made her seem taller. Yet now as she scooted toward Winnie with small, careful steps, scrutinizing the panic in her face, Winnie couldn't ignore the wisdom and years coming from her. The concern and frailty that reminded her of her grandmother.

Hortense wasn't psychic like Winnie. Though she loosely believed in Winnie's ability, she couldn't see the filaments at all, and she couldn't know what Winnie was running from. So there was no point in asking what Hortense would do, yet the question almost bubbled out of Winnie anyway.

She clamped her mouth shut until the urge faded—she didn't want to know how it felt for Hortense to dismiss her too. She was still raw from her conversation with Marcel.

"I'm not being chased!"

"Hmm." It was Hortense's way of saying she didn't believe it, but with nicer language. She waved Winnie over to the small kitchenette and makeshift altar in the back. "I need you to finish dressing these candles for me today. I have a feeling we'll need them."

The task sounded more interesting than the usual, stocking shelves and staring at the cigar-smoking rat until someone came in. However, dressing candles was something customers asked of *Hortense*, as a kind of priestess. It was uncharted territory for the seventeen-year-old resident psychic.

Winnie paused, nervous. "Finish them? By myself?"

"Yes, my hands are hurting me," said Hortense quickly,

massaging her thin, wrinkly fingers for show. "I thought you'd be happy for something else to do, but if you don't want to learn, then I can—"

"No, I'll do it!"

She rushed forward. On the low table sat a collection of thick candles of varying colors, some in glass containers marked by saints, and bags full of herbs and bottles of oils beside them. The crystals had been pushed back to make room for a mortar and pestle. She had an idea of how they'd look in the end, just from being the one who stocked and arranged them, and guessed it wasn't the physical effort that would challenge her; instead, it was the combinations she'd have to learn, remember. Which herbs paired with which color candles, and how the oil factored in, she couldn't have said.

"You want to start with the herbs first, they carry energy with them." Hortense's voice was firm as she waved her hands over the collection and pressed a bag into Winnie's hands. "Everything grown in nature has spirit, has intentions, can be drawn or repelled."

Winnie wasn't sure she believed any of this had true power, candles and magic oils and flower petals, but evidently many people did—the candles sold well. Even Apollo Rathbun had bought a crystal when they came poking around the shop, calling her a fraud.

Did they believe in the power of blessed candles too? Did Cyrus? There was something about that family, those two cousins, that kept hijacking her thoughts, and she couldn't escape. She found herself wishing that she could just ask Apollo if they knew about the box, what Cyrus might do with it.

She wanted to read them again and divide the premonitions from the dreams once and for all.

". . . these things can act like magnets if you're smart, good and ev—are you listening?"

Winnie snapped out of her daze and nodded, crooning sweetly, "I always listen to you."

From then on, she refused to let her thoughts drift, to think about Apollo and that look, Cyrus and *that* look, blood surging from her mouth. She took notes on the old woman's instructions, which herbs to sprinkle like she was seasoning a dish, which oils to layer on top as a sealant. Some candles were to be engraved with particular symbols or words like *love* or *power*, and carve Winnie did, long after Hortense patted her arm and said goodbye.

Basil, blackberry leaves, palo santo shavings, and garlic. Again and again, on loop in her thoughts, until it became automatic, unthinking.

So deep was she in her work that Winnie didn't hear the bell over the door at first. The approaching footsteps. It was only when a hand touched her elbow that she leapt and turned around.

"Excuse me!"

A customer waved a pair of silky raven feathers in front of Winnie's face. She was middle-aged, with hair the color of wheat and an apologetic smile when she noticed the candles and what she'd interrupted. The beads clacking around her wrist filled the shop.

Winnie wiped her hands on the towel and stepped away from the altar. "Will that be all?"

The sun was already low in the sky as she came around to the register, and it would only be a handful more candles, a few more sticks' worth of palo santo shavings, before she could close for the evening. Then, of course, would come the piles of homework. She might not have a chance to visit a pawnshop and rid herself of the box, of the Rathbun cousins, until the weekend.

"Do you have any more cemetery dirt?" asked the woman in a whisper, a furious blush on her cheeks. "I didn't see any on the shelves. I know sometimes Hortense is quiet about it."

Despite the woman's embarrassment, Winnie nodded with a bland smile and strolled over to the supply closet. She was schooled in such requests. More cemetery dirt, more rainwater, more teeth and other bones, they were all things she'd been asked before.

"Just a sec!" she called over her shoulder.

Cemetery dirt came in cute little jars stored on the bottom shelf, collecting dust because Hortense preferred people ask rather than have curious—and *angry*—strangers poking around. No one ever told Winnie what they were used for, but she wasn't sure she wanted to know either.

She threw open the door and squatted, her knees twinging with the effort after so long standing straight, and flinched.

A draft moved through the shop. "*Siggy, guqqgi hiib.*"

Sitting on the bottom shelf, right beside the jars of cemetery dirt, was a pillowcase wrapped around something small, heavy, and rectangular. *Her* pillowcase, a soft shade of yellow with white stars on it. It, and the thing inside, should have been sitting quietly in her basement but was now, inexplicably, impossibly, here. Waiting for her.

"No . . ."

Her voice was hardly audible.

Then, with a steadying breath, she reached past the box, grabbed the little jar of cemetery dirt, and slammed the closet door shut behind her.

No, now wasn't the time.

"Here you go!" Winnie rang the customer up and watched the woman depart with unerring calm, though on the inside she was tumultuous.

It might have been better to hand the box over to the customer as a gift. Let it be someone else's problem. But then Winnie considered the customer opening it, trying to store something inside. Perhaps the light lying in wait might kill her instead. Lying was one thing, but Winnie couldn't imagine transferring her fate onto someone else.

Winnie worried her lip at the thought before slinking back over to the closet. The cuts on her fingers throbbed just looking at it, finding little drops of blood where she'd touched it last night. Her hand hovered over the case, hesitating.

"It's not possible, it's not possible, it's not possible." Yet the chances she and Hortense had the same bedspread, or were being tormented by the same box, were slim.

Then she pulled the fabric back to reveal its contents, and her heart sank.

The box made of bone belonging to some large creature, carved and awful, was truly here. The box that wasn't in the supply closet when Winnie had poked around for supplies just the day before yesterday was right here, waiting in the Red Hourglass for her to find.

It had *followed* her. And then she was forced to picture Hortense making the mistake of opening it next.

"*Oyab xgyyj ceji ez ucfbihhuyz, guqqgi hiib.*" The whispering sound scraped against her eardrum. "*Ez ucfbuzq lyb ci qy lyggyv.*"

She ran her hands down her face and sat, legs splayed, on the floor.

There was no way she hallucinated walking to the basement. Winnie Bray had never hallucinated a day in her life—she had extra sight to see the filaments, yes, but this wasn't like that. No way did she pantomime bagging the box, carrying it downstairs, all while it was still scratching and gnawing and skittering and—

"Shut the fuck up," she hissed at it.

And to her surprise, it listened. It stopped all its noise, and then the hairs on her arm rose. They were alone in the shop, just her and the box, and she couldn't shake the feeling that it was looking at her. Listening to her. Waiting for her to do something.

But what?

With a hopeless shrug of her shoulders, Winnie sighed. "I don't know what you are, or where you came from, or what you want from me. Why are you even following me?"

"Oyab xgyyj ceji ez ucfbihhuyz."

The sounds brushed against her like spiders, crawling all over her body, into her ears, down her spine. Slipping deep inside until it made her bleed out. She shivered and leaned away.

Was she supposed to read it again? Winnie always saw something new when she read people, but they were *people*; and not all objects could be read, but the ones that could had never shown futures before. Objects weren't complex—they didn't carry their own thoughts, feelings the way this one did.

And it felt . . . hopeless. Touching this skittering, whispering thing made Winnie feel hopeless.

If the box could follow her from her basement to the Red Hourglass, there was nothing to stop it from appearing at school or following her across an entire ocean, transporting itself into Cyrus's hands and rending her apart. This thing was destiny, pursuing her, and she couldn't pretend that her sight wasn't always, *always* right in some way.

"Qewi ezyqsib gyyw."

"Unless . . ." She worried her lip again.

Unless she missed something, which happened sometimes. Maybe she'd misinterpreted her death, and by looking again, she'd find some new context. A feathery pulse, a way out.

Winnie pressed a single finger to the box and gasped. Lightning raced through her arm and made her heart stumble in her chest. The muscles in her throat clenched, and her eyes burned and rolled back until she saw . . .

Nothing.

Nothing at all.

She blinked and stared at her finger.

The lightning was receding from her skin, tension melting away as if the box was refusing her. As if a wall had been put around the future, blocking her cursed sight from knowing more.

Or, she considered as she sat back on her heels, she'd seen all there was to see, and there was nothing else of her to sift through.

CHAPTER 10

Forging an Accomplice

While her friend-by-association group occupied themselves by talking about Senior Formal, Winnie sat on the uncomfortably scratchy tartan blanket and desperately browsed every social account in the city under the name *Apollo*. Searching for them was better than watching Kristina and Yas wrapped up in each other, Yas stroking Kristina's ankle idly with her thumb as "friends" did while Kristina twirled a finger around a lock of Yas's hair.

The only sure way to find Apollo was through Cyrus, and she wouldn't go near him with a ten-foot pole—apparently a knife wasn't enough. Yet she had to know what Apollo knew. They might be the key to saving her when the time came.

The solar eclipse, the chasm, the bright light. She, Apollo, and Cyrus were right at the center of it.

"Wait, I'm lost—so how many formals are we going to?"

No one was listening to the live music they'd come to see. No one was really interested in a cover band delivering slow, depressing renditions of Stevie Wonder and Michael Jackson; it wasn't anything to dance to, but it was decent ambient noise while they said goodbye to the summer sun. The first day of autumn was also their last Thursday to lounge on a blanket by the water, listening to free music, until June.

A boy from Kristina's neighborhood named Jeremiah leaned

back on an elbow and plucked a grape from the tray at the center of the blanket. He went to St. Ignatius, an all-boys' school, and with Yas and Kristina, he was deep in the complicated calculations that came with private Catholic schools and the restrictions on who could and couldn't go to homecoming, who students could and couldn't bring as dates. Jeremiah couldn't take his own classmate, but together they *could* bring Kristina and Yas.

"*One* lavender formal!" Kristina clarified, entwining her pinkie finger with Jeremiah's in promise.

It went without saying that Winnie wasn't going. Clinging to someone's arm and dancing meant a lot of skin-to-skin contact, meant her skin on fire and her eyes claimed by sight that would only lead to her picking apart a person's whole life. She'd see too much. And besides, she didn't have anyone anyway.

Kristina ate another brownie. "My vote is for Kavanaugh, since it's practically on Niagara Falls."

"Win? What about you?"

Winnie looked up from her phone to find her cousin waiting. Trying to include her when she didn't want to be included. Yas and Jeremiah both had already tried to set her up in the past, and it never panned out. A girl from Beaufort who thought it was weird that Winnie knew so much about taxidermy. Winnie couldn't tell the truth about the Red Hourglass, and so she was accused of conferring with demons. Jeremiah's pick had been a guy from St. Ignatius whose body spray was nauseating. When he'd touched Winnie's hand, she flinched at the pain of it and at knowing he'd call her a freak before the night was done.

That was how it always went, how she always ended up alone. All the little crushes never amounted to much when she had to stay out of reach.

"Huh?" she asked.

Yas took her time to watch the seagulls flying overhead. "What if we all go to Kavanaugh?"

All was doing the heavy lifting.

Kristina was the first to catch on. "Yeah, two formals back-to-back is kind of a lot."

"Oh god, no," Winnie grumbled, waving a dismissing hand. "I don't even know if I want to go. I was thinking of skipping."

No more being set up, feeling more alone in an effort to be less. In a matter of weeks, that box would try to kill her, and if she failed, she didn't want to waste her last moments cringing away from some stranger. She'd be dead before her cast even came off—she'd rather spend it doing something *important*.

Like trying to stay alive.

So she returned to her phone, to what might be her only chance: the Rathbun family. There was a fluffy obituary in the *Buffalo News*, the mile-long article talking all about Theodore Rathbun, the perfect patriarch. The Rathbun family wasn't just a part of Buffalo history—they *were* Buffalo, apparently. They, along with a few others, built this city from the ground up. The Central Terminal was dedicated to Theodore's great-grandfather. His loss was a loss for everyone, a piece of history from Buffalo's renaissance.

Blah, blah, blah.

There wasn't a renaissance, in her humble opinion. The whole city looked like it was trapped in the 1890s—every building was squat and crumbling and begging to be torn down. The streets had seen better days decades ago. But Mayor Walter White attended the funeral of Theodore Rathbun. He spoke to the grieving widow personally instead of sending letters or an email. That family was important, it seemed, and they had a big fat mansion on Millionaire's Row to prove it.

That's what the *News* forgot to mention—that the neighborhood full of chic office buildings and foundations and mansions wasn't just called Bryant. It was *Millionaire's Row* to the rest of the city, because normal people didn't live there. They drove past it. They walked through it. They collected its garbage and mopped its floors and even built the homes that now stood proudly above the city.

And if she didn't find Apollo, Winnie had no choice but to head there tomorrow after work. Apollo probably didn't live there, but according to the obituary, Theodore Rathbun had only two sons, Richard and Edward, and four grandchildren—including Apollo and Cyrus—so surely someone other than Cyrus would know where to find the green-haired heir.

Then as if thinking could conjure them, Winnie caught a glimpse on the edge of the crowd.

Apollo was hard to miss. Such an ugly, *hideous* shade of vomit-green stood out. Their heavy black hoodie seemed to absorb all the light, and the chains dangling from their baggy black pants jingled at the perfect frequency for her to hear.

Yes, it was definitely them, definitely that curl to their hair, especially at the nape of the neck. The jewelry in their ears, on their wrists, on their fingers—Apollo was draped in silver and had turned themself into a shiny bauble that Winnie couldn't help but track, and all over again she heard their voice.

Calling her a fraud.

"Be right back."

"What—" Yas started.

Winnie was already up on her feet and stomping through the crowd of picnic blankets and lawn chairs, children playing catch or sprawling out on the grass. She made a beeline for Apollo as they retreated from the show and headed toward downtown.

"Hey!" she shouted, surprised by the bass in her voice. Surprised by the anger she felt when they didn't slow.

Up close she spotted tiny white pods nestled in Apollo's ears; they didn't hear her approach, wouldn't notice her gaining speed until she cut them off.

Apollo drew up short. "*Watch it—*"

As they snatched the earbuds out, their eyes, such a delicate shade of hazel, narrowed on Winnie. Their lips dabbed with red-tinted gloss pursed into a perfect bow-shaped pout. A glower. She couldn't fathom how those visions would ever come to pass, that she'd ever tolerate being near them.

"Oh," said Apollo flatly, as if they heard her thoughts and felt the same. "It's you."

She raised her pink-casted arm for them to see. "Yes, *me*."

That softened Apollo a little bit. Softer than Cyrus had been when he saw it. Softer than even Yas when she'd walked out of the ER. Winnie pictured Apollo's bewilderment when she'd broken it, their frantic guilt as she'd climbed to her feet. Yes, she could use them to foil Cyrus and save herself. Others might have fallen prey to Winnie's premonitions, but *she* was different. Clever. Only now, having cornered them under the skyway, alone in the shadow and hiding from the setting sun, she realized she didn't know what to say next. *Help me? What do you know?*

Her mind went blank with Apollo staring back at her. She couldn't remember if they'd been this tall in her premonitions, or if it was just platform shoes. Looming over her, just like their cousin, was Apollo dangerous too?

They slipped their pods into the case and waited, not so patiently.

Floundering, Winnie put her hands on her hips. "Your cousin's a bad guy, you know that?"

Apollo startled at her words, and then their eyes dimmed again. Like they had to force the coldness in them, like the sharpness didn't come naturally but was carefully curated instead. "I know. Sorry about your arm."

And then they stepped around her and walked away. Just like that, no goodbye, no asking what she really wanted.

Sorry about your arm.

Apollo kept walking, chains clanging down the street, retreating farther and farther away from the sun and the music and the liveliness of the event. And just like at the Red Hourglass, they got to have the last word while Winnie stared, speechless.

So she ran after them. In several big strides, she arrived at their side and tried not to register how they scowled when they saw her. *She* was not the problem; she wasn't the trouble that had befallen their stupid family. Their stupid family was the trouble befalling *her*. Apollo had walked into her shop and started all of this, not the other way around.

"What do you want?" they snapped, picking up the pace. And with their long legs, so much like Cyrus's, it was hard to keep up.

She didn't like comparing them, Apollo and Cyrus. They didn't feel like they should be compared. One could pull her from the chasm, while the other would bury her in light.

Winnie rushed forward. "Whatever he's looking for, make him stop."

"Oh yeah? And what's that?"

She paused her walking to fish the illustration from the bottom of her tote bag. She'd been carrying it around everywhere—her wallet, her keys, her bus pass, her phone, and this dangerous flyer—just in case.

Then she scurried after Apollo, already halfway down the block, and held it in front of them. "This."

They drew up short. Stared at that paper for a long time but didn't touch, like it was acidic. Like it might burn them the way she'd been burned. Winnie couldn't be sure, but she thought their fingers trembled. Fine fingers in so many heavy rings, the nails freshly painted. Dark nails that would hold her close—

"What is it?" Winnie forced herself to ask. "What is it for?"

"Where'd you get this?"

Apollo *recognized* the illustration. They finally took the paper from her and kept staring. They knew about the box. Next, she needed to know if they had an idea of what waited inside. If they knew what was coming and how to stop it.

She snatched the flyer back. "I found it."

They stood there for a moment, chewing on their tongue, studying her face. Their gaze passed indulgently over her eyes, her flushing cheeks, her mouth. Finally they scoffed. "Liar."

And then Apollo kept on their way.

"Hey!" She started after them again and could've sworn this time they waited for her to catch up.

"And not a very good one—"

"Not true." Winnie bristled. "I'm an excellent liar."

They gave her a hard look and scoffed again. And kept walking, although this time, she confirmed their effort to move a little slower, to let her follow. She wasn't imagining it.

"What? Did you get a vision? Am I gonna die?" Apollo teased with a smirk.

They'd never help her if she told the truth. No one did.

"Actually, yes," she answered plainly.

Apollo stopped walking for just a moment, just to narrow in on her and her frankness, and then their scowl returned. The jest was over, and they were no longer in a laughing mood. "That's not funny."

"No, it isn't, which is why I'm not joking." Winnie wouldn't give up. She couldn't. "And if he doesn't stop, I'll die too."

It wasn't such a leap to think Apollo might die in the light—Cyrus was *their* cousin after all, and they'd come to 483 Heritage looking for that box together. Still, this lie made her feel ill.

"Sure—"

"You know I'm right," she snapped.

She was gambling on that look on Apollo's face when they first saw her in the house. They didn't know how she got there, and this was perhaps the time to show it. To really prove it and hope that they, unlike everyone else, might listen.

All she had at this point was hope.

"How exactly are we gonna die? How do you know?" Apollo asked, taking a charged step toward her. And Winnie foolishly took a charged step toward them instead of away. Before she could answer, they added, "And *don't* say you're psychic."

Winnie clamped her mouth shut. As she tried to think of another response, how to lower their defenses so they'd answer her questions, Apollo shook their head like this confirmed she was a fraud and turned their back on her. It wasn't that they didn't believe her; they just didn't *want* to believe her. They wanted Cyrus to be a good guy, but he wasn't, and it wasn't Winnie's fault for saying so.

"How do you think I found you at the house? You think it was a coincidence?" she shouted at their retreating form.

Apollo shrugged. "It *was* a coincidence."

"Then watch me do it again."

They gave her a long glance over their shoulder, and Winnie raised her broken arm again for them to see. She let Apollo linger on it. Let their eyes betray them as a soft thing to be twisted to her demands. If they wouldn't willingly be her accomplice, she'd *make* them, forge them with her own hands if she had to.

"You owe me," she said, "and if I'm wrong, all you lose is five minutes."

She watched them deliberate, trying not to think about how close they still stood to each other now, and how close they'd stand to each other again. The shadows cast by the setting sun carved out the edges of their face, their jaw, as they chewed their tongue again in thought.

Winnie didn't know if she was running *toward* her destiny or away. If it was a smart gamble to hitch her horse to Apollo, pitting the cousins against each other.

Apollo sighed finally, begrudgingly, and nodded toward a café on the corner. A local chain and Winnie's favorite, in fact, because nothing tasted more like courage than their espresso shakes made with too much caramel, white chocolate, and cream, just the way God intended.

"Fine," they spat, stepping into the crosswalk, not at all menacing like Cyrus. "Follow me."

CHAPTER 11

Perhaps, Maybe, Might've, by Happenstance

"So how does this work?" Apollo asked as they dropped down onto a sagging blue couch. The café was empty, no one but a disinterested employee around to listen to them get their future read again by a psychic girl who couldn't possibly be psychic yet still knew too much.

They didn't believe in psychics, but they also didn't really believe in coincidences either. Not like this. Like finding the girl in the house at the same time Cyrus wanted to investigate. Like Cyrus inviting them to stay at Rathbun Manor, no strings attached. Like their grandfather and her father dying in that same house on the same day in connection to some mysterious heirloom Apollo had never even heard of, yet Cyrus wanted and she wanted to keep from him.

They swirled a green tea bag in a cup of steaming water and watched Winnie approach the armchair at their side. Her faux locs swayed in time when she stepped around the table, the sickeningly sweet perfume of vanilla and cherries drifting their way when she sat, and she adjusted the big, clear glasses on her face, oblivious.

Apollo tried not to breathe her scent in too deeply, which instead transformed to them not breathing at all. "Did you hear me—?"

Winnie put up a single manicured finger, almond tips painted a deep, deep purple, and took a sip from her own drink, some huge, milky abomination with far too much whipped cream and caramel syrup running down the sides to be healthy. Coffee at this time of evening. Her lashes fluttered, her eyes drifting shut in bliss, leaving Apollo to do anything but stare at how smooth her skin looked, how it wasn't a stretch to call her *pretty*, even under the terrible lighting.

Perhaps she grifted *because* she looked like that. Doll-like, innocent, smelling like dessert, all so she could get away with it.

Apollo would keep their guard up.

They focused on the picture she'd dropped on the table. The antique box with the carved faces, another copy of the drawing they'd found in their grandfather's desk down to the nonsensical text and the faded annotations on the sides. And of course they recognized Cyrus's phone number haphazardly written at the bottom.

How did she get this?

Maybe she'd stolen it, picked it off of Cyrus's body in the fight, though that didn't seem likely. She could have just found the flyer around or printed it from somewhere online. Or maybe she was lying about this like she'd lied in the fortune reading, and she was lying about the box killing Apollo just to corner them . . . For what? What could Apollo possibly have that she wanted when *she* was the prep school girl bound for the stars?

"I need your hand," Winnie said when she finally set her cup down and leaned forward. "And then you can ask me a question. Something you know the answer to. Don't ask me what you're gonna be in ten years—you won't know and probably won't like the truth."

Her tone was all business, and as she removed her jacket and set her tote bag aside, she sent more wafts of herself toward Apollo that they had to fight to resist.

They faked a cough in the crook of their elbow just to sneak an inhale.

Winona Bray was dangerous. Like an angler fish, a bright lure in the dark that only led to sudden death.

Apollo took out their phone and set a timer for five minutes, propping it up between them on the table so that she could see. They wouldn't let her sink her teeth in them.

"How is reading my palms gonna tell you what I had for dinner two nights ago?"

She smirked. She looked annoyingly confident about being able to do something no one in the world could. How about you let me show you?

When Winnie took their hand, she didn't actually look at the palm. Just like last time. She winced at Apollo's touch, her right eye twitching as she stared into the distance. Her gaze glazed over, and her irises slowly drifted up and nearly rolled into the back of her head. Her throat tightened for a moment, like she was fighting against this feeling, against *Apollo*, but then she let out a tight breath.

It didn't seem pleasant.

Apollo felt nothing but the coolness of her hand, her grip loose on theirs.

"So?" Winnie asked, shifting her head toward them but not really looking at them. Not with her eyes still rolled back. It was creepy. "Your question?"

They cleared their throat and repeated, "What did I have for dinner two nights ago?"

Her head turned ever so slightly, and immediately she replied, "Pizza and wings."

The charm and softness that usually adorned her voice was gone, replaced by vacantness. Like she did this every day, which they supposed she did. She met countless people every day; making shit up was business as usual. She could be lying to Apollo right now.

"Okay, we're in Buffalo. That was a bad question—"

"Although *you* didn't eat much," Winnie continued as if she hadn't heard them. Then she frowned and added, "You looked sick. Are you okay?"

Apollo coughed again and pursed their lips in thought. Just saying they looked sick didn't convince them of anything. The clock on their phone continued to count down. "What's my sister's name?"

She again shifted her head, like she was reading Apollo's whole life written in the air. She answered quickly, "Artemisia." The corner of her mouth twitched up, smirking again. Before Apollo could snap back, she added, "You're a twin, fraternal. Older. And you still talk every day. How cute."

They didn't like how she said it, didn't trust her to mean it.

Apollo drummed the fingers of their free hand on their thigh. "Any others?"

"A brother," Winnie said without hesitation. She stretched her neck left and right, as if she was just getting started. "Orion. And your parents are Richard and Elizabeth—your mom's Black, and your dad's family would have minded if she hadn't come from money too. That's how you're related to Cyrus. And all of this can probably be googled, by the way. Your questions suck."

They resented that, lips curling. They didn't sit around thinking of ways to test a psychic. Even as they tried to come up with something else, something she really wouldn't know, their thoughts hooked onto the idea that Winnie might have googled them. They both liked and hated it.

"Although . . ." She squinted and leaned forward. Her locs

trickled and swung forward like pendulums counting down. "You don't live with your parents and siblings anymore. Interesting. *You* are staying at the Rathbun house with Cyrus. The big one on Millionaire's Row. Just moved in last week, actually."

They blinked. *Millionaire's Row? Was that what she called Upper Bryant?*

Without waiting for any reply, she inched forward again, nearly hanging out of her seat, and chewed her lower lip, like something interesting caught her eye.

"You were arguing with your dad recently. There was a phone call from school; they had you in handcuffs in the hall. You had a black eye and—"

Apollo snatched their hand away. This wasn't fun anymore—they didn't understand how she did it, but they didn't want her prying into their life. Whether Winnie was truly psychic or not, she knew more than enough, more than they were ready to share. It didn't matter how soft her voice, how she fluttered her dark lashes, the cast on her arm.

No.

She didn't get to know about the fight. She didn't need to know about Patrick Barnes, what Apollo did and how good it felt, how Cyrus went and covered it up without them asking. Helping Apollo as if he could coerce their loyalty from it.

Together they sat in silence.

Apollo took a sip from their piping-hot tea, letting it burn their tongue just to soothe their parched throat. And in the corner of their eye, they watched Winnie press the heels of her palms into her sockets, wiping the last dregs of Apollo from her sight.

Her demeanor was nonplussed, taking up that massive swirl of sugar and coffee again, instead of smug like Apollo expected. She sat there as if she knew she really was psychic and whatever pain, disorientation that came with it was par for the course. Apollo shivered.

At the shop, her eyes had gone shrewd and calculating, her mouth carved into too perfect a smile, and it'd made them feel like she was lying. But right now, she simply looked tired.

"Believe me now?" she asked as she slumped back into her seat. One fine eyebrow arched.

I'm starting to.

Rather than admit that, they grimaced. "Let's say I do. What do you want from me?"

They didn't have a clue what Winnie expected of them. Did she expect Apollo to tackle Cyrus, lock him in the creepy dungeon, and leave him there forever? Did she know about the creepy dungeon? Did she expect Cyrus to care what someone with a *track record* had to say?

If Morning Star—the heirloom, whatever—was going to kill them, kill her too, why would she waltz right up to Apollo instead of keeping her distance? She was allegedly psychic, couldn't she just save herself and leave them to perish?

"I want your help." She picked at a loose thread at the end of her sleeve and didn't look up to see Apollo's reaction. The bravado of the fortune teller dissipated. "To stop him."

Those four innocent, vulnerable words hurt Apollo to hear, for all the wrong reasons. People didn't want their help. Nobody trusted them with anything. Apollo was someone to be handled, kept under control, something wild and unpredictable to plan against. Apollo couldn't even save themself without police getting involved—their help was a curse.

Winnie went on. "I mean, what is it? Why does he want it?"

The folder from Cyrus included photocopied pages from their grandfather's notebooks, and they'd gone late into the night flipping through it all, trying to wrap their head around it. Grandpa Ted seemed to think that the box harnessed the power of a star, based on plans from his great-grandfather. He talked about energy and equations, unlimited and stronger than the sun, right in the palm of his hand. Where the first Rathbun had carved a place for the family with real estate in the early 1800s, now Cyrus, in Grandpa Ted's steps, wanted to take them into tech. *Energy? Defense? Space??* he'd scribbled in the copies' margins.

But those were all just theories, dreams, about something neither of them had ever seen.

"It's a family heirloom," said Apollo with a sigh, rubbing their temples and trying to remember whatever words Cyrus had used or highlighted. They didn't know how to help her. They wanted to, wanted to prove they could be good, but that didn't mean they knew what *good* looked like. Especially when they'd already decided they wanted no part in this the moment they found that dungeon.

"No, I know that, but like, what's *in* it? Where'd it come from?"

Apollo straightened on the couch. "Do you know where it is?"

Her eyes sharpened, defenses up. Quietly, she replied, "I didn't say that."

Winnie was lying again. She might be able to read Apollo like a book, but they were fast learning how to read her too.

She couldn't sit still. Fidgeting in her seat, some battle waged plain in her eyes, under her skin, as if she was trying to weigh how much she wanted to tell Apollo. As if *they* were untrustworthy and not the other way around.

Just like everyone else saw it.

Apollo hardened. "Look, *you* came to *me*. There's only so much I can do if you don't tell me what you know. I don't even understand what it is, so it's not like Cyrus'll listen if I just say, 'Hey, stop.' He wants glory, and he won't stop until he gets it. But I think it's how my grandpa died. And your dad."

"My dad?" Winnie's brows rose, and she waited for them to say more. Not that they knew what to say about that either, or even how the box was related to the fire. It took several starts and stops before she managed to mumble through gritted teeth, "Perhaps, *maybe*, I *might've* found *something* at the house, by happenstance."

Oh my god, she's infuriating.

"'By . . . happenstance'?" Apollo cocked their head.

She pushed the flyer away from her and ignored them. "But when I touched it . . . I'm not all-knowing. I can look around, but sometimes if the vision is strong enough, I just see people in a place, hear what they're saying. It would take a long time to follow how they get to a particular moment, and I can only hold on so long when it hurts. This time, with so many pieces . . . I don't know why he opens it, or how this pure light spills out—"

"'Why *he* opens it'?" They swallowed. "You mean Cyrus? Is that how we die? Whatever's inside kills us? *Cyrus* kills us?"

She flushed.

Apollo had found themself leaning in closer, transfixed by whatever siren quality Winnie had to her voice until that last part. There was something alluring about the way she described what she saw and how, this arcane ability that was impossible and didn't exist in the world and yet had to be real all the same in her. And why her? It undercut how devious she was underneath.

But she'd seen them die and was here to warn them. She didn't ignore them like everyone else did.

Before Apollo could say anything more, sort through all their questions and thoughts, the lone barista approached. She wiped her hands on her black apron and sighed.

"We're closing now, so I'm gonna have to ask you to get going."

Winnie nodded absently, still fidgeting with the ends of her sleeves. And Apollo took her in anew, how the armchair suddenly seemed to swallow her, how she fought to stand. If they were someone else, they might have comforted her.

Instead, Rathbuns only knew how to break things.

Now pure light from a box was going to kill them by Cyrus's hand. Was that what happened at 483 Heritage Street? Light and a fire?

The barista retreated, and Apollo followed Winnie and her nearly finished drink outside. They rubbed the teeth of their house key against the pad of their finger to keep them grounded, to stop them from reaching out to her. Or bolting. Apollo was only freshly independent, on their own, ready to figure out what they'd become, and the answer was awful: dead. Would their parents finally be relieved?

Standing beneath the streetlight, Winnie looked like the angel of death. The light provided a halo that invited Apollo to turn into a moth and make it easy. The dainty chain around her dainty neck, the charms in her locs that glittered, her apparition was plaintive and saintlike. She wanted Apollo to come willingly, valiantly, to their death instead of resisting, and somehow they didn't immediately refuse.

Somehow Apollo *wanted* to offer their help, even if it turned out to be a hoax. Even if Winnie was both a liar and telling the truth. Even if they were forsaken, Apollo wanted to be her only hope.

So they took that step toward that light. "Are you working on Saturday?"

The invitation surprised Winnie, who glanced up from reading a message on her phone to search Apollo's face. "I . . . I'm not working, no."

They hesitated. Playing hero hadn't worked out so well last

time—heroes didn't need their moms to talk them out of handcuffs because they bashed a boy's face in. Big cousins didn't buy heroes out of pressed charges. Apollo was more than a tragedy in the making, even if their family didn't see it that way.

If the box was dangerous, they'd hide it. Destroy it. Pretend they never saw it and make it so no one ever found it again.

"Good. Then I'll meet you at your shop at noon. Bring whatever you 'perhaps, maybe, might've found *by happenstance*,' and we'll go from there." Every word sounded like a question, Apollo was so unsure.

Being a hero was unfamiliar ground.

But Winnie's eyes brightened, and she nodded eagerly. Their heart panged to see it.

So somehow, they would betray Cyrus, who'd settled their debts, all while living under the same roof. Stab him right in the back—Apollo could totally do it. It should be easy for a delinquent like them, right?

She walked away without another word, and Apollo was left watching her form, her hair swishing down her back as she drifted from the light.

Apollo Rathbun believed Winnie. They didn't just listen, but they sat there without some smug look on their face, and listened, and *believed* her. Put real, live faith in Winnie's words. In her power. In *her*, like no one else had.

As she hurried back to Canalside, Winnie realized she couldn't remember the last time someone had really believed the truth from her lips. Or most of it, anyway. Hortense, maybe, but she'd never told the old woman's fortune and the old woman never asked. And though she sometimes suspected her family did when she slipped up, they'd never admit it. A girl who could see the future, including all your mistakes, was more terrifying than death itself. Yet Apollo did it without flinching, without knowing her at all . . .

Even if she'd hoped for it, she wasn't prepared for how it felt to have someone just listen.

Her cousin and friends were still standing around when Winnie returned, the picnic blankets rolled up and loaded haphazardly into Jeremiah's trunk. Yas idled on the sidewalk, scanning the park, switching her weight from leg to leg impatiently.

At the sight of Winnie coming down the block, her expression went from relief to a wide grin. Her eyes bulged as she rushed forward and seized Winnie's shoulders.

"What was that about?" demanded Yas breathlessly, giving her a shake.

"What was *what*?" Winnie said, blinking, innocent.

She, however, knew exactly what her cousin referred to. It was now twice that Yas had seen Apollo, without even knowing about their visit at the Red Hourglass. Apollo wasn't still a stranger, but Winnie didn't know how to explain them, choosing instead to just shrug and squeeze into the back seat of Jeremiah's car.

Yas followed and pressed in close. "You have to tell me."

Winnie pretended not to hear, so her cousin pinched her, right on her ribs. *"Ow—!"*

"Are you, like, into them? Want to ask them to join us for Formal? We still have room in the limo."

"No, and no." She grimaced at the horror of such an idea.

Rather than that be the end of it, Yas closed her eyes, a pained look crossing her face. "Okay, but *please* don't tell me you're into the landlord."

Her stomach clenched, thinking of Cyrus and the knife. What might have been a kiss or a curse.

"Yas, shut up."

She didn't want to talk about dates or Formal—she only wanted to cling to this weightlessness, this strange unburdening that had overcome her body, for as long as she could.

When Jeremiah arrived at her house, Winnie murmured a goodbye, scurried inside without meeting Yas's eyes, and tried not to overthink it: putting herself out there, Apollo softening when they saw her arm, the sun setting their eyes ablaze when she told them they would die.

"Qsibi uh zy fgez qseq dez eddyazq lyb ci, guqqgi hiib. Qsibi uh zy fgedi oya dez baz vsibi U vugg zyq luzj oya."

Ignoring the persistent whispers of that carved box now nestled in her sock drawer after its discovery at the Hourglass, the sensation of wind and feelers brushing against her, Winnie crawled under the blanket and replayed Apollo's words. *I'll meet you at your shop at noon.*

It wasn't so hard to believe someone would finally listen to her. That there'd be someone in this place who cared what she had to say.

Yet she tried to steel herself anyway. Just in case.

April 1907

The dreaded box from Rhodesia sat on a table among other boxes carved from bone, one from marble, another from limestone, but there was only one that whispered to Alexander. He didn't know when the whispering started, but there it was, even now, even in his sleep.

Though he'd replicated its form as best he could, spent hours upon hours late into the night carving—*always* carving lately—he could not manage a perfect one. He wasn't sure that he ever would, but he wanted to try, to figure out exactly what it was about this vessel that was so different from the rest. Inside was something momentous, powerful and dangerous, and after the mishap with the president, he sought to build a better vessel so he could control it lest *he* be speared with light or spewing blood too.

If he mimicked the exact specifications, or remade it bigger or thicker, would that create some new but vital pathway he couldn't see? Would that help him understand?

This box, like everything around him, was of the material world and obeyed *science*, yet he was afraid that he never would understand, that he might die still ignorant. Insignificant. And thus without a monument to his name.

Sometimes when he slept, he swore the box sounded like a ticking clock just to mock him.

It sat among its counterfeits and whispered loudly to him,

until he felt the very words coming from all around and inside him, the breaths tickling his muscles. He wasn't sure he always understood the words either; they were in a language not of man. None of his linguistic texts, his anthropological references, none of his letters and university visits could seem to unravel this box or give him any bit of headway.

How could he tame it, then? How could he bend this thing to his will?

"*Oya hiiw qy qeci vseq oya dezzyq*," was all it told him from the stained oak table, and he continued to stare at it as if the room was spinning, as if the very flaps of the lid moved with its speech. Sometimes when he braved opening it again, just a crack, all the objects in the room *did* fly at him, or the force of it sent him falling away while his pitiful boxes carved from wood caught fire. Sometimes Alexander felt like *he* was spinning and not the other way around.

A disturbance broke out on the floor above him, tearing through Rathbun Manor while he watched the twisting, turning of the very air around him. Light made thick and visible, refracting on nothing, and he had no idea if it was his imagination or real. Alexander had been sleeping poorly or not at all, but also suspected that the box had its own gravitational pull, and inside was a core far denser and more powerful than should be possible. When he exposed this mystery at last, he'd become legendary to the field of physics.

"*Where is he?!*" a voice bellowed through the muffle.

The cellar door wrenched open then, sending down a ray of soft light and the clamor of footsteps.

"I've had enough," said his eldest son, Joseph, a new severity in his voice. "Father, I've had enough of this. We could feel the earth trembling all the way in Delaware Park today."

His gait was angry, heavy, and in the span of seconds, Alexander thought he could feel his son entering the box's orbit. The boy didn't seem to lean with the weight of it, to let it tamper with him the way it seemed to tamper with Alexander, but then again, he wasn't sensitive to science. He was bullheaded and aloof simultaneously.

It turned out that Joseph had a weaker constitution than Alexander had hoped, and it was for this reason Alexander had to keep the box away from him. His boy would squander it on his esoteric interests, trying to summon magics and fairies instead of rooting his work in the real world. Where real people would see it. For this reason, Alexander went to painstaking lengths to record his tests and theories and sketches in these manuscripts—so *real people* would read them. What were angels to a physical thing such as this, of matter and space, with a mass that pushed and pulled?

"You missed Isabelle's wedding," stated Joseph, and though Alexander refused to look up from his work, he knew the boy had a scowl in his brow.

See? he thought, feeling validated. *Weak.*

Even when stern, his son lacked the proper bass in his voice to be truly terrifying, especially to Alexander, his elder. When Alexander knew better.

"Her wedding is next week, the fifth." Alexander set his paper and charcoal down and rubbed his eyes. Littered across the floor were his imperfect illustrations, new angles and new shadings that tried to capture the refracting light and thick air but failed. Perhaps his eyes really were tired, and that was the explanation?

Joseph threw a newspaper right on top of the counterfeits. "Today *is* the fifth. You haven't left this cellar in a week."

Alexander froze.

The date was there in print, inexplicably. And when he finally—*finally*—looked up at his boy, to see what trick this might be, he didn't see any trace of a boy at all anymore. There was silver along the edge of Joseph's ear. His blue eyes were weary, dim and stricken by the lines of time. He looked older than Alexander remembered him, though he was sure that Joseph was still a boy. He had to be.

Alexander hadn't been distracted for so long.

"Did you convince the paper to do this? Why—?"

Joseph tossed back his head and released a bitter laugh. "Why would I when your obsession can do this for me? You haven't bathed, you haven't eaten, your suit hangs on you like rags. *I* have been running Rathbun Mining for years now while you continue to chase this fantasy . . ."

Alexander didn't want to hear him speak about fantasy. Not when he was the one who brought up magic and superstitions.

"Oya dezzyq syfi qy dyzmaib. Oya dezzyq syfi qy qeci ci. Qsuh uh zyq e hidbiq ciezq lyb oya. Oyab illybqh ebi laqugi . . ."

Joseph's ranting was too loud—it was talking over the box, right as it was telling Alexander something important. It could be sharing secrets of how to conquer it right now, and he might never know if his fool of a son didn't cease his yammering. Yes, Joseph may have looked older, but he still behaved like a *child*.

Alexander considered himself a gentle father, but in this instant, he wanted only to throttle his eldest.

"I've requested a visit from Dr. Myers to have you evaluated, and—"

Here, time and somehow space was curving around this object, and Alexander could hardly taste the dust from it without his family inserting themselves. They didn't understand that he was on the brink of greatness. And they weren't worthy of the secret he was so close to unraveling.

"*Oyab vybw uh laqugi*," it was saying. "*Oyab guli uh laqugi. Vseq oya ebi uh zyqsuzp defexgi yl dyzmaibuzp, yzgo xiuzp dyzmaibij.*"

Yes, Alexander could hear it, could nearly understand it. It was speaking right to him, in a frequency only he could understand. Joseph couldn't fathom that his father was a great man who would give his life to this and build his monument.

Scientia vincere tenebras.

"Oya qsuzw oyabhigl e dyzmaibyb xaq oyab ebbypezdi uh oyab jyvzlegg. Oyab ebbypezdi, oyab pbiij, xyqs ciezuzpgihh. Yzgo oya vugg xi dyzmaibij xo jieqs. Xo ci—"

"Now, come upstairs. I've had the servants draw you a bath." Joseph rested a firm hand on Alexander's elbow.

He smacked the hand away. "Leave me in peace. Get out."

The boy startled, and moved to try again, but no, Alexander meant it. He meant to be alone with the box, to understand and translate its message. He meant to crack this code or die trying. To be great or die trying. Something Joseph's degenerate, lazy, and pampered generation didn't understand.

"Father—"

"Get OUT!"

Alexander shoved his son hard. It was enough to make Joseph stumble back and fall. His head collided with the cement wall with a *crack*, and his eyes swam as he sank, his feet splayed out in front of him. It took a long time for his gaze to focus again.

Alexander sat still, unsure if he should help but unwilling to step away from the box in case he missed something. He just—his family was always getting in the *way*.

Joseph sprawled at the base of the stairs, his fingers floating up to the back of his skull. They came away spotted in red. From the sheer violence of it, he then gaped at his father, while Alexander turned away. Back to the box from Rhodesia, the family's salvation, otherwise what was the point of all this?

"Oya ebi zyq e pbieq cez."

Yes, yes, it was all becoming clear. Alexander nodded, his jaw tremoring. He thought he was finally getting it. "Yes, I am."

"Oya ebi ezoqsuzp xaq pbieq."

"You're wrong," he whimpered, tears trickling down the sides of his face. In a fit of rage and desperation, he shoved all the other boxes, the counterfeits, away. The box was letting him in, as if only to taunt him; for all his sacrifices, he had nothing to show.

It all crashed at Joseph's feet, stirring the boy, who then scrambled up from the floor. He marched angrily up the stairs, and the walls seemed to shake when the door slammed shut behind him.

"Oya, vsy vugg xi dyzmaibij xo vybch, vseq ebi oya vybqs ul oya dezzyq qeci ikiz qsic?"

Alexander was alone when he raised the chisel in his hand. He was faintly aware of the rest of his family storming out of the manor, leaving him finally, blissfully, alone in the quiet below. With the flutter of air that teased him, wrapped around his neck, and hurled poison in his ear. "All I wanted was to . . . Perhaps you're right."

Then he shoved the blade into the side of his throat. Deep. The pain swelled in him, and out poured misery. Out poured his failures, the truth that he wasn't a great man at all, that the box wasn't just power but also truth, and truth always won.

Again and again, while the box watched and whispered, he took the blade out and dug it right back in, knowing that he had finally succeeded at something.

CHAPTER 12

Fire Is Fire

By the time Winnie reached the streets of Elmwood, she was late. Her bus hadn't shown, which left her trekking halfway across the city, and then she'd stopped for an espresso shake, *extra* caramel sauce. For fortitude.

Now, as she walked beneath the tree canopies, in and out of the sunrays shining through, it had occurred to her that maybe she *should* be afraid of Apollo, of people like them. Not the mullet and eyeliner, but Rathbuns, people with power or proximity to it. They might not have been the one to break her arm, but they lived with the person who did. And she'd been foolish enough to reveal her hand, that she had what Cyrus was looking for, while they readily offered to help her.

It wasn't that she trusted Apollo either. She just couldn't bring herself to be *afraid*—that vision of them in handcuffs and with a black eye aside, Apollo was wiry. Fragile-looking. Clearly susceptible to persuasion. Meanwhile Winnie's harmlessness was merely a mask. She came armed with the future and her pocket knife, the one she'd apparently come to threaten Cyrus with.

If Apollo tried anything, sinking a blade deep into the soft of their thigh would be easy.

She found them leaning against the trunk of an old elm tree right in front of the Red Hourglass. Their long black cardigan and cropped tee shirt flapped in the breeze, exposing a hip bone, while they focused on the phone they held aloft. Winnie picked up tinny replies from whoever was on the other end of the call, probably their sister, as she neared.

The instant they noticed her, their smile shuttered to a blank mask.

"I'll talk to you later, I gotta go," Apollo murmured before swiftly hanging up.

A couple of power walkers in neon polyester strutted past them on the sidewalk. All the cars parked along the block were empty, the streets quiet. Then it was just them two.

"Shall we get this over with?" Winnie took a sip of her shake with measured calm, in an effort to appear disarming, though it didn't seem to work.

Apollo eyed the strap on her shoulder, the backpack she carried, with suspicion. And when they pushed off the tree, her heart beat faster in response.

She tried not to think about how it reminded her of *that* part of the box's vision where they'd been too close, huddled in the dark. How Cyrus would try it too at knifepoint. Forcing herself to remain still, she stared at their shiny hair, wet and freshly cleaned and in neat, green ringlets.

Apollo was nothing like Cyrus, she told herself. For better or worse.

"You got the box?" they asked as they pivoted to the street, their car keys ringing in their grip.

She cleared her throat.

Parked before her was an old Volkswagen bus, the sides eaten away by rust, the chipped green paint peeling in sharp edges. Apollo rounded to the driver's side.

"I didn't say I have *it*, I said I might've found something—"

"And I already established that you're a bad liar. When you lie, you smile like you're planning to rob me." The van rattled when they climbed inside. "And if I'm wrong and you *don't* have it, I'm sure you'll get a vision of me leaving you on the side of the road."

They waited, watching her through the window to see what she'd do.

Winnie huffed, reluctantly pried the passenger door open, and hauled herself up. The van felt like it was held together with duct tape, and upon second glance, she realized the rearview mirror actually *was*. Her seat belt had a little give when she buckled herself in. The cushion wobbled beneath her as she tried to get comfortable.

If she hadn't already seen her future, she'd think she was going to die in this van.

"So I was thinking Letchworth State Park?" Apollo turned the engine on and glanced her way with an arched brow. They had a striking profile, sharp and fearless, that made her mouth go dry. "Cyrus would never find it there, and it'll be pretty empty this time of year."

She nodded and clutched the little handle over the door. Just in case. It too felt loose. "Fine. How old is this thing?"

"Old."

When Apollo threw the gear in drive, the van set off far smoother than Winnie expected. Than Winnie thought capable. It rumbled its loudest and most violent at red lights, when it was at a standstill, but dulled to a hum when they drifted onto the expressway.

She sipped her coffee, letting the sugar coat her taste buds and soothe her nerves. Caffeine filled in the heaviest, hollowest points of her body until her grip loosened.

"So you really believe me?"

Apollo shrugged. "I don't know how you know what you do,

but you're right—Cyrus's getting into something weird, and I don't want to die."

Winnie nodded and lapsed into silence, gazing out the window and trying not to feel guilty for lying, while Apollo drummed their fingers on the steering wheel to imaginary music. Because the stereo probably didn't work. It would take some time to arrive at the park considering how the engine rattled, if it wasn't already shedding parts by the mile. Its noise drowned out the box's hissing, though, and this flavor of quiet seemed better than making forced conversation.

What's your favorite color? was a silly question to ask when she was trying not to die young. And while she was curious why Apollo would ever drive such a wreck when they came from money, that was simply too personal.

She took another sip of iced coffee then, let the gurgle of the straw fill the car, and tried to relax. It was impossible.

"How do you drink that? It seems so sweet." Apollo grimaced.

"That's the point," Winnie quipped, taking the time to finish in one loud, big gulp. The whipped cream and ice settled happily in her belly. "The box makes noises, you know. Makes it hard to sleep, so I need the sugar *and* the crash."

"Noises?"

She stifled a yawn at the thought. "Whispering, scratching. It sounds like there's something trapped and trying to get out, but all around me, all the time. And when I touched it, I saw . . ."

She made an exploding gesture with her hands.

It was weird, talking about her ability, out in the open. Until now, it had been relegated to silence, hidden in the back room of the Red Hourglass. It was like being naked, sharing a secret with someone who might run and broadcast it as soon as they left her sight.

"What do the whispers say?" Apollo's brow furrowed. She silently appreciated how expressive their face was.

"Dunno. I forgot my demon box translator in my locker."

They just shivered. Actually *shivered*, instead of rolling their eyes or snorting or laughing at her. "That's terrifying, to think there's something alive in there."

Winnie didn't know what to make of that, any of Apollo's reactions. They might know more than they let on, so she decided to say less about it until they showed their cards.

She pursed her lips and glanced into the back of the van. The interior looked far better than the exterior at least, a lush, shaggy black-and-white rug that seemed clean, an assortment of pillows and blankets that looked comfortable. Fairy lights hung around the windows. Boxes were wedged neatly behind the driver's seat.

"What's all that?"

Apollo glanced in the rearview mirror. They were venturing farther from the city now, deep into empty roads that wove around the forests and towns at the heart of Western New York. Winnie rarely came here except on school picnics or for the occasional family reunion; it certainly wouldn't have been her first idea for handling the box, but no way Delaware Park, full of soccer teams and smack-dab in the middle of the city, was an option. Apollo made a good call.

"Camping, for road trips and stuff," they answered hurriedly, like she'd flustered them in asking a tricky question. There was nothing else to see, nothing else to distract them for a mile. "I want to travel, see other places, so I'm fixing this thing up. I got a camper's stove and everything."

"And you'll sleep back there?"

They nodded proudly.

Winnie supposed it *did* look cozy by some stretch of the imagination. Maybe even cozier than some motels she'd stayed at on family vacations, the beds she was forced to share with Yas that smelled like cigarette smoke. But she couldn't imagine being alone for days, parked on the side of an empty road. She couldn't be herself around her family, but they were still *there*.

"Sounds lonely. And uncomfortable."

She hadn't intended to say it aloud. What Apollo did when this box problem was over was none of her business, she reminded herself.

"I have two younger siblings, and my parents are always on my case," quipped Apollo with a smile. "I think I'll manage."

She turned to face forward. "They on you about college too?"

People like the Rathbuns were probably legacy students at some Ivy League, their applications routed to a special pile where deans knew them by name. Winnie's mom was strict—a degree from a four-year college at minimum, no exceptions—but Apollo was probably promised to Yale at birth or something. She snorted, imagining the jangle of their chained pants and that awful mullet on a posh New England campus.

Apollo loosed a soft breath. "No, I'm not in school actually."

"But I thought . . ."

It had only been weeks since she'd seen them grace Kavanaugh's campus one morning before swiftly disappearing, which everyone assumed was a transfer. Whisked away to some prep program even more elite, exclusive, perhaps. It happened occasionally.

Instead, they whispered, "Got kicked out. After getting expelled from public too."

Then a thick silence filled the car, and Winnie's cheeks flushed. She shouldn't have asked. She shouldn't have *spoken*.

Apollo remained stiff in their seat, focused on the road and sneaking glances at her to gauge her reaction. Her mortification. And she stared straight ahead while aware of their every movement.

This was why people didn't want her to open her big mouth. She didn't say good things that they wanted to hear. If she kept it up, she'd blow it and really be on her own.

"I'm sorry, I shouldn't be so nosy—"

"No, it's okay," Apollo tried to say, but it was too late.

Winnie shifted to stare at the tree line growing thicker, at the painted park sign up ahead. Her time was better spent enjoying the leaves that were beginning to change, the array of colors that welcomed her in. Buffalo inspired these bittersweet feelings in her, that she couldn't wait to escape, but also, in death or in departure, she'd miss this beauty. She refused to think about Apollo, the black eye and handcuffs, what they did to be *expelled twice*. She wouldn't picture them lying under polychromatic trees in their cozy van, alone but completely themself, while Winnie would be doing parlor tricks in a new place for strangers' approval.

Nope, she wouldn't bother with any of it.

The moment Apollo put the van into park, Winnie threw open the door and leapt out. The air was fresh in the woods, clean and comforting in a way she forgot air could be. Not even on Kavanaugh's campus were her breaths so crisp, the space so quiet. There wasn't any noise at all except for the box in her bag and Apollo's time machine rattling as they climbed down and locked the doors.

Apollo eyed her a beat too long, peevish, a scowl on their face, before fetching a small shovel from their trunk. "Let's do this?"

She swallowed and hurried forward.

✦ ✦ ✦

The freshly dug hole was a miniature grave, and Winnie couldn't stop staring at it and thinking about what Apollo said during the drive. *That's terrifying, to think there's something alive in there.*

The box was quiet when she reached into her bag to retrieve it, solemn as if it knew what they were planning. As if it was afraid, or perhaps appalled that they hadn't even sprung for a tombstone, though the whole point was to make sure it wasn't found ever again.

More likely, she considered as she closed the bag, the box still wrapped in its pillowcase and tucked under her arm, was that this thing was simply watching her again, waiting to see what she did next.

It couldn't be this easy.

"Here."

With Apollo eyeing the case, she flashed the blood-dotted fingers she'd snagged that first night. They were still bleeding and slow to heal, as if something was reopening the wounds in her sleep. "I can't figure out how to touch it without getting cut. This is a week old, and it's still bleeding."

They opened the pillowcase and snuck a glance. "I think that's called hemophilia."

"I don't have hemophilia," she snapped.

With slow caution Apollo ignored her and reached inside, as if it might bite. In the daylight, the material looked even more luminescent, the dirt in all the grooves faded. The carvings were still strange, grotesque, and the waves beneath the serpent began to look more like a mass of people, screaming. Winnie turned away—she didn't want to look at it any longer than she had to.

"It's . . ." Apollo gulped. "Smaller than I expected, but definitely the box from the sketches. I've seen this script in my grandfather's notebooks."

Winnie rubbed her arms to fight away the chill the box had given her. "'Notebooks'?"

They sat in the grass. "Family heirloom, remember? My grandfather was studying it; we found a bunch of his notes in the attic." They turned the box over and studied its sides. "The theory is that there's some serious natural resource inside. Some sort of energy. Cyrus wants to eventually extract it."

"For what?" She frowned.

"Tech, research, the government, weapon manufacturers—it's unlimited power in a box, according to that theory."

Winnie scoffed and dropped down beside the grave, annoyed that she hadn't guessed as much. "It's always money."

There were always these things cropping up, inventions and creations and oddities that were dangerous, that killed people, and you were never supposed to bat an eye because the people who died were acceptable collateral damage. The Cyrus Rathbuns of the world weren't expected to pay the price for their own ambition; it was people like Winnie and her family—her father. That the Rathbun patriarch might have faced a similar fate felt like a rarity, a fluke, and clearly, it still didn't change anything. It didn't stop what was coming.

Why was her life an acceptable building block for Cyrus's rise to fame?

"Can I open it real quick?" Apollo asked, oblivious to Winnie's brooding, holding the box up to their ear and giving it a shake.

"No."

They set it down in their lap. "But we don't die here, do we? What if it's only dangerous because Cyrus activated whatever's inside?"

Winnie climbed to her feet and backed away. "In my vision, this thing tears a room in half when it's open, and just watching made me feel like I was on fire. If you want to take that risk, go ahead."

Her voice was strong, and that seemed to convince them, even though she didn't give any details about *how* they'd die. Because she didn't know. Because at the end of the day, all Winnie knew how to do was lie. She wouldn't allow herself to feel guilty now; she'd never seen her own future until she touched that box, which meant that this premonition and its rules were uncharted territory. Maybe Apollo was right, and they could raise the lid without killing her, but maybe she'd changed her fate, *accelerated* it, simply by telling them. She didn't want to chance dying here either.

Apollo's understanding was a dark look on their face as they dropped the box into the grave. "I'm sorry you had to see that," they said softly, scraping dirt into the hole. "It must have been terrible."

Winnie hadn't bothered to mention the shadow the size of a planet moving through the sky, the solar eclipse, her vomiting blood. So they should have comforted her, Apollo's empathetic and oblivious words, but they didn't. She was too far out of reach.

There was no fanfare to burying the box. Its sounds faded to silence. Nothing had launched itself at her, scorched her, torn through the ground and tried to swallow her whole. Once the box was fully buried, there was *nothing*.

Her breaths didn't come any easier when they were back on the trail.

"I didn't think it'd be that simple," Winnie admitted finally, keeping her eyes on the ground. It was done.

Apollo shrugged like it was nothing. "Glad I could help."

"I expected it to put up a fight, but I guess I could've done that myself. It's over now. It's buried, so thank—"

“Shh!” They put out a hand to stop her.

She balked. Did they just *shush* her? In the middle of her gratitude? Smacking their hand away with her cast, she pressed, “That was rude—”

“*Winnie.*” Apollo’s voice was low and sharp, a forceful warning. It was the first time she’d ever heard them use her name, and she didn’t like it. “Look. Up ahead.”

And when she followed their gaze, she understood why.

The box was sitting right at the end of the trail, where fields opened up to picnic pavilions and washrooms. Right where anyone could have stumbled across it and picked it up.

“*Oya dezzyq xi buj yl ci.*” A scratching sound raised the hair on the back of Winnie’s neck.

“How did it do that?” Apollo whispered to her, as if they were afraid of being overheard.

She just dropped her head into her hands and groaned. “I knew it was too easy.”

It was playing tricks on her again; just as she’d tried to leave it in the basement and it reappeared at the Red Hourglass, the box made them think burying it would work. It was devious.

In a flurry, Apollo grabbed the thing from the dirt and stormed to the back of their van. The old metal door creaked on its hinge as they fetched something from inside and slammed it shut. Then, without another word, they marched off, pants jingling, toward the row of pavilions.

“Apollo?”

Winnie darted after them, once again struggling to keep pace with their long strides. Especially when they were angry. Scared. They didn’t look back at her.

“What are you doing?”

“What do you think?” they snapped, strolling right up to a

pavilion. Winnie glimpsed a white plastic bottle—*lighter fluid*—in their hand. "I'm gonna burn it and scatter the ashes out the window on the drive back."

Her eyes widened. "Don't you think we should—"

To her surprise, they slowed. And turned to her. And the anger that seemed to burn in them vanished to unnerving zeal. Brightness that gave her pause. "Okay, do you have a better idea?"

No, she didn't.

She didn't know anything about this box, other than the fact that it was fucking with her, playing with its prey before the kill.

Taking her silence for agreement, Apollo tossed the box carelessly onto the grill, flicked open the lighter fluid, and doused the lid. Winnie suspected it wouldn't work—*the box had survived the fire at 483 Heritage, hadn't it?*—but she also didn't know what would happen if they tried again. Maybe another fire, a *hotter* fire, would end this. Maybe, hopefully, she was wrong. Fire was fire, after all.

"Guqqgi hiib, oya dezzyq xi buj yl ci. Zyq xo lgeci yb jubq yb sujuzp."

She grabbed Apollo's sleeve. "Wait, do you hear that?"

"Hear what?" They glanced between her and the box, exasperated. "I don't hear anything. It's probably just the wind—"

"I don't think it's gonna work."

Apollo snorted and fetched a matchbook from one of their deep pockets. "Well, it's worth a try anyway, isn't it?"

They weren't listening. Nobody ever listened to her.

Winnie kept her eyes, wet and waiting, on the box, because she was frozen in place, torn, knowing this thing was dangerous, remembering how the light would pour from it and invade everything. The blood spilling from her mouth, her collapse, *flatlining*. But then . . .

There's something alive in there.

Could it feel pain? A living thing that could give warnings and move itself to new places, following her, never letting her escape—would it feel the fire, even if it didn't burn? The box could do the impossible, like her. The box was *like* her. She should be studying it, trying to understand it, not—

The match struck. Apollo dropped it onto leftover charcoal, and flame erupted on the grill.

She lunged for it. "No!"

Apollo seized Winnie around the middle before she could sink her hands into the fire and wrenched her away. "What are you doing?!"

Their shouts were drowned out by sudden panic mounting in her, that the box would be lost, that she'd be alone again, that it could *feel* flame licking its bone the way she felt that light shredding through her own, and maybe her father too. Her breath cinched until she saw—

Nothing was happening.

"Vibi oya elbeuj, guqqgi hiib?"

Her mouth fell open. Beside her, Apollo was still shouting, even as they released her. "What is wrong with you?"

She didn't know.

Winnie just shook her head, confused at how the fear had risen out of nowhere and gripped her instantly. Irrational and all-consuming fear of being separated, of the box being destroyed. It didn't feel like *her fear* at all, now that she thought about it. It felt conjured. A lie.

"I don't know, but it isn't . . ." Winnie swiveled Apollo around.

The box wasn't burning. The rational part of her mind had suspected it wouldn't, yet something had taken over her body anyway and left her limbs feeling alien. It was strange, watching the flames lick at its sides, waiting for the fire to do what it should. Waiting for the box to behave like it should while knowing deep down that it wouldn't.

It only wanted to mess with her.

"Oya hsyagj xi."

Gaping, Apollo backed away from the grill slowly. Cautiously. And beside them, Winnie followed, clasping her hands together in case there came another urge to grab it.

"How did you know?" Their voice sounded haunted.

"I found it in the house." She realized she was trembling. "I don't know why I—it made me do that."

Together, they watched as the fire failed to consume it, as charcoal faded to bright orange and became cinder, the box looking exactly the same as before they started. Unchanged as it was when she found it in the basement, and once again surrounded by ash.

In the stillness, with hesitation, Winnie extended a hand to finally touch it. "Cremations burn at a higher temperature. Maybe we could . . ."

Apollo kept their distance, kept shaking their head. "I'm not breaking into a funeral home."

The box was cold as ice when she touched it. Her hand pressed flat at the side, as if it hadn't just sat over a fire and been doused with lighter fluid. Behind her, Apollo scowled, terrified.

"It's cold," she explained guiltily before stepping away.

A long, tense moment passed before they finally came closer. First they peered over Winnie's shoulder, alternating glances again between her and the box as if this was all somehow her doing, as if she and the box were conspiring against them. It made her feel dangerous and alien and also protective of the thing.

They extended a hand like it was a wild animal. "That's impossible—"

In a flash, Apollo yelped and whipped around. The shout was loud and feral enough to make Winnie jump. A pace away, they gripped their wrist close and glared at the box, biting back a curse.

"What? Apollo, *what*?"

Doubling over, they hissed. One loud exhale after another, while she could only watch helplessly. Confused. They flailed their hand again and again, the flesh of their fingers and part of their palm rapidly turning red.

"It fucking burned me," they growled through gritted teeth. Then they reeled away from the box—from *her*—and dropped on the metal picnic table, shaking.

Winnie glanced at the box, Apollo's pained face, her unmarred palm, and the burn on their hand. "But I *just* touched it, and it's cold as ice. It couldn't have—"

"Tell that to my fingers!"

Which she couldn't if they were still shaking. So she seized their wrist to get a steady look. The skin radiated heat and looked achingly raw, but as she held on to them, she realized her mistake. The strings of fate that comprised Apollo took hold of her. She'd done it without thinking, but now *she* was burning while a vision forced its way up her veins and into her eyes.

Winnie was no longer studying Apollo's hand and instead was watching them drag a wooden chair through a hallway lined with doors and tan lockers. A school. She knew she should look away, but there was a lone boy riffling through his own, hunched over and unaware, or pointedly ignoring the screech of wood against the concrete.

He didn't see Apollo's hand tighten around the back of the chair. He didn't see Apollo swing for him, but Winnie did.

She let go and staggered away the moment the chair made contact.

“W-what did you see?” Apollo groaned. Their eyes were unfocused, chest trembling with frantic breaths. “You saw something, didn’t you? Your eyes did the thing.”

She shook her head. “N-nothing. Come on, we need to take care of your hand.”

CHAPTER 13

A Preposterous Question

Apollo dreamed of fire.

The halls of Rathbun Manor were burning, flames climbing the walls and licking the decorative drapes, the massive painting of Josiah Rathbun, one of the first to settle in Buffalo, over the mantel, devouring the antique wood and velvet chairs along the grand manor hall.

It was only a dream, they knew, even then, but still they felt the heat against their skin. The fire gnawing at fat and flesh and bone. Their lungs spasmed from the hot air, eyes stinging from black smoke, and it brought them to their knees.

"Help . . ." The voice was faint over the roar of the blaze, Apollo's hissing breaths, but it sounded familiar, soft and plaintive. Angelic.

It sounded like *Winnie.*

On their hands and knees, Apollo eased down the grand staircase. The dusty banisters were nothing more than skeletal, a strong push away from buckling. The walls threatened to bring the ceiling down on them.

"I need your help."

It was a mistake for her to ask them—Apollo had never saved anyone before. Couldn't save anyone. All they could do was break: their parents' faith in them, Patrick Barnes's jaw and cheekbone,

their future. If Apollo hadn't been expelled, if they hadn't swung the chair, they wouldn't have even needed to crawl into Cyrus's hand.

They wouldn't be at risk of *dying*, if what Winnie saw was true. Winnie might be a liar but she wouldn't lie to them; not now, anyway.

"Do you believe me?"

They wanted to refuse, say no.

Winnie Bray had been nothing but scheming and mischievous since the moment they met, a sharp darkness in her doe eyes, but there were also brief moments when Apollo glimpsed between the gaps in her armor and thought they saw just a girl in trouble, in need of saving.

Apollo wasn't a knight. They didn't know how to slay dragons.

They descended the staircase, right into the hell of the grand foyer. Gold leaf on the chandelier was burning, raining down on them like the heavens were on fire. Billowing flames worked on eating through the ceiling beyond, and there was no doubt in their mind that it was coming from the study. Their grandfather's study with its wall of books and dark wood furniture.

"Apollo, do you believe me?"

The only thought on their mind was to get to her, to pull her to safety.

When Apollo crossed the threshold of the study, Winnie wasn't waiting for them. She didn't lie on the ground or cower in a corner. Instead, there was only the antique box, *Morning Star*, sitting right in the center of their grandfather's desk. It felt posed, poised as if it had been plotting. It had faked her voice, knowing Apollo would follow. There was no expression, but Apollo could feel eyes on them while flames danced out from under its lid like the face of a biblical angel.

A creature that simple humans weren't meant to behold.

"I want you to help me," the lid said again in Winnie's sweet lilt, while the flames that should have burned it wouldn't. "*The devil was also an angel.*"

Then the lid flew back, wide open with a sickening, squelching *crack*. Like a skull cleaved from a neck, like the fracture of a jaw under fist after fist after foot—

Apollo jolted awake from the nightmare and fell out of bed. Heart hammering in their chest, they landed painfully on their shoulder, knocking their dazed head against the antique nightstand, and groaned.

Thoughts of the box had followed them long after they'd dropped Winnie off yesterday. The uncanniness of it clung to them like a bad smell. They couldn't help replaying the burial, its sudden appearance on the trail, and Winnie trying to save it. If Apollo hadn't acted fast, she would have burned herself.

Or would she?

There was clearly something strange about it. And her. It wasn't just that the box wouldn't burn, but it was the *way* it hadn't, how it seemed to glow sinisterly, the light creating a thin buffer to keep the flames from touching it—it was unnatural. Just like a girl being able to tell the future.

The very same girl who stood in the light and had asked for Apollo's help like an angel.

The devil was also an angel.

With a tired sigh, Apollo pushed themself up and sank down into the mattress. The bed was old and uncomfortably soft, and somehow the clean, new sheets still smelled of old dust. It was already hard enough to get any sleep here, especially without Artemisia's snores to lull them as she'd done for eighteen years straight, but now there was the nightmare to contend with.

They had *Winnie Bray* to contend with. Just as much as the

box disturbed them, Apollo had to consider if she was lying. If they were being taken for a fool and it was all just a trick.

Yet Winnie had been so gentle yesterday after Apollo burned their hand. She didn't behave like it was a trick, like there was something she'd get out of it. They'd even examined her hand—though Apollo had watched her touch it, she was really, truly fine.

Then they'd mentioned the first-aid kit in the back of their van, and she'd pulled them by the sleeve, sat them down on the edge. She was careful, trying so hard not to touch their skin as she cleaned the burn and wrapped it in bandages. She couldn't even look them in the eye as she muttered, "I'm sorry it hurt you. I don't know why I'm . . ."

I don't know why I'm different. That was what Apollo had expected her to say, except she stopped herself. Instead she just smoothed out the tape and smiled.

The burn hadn't even hurt Apollo anymore—they didn't need her to do any of it, but they let her. No one was ever gentle with them, no one ever treated them as soft, someone who could be hurt. It was why they'd donned this shell in the first place.

Afterward, Winnie had carried that pillowcase full of poison around to the passenger seat and tossed it over her shoulder—*Thanks for trying*—like it was the end.

So Apollo couldn't stop themself from suggesting they meet again today, try something new.

"Pitiful," they admonished themself because no one else was around to do it, before getting ready.

To make the bed, first they had to gather all the papers Cyrus had given them and one of the notebooks they grabbed from a box in the attic. They were sure it hadn't helped with the nightmare, falling asleep to readings of megajoules and the differences between nuclear fission and fusion, the equations and mechanics that went into building an atomic *bomb*.

Why would Cyrus want any of this? What would he do with it?

Like the demon core? had been scribbled into the margins of the box's drawing in Cyrus's shaking hand. And when Apollo had looked up the phrase themself, they couldn't reconcile what they saw with what Cyrus wanted to market and sell.

People had *died*. Scientists and their assistants grew sick, were endangered by something they thought they could control, could master . . .

"Apollo? You awake yet?"

Cyrus's voice floated up from the basement. The old air ducts made it easy for them to shout messages to each other, with every whistle and breeze broadcast through the manor. It most surely meant that central heating was probably nonexistent, and they'd have to find someone to fix it before November came around. His words sounded tinny, like a ghost talking to them through dimensions.

Apollo shuffled over to the little vent by the bathroom door and squatted. "Yeah, what do you want?"

"Come down, I need your help with something."

After that nightmare, the words made them wince. They didn't want to see anything he was up to—judging from their bandaged hand, nothing good could come of it.

Still, curiosity made them throw on a sweater and the furry indoor boots that Orion gifted them last Christmas and drift down the stairs. The manor was so empty, lifeless, compared to their old house that every step filled the walls. They were used to two siblings fighting and screaming at each other, their parents issuing warnings, *beeps* in the kitchen, the low television in the living room, waking up to Motown on Saturday mornings—*noise*.

Here, there were no smells of a delicious breakfast underway or even their dad's instant coffee wafting up the stairs. All they smelled was dust and old wood and mildew. It didn't seem possible to be homesick in Rathbun Manor of all places, but the widening gap between them and everyone else left them feeling adrift.

Something banged around in the basement, and they followed the ensuing grunts and curses down, until they reached that door. The once-hidden black door to their grandfather's dungeon that was now wide open.

Standing on the threshold, Apollo said, "I'm not coming in there."

Another crash and clatter as a toolbox fell over and emptied across the floor, and Cyrus's head ducked into view. "Why not?"

They only arched a brow. It should have been evident.

"Oh, will you grow a pair?" Cyrus snapped, throwing his hands out in exasperation. "I can't do all this myself, which is why I'm *paying* you to help me. Do you want the money or not?"

He spoke as if he'd never been punched in his life, and lately Apollo wanted to be the one to do it. His brows even rose in challenge, because he knew that they couldn't exactly refuse, and he had a carrot worth dangling. Their savings were drying up; a week out, and their parents still weren't budging.

Apollo couldn't pretend forever—they were really, truly, on their own.

"Damn, dude." They acquiesced, stepping into the main vestibule.

They hadn't returned to the creepy dungeon since the day they discovered it. In that time, Cyrus had managed to replace some light bulbs and set up lanterns for the rest, so that the long, dark hall was finally illuminated. There was still an inexplicable breeze underground, but now they glimpsed the several rooms branching off. And with its ornate rugs, Gothic sconces, and crown moldings, it looked less like a dungeon, or the Prohibition tunnels mentioned in that article clipping. It appeared just like an extension of the manor.

Which had the effect of making Apollo feel even *more* uncomfortable—what was their grandfather doing down here that he needed to hide it?

Cyrus waved them impatiently from the first room on the right and disappeared back inside.

Their cousin's noise made it less unnerving, with his shuffling about, talking excitedly to himself. His grunts were a beacon for Apollo to trace, for them to lower their hackles.

The room was small and a sore attempt at cozy, with lush velvet chairs and a single full bookcase. The rug had been rolled back and shoved aside. Against the wall was a stack of cardboard boxes like in the attic, coated with thick dust from time, and Cyrus was pulling out the contents: silver serving trays and matching goblets, bottles of wine surely turned to vinegar, and unlabeled jars with dark liquid. There were faded yellow recipe cards and scarves and a rust-spotted knife.

Written on the side of the box was CEREMONIAL.

Nope.

"Is this what you wanted to show me?" asked Apollo tightly.

Cyrus grinned at them. "Cool, isn't it?"

They wanted to stomp out and slam the door behind them and not deal with any of this anymore. If Winnie was right, just being anywhere near their cousin was a liability.

But Cyrus didn't have the box; *she* did. So maybe if they kept it that way, they'd be safe.

"'Cool' isn't exactly the word I'd use. Look, can you make this quick? I have somewhere to be."

He frowned. "What? With who?"

A devil.

An angel.

Apollo didn't know which. And rather than answer, they stepped farther into the room to appease their cousin and scanned the bookshelf.

The Holy Books of Thelema. The Emerald Tablet of Hermes. A Treatise of the Philosopher's Stone. Three Books of Occult Philosophy. Kybalion.

Hairs rose on the back of Apollo's neck.

Cyrus wasn't cowed. "I said, with who? Is it that girl? Winona?"

Hearing him say her name felt strange. He said it harshly, with an accusation attached, even though she hadn't really done anything wrong. Apollo felt the urge to protect her from him anyway.

"No, I'm seeing Art. Why would I—?"

"What do you think of her?" Cyrus prodded instead, not looking up as he continued filtering through the box. "Would you ever be into someone like that?"

It was such a preposterous question, Apollo couldn't help but snort. What did they think? She was a liar and a trickster, and because of her, they'd burned their hand, couldn't sleep, and couldn't even trust their own family. And she went to *Kavanaugh* of all places. Almost everything about her was a nonstarter, and they'd only known her for a week.

Apollo had their fair share of girls to pine after, wanting to both be like them and be with them, but *Winnie*? No. Impossible. Why would he even ask such a thing?

Then they whipped around. "Wait—would *you*?"

Cyrus didn't laugh. He only shrugged and said, "What if I said yes?"

"But she's . . ."

They didn't intend to sound so disgusted. It wasn't that Winnie wasn't attractive—of course, she was. She knew it, too. But more than that, she was also devious. And rude. And bossy. And entitled.

Just like Cyrus.

"Yeah," their cousin said with a dreamy smirk, as if he knew exactly what they were thinking, "she is."

Apollo's stomach soured at the thought of those two together. She'd certainly get under Cyrus's skin, and his temper ensured anything more was unrealistic. Wishing they'd never heard this and feeling strange, they stepped away from the bookcase and pushed the hair from their eyes. "Well, good luck with that. I don't know how she'll take it, considering you broke her arm."

They tried to sound carefree, like it wouldn't matter to them either way, but it was difficult for some reason.

Still, Cyrus didn't notice. He only scowled and gestured to the boxes. "Like I'm taking girl advice from *you*. Anyway, whenever you're done hiding behind your sister, I want you to empty out this room. I'm building a lab."

CHAPTER 14

(Not So) Ridiculous Prophecies

This time, Winnie was ready when Apollo walked through the door of the Red Hourglass. Sundays at the shop were usually slow, so she passed the hours before straightening things on the shelves, inventorying anything that might be useful.

And right as the clock struck two, the bell chimed and a cool autumn wind gusted inside like she knew it would. They darkened the doorstep and glanced around at the curios, green hair dripping onto the shoulders of their oversize hoodie. Then, after a languid moment, their gaze landed on her, and they nodded.

"Hey."

Winnie slid the Government and Politics printout she'd grabbed to look busy aside and nodded back. Cool, aloof, *normal.* "How's your hand?"

Amid the all-black, the neat bandage stood out, as if it really was her fault that Apollo had been burned, and the world wanted her to know it. She should have anticipated somehow that the box would hurt them—wasn't that the whole point of being psychic? She should've known that, like how she knew she was alien, unlike them.

The box wanted her to know it, was forcing her to admit it to herself.

And that was why she'd decided to leave it at home for this.

Apollo drifted slowly through the aisle, squinting at the case full of wet specimens. Their nose wrinkled. "Fine. How's your arm?"

Ah, their guilt for mine.

She tucked her lip between her teeth. "Fine."

It was her idea to come to the shop this time. Apollo had seemed eager to help her despite their injury, and while she should have refused, a small part of Winnie couldn't deny that she liked the company. That she didn't feel so alone in bearing this secret for once.

Even if it was all based on a lie.

Apollo was only helping her because she'd told them they were going to die. Their alliance was one of necessity rather than any desire to do good, so it was in her best interest to shove down the shame that kept rising in her chest until the problem was solved. If they got rid of the box, Apollo need never know that they weren't in danger. That Winnie was a liar, through and through.

"So, what's next?" they asked, finally arriving at the register. Back in the same positions where the two of them had met.

Though nothing had really changed, Winnie noticed now how the green of their hair brought out green tones in their eyes. She'd been too distracted then by the sheer force of their presence, but even the bare skin on their collarbones, where she might one day press her hand, seemed delicate and warm and scandalous to look at.

She had to remind herself that Apollo wasn't as soft as she'd once thought. The chair had *snapped* when they brought it down on that boy, and the desperate fury in their eyes said they didn't finish there. That could either come in handy or be a risk.

"Well . . ." She pivoted quickly toward the bookcase.

After the fire failed, it made sense to table destroying the box. There also wasn't much of an option to hide it, seeing as it could find her anywhere, anytime. Instead, Winnie had proposed looking for a solution *here*, a place uniquely suited for problems like this.

"The box is supernatural," said Winnie now as she pulled a book from the shelf. *Tillie Hartmeyer's Encyclopedia of Magical Objects.* "And we happen to be in a place specializing in the supernatural."

Apollo's brow seemed to arch even higher at that. "Is that so?"

It didn't matter this time if they put on a show of pretending not to believe her. Yesterday, they'd covered that box in dirt and watched it reappear half a mile away. Winnie had pressed her hand to it after it sat over a fire and didn't get burned. It was those justifications that won out before she could say anything more, because Apollo just sighed and strolled over to the case anyway.

Tall and remarkably lithe, they reached up to the top shelf, where she always used a ladder to restock, and grabbed a different thick book with their silver-laced fingers. The movement perfumed the air with peppermint.

Apollo's wrists were slender, pale, and blue-veined, like a sickly Victorian child. Dark circles bloomed under their eyes, making their cheekbones appear sharp and a little feral.

She swallowed and marched off to the reading room, keenly aware of their following steps.

"Anyway, I figured maybe if we know what we're working with, we'll have some idea of how to stop it from . . ." She waved her fingers in the air. "Doing whatever it's doing. Messing with us."

Apollo flopped onto the violet pillows, exposing more collarbone. "Considering you almost launched yourself into a fire, I think it's doing a bit more than just 'messing' with us."

They opened their book.

It was a collection of prophecies from around the world, predictions of world-ending floods and balls of fire raining from the sky. Winnie had always avoided thinking about these kinds of stories, in part because it seemed awful to consider there might be other psychics in the world and she couldn't find them, and also because there might be none at all. The world hadn't ended yet, so they were either wrong or dead—neither particularly useful to her.

She perused the table of contents of her own book on magical items. *Fabrics, plants, jewelry, stones, living creatures . . .* And cracked the spine on the section detailing boxes and containers.

An easy hour of silence lapsed between them as Apollo read, their brows knit in concentration, and Winnie tried. It was harder to focus lately with the exhaustion racking her bones, the box's constant scratching that gave way to horrifying dreams of blood and darkness when she *did* manage to sleep. She needed coffee, something stronger than coffee, and besides, the encyclopedia wasn't saying anything about boxes that could spew light, jump from place to place, and whisper.

"Listen to this. 'Boxes, jars, and other vessels are often infused with magic to help protect or restrain the objects within. Inscriptions can indicate which, as unauthorized persons or methods of opening can be dangerous to the wielder and others around them.'"

They snorted. "Oh, it's dangerous, all right."

The entry ended there without mention of *which* inscriptions were good or bad, though it hardly mattered since they were indecipherable anyway. With a scowl, she then flipped directly to the index, devoid of key words like *motion*, *sound*, or *light*, excluding a small passage on selenite crystals that could be charged by *moon*-light. Hardly the same.

And after every few sentences on cursed dolls, she found her attention drifting back to Apollo. They draped across the pillows like some androgynous Greek sculpture in a museum, where they should have been fed grapes and crowned in a laurel wreath instead of . . . this.

It was distracting.

She slammed her book shut and rubbed her eyes.

"How long have you worked here?" asked Apollo as they flipped through illustrations.

"About a year."

"And how long have you been psychic?" Finally, they glanced up.

As if a spotlight, or sunlight through a magnifying glass, had pinned her in place, she squirmed. Her fingers pulled thread out of a hole in her jeans. "Why . . . why do you want to know?"

No one had bothered to ask her that before, but from them, it sounded like an inquest. Sometimes it seemed like they wanted to catch her in a lie, and some days she wanted to be caught. She wanted someone to care enough to catch her.

Apollo tapped the book with their index finger. "Well, this says that some cultures revere prophets, and others revile, cast out, and kill them. It depends on the source of their vision—so how did you become psychic? Were you just born like that?"

Born cursed.

Was she born different or made?

Winnie straightened and leveled her gaze on them. She didn't actually know the answer, since she'd been seeing things as long as she could remember, but she didn't like the question either—there wasn't anything wrong with her, and she didn't deserve being reviled, cast out, or *killed*. "I don't think you're going to find me in that book."

They studied her for a long time, her posture, mulling over her words, and though she wouldn't back down, Winnie wished she could read them now. Lay her hands on that carved face and know exactly what they thought.

Then Apollo laughed. The sound made her stomach flip.

"Yeah, this is no use. A few chapters back, it said someone once predicted that a giant sun-eating serpent lives in the Earth."

She froze.

"Apparently one day, it'll hatch."

The carving on the box flared in her mind, a snake curling in the sky above a throng of screaming people. Her vision, the ground cracking and something huge undulating through the clouds.

"Yeah, how ridiculous. Who said it?" When she tried to laugh with them, her voice sounded forced, unnaturally high. She watched them, trying to gauge their reaction and if she was transparent, though they didn't seem to notice. Would they still laugh if they knew it might be true?

"I don't know, it says anonymous."

The disappointment was hard to brace against. She was still the only psychic she knew, and if her vision was as grand as it sounded, maybe the last. A savior the world didn't deserve.

Apollo tossed the book aside, never noticing how long it took Winnie to loosen her muscles and breathe again. "How about we walk through everything you've seen instead? Maybe you missed something?"

Every second they came up empty was another second the box might win; it might grow tired of her and present itself directly to Cyrus next, transport itself right into his hands. Maybe that was why she'd one day pull the knife, to get it back.

Picking up a notebook and pen, Winnie nodded.

"What was the first thing you saw?"

Immediately, the pen stilled in her grip.

You. They were so close, it felt taboo. Her eyes should've rolled into the back of her head. If her hand was touching them, she would've been in pain; so why did she look so eager? Anticipating something that could never be?

After that was . . .

Writing as neat as she could, she answered, "A solar eclipse."

"Very original." Apollo searched on their phone and stiffened. "Total solar eclipse . . . Three weeks away."

Their words hung in the air. They didn't look at her, and chewing her lip, she didn't look at them. There wasn't much to say when they both understood what that meant.

A countdown.

She wanted to crawl into a hole. She wanted to throw open the door and start running and not stop until she hit water or her legs gave out. None of this was fair, not her sight, the visions, the box, having less time than she expected.

"Are you sure that's the day we . . . ?" Apollo pouted, refusing to say the word. They were too pretty to grimace.

She'd roped them into it with her awful tongue.

The truth was bubbling up her throat, threatening to spill like vomit. She had to tell them, to absolve them of this chain that she'd put around them, tying them together. Lying was supposed to be easy, and yet . . .

"What else happens?" they asked hurriedly. "Maybe the eclipse is only the start."

Winnie pushed the locs from her shoulder and cleared her throat. "First was the eclipse, and then . . . an earthquake. I was in some room, but I've never seen it before. The earthquake destroys most of the stuff inside, so I only really saw the box. And Cyrus's hand opening it."

In a matter of weeks, somehow, Cyrus would get the box, and all she had to go on was the knife at his side and herself, rising up to meet his face. Did she give it to him? Maybe he seduced her into handing over the weapon that would kill her. At least Apollo would be far away, it appeared.

Dropping her pen to press the heels of her palms into her eyes, she added, "When it opens, I bleed out. Like *gallons* of it."

"Pleasant," Apollo muttered, tugging absently on a dangling earring shaped like a safety pin. "And where do I come in?"

She stiffened. "You . . ."

You don't. This was the time to tell them. If there ever was a time, before they got too far, before they helped too much. Winnie might selfishly lead them to their death right alongside her—just because she hadn't seen it, didn't mean it wasn't so.

They came a little closer, minty and warm, the cushions of the pillow sinking with their weight, and picked up the notebook. "Is this a joke?"

Winnie's vision swam; she'd been holding her breath, biting her tongue to keep the truth from spilling out. Nausea gripped her as she pressed her clammy hands to her neck and turned her head to see what they were squinting at.

- Hygeb idgufhi
- Jebw byyc lagg yl xyywh
- Iebqsmaewi
- Dobah yfizh qsi xyr
- Gupsq

It was undoubtedly her own handwriting, but she couldn't read it back to herself. All the words she'd scrawled were suddenly foreign, as if she'd written them in a trance, as if the box was still messing with her from afar.

"I didn't write that." She was searching for an excuse and came up empty. Apollo was the only person who believed her when they shouldn't have, and now she was *losing her mind.*

However, they didn't look angry. They kept squinting at it, lips still in that pout that she realized meant they were thinking. "I've . . . seen this before."

Winnie blinked. Of all the things she expected them to say, it wasn't that.

Groping for some understanding, she reached for her bag. It might have been her fatigue that made it hard to read, her mind imagining something that couldn't be, and she had another energy shot buried somewhere inside.

But there, at the bottom, was the box and its pillowcase again. It had brought itself to her, sitting quietly the whole time they were here. *It made her do this.* She squeezed her eyes shut, waiting for the room to stop spinning.

Apollo rose excitedly onto their knees. "I've seen this before! I know where to look next—"

She might be sick.

"Hey, are you okay?"

The cushions around her shifted again, and her face was flush with heat. When she pried open her eyes a sliver, she saw Apollo's brows knit with concern.

They quickly pressed the back of their hand to her forehead.

Such an innocent gesture, just trying to check on her, to see if she was ill, a normal thing people did for someone they cared about.

But Apollo still didn't know Winnie well at all, and Winnie wasn't normal. The only reason they were in this mess to begin with was because of how *ab*normal she was. The instant their fiery skin touched hers, there was a starburst behind her eyes.

Apollo in their van, sitting at an intersection. They drummed their fingers impatiently on that raggedy steering wheel, nostrils flaring, chewing on their tongue.

They looked angry. Something was wrong.

When the light turned green, they accelerated, and a dark mass approached on their left. Growing bigger, moving as fast as a comet.

The crash was loud and sudden.

Apollo's van went into a tailspin, the truck that hit it refusing to slow. Refusing to consider the fragile body in the heart of the wreck. The *crack* of their skull reverberated through Winnie's own as she flinched away.

"I'm sorry!" Apollo's eyes were wide. They tossed the notebook aside and backed away from her, hands raised. "Shit, I forgot, I'm sorry."

Her mouth was dry when she tried to swallow.

"It's okay." There was no way to survive in that piece of junk. Just witnessing had birthed a headache that felt like it was splitting her skull in two. She massaged her temple. "You're right, I'm not feeling so great. Can we pick this up another day?"

Something in them deflated when she said it. Their shoulders slumped as they looked between the notebook and her, and then they mumbled, "Yeah, sure. Should I even bother asking what you saw this time?"

Bang.

They'd seemed so proud of that van, all the camping gear in the back, their plans for the future. The only reason she'd seen them lose it all was because they were foolish enough to reach for her.

Reach again, some part of her wanted to say, but that was horrid and the root of the problem. She couldn't have anyone close because she was awash with death.

This time, she didn't have to lie at least.

"Be careful at the intersection of Main and Bryant." Winnie

gathered her things and refused to look at them. She couldn't bear to see how her curse would forsake them too. In some ways, she'd been hoping they'd escape. "Some asshole runs a red and . . ."

You die, for real this time.

She hoped they could understand without her having to say it. It was hard just saying the truth, waiting for them to finally call her a fraud or sick or a freak.

Instead, Apollo saluted. "Aye-aye, Captain."

Pain lanced through her heart.

Everything Winnie predicted about others came true. Even if they believed her, Apollo could only stay vigilant so long. It was only a matter of time.

Everything she touched died, including them. To save herself might be in vain too.

September 1911

Joseph Rathbun glanced around the cellar, standing in the exact same place his father had died. It was his first time down here in years, and it felt strange.

Died wasn't quite the right word to use because it sounded like happenstance, but the truth was harder to put into words. This was the location of his father's untimely demise wrought by his own hand. His own hand, wielding a carving knife that nearly separated his head from his shoulders. The old man wasn't well toward the end, and the guilt of leaving him to his own devices had haunted Joseph in the years since.

Some nights when he couldn't sleep, he thought he heard his father's ghost whispering in the walls. And out of respect, he ignored this dank, dark hole for as long as he could.

Now he walked the length of the cellar, marking where his father's blood had stained concrete, while an architect wrote notes and took measurements, because he was going to renovate it.

"I'm sparing no expense here," he reminded the woman, beaming.

Inspired by the correspondences with one of Crowley's associates in Switzerland, having met up with the occult master and a few of his friends in New York City, Joseph was finally going to pursue his own path with the Rhodesian box in earnest. He'd taken enough time to mourn publicly and agonize over failing the father who'd been lost long before the dismemberment. To be honest, aside from planning the funeral, from the *cleanup*, nothing really changed for him in the aftermath—he still had to handle the family's finances, ensuring his mother was well cared for, his sister settled. The mines' leases were all closed by now, and with the remaining funds, Joseph set up Rathbun Steelworks, which at least was breaking even.

Taking into account this and rent from the old Exchange building occupied by the city, money was still trickling in. Reduced to droplets, sure, but this gamble would pay off.

His father hadn't listened to him back then, back when Joseph had first brought the Rhodesian box home. Alexander was a man of science, believing that modern applications of physics and chemistry would reveal to him secrets of something that was not modern or scientific at all. What he should have done, had he listened to Joseph at all, ever, was consider a more *ancient* science.

Arcane knowledge for what was obviously an arcane artifact.

Alchemy.

Alexander Rathbun was a businessman with more ego than acumen, who decided on a whim to fashion himself a modern scientist; Joseph was far more reasonable.

"Should I follow the specifications exactly, or would you prefer some alterations and suggestions?" The architect, Florence St. John, raised her clever gaze to him. She'd come recommended from an esoteric circle who built houses for their practice in California and therefore hadn't batted an eye at the request. "For example, we can excavate below and have additional chambers in a lower level."

Joseph stepped into the corner that he'd envisioned for his main chamber. The *ritual* chamber. The very thought made him antsy with excitement, ready for the chance to prove his father wrong. Cost be damned. He closed his eyes and tried to picture it: a proper place dedicated to the box. He would no longer have to crowd around his small study with Mayor Fuhrmann and his friend Bernard Kellogg, trying to understand its secrets and be imbued with its arcane knowledge. They wouldn't have to deal with children darting in, their noisy crying, Joseph's wife, Carolina, popping in for questions and tea. They could *recruit*.

"A lower level to hold things such as the library or laboratory would be helpful, yes," admitted Joseph, embarrassed that he hadn't considered such. He was still thinking small, still cowering, long after his father was gone—but no more. "Howard Sutton, a confidant of Crowley, only provided specifications for the ritual room, but I want this to be perfect. A legacy."

"Of course."

No, not want. *Need.*

He was going to build his own lodge here, a society to rival the Freemasons, centered on his discovery. It would be frequented by members of the Chamber of Commerce, a senator or representative—men of great importance gathered in *his* home, around *his* discovery, sharing their secrets of power, the Rathbun name climbing higher than any mine would take them. Transmuting coal to gold would be child's play for the Rhodesian thing, when they could sublimate their very forms. Evade death altogether.

Joseph was certain that this box was the philosopher's stone. It was the very essence that alchemists like old Albert Magnus and Thomas Aquinas were talking about, searching for. And he'd done it. Was it not alkahest at its purest that seeped out when the box's lid was cracked open?

The architect tucked the folded floor plan under her arm and turned to him. "So what scale do you envision? How many people?"

He faltered. Dreaming wasn't so new to him, but discussing it as if it was reality, an intangible want transforming to a true thing, was something he'd yet to prepare for.

"When this is done and word spreads," he began, rubbing his chin as if that might massage the words to come easier, "learned people of esotericism from all over the world will travel here to witness the stone. Rathbun Manor will become a center for studying it, using it, begging to be healed, craving membership to what will be the most exclusive society. Twenty-five and no more."

His circle would hold the key to enlightenment, enough to make the likes of Crowley green with envy.

"And these inscriptions here?"

Joseph drifted closer and glanced over the mock-up she held, appreciating his own improvements upon Crowley's *Goetia*. The man was a voracious reader but sloppy, distracted where it mattered most, in Joseph's opinion. He couldn't make a lodge work, couldn't make esotericism work, and squandered his English aristocrat money while he himself hardly worked a day in his life—Joseph was different. *Built* different.

"Yes, I will need them engraved into the flooring of the entry chamber. Not just painted—they shouldn't be easy to wear away, you understand. Perhaps some gilding might help. And on the ceiling too."

The architect scribbled diligently in her notes, and Joseph couldn't help but notice the silver cross around her neck. A woman of God doing work primarily for the people who reached beyond Him. Ever since its discovery in the mine, Joseph suspected that his box and the alkahest inside perhaps were not of the Christian God or devil; it *had* to be older than Christ himself, maybe even older than man, than Earth. When he held it, it weighed heavy like creation set deep within whatever had come *before* time, *before* space. Soon, Joseph would teach his philosophies on this—did she realize? Did she care?

As if to intentionally prove his need for a private space, his new baby, Charles, wailed upstairs.

He clenched his jaw. "And I'll need it to be soundproofed, of course."

"Yes, I hear that. I'll have new plans drawn by the end of next week." She shook his hand and headed for the stairs.

When all was ready, armed with the box, Joseph would lead the world into a new era. Alexander had wanted to elevate himself into a great man, but Joseph was more ambitious than that; he would take the box for what it was—the philosopher's stone, the holy grail, alkahest of legends—and bring himself higher, to something *greater* than man.

Time would prove it.

CHAPTER 15

Step Aside, Marie Curie

Winnie dropped down at their large, circular table with a pile of books almost bigger than her.

It had been three long days since Apollo last saw her, since she'd mentioned the eclipse and they'd foolishly touched her face, and they didn't bother to hide their relief now. She seemed to be feeling better, still looking a little pale but eyes astute, *focused*, and some sick part of them preferred being here with her at the public library, trying to be her hero, trying to thwart death itself, rather than helping Cyrus clean out the dungeon.

It had been three long days filled with nothing but hauling around boxes and furniture, and they were sick of it.

Apollo scanned the stack and felt energized. Most of her choices were collections on occult symbolism, with the hopes that the heirloom's engravings might indicate its original purpose. Understanding what it was trying to protect or hold back could tell them why it followed her, unburying and teleporting itself, how to stop the light from killing her.

And of course, Winnie included one textbook on *material science* as if that carried equal weight. As if the box that didn't burn her but burned them could be broken down into compounds and equations.

She pushed her glasses farther up the bridge of her nose and raised her fine brows expectantly. "What?"

"Step aside, Marie Curie," they murmured with a smirk.

Her glare made Apollo go back to their own books and stifle a chuckle. They'd grabbed just two, inspired by her list of visions that neither of them could read because it looked identical to the stuff in their grandfather's journal—a book on ciphers, and a tome of poetry. If the writings couldn't be touched by a translator app, perhaps they needed decoding instead. And the sheets of poems from the dungeon were incomplete; they had to be important for their grandfather to leave them there. To try encoding them in the first place.

Beside them, Winnie took out a notepad and pen. Of course she was taking *notes*.

She continued to scowl at them. "How about you just focus on your . . . Longfellow collection?"

Something about the jab felt like a challenge from her mouth, and Apollo wanted to say something witty back. Something to draw her ire, just to see what it looked like.

"You can find all manner of things in poetry." They wriggled their brows for effect.

Her scowl deepened, and her full bottom lip puckered out, which made Apollo feel like they'd won somehow. They wondered what Cyrus would have said in their place, if he'd also like her note-taking, the annoyance on her face.

What if I said yes?

"I just want to know what it's made of," Winnie grumbled in the silence. "How it's doing all this. What if the same thing is in *me*, making me . . ."

She didn't have to finish her sentence.

Apollo leaned back and shrugged. "Well, if all else fails, we can always dissolve it in a bathtub like a body. It *is* alive and made of bone after all."

"I'm not having that in my search history, but you can try."

They laughed. A hearty, full-bodied laugh, loud enough to earn them reproach from the librarian on the floor. They didn't mean to, and Winnie clearly didn't intend to be funny, but she was. And her expressive displeasure only made it better.

So Apollo turned in earnest to Longfellow. She didn't know that they weren't reading for poetry's sake—they were more of a Blake kind of person. Instead, they went straight to the lines from the first sheet they'd grabbed to see if there was any connection to the box. To see if the scavenged pieces from their grandfather's dungeon might help point them in the right direction.

"To know a secret that the Gods would keep."

It turned out that the page belonged to a long—*fifty* pages long—poem by Henry Wadsworth Longfellow called "The Masque of Pandora." Not that Apollo was so well-versed in mythology, but it seemed a useful thread to follow. Pandora, a box that ruined your life. Easy.

Scanning through it proved less fruitful. Unfortunately, Longfellow didn't provide any ideas on what to do with the box. How to dispose of it. Or where it came from besides "Zeus."

Sick flow though.

Still they read once more, closely this time, about Pandora, menaced by dreams to open Epimetheus's forbidden box the same way Apollo was menaced by dreams of Rathbun Manor on fire, and it made them think about Winnie's ability. Why *she* wasn't burned, why *she* could see the havoc it wreaked. Maybe *she* was supposed to be the one who guarded it, like Epimetheus, and Apollo was her Pandora who'd curse the world. Maybe they had a connection, their fates intertwined.

Apollo considered the bags under her eyes, how she looked more and more like a fortress. Impenetrable. They didn't know how much information she was sitting on, what secrets she was keeping, shouldering alone, but she was definitely hiding something.

They turned to her. "How does this whole psychic thing work?"

Winnie stiffened in her seat, just as she had the last time they asked about her ability. Her gaze hardened on a spread of symbols Apollo had no chance of recognizing and didn't seem particularly useful either. "Why is that relevant?"

"How *isn't* it relevant? You saw something—how am I supposed to stop it if I don't understand how it works?"

Her jaw shifted, her teeth working on her lower lip, and Apollo tried not to spend too much time noticing these things. Thinking about *why* they noticed these things. Just being here with her, considering what Cyrus had told them, felt weird. Traitorous. But it was hard not to see the subtle slump in her shoulders, how there was a steady waft of the scent of cherries toward them because of the library's infernal air-conditioning.

"I'm not supposed to talk about it, you know," she conceded, turning the page in her book without looking at it. "I told you, it's not this foolproof thing that makes everybody happy and saves the day. Sometimes I see death and carnage but don't have a time stamp or a flowchart to stop it."

And Apollo's chest panged as they listened and wondered how many times Winnie might have seen death, had to corner people and beg them to listen. They'd been so unwilling to believe her, but they were all she had. Did her premonitions always come true, or was believing her enough to prevent catastrophe? Could Apollo be saved?

"Is it only through touch?"

She pretended to read but was flipping pages far too fast to be convincing.

"Can you control what you see? What if you looked ten years into the future?"

No answer.

She was making this difficult, but Apollo could be stubborn too. They had enough skin in the game not to let her win. She couldn't be evasive forever.

"Do you often see your own future?"

With no response, they started to wonder if she was even listening. If she had some other special ability to block them out completely. Winnie's gaze focused so deeply on the book, squinting in concentration, that Apollo thought it was within the realm of possibility. Certainly no stranger than the heirloom.

They shuffled their seat closer, enough that the knee of their jeans grazed hers, and when she rounded on them, their faces were only inches apart. Apollo felt like they were toeing the edge of a precipice.

"*What?*" Winnie glared.

"When did it start? Do they always come true?"

Though they'd made sure there was no skin-to-skin contact this time, Winnie reasserted some distance between them, sliding her chair away rather than answer. It left Apollo in a cloud of her scent, while they watched the flush rise up her cheeks, the flutter of a pulse in her throat. It was . . . exquisite.

"Five minutes before this conversation," Winnie lied, making sure the edge in her voice conveyed that even this answer was begrudging. And when she forced herself to meet Apollo's eyes, they forced themself to focus on her words, their cousin, anything but admiring the pull of *her*.

Cyrus, Cyrus, Cyrus.

They nodded seriously. "Is anyone else in your family psychic?"

"Everyone, including the raccoon stuck in my attic."

Apollo pushed her book away, their arms longer than her reach, and something in their pleading expression made her take a deep breath. She closed her eyes to gather herself.

"Everyone's afraid of it, actually, like they think I'm cursed. And maybe they're right—is there anything more torturous than seeing the worst day of someone's life before it happens and knowing you won't be able to stop it?"

They reached for her shoulder but then remembered themself and stopped it. Their hand fell away before she could flinch, before they forced her to apologize for rightfully flinching away. She stared at the hand anyway like something was wrong.

"This time, you'll stop it," they offered with a grin to distract her. And they'd meant it, because Apollo refused to believe life could be so consistently awful, especially after they'd committed to being a hero. "*We'll* stop it. I'm far too cute to die young."

Just as they'd hoped, this managed to get under her skin.

Winnie arched a brow in a play at skepticism, but the flicker of her gaze to Apollo's hair, to the wolfish cut that adorned their eyes and cheeks, tracing their jaw and neck, betrayed her.

"Hardly." She gave that blithe smile of hers, though it had none of her usual conviction, and took another sip from her massive sugary coffee.

"Liar."

If Apollo wasn't convinced that Winnie couldn't stand them deep down—whatever she'd glimpsed when reading them seemed to repel her—they'd think she found them attractive. Just a little. Something about Apollo appealed to her, made her glances linger, even if she'd never admit it to herself. It wouldn't amount to anything, because prep school girls and prep school rejects didn't go together, and they'd never tell Cyrus, but for some reason, they liked how she looked at them. How effortlessly they rattled her.

In response to their smirk, Winnie flipped her locs, smacking Apollo with the gold-tipped ends and a wall of ripe cherries. "Now, will you *shut up* and let me read?"

It was her raised voice this time that elicited another *Shhhhhh!* from a passing librarian. There weren't many other people on the floor, but it seemed just like this place to hate their presence. They had books, they were reading—wasn't this the point? But unlike Apollo, Winnie seemed to retreat into herself at the rebuke, even as the white librarian with her pinched, scowling face marched away and ignored the other table across the floor having a far louder, spirited debate about a murder mystery.

"You know," Apollo started again when the librarian was afar, "it's not fair that you get to know everything about me, and I know nothing about you."

Like what did you see when you touched my hand? When you lied and said it was nothing?

"Let. It. Go." Winnie bit out each word, baring her teeth. It was a warning for Apollo to back off. Earlier, she was all jokes, but now she might bite.

So bite me.

Incensed, they rose from their seat and stormed off. They hadn't imagined the moment in the park—Winnie's rapid blinking, her irises rolling into the back of her head. Exactly like the shop and the café, when she'd somehow pinpointed the end of a fight they had no interest in rehashing. Did she see the full argument with their father, or the brawl that preceded it?

Didn't Apollo have the right to explain themself?

They landed at an inventory computer to look for anything on psychics. Clairvoyance. If she was going to be like this, then they'd find their answers elsewhere. Like how often she could read things compared to people, what kinds of things she could read.

The extensive list the library carried, however, posed more questions than expected. Ed and Lorraine Warren were a running theme, and now Apollo reconsidered if perhaps the heirloom was possessed. A spirit able to move about, infecting their dreams like a virus and whispering to Winnie. Maybe an exorcism was needed—surely, they could DIY that.

They grabbed a book and strolled back to their table, somehow even more frustrated with Winnie than when they left. They finally accepted that she most likely *knew* they were going to that house with Cyrus, and this was how she beat them there—by looking into them and then lying to throw them off her trail. She might be doing it again.

Winnie Bray was a menace and way out of Cyrus's league.

"I hope you're ready to be serious," she said when Apollo sat down.

However, when she noticed the new book, her shoulders rose. They climbed to her ears as she glared at the large CLAIRVOYANCE written along the spine. The look she gave Apollo next felt like daggers, could have drawn blood.

"What are you doing?"

Rather than answer, Apollo put on a great display of opening it, of slowly skimming the table of contents with one languid finger. In the process, they leaned closer too, *accidentally* putting it right in her pretty, annoying face.

"Well, you won't work with me, so I'll find the answers myself," Apollo sniped.

It was very likely that the author of the clairvoyant book was a sham—there was no way another like Winnie walked the earth. She seemed special to them, somehow, one of a kind to protect. But if all they got from this was another rise out of her, so be it.

"Not everything can be solved by taking a sledgehammer to

it," they added, sticking up their nose at the large photo in the textbook before her. Printed on a full page was a person swinging the tool at a structure made out of what looked like concrete blocks.

Winnie didn't follow their glance though. Instead, she seethed and muttered under her breath, "Why don't we take a chair? Since that clearly worked out great for you."

Apollo's lungs stopped working. Their heart stuttered. They stared straight ahead, eyes glazing over, as her words settled in. Of *course* she saw the fight. Of course she knew, and her antagonism made all the sense in the world. She didn't find Apollo appealing—she was afraid of them, with good reason.

For the rest of their life, even with a total stranger, Apollo would be forever defined by their viciousness. Patrick Barnes was not a good person, but somehow Apollo had to wear that shame.

Winnie rubbed her eyes and sighed. "Apollo, I'm sorry."

They couldn't draw a single breath. It wasn't that she'd said it, but that it was so easy for her *to* say it. Just like Cyrus, throwing it in their face. And she was right—it was nobody's fault but Apollo's. That was how everyone else saw it. They'd never get the clean slate to be a hero, and they were foolish for thinking so.

"*Apollo*," Winnie tried again, swiveling in her seat. They felt her hand on their arm, her skin warm through the cotton of their sleeve. Her knees pressed in their thigh. She was heady, sweet. "I'm sorry. You were being really annoying, but that wasn't fair. You're right, you should know this too—so what do you want to ask me?"

They didn't know how to hold grudges.

Apollo nodded roughly, breathing shallow. They no longer wanted to read the book. Or ask her anything. They didn't even want to get a rise out of her, or be near her. They'd provoked the little lamb by their side to see if she might bite, and bite she did.

All Apollo won from this little game was the feeling that they might cry.

Mulling over their words, they asked flatly, "What happens if you touch it again? The heirloom? Do you see different things? *More* things?"

She lifted her backpack and pulled out the box, setting it on the table between them. A shared secret. Like they were partners. And unlike Cyrus, her apology actually seemed earnest. They didn't want to give their forgiveness, but she coaxed it right out of their chest.

"Usually, objects are one and done," explained Winnie, and the effort of just saying it aloud showed plain on her face. Apollo told themself they didn't care. "I tried again a few days ago and nothing happened, but I can try now."

Her hands hesitated over the carved lid for a moment. Rather than watch her wince in pain, Apollo grabbed the book on ciphers that they'd pushed aside and opened to page one. There were various types, it turned out, some of which were simple but laborious to undo and others that required *math* and *algorithms*, which seemed to be more Winnie's speed. Just like they weren't a hero, Apollo wasn't a genius either.

If they couldn't figure this out, then maybe Apollo was just a nuisance here too.

She slumped back in her seat. "Nothing. It's blocking me."

Apollo kept reading. The truest way to decipher a text, it said, depended on its type of cipher, but the keys could look like anything—a number, a word, an alphanumeric scramble. There were some that carried on for fifty characters, and others that relied on sophisticated calculations they'd need a *program* to run. Sometimes keys were hidden in pictures, the book said, that only the intended would know to find. Without the key, it could take days, weeks, months, or even years.

"May I?"

At Winnie's assent, they picked up the box and examined it again. The carvings were all as morbid as they remembered, especially the mass of wailing people and rivers of fire welling up from cracks in the ground. At the top, among the waves of what might have been wind and clouds, was an inscription: *Lbii qsi Hqeb, Haccyz qsi Hibfizq. Uz qsi exohh U xigyzp, qy qsi exohh U biqabz.* It didn't resemble any example keys in the book, but perhaps it was a hint. Or, if Apollo ever managed to decipher it, they'd know exactly what this box was up to. What it wanted. How to break it.

They turned the page.

Other keys, it said, fit neatly into a table like this sample:

A	B	C	D	E
M	E	J	T	K

Apollo's mouth fell open.

"What is it?" Winnie put her phone down.

Before they could answer, pain spiked through their fingertips. They hissed.

It felt like razor blades slicing through skin—but how? The box dropped from their hold, back onto the table, making her flinch. Her eyes narrowed on the blood beginning to well and she nodded with familiarity, because of course, it had happened to her first.

Winnie offered a tissue, but Apollo only crumpled it. An idea was taking shape, and their excitement was too much to contain. Everything she'd said was forgotten.

"The box is using a cipher. A substitution cipher."

"But why?" Despite her skepticism, she was leaning closer, looking between the cryptography book and the inscription and them.

They took a beat. "Maybe it wants to be known. Maybe it wants someone to put in the effort." Her shiver mirrored how they felt saying it, just theorizing it, because that made it more real. More lifelike, if true. It was communicating with them, which was horrifying and thrilling at the same time. "But *I* know how to decipher this now—I know where to find the key, and I need a psychic with me."

First, she blinked, big doe eyes processing who they could possibly mean. Then it registered, her grin conspiratorial and magnificent.

Their heart stirred in their chest. And that was when Apollo realized they were in trouble.

CHAPTER 16

Grandpa's Creepy Dungeon

"Why are you dressed like a spy?"

Apollo leaned against their van and took in Winnie's outfit. She'd used the occasion to dress like a cat burglar on a diamond heist, in a nice dark shirt and cargo pants, and even ditched her glasses for contacts. She didn't know what awaited her in Rathbun Manor, in the *dungeon* as Apollo had called it, but she figured if she was ready to contort herself around dangerous lasers and booby traps, then she'd be ready for anything.

She arched a brow. "Why *aren't* you? Considering what we're about to do, *I'm* blending into the shadows. The least you could do is wear a hat—anybody a mile away can spot you. Your hair's practically fluorescent."

They dressed the same as always, wearing some loose shirt with a stretched-out neckline. Androgyne and futuristic punk at the same time. She tried not to feel appreciative of how they knew to drape the long, lean lines of their body, how the dark gray turned their skin warm and inviting.

Because they had a job to do. And Apollo was Apollo.

"Come on, you're twenty minutes late," they said instead of entertaining her question, pushing off the van and starting for the front door.

Rathbun Manor stared down at her, and she stared right back. The tall, white-painted face was covered in ivy like some ancient dwelling, the kind of place that had history and legacy, where a family wasn't threatened into leaving every generation. It exuded staying power that intimidated as much as it annoyed her. With its massive windows gilded in brass, sprawling yard and cobblestone walkway, the bold, white columns framing a large red door, it was undeniably beautiful.

It was the kind of house that people on reality TV lived in, where her Kavanaugh classmates grew up and hosted their sweet sixteens that she was sparingly invited to.

And this was where Apollo lived, their rusted hunk of metal parked crookedly in the driveway.

The mansion was surrounded by tall hedges that separated it from its neighbors. Once there were other wealthy families sharing this street, sharing the air that smelled like money and greenery. They didn't need fences to keep the poor out. Now, none of the other lights were on. An eerie silence made the hair raise on her arm.

She hurried after them. "Are you sure this is okay?"

"Why wouldn't it be?" Apollo opened the front door that was readily unlocked and held it wide for her. "Cyrus is at a dinner with his department head tonight, so we should have the place to ourselves for a bit. Don't want him to know we're poking around."

They wouldn't meet her eyes as they latched the door behind them and flicked on a switch. It was a marked difference from how they'd been at the library, spirited and familiar, but she reminded herself that the change was her fault.

Why don't we take a chair? Since that clearly worked out great for you. She still didn't know why she'd said it, or how to ever take it back. She knew only that once again her big mouth had pushed someone away, and they didn't deserve to be judged by a serial liar.

A massive crystal-and-gold chandelier illuminated the grand

staircase and faded wooden floors of the foyer. Winnie tried not to gawk at the tall ceiling, tried to look as if she was invited into historic mansions to read things every day. Even if she wasn't sure this plan would work.

Apollo seemed to have more faith in her ability than she did these days.

She attempted an unimpressed nod. "Show me the way, then."

They brushed past and led her to the cellar door down the hall without another word. The dark was heavier below. Even with the main light on, there was so much it didn't reach. They wove through dusty boxes and paint cans, a maze full of garbage and antique wood furniture stacked high, that actually made the house feel lived in rather than staged.

Then came a black door.

"Here we are," said Apollo as they jerked it open. It whined on its hinges. "Grandpa's creepy fucking dungeon."

She grimaced. "What do you think he used it for?"

"Hell if I know." They seemed to hesitate at the threshold, like they didn't want to go inside any more than she did. It looked haunted. "Cyrus is turning it into a lab. He's moving in all this equipment for *experiments*."

Inside, a warm yellow light flooded a round room. She could see a dark hall reaching beyond, deeper into the belly of a beast. An office printer sat beside a table with a large containment box, empty, with black rubber gloves inside. A plain wooden chair had been pushed next to a cabinet in the vestibule, and carved into the wood floor were a bunch of symbols.

Apollo examined it all. "I'll look for the key and see if I can break some of this to slow him down."

"And I'll try to find a vision." Winnie tried to sound calm, confident, but her hands were shaking. Everything about the dungeon, this room and whatever lay beyond, gave her the chills. Triggered her flight response. Still, for Apollo, she squatted down and pressed her hands flat to sigils.

The grooves were big enough for her fingers to fit in, but it was all cold. Unlike the fire of people, objects carried only a small spark, like static from a light switch when you were wearing socks, but here was nothing. They could be here all night waiting for something to grab her.

She looked up at Apollo and shook her head.

They nodded over to the cabinet, which was topped with old, yellowing pages torn from a book and newspaper clippings. One faded headline read GRUESOME DEATHS DISCOVERED IN CONNECTION TO BOOTLEGGER TUNNELS. It was dated in 1923, from the Prohibition Era, and included a photo in black-and-white of this exact vestibule from an angle that made the dark hall look like a gaping maw. A den of crime, of *death*.

Still no fire, no vision to grip her.

"That was my great-great-grandfather," Apollo said over her shoulder. "And apparently his father before him died here too."

Winnie set the newspaper back down and ran her fingers along the edge of the furniture. A spark caught fast and bright, seizing her hand and dragging her consciousness down into it. Her vision faded to a dimmer version of the vestibule, one without the modern equipment, where the carved box sat luminous, right on this same cabinet.

A woman inched inside, a box of laundry detergent tucked under her arm. She wore a uniform, a crisp white shirt and black pants, and she looked nervous. Glancing back and forth, up and down, like something might snatch her.

She looked *familiar*, like a ghost that Winnie had once known.

The box was whispering to her as she drew closer, her hands trembling. Hesitation seemed to cross her face as she looked at it.

But then she grabbed it, shoving it inside the laundry detergent and giving a cursory look around in case anyone saw. Her footsteps backing away, running, were quick, careful. And Winnie kept staring at her face, from every angle, the worry on it. Yes, she looked like—

"You see something?" Apollo was standing close when she let go.

Winnie backed away from the cabinet and rubbed her fingers on her pants, wiping away the feel of this place. "My grandmother stole it."

They cocked their head. "What do you mean?"

"The box used to be *here*," she insisted, gesturing to the cabinet. "In this room. I watched my grandmother take it away. She was younger then, but it was definitely her. I guess that's why it was at . . ."

What she saw didn't make sense, didn't seem *possible*, and yet it was there, plain as day. Her grandmother wasn't a thief, she didn't steal—and yet she'd pilfered the box from this mansion and brought it to 483 Heritage Street, and Cyrus was right that it had been a Rathbun heirloom. It only left Winnie with more questions, like how her grandmother knew this family and why she took it in the first place.

"What do you think it means?" Apollo shuffled through the papers, lips pouted in thought. They had yet to find the cipher key, and her premonition didn't help.

Winnie stood at the edge of the long hallway. "I don't know, but let's keep going."

She didn't wait for them to lead the way. With both her hands out against the textured wallpaper, she glided into the dark. The lights flickered on after her with the flip of a switch, making the shadows dance ahead, and Apollo kept their distance behind.

"Are you still mad at me?" She wrapped her fingers around a light fixture, looking for a spark. "I really am sorry."

They eased slightly closer, brow furrowed. "Why would I . . . ?"

They had every right to be, there was no need to pretend—it wasn't fair that she knew their secrets while she gave nothing in return. While she'd lied about them dying, warned about a car accident that clearly didn't happen, pushing them around and making them carry this weight so that she wouldn't be alone. Judging them for a feral fight while they were trying to *save* her.

Winnie raised her shoulder. "I know what I said was messed up, but I really don't care what I saw. You don't have to explain yourself to me."

Apollo slowed.

"And that guy probably had it coming."

They nodded and said quietly, "He did."

"Was it because you're . . . ?" She started to ask, but seeing how Apollo looked moments away from jumping out of their skin, she pivoted. "Honestly—"

A door shut upstairs, dislodging dust over their heads. Together they froze, while the soft *tap* of shoes rang through the big hall, crossing from room to room. Their eyes locked. Someone came home.

"Cyrus," she breathed.

Apollo tracked the creak of footfall with their gaze, craning their head and frowning at their cousin's whereabouts. Alertness replaced the discomfort of their conversation, and Winnie dampened her disappointment. Then they stepped around her. "Let's hurry up. I don't want him to know we're here."

Winnie followed them into a small room and started touching

everything—she braced her hands around the doorframe and seized another decorative sconce. Apollo stood guard in the entrance, menacing and sharp, while she groped the soft velvet seat of a chair and opened the flaps of a dusty box.

"And no," they said softly, giving her a friendly but distant smile, "I'm not mad at you."

"Then why—?"

The moment she plunged her hands into the box, its objects flared like firecrackers. Her fingertips stung. The mouth of a cup lanced through her palm as she closed around it, and the round metal handle of something else shot up her arm.

Light blazed in her eyes and only faded when she was looking at a middle-aged white man. He wore a heavy, dark cloak, the hood obscuring his brow; in one hand was a silver cup, and the other held a knife. Not a kitchen knife or like the folding pocket one that she had—this was polished silver and ornately carved with a winding grip and jeweled pommel, catching in candlelight.

He held it up before the cabinet, a mock dais where the carved box still sat, and he was chanting in some language she didn't understand. A small congregation of other white men in cloaks watched on.

It looked disquieting. Vulgar.

One of the members knelt before their leader, gripping a coarse rope that tied around the throat of a lamb. Young, with soft white wool and shiny dark eyes looking at all of them. It trembled in fear.

"Winnie." Apollo's voice sounded distant and strained. "We should go."

She nodded absently but didn't want to let go. Not until they got something *important*. They still needed the cipher key, and how she had to find the box's connection to her grandmother.

With swift, sure movement, the priest brought the knife across the lamb's throat. None of the onlookers flinched. Blood speckled the white wool as the lamb's legs buckled, and the man positioned his chalice underneath to collect it. Red pouring and pouring like wine.

"A sacrifice," he said in a deep, commanding voice.

"A sacrifice," the others echoed.

"*Winnie.*" When she withdrew, she found Apollo's face close to hers, eyes bright with alarm. "He's coming."

The main cellar door swung open with a loud *creak*, followed by the soft *tap* of Cyrus's steps descending the stairs. He was drawing close now, so close that they wouldn't have time to run out without being seen, but it was enough to hide inside. Which meant that she still had time.

"Not yet."

Winnie went to the bookcase, pulling book after book in search of another spark. There had been a cult dedicated to serving the box, trying to earn its favor through animal sacrifices, and she'd bet money it was tied to the deaths mentioned in the newspaper. If someone was willing to build a following for it, sacrifice for it, consecrate these creepy rooms for it, then they'd have researched where it came from. Maybe they had theories about what it wanted and knew how to talk to it.

"What are you doing?" Apollo whispered in a hurry, throwing a glance over their shoulder.

She grabbed another, *Kybalion*. And another, *Emerald Tablet*. If none of these books gave her anything about the box, the cult, why her grandmother was even here, then they could still hide in the dark until Cyrus had gone. "Bet you wished you dressed like a spy now. Get the light, we'll wait him out."

Surprise flashed in their eyes, but they scurried to the switch with a grin. Like they enjoyed her daring. Cyrus's shuffling footsteps were drawing near. The sound of them on the concrete floor grew louder as he reached the black door, the dungeon's vestibule. If he caught them, they'd have to explain being together, being here, and he'd know she was up to something. That she wasn't such an innocent bystander after all.

When Winnie pulled the last book from the shelf, it didn't come away. Instead, something clicked. The whole bookcase popped forward, unlatching like a door. An opening to a secret passage.

The light went out at the same time Cyrus bellowed, "Hello? Anybody in here?"

Apollo scrambled toward her. Her pulse was frantic in her ears, threatening to give out, as she swung the bookcase open and dashed inside, grabbing a fistful of their loose shirt to follow. It was a corridor thrown in complete darkness, a little claustrophobic, but they would hide and wait for hours if they had to, until Cyrus left.

The last thing she wanted was to have him know she was investigating him and suspected his whole family of malice.

"Come on, hurry!"

Apollo pulled the secret door shut and immediately crashed into her. The walls were narrow, and their hands floundered for purchase as Winnie tried to right them, hoping they didn't yelp, she didn't squeal. If either so much as *breathed*, Cyrus might hear.

"Apollo?" His voice was in the room they'd just left, on the other side of the bookcase.

Tangled in the passageway, Winnie and Apollo froze. The air was warm with their body, the frenzy of escape. Her heart pounded in her throat. She held her breath and stared at that door, waiting for it to pivot and expose them. Waiting for Cyrus's smug face to catch her.

Instead, he retreated. His shuffling gait carried him farther away from the bookcase, the room, until they heard nothing at all, but the dungeon door clattering shut. Then he was gone.

It took a moment for Winnie to reinhabit her body, for her eyes to adjust to the gloom. Their clambering had left her flushed, trying to catch her breath, hair sticking to the back of her neck. But there was more than that—Apollo's hand had curved around her ribs to stop her from falling, and now it burned through her shirt like a brand. The other braced against the wall, effectively pinning her in place as they folded over her, shielding her. And she held their middle to balance them.

"That was close," Apollo snickered, so near their breath tickled her cheek.

Winnie gave an incredulous, airy laugh. "I shouldn't have kept going. That was reckless."

"It was." Through the dark, they seemed to stare down at her through long lashes but didn't move away.

And she didn't let go.

Apollo leaned down, hovered for a moment in hesitation, and then pressed their mouth to hers.

Sudden and ensnaring, the kiss made Winnie's mind go blank. Apollo's body melted against her, coaxing want from somewhere deep in her bones. She didn't know the last time she'd been kissed, and never like this—*this* made her hands cling to keep them close, her lips part to taste the cinnamon and heat on their tongue—

They tensed. Blinked and jerked back an inch, as if they realized where they were, what they just did.

"I . . . ," Apollo stammered.

Coming back to her senses, Winnie gaped. Where the stretched neckline of their shirt had dipped further, her hand had floated up to lie flat beneath their collarbone. Savoring the feel of *skin on skin.*

The heat of Apollo suffused her palm, but it didn't burn. The kiss hadn't burned. She wasn't seeing—hadn't seen—anything but them in this corridor, here in the present, pressed together just like in her premonition. In fact, she wasn't reading them *at all* now.

Her brow furrowed. "Why can't I—"

"I'm *so* sorry," Apollo gushed as they extracted themself from her. Even in the dark, she could tell they were blushing. "I wasn't thinking. *Again.*"

She only stared at her hand, unsure of what to say. Beyond the kiss, they didn't seem to notice what else just happened—what *hadn't* happened—as their gaze swept over her face, flicked back to her mouth one last time with a grimace.

They turned away. "We should get moving."

The corridor was short, lined with bare wood-paneled walls and cobwebs. It fed into stairs coated in thick dust, and they each took careful steps to avoid creaking and risk letting Cyrus know that they were here. That they were in the walls, kissing and being kissed, which somehow felt more dangerous than investigating him and ruining his plans for the box.

In a fog, Winnie followed Apollo up, watching as they pressed their ear against the door. When nothing sounded, they pushed it open and peered outside. Light filled the seams, and she had to cover her eyes as she stepped into another room.

It was a study.

She crept out from behind a wall of old, leather-bound books, where one yellow copy—the door's trigger—was left ajar. The room was all dark wood floors and antique leather armchairs. An old, stately mahogany desk sat by wide windows, on a nice, expensive rug. Nothing about it seemed particularly special, or out of the ordinary, except that Winnie recognized this wall of books, this shade and cut of flooring, this arrangement of furniture.

Riffling through the desk, Apollo raised a small scrap of paper. "I found the cipher key." Then they waved for her. "Come on, the front door's right through here. We can slip out, and I'll drive you home—"

"This is the place." Her voice came out a whisper, but not because she was thinking about Cyrus and afraid of being overheard. She simply couldn't say it any louder.

"What?"

Winnie turned in a circle, absolutely sure now, the blood draining from her face. "This is where it happens. This is where it ends."

Apollo had made a *huge* mistake.

Still parked outside of Winnie's house long after she'd already gone inside, they pressed their head to the cool steering wheel and waited for their thoughts to clear. The evening hadn't gone anything like they'd expected. They didn't even really *know* what they'd expected—finding the cipher key, Winnie reading some of their grandfather's things and finding a link or a way out of this mess, perhaps.

"So why did I do *that*?" they groaned to the empty van.

They'd kissed her.

It wasn't part of the plan; it wasn't even a conscious decision. She had this daring, devilish look in her eye when she'd marched deeper in the dungeon Apollo could hardly brave, and when they'd heard Cyrus coming, she didn't flinch. She kept looking. She'd unveiled a hidden door, and then they were crammed into that tiny passageway, adrenaline coursing through their veins. Her perfume and her breathy laugh when they'd realized they escaped?

It was intoxicating. *She* was intoxicating.

Their mind just emptied and forgot they weren't supposed to touch her, that any magnetism they felt was all in their head.

Apollo didn't realize what they were doing until it was already done, until there wasn't any space between them, and their nostrils and hands were full of cherry and *her*. Craving had cracked open in them at the taste, and they realized they wanted more. And there was a moment during the kiss where they thought they'd felt her smile, but in the study, she had this strange look on her face.

The look that something was wrong, *before* she recognized where she was.

Apollo flushed all over again and tried to think about the rest: Winnie would die in their grandfather's study, her grandmother had stolen the box from their family, and their great-great-grandfather Joseph Rathbun led a *cult* surrounding the box, replete with sacrifices and creepy chanting. At least, the description seemed to fit. Ritual chamber, mass death, and their families entangled for multiple generations over this thing.

In the breast pocket of their overshirt was the key to the cipher. It was only partial, they realized, smoothing out the torn edge, but it was something they could reconstruct with time. Decipher the seal on the box and save Cyrus and Winnie from the dangerous light that lurked inside. Apollo Rathbun, hero of the century.

The phone lit up in their lap. Artemisia calling.

"Yeah?" Apollo answered before trying to rub the steering wheel's indent from their forehead. "What's up?"

In the video call, their sister lounged comfortably in bed, welded to a mountain of pillows. She squinted at the screen. "I can sense when you're in trouble. What's up with *you*?"

What isn't?

They didn't want to tell her about the box, about Winnie's

predictions that included them dying. Their sister might actually believe it, take it seriously, and worse, insert herself between Apollo and whatever supernatural forces might take their life. They definitely needed some help, couldn't manage this alone, but not with the part about fighting fate. So what else did that leave?

"I, uh, need some advice . . ." Apollo groped for the words, hating themself. "So, there's a girl that Cyrus might be into—"

"What did you do?" An accusation.

They closed their eyes to brace themself.

"*Apollo!*" She broke into giggles. They heard her shuffling to sit up and knew without looking that she was shaking her head and grinning. That she was enjoying the whole mortifying ordeal. "I can see you blushing from here. You scoundrel. Damn, who is she? Can I meet her?"

"*No.*" They ran a hand down their face. "Did you hear me? Cyrus—"

Artemisia scoffed. "Who cares about Cyrus? My twin is a rake! A reprobate, a—"

"Lay off the SAT terms."

Her laughter only grew, and something about it made them feel at home. Safe. They breathed a little easier with her teasing, even as they hated the position they were in.

"Well, you should tell Cyrus and rub it in his face as payback for paying off Patrick's parents." She was no longer grinning.

Their sister was the only one who knew the full story. That Patrick was dedicated to making Apollo's life hell, always giving them shit, trying to break them down. Perhaps because he was miserable or bored, it didn't matter—everyone made excuses anyway. No one believed that one day he was going to kill them; they only pretended to care when you became a face on a mural, but people like Apollo didn't get murals.

And when that wasn't enough, when they wouldn't break, Patrick then turned his sights on *Artemisia*, so Apollo swung.

Cyrus didn't understand that the only reason Apollo was expelled from public school was because they walked away with a black eye and busted nose while Patrick was wheeled into an ambulance. It didn't matter what he did first; suddenly there was zero tolerance for violence. There wasn't a point in Artemisia even trying to defend them—everyone had convinced themselves that Apollo started it, that they had been the problem the whole time. Getting booted from Kavanaugh right after over dress code violations was the cherry on top of a shit sundae.

Now that Apollo kissed Winnie, she very well might call them a problem too.

"It's a little more complicated than that. She probably hates me now, I'm pretty sure." Their words fell heavy like a stone. They knew what happened when they touched her, and yet a quick impulse threw it all out the window. Winnie would hate them, avoid them, and they'd deserve it.

Artemisia just shrugged. "That may be so, and I don't know her, but she probably hates Cyrus more."

"And speaking of the devil . . ."

As if he could sense them talking about him, Cyrus was calling on the other line. The screen danced with his phone number again and again, and when Apollo hit ignore, he called right back.

"I'll call you back." They sighed and hooked their phone onto its mount, turned on the engine, and answered, "Hey, Cyrus, what's up?"

Skipping the greetings, their cousin's voice was sharp when he asked, "Where are you?"

The van rumbled in reply. "Went out for a drive."

"With who?" asked Cyrus.

"Why does it matter?" Apollo snapped.

Even if he *knew* they were running around the city with Winnie, smelling her hair, kissing her, it wasn't any of his business. They didn't have to answer to him. His money wouldn't hang over their head forever.

The turn signal clicked as they waited for Cyrus's answer, as if he was staring at the phone and confused who'd spoken.

Finally, he said, "I think I heard something in the walls. When are you coming back?"

"I'm five minutes away. Can you wait that long, or do you want to stand outside?" Apollo's voice had an unintentional edge. Right now, they wanted nothing more than to keep driving, or turn back and beg for Winnie's forgiveness, or throw themself at their parents' mercy and be done with all this.

"*Fine,*" Cyrus seethed instead, hanging up without another word. He was getting on Apollo's last nerve.

At the green light, Apollo moved through the intersection and rolled their eyes. Cyrus had inserted himself into Apollo's life and now thought he owned them. How wrong he was. Apollo was past outbursts of violence, but that abrupt phone call felt as if their cousin was *looking* for a fight. They were headed toward a dangerous precipice and would go over the edge soon if he kept it up.

We're family, Apollo tried to tell themself. *He's basically taking me in, trying to help me—*

Streetlights caught on something moving fast in the corner of Apollo's eye, and they slammed on the brakes. Their breath caught.

A black car with its lights off flew through the intersection, less than a foot away from clipping the front of their van. And with their heart racing, eyes wide with panic and disbelief, Apollo glanced up at the street signs just to be sure.

Be careful at the intersection of Main and Bryant.

"No . . ."

Winnie had just saved Apollo's life. She'd braved their touch and saved them from certain death. And now, with the partial cipher key in their pocket, they'd do anything to return the favor, cousins be damned.

May 1923

Rathbun Manor was empty when Charles arrived home from school. He spent time with his friends at Kavanaugh upon dismissal like always, but it wouldn't matter; the manor was often empty. Kit, his eldest sister, was married now and seemed quite happy in her domestic life; she rarely visited, and Charles rarely saw her, but Sarah, in the middle, often went over, preferring to stay there for days or weeks at a time.

And it was only a few years until Sarah left for good, so Charles got used to being alone.

His mother went to parties, it was all she did—visiting her friends for lunch and then *their* friends for dinner. Despite the Prohibition, or because of it, she often came home late in the night, slurring her words, and slept late into the morning, long after Charles dressed and sent himself to school. He suspected it was how she coped with being unhappy or ignored, since there was hardly anyone to care or notice. His father, on the other hand . . .

Well, Charles saw his father least of all. Even though Joseph Rathbun spent the most time at home, he was never *present.* The pile of unpaid bills collecting on the dining room table was proof of it, like a wooden cross to ward off vampires.

"I'm home," Charles announced to the manor's quiet, empty halls, greeted only by the echo of his words. Only by himself.

Were it not for Mrs. Vance, the housekeeper, he didn't know where he'd be. He was twelve years old, no longer cute, and deemed too old for a caretaker; his father's parents were dead, and his mother's parents lived all the way in Rochester and hardly expressed any interest in whether he was fed or dressed. If the unexplained earthquakes plaguing the city finally leveled Rathbun Manor with him inside, how long would it take anyone to even *think* of looking for him?

He dropped his bag on the runner and kicked the door shut behind him.

Today, there was no one around to notice the massive hole in his trousers at the knee, the grass stains and dirt streaking along both shins. He'd gotten into another brawl just outside Kavanaugh's gates with Antoine Rochefoucauld, French and insufferably valiant, and he wished there was someone here to scold him. To tell him to wash up as soon as he came in, to tend to his studies, yell at him for his terrible German scores. Someone at dinner might order him to mind his manners or eat his vegetables. Their gaze would catch on the blood on his knuckles and crisp white collar and frown in contempt. Another uniform ruined, another letter sent from school.

Perhaps he might have lost his allowance, perhaps he'd be punished with the task of scrubbing his own laundry.

Something to prove he existed.

But like always when he came home with some rip in his clothing, the pants seemed to mend themselves by morning. The dirt scrubbed itself free. Mrs. Vance and the servants hardly acknowledged him, and he'd learned never to acknowledge them, so there existed a strange impermanence to everything Charles did in Rathbun Manor; when he rearranged his father's books in the study, turned them all with the pages facing out or upside down, they made their way back. When he spilled his mother's jewels, they were righted, neat in their receptacles.

If his mother even remembered the pearl necklace that Charles broke—he'd actually snapped the chain, he was so angry—well, he never heard a word. She never said anything. There was a new pearl necklace and a new bill at the top of the pile, and Charles's father went flitting from his office downtown to the cellar without noticing. The door was always locked, and the message was clear: Charles need not enter.

"How was your day, Charlie?" he asked himself as he sulked his way to the reception room and dropped into an armchair. "It was fine. Welcome home."

He did not feel welcome though; he felt like he was sharing his home with ghosts. *Imposing* on them, actually.

There were other things that contributed to this feeling; often sounds carried through the ventilation of Rathbun Manor. Sometimes he heard voices whispering to him while he read or tried to sleep, voices from people somewhere in the house that he couldn't see or ever find. When he told Sarah, she'd only laughed at him, though the amusement didn't reach her eyes; she knew something, and that was why she rarely came back.

A bell rang, informing Charles that it was time for dinner. He took his place at the long table, eating while he counted the stack of invoices still in their envelopes and listened to the whispers.

He couldn't remember the last time he saw his father. Other boys his age were already being introduced to their families' businesses, taken under the wings of elder brothers or fathers—Daniel Kellogg spent his summers managing the factories, and Michael Hawley already bought his first piece of real estate. Charles, on the other hand, could hardly remember what Rathbun Steelworks *did* anymore. Was his dad's hair dark or silver now? How tall was he really? What was his voice like? His laugh? His only recollections of Joseph Rathbun came from the noble portraits over the mantels and in the halls.

All he cares about is that box, Kit had said to him once, in a strange bout of candidness. Neither he nor Sarah even knew what box she meant or why.

"*Let me in.*" A voice floated up from the cellar, through the air vent.

Charles rose from his place at the table to go and close it when he noticed in the corner of his eye that the cellar door was cracked open. Just a little, he realized, and figured his father must have forgotten to latch the handle and lock it in a hurry, but still Charles took a step and pried the door open farther.

"Daddy?"

The cellar was the only place he and his sisters weren't allowed to be; he could run around Steelworks, climb the shelves in his father's study, make a mess of Sarah's room or his mother's vanity table, but the *cellar* was off-limits. Even his mother didn't go down there, for as long as he could remember. The forbiddingness scared him a little, but he wanted to be yelled at.

"Daddy? Are you down there?"

There was no reply.

Charles pushed the cellar door wide and stood on the top step. His mouth twitched in a grin at the dare. He pictured Sarah coming home and catching him all the way at the bottom, and perhaps she'd run to their father the moment he walked through the door, and then his father would finally look at Charles and rain hellfire upon him. Maybe Charles would even *take* this alleged precious box and hide it, just to make sure someone noticed.

Then there came a muffled cry from somewhere farther below, the moan of a ghost, a stranger, immediately followed by a louder shout.

"LET ME IN."

Charles recognized his father's voice after all—it sounded like prayer. There was reverence, afraid and desperate, that Charles only expected in church, which felt unusually intimate since he'd never *seen* his father go to church. Yet now there was more emotion and color to his voice than Charles had ever heard before.

A light flashed from the bottom of the stairs, and then the manor trembled like thunder after lightning. Charles gripped the stair railing tightly and hesitated—he hated earthquakes, and the middle of a staircase was a dangerous place to be when they hit. Sense told him to forgo exploring the cellar for safety, but then came another flicker from below, from beneath a black door, as if to entice him.

Intrigue him.

If Charles interrupted his father, he would *definitely* be in trouble . . .

So he descended the stairs, sure to make every step as loud as possible. He landed on the cellar floor with a stomp, pain reverberating up his legs. Somewhere behind the closed black door, he heard a shuffle, the sound of something dropping to the ground.

He grinned widely.

Angry parents were better than none at all. It was better to be detested, *loathed* even, than invisible.

"Daddy," he sang at the top of his voice.

As he marched toward the door across the cellar, he tipped over a box with his elbow—*oops!*—and knocked a cracked vase with his hip so that it fell to pieces. Its shatter filled the whole house. All the way to the chamber door, he shuffled and rumbled and did anything he could to make his presence known and loathed. To make a mess.

"Are you in there?"

Hurried whispers he couldn't decipher carried on inside. Whoever was there—and he was sure it was his father at least—knew he was coming. They couldn't ignore him forever.

He shoved the door open clumsily and paused at the threshold.

Charles didn't know what to expect—he'd never even *been* in the cellar, much less through the door, where Joseph Rathbun spent all his time. It was dark inside, illuminated by a lone candle even though the house had proper wiring by now. The room was mostly empty, with only a low cabinet on the far wall and a corridor opposite, descending. On the cabinet, beneath the nub of a candle, sat a lone white box. It was engraved and glowing.

A draft rippled through the now-silent, dark corridor and sent shivers down his spine.

If Kit and Sarah were home, he'd brag all about getting close to the thing their father loved more than them.

The box seemed to pulse with light. It had an attractive, dangerous quality, precious, like if he touched it, he would be in extreme trouble. And if he *smashed* it, well, hopefully that was an unforgiveable offense he'd be willing to do.

But where was his father?

It was odd to leave this special thing here, unattended, with the door open, but then again, maybe Kit was wrong. Charles had heard about unassuming tunnels beneath houses and businesses. Prohibition had made people careless with these secrets—like his mother stumbling through the house at dawn—and he supposed his father was no different.

What else would a man do in his basement bunker with his friends?

The box meant nothing, then.

"*Jyzq oya vezq qy gyyw uzhuji?*" A whisper tickled the back of Charles's neck, muffled and carried on the wind, as he stared at it.

He whirled around to trace its source and, in the mouth of the corridor, glimpsed a white hand.

"Daddy?"

Charles grabbed the dying candle and inched closer.

The hand belonged to a corpse, half slouched, half lying in the dark, making it easy to miss at first. And it wasn't just any body, Charles realized when he gasped and staggered back, but the corpse of his father.

Joseph Rathbun's eyes were missing from his head. The sockets bore only liquid, though that seemed to be the least of his problems, because his face had been *peeled* in chunks and strips like an orange. Skin hung from his face, leaving behind muscle in his cheeks, the tendons of his jaw, the full exposure of his grinning teeth.

And he wasn't the only one—lying in the corridor behind him was a collection of other dead men, their bodies contorted and melted and fallen to pieces in the shadows. No longer people, but liquified meat from a butcher.

Charles didn't bother to scream, because no one would have heard him; no one was ever home. With grim determination, he backed out of the cellar and wiped the tears rolling down his cheek on his grass- and dirt- and bloodstained uniform.

He didn't understand what had happened here; he didn't *want* to understand.

Transformed into the man of the house at only twelve, his mother absent and hard to get ahold of for another two days, Charles's first instruction was to remove the bodies—at which point, the city coroner so kindly informed him that there were eight total, including all his father's friends—and then seal the vestibule and the corridor beyond. A heavy padlock was placed on the door, and he himself would mind the key for the rest of his life.

Alcohol poisoning, Charles had told everyone, ready to carry the truth of what he saw to his grave.

CHAPTER 17

Just Friends

Winnie stifled a yawn as she dragged herself into the kitchen, exhaustion deep in her muscles. It hadn't been too late when Apollo dropped her off at home on Friday night, but then she'd stayed awake, thinking. About her grandmother Catherine stealing the box, Apollo's great-great-grandfather leading a cult, Rathbun Manor's secret passageways. Lying in bed, shifting left and right, staring at the ceiling, doing her homework on Saturday and folding her laundry on Sunday, she stayed in all weekend and replayed the night again and again.

Apollo had kissed her and didn't seem to know why. She'd been kissed and had touched them yet hadn't read them. *Couldn't* read them. She put her hands on someone, and for once, all there was . . . was silence.

Velvety silence.

It hadn't made sense when she saw it in her vision, and it didn't make sense now. Even knowing that the study in Rathbun Manor was where she'd die, her mind could do nothing but replay the moment she'd noticed her hand on Apollo's sternum, their heartbeat pounding beneath her fingertips. Crammed together in that tiny passageway, Winnie had felt craving instead of pain. Was her curse broken? How? Why could she read the things in the room but not them?

She fought another yawn and pivoted to looking up the

symptoms of sleep deprivation. How long she could go before her body broke down, how to fight it when coffee no longer helped. Delving into online forums of techniques that sounded like torture, she didn't notice her brother sitting at the table until it was too late.

"Yas has been looking for you," said Marcel, with his own cup of coffee. Black and bitter, not a drop of sugar or cream, like a monster. "And I noticed you haven't been walking home lately—whose van was that, Friday night?"

She jumped. "I was helping a friend with something."

"Since when do you have friends?"

Winnie only scowled and ignored him in favor of heaping teaspoon after teaspoon of sugar into her own mug, followed by enough milk to drown out the taste of coffee altogether.

According to the clock over the stove, it was late. She was late to rise, thinking about that silence until she dreamed of the light. The rattle of the walls and crackling earth underneath, hatching a massive, devouring serpent from the depths while the sky darkened above. She needed to leave for Kavanaugh soon, which meant looking like she hadn't stayed up all night replaying Apollo's mouth on hers.

A perfectly normal kiss under perfectly normal circumstances.

Everything was fine.

"It's good you're busy with friends though," Marcel continued, tossing her a wink. He didn't sound like he actually cared either way, but just wanted to rub it in. "I was starting to think you were turning into Mama."

The blend of sugar and coffee warmed the pit of Winnie's stomach. It took her a moment to finish savoring the sensation, to raise her head with her lids still heavy, as she asked, "Mama? Why?"

She didn't have as many memories of her grandmother as he

did. Catherine Casey had been both severe and doting, a woman known throughout the neighborhood for her roses and their thorns. When she thought of her, Winnie really only had bits and pieces, while Marcel had been older when she died.

He shrugged. "You know she was always telling stories, into all that woo-woo stuff. Y'all are a lot alike."

And then he rose to grab an orange from the fruit bowl on the counter while Winnie remained standing there, brows knit, staring at his back.

Her grandmother, into *woo-woo* stuff. The same woman who dragged everyone to church on Christmas Day, who'd opened her bed to Winnie when she had nightmares and taught Marcel how to clean fish—*she* was a liar?

And a thief, Winnie added mentally, thinking of that vision, how a young Catherine had made sure she wasn't being watched, followed, as she swiped the box right off its pedestal.

Was she psychic then?

Winnie took a big gulp of coffee and moved to finish getting ready for school. Her brother leaned against the doorway with a grin that reminded her of a shark: unnerving. He didn't even have to say anything for it to give her goose bumps.

"Can I help you?"

"So, is it a friend or a *friend*?"

She pushed past him but didn't have to glance over her shoulder to know he was still grinning, probably texting Yas to figure out more to hold over her head later. Instead, she called out, "Say anything, and I'm telling Mom about the *oregano* you keep in a boot in the back of your closet."

The box was sitting on the shelf in Winnie's locker when class let out. Bloodstains from Apollo's fingers still marred the front.

"*Guqqgi hiib, syv cads gyzpib jy oya qsuzw oya dez bihuhq?*" A breeze carried down the stuffy hall.

She'd drifted through the day in a fog that seemed to be growing slowly. Ever since she'd found that thing in the basement, the nightmares were getting more and more visceral, and the exhaustion was eating away at her mind. She felt completely unmoored now, floating away, the ground just out of reach. Weeks of floating down the halls, in and out of classrooms.

The semester was far enough along that the air at Kavanaugh was frenetic: Teachers were trying to prepare them for unit tests, SATs, and college apps. Lockers clattered, books slammed down, and students groaned in every inch of the hall. Everyone in every year was tense and ready to snap.

Except Winnie. When she should've been thinking about Cambridge, she was thinking of the carved bone box her grandmother stole.

That would kill Winnie—was this retribution?

She shoved the box into her backpack and shuffled outside, through the gates, and only loosely paid attention to the rustle of footsteps on grass. She bit onto her knuckles to smother a yawn and made a note to grab an energy shot before the shop.

"My *god*, you're impossible to get ahold of these days." Yas widened her eyes in exasperation. With the chilly autumn weather closing in, she wore a long black leather trench coat that shone in the sun. And when she saw Winnie's face, she flinched. "Yikes, you look like the living dead."

"You live two streets over," Winnie pointed out, ignoring the last comment. "It's not hard to find me."

Yas gave a withering glare. "Well, you certainly aren't home very much. I almost came to your work, I was so *bored*."

The thought of her cousin poking around the co-op grocery store where she most definitely *didn't* work made Winnie straighten. "Aww, you miss me?" The cloying sweetness of her voice was enough to make Yasmine huff.

Though they were both friends and cousins, Yas always had someone else—she was Winnie's best friend, but Winnie wasn't hers. And Winnie would never be hers when she had to bite her tongue every time a premonition cropped up. Sometimes she didn't want to be made to feel so lonely. But now that it was the other way around, now that *Winnie* was busy, her cousin had finally noticed.

Yas fell in step beside her. "We both know you don't have any other friends—"

"Why does everybody keep saying that?"

"—and I know you're not just bagging groceries and doing homework, so what's the secret? Is it Apollo?"

She felt her face burn, even as she refused to say anything.

Winnie struggled to reconcile such goodness, the tenderness of that *kiss*, with what she saw of Apollo—the arc of the chair, the dark determination in their eyes. She had never seen anything like it, how cold and calculating they looked instead of the bright and warm and effervescent person she knew. With her, Apollo always had a sort of levity to them, even a sort of skittishness, like they were more afraid of the world than being the danger in it. She hadn't thought they could explode.

"It is, isn't it?" Yas had a sinister grin so wide that Winnie could see her molars and the gap where her wisdom teeth used to be. "Why didn't you just tell me?"

It wasn't that Winnie enjoyed working together—she didn't like skulking around in their grandfather's creepy dungeon, hiding in walls, spending hours staring at books in a library. Yet, she didn't *hate* her time with Apollo either. They didn't grate on her nerves or wear her down like they tried to. She liked having someone there to shoulder the burden.

She liked being listened to and believed. Lately, she felt less . . . lonely.

But neither Apollo nor Yas needed to know that.

She nodded to the street and backed away, to get out of this conversation before Yas pressed for information she couldn't hide. "Because there's nothing to tell."

"Liar!"

"Gotta go!"

The bell over the Red Hourglass's door chimed and heavy footfalls clamored in.

"Have you ever noticed how bright the sun is?"

Sitting before a coffin-shaped shelf to sort through a large box of books, Winnie startled. Apollo stood in the doorway with a scowl, ethereal and backlit by the setting sun. It wasn't bright enough to be wearing sunglasses out of necessity, yet they pulled them away gracefully and flipped the hair from their face.

The black ruffled layers of their clothing made them look taller and more alien than she remembered. Than they did Friday night in the dungeon, in the secret corridor.

She turned back to the shelf to keep from staring. Her heart fluttered in her chest.

"I got this for you." Apollo marched deeper into the shop, a large drink in hand and swirling. The ice jingled before her like a bell before a dog, and in a trance, she rose and followed them through the narrow aisles.

"For me?"

Rather than address the kiss, or their presence, considering they had nothing planned today, Apollo just offered her a straw. "Ordered the sweetest thing on the menu. How'd I do?"

Winnie blinked at them, stunned for a beat, and took it. The drink was an onslaught of caramel and cream, so delicious her lids fluttered shut. She was close to trying out a torture technique at the start of her shift just to stay awake, and this was exactly what she needed to get out of it.

"It's perfect." Her voice was a whisper.

"Good, you deserve it," said Apollo as they leaned against the counter, taking a sip from their own drink. Just like before, they were back to avoiding her eye. "You saved my life."

Her brow furrowed.

"The accident? Main and Bryant? Someone almost hit me."

She didn't move. She couldn't do anything but stare at them, waiting for it to make sense.

"And because you warned me, I was careful. I stopped in time." They beamed. "I'd hug you, but well, I can't, so you'll have to settle for my undying devotion instead."

She still didn't understand.

Winnie could hope all she wanted for a different outcome, but her visions of others *always* came true. Yet, Apollo was here, and they looked fine—in fact, they looked better than fine. Better than she was doing. "But . . ."

She didn't know what to think. She should have been happy that, for once, she'd managed to avert a death instead of watching it twice. It was exactly what she wanted—if Apollo could be saved, then she could be too. Together they could stop this prophecy.

Yet something about it didn't feel right. They were missing

something, some context, something that told her why Apollo was special.

All she managed to say was, "I'm happy you're okay."

Apollo shoved their hands into their pockets and looked around the shop, returning to that case full of wet specimens that they seemed to like so much. They chewed their tongue in thought, like there was more they wanted to say and needed to work up the nerve. The elephant in the room, the big gap between them.

"And I should say again how sorry I am for, uh . . ."

"The kiss?" Winnie raised her chin.

"Yeah, *that*. Chalk it up to the heat of the moment. I wasn't thinking and forgot all about the psychic thing." Scarlet rose above their collar, all the way into their ears.

She cleared her throat. "About that, I didn't—"

"And it won't happen again," Apollo added in a rush, still avoiding her eye.

The certainty behind those words pinched her lungs, and it took a moment for Winnie to gather her thoughts again. "That's not . . ."

Her cheeks warmed when she thought of the feel of them. The physical realness of them. *It won't happen again.*

Winnie shook her head and tried again. "I didn't read you. When we kissed. I didn't see anything."

A long silence filled the Red Hourglass as her words sank in. And then finally, Apollo turned and looked straight at her, understanding.

Either Winnie's ability was growing erratic as her demise loomed closer, or Apollo was the one who was changing. There wasn't any difference in their face, anything noticeable on them to indicate why she couldn't read them when they'd touched.

"It's broken. I read you here a week ago just fine. I should have seen something—I always see something—but that night, there was only—" The words were falling out of Winnie's mouth faster than she intended, like if she spewed it all up, it might not taste so bad. But she had to stop herself before she said the wrong thing.

Apollo took a step toward her and repeated slowly, "You couldn't read me?"

She nodded impatiently.

Another step, and then they offered their hand. "Maybe it was the adrenaline. Read me now."

She stared. Their palm was there, within reach, the skin pink but smooth where the burns were still healing. And offered to her instead of something she requested or something pushed upon her without warning. Apollo was opening themself up to be read by her, *seen* by her, even when they knew and understood the full truth of what that meant, what she might find. As if they had nothing more to hide.

"I want you to," Apollo urged, unblinking.

So with just her fingertips, Winnie grazed the center. It should have been enough for a spark to catch and burn through her. It should have seized her tongue and blacked out her eyes. Instead, Apollo was merely warm and ticklish.

"Maybe . . ." She squeezed it like a handshake, trying to coax a flame, an image, a sound, an inkling.

Nothing.

"Can I?" Apollo raised their brows and, when she agreed, rested her hand slowly on the base of their neck. She felt them gulp at the sensation. "How's this?"

In the quiet of the shop, it was a peculiar intimacy, their hand over hers, right at the crook above the collarbone, where their pulse felt strongest, body liveliest. More intimate than any kiss. It burned Winnie, but not the way she was used to. Not acid tearing its way through her veins, but something heavier, stirring in the pit of her stomach. *Courage.* It was still an invasion of her senses, only now her body was colluding against her.

In a rasp, she answered, "Just you."

And as she took her hand back, Winnie realized she *wanted* to look into Apollo's head to see what happened next, where this might go.

"Well." They coughed, their ears a deep red. "Uh, good to know."

Unsure of what to do with herself and afraid of what she might say, how she might keep looking at them, Winnie turned toward the coffin-shaped shelf, the box of books she'd abandoned on the floor. "Well, I guess I'll get back to this. How is the cipher going? Was the key useful?"

Apollo shrugged. "It was only partial, unfortunately, so that means I have to just try combinations until the words make sense. Like hangman. There are some decryption apps, but it would take too much time without a full key." Then they vaulted out of their seat and took the box of tarot cards from Winnie's hand. "Here, let me help!"

She eyed them warily.

"You seem tired," they mumbled, turning away so that she couldn't see their expression. Analyze the agitated way they reached for another item to stock. "And besides, I feel weird just sitting around all the time while you work. Get some rest. I got this."

The silence stretched on as Winnie took only a step back and continued to stare. *It won't happen again.* In her experience, people weren't nice just for niceness's sake, filling potions and magic oils and vials on a shelf at a business they didn't work at. Especially for people they *didn't* want to kiss. How was the person who'd gripped that chair like a life raft the same one who so tenderly offered to bare their secrets?

"You saved my life, remember?" Apollo added when she didn't move. "Friends let friends help."

She scoffed and finally relented. "Is that so?"

"I think that sneaking around my grandfather's creepy dungeon, trying to stop my cousin from causing some apocalypse, and letting you poke around in my head definitely doesn't make us strangers."

These weren't the normal circumstances in which people became friends, that forged strong relationships that you could fall back on. If they stopped Cyrus—*when* they stopped Cyrus and the box—would Apollo still call her a friend?

Just friends?

Still she was tired and appreciated the break, so she retreated until she was in the reading room, dropping down on the mass of pillows. She tried to think about the box, replaying that vision in Apollo's grandfather's study where she'd meet her end, looking for a clue, something she'd missed. An idea of what to do next. It took no time at all for her eyes to shut, catching one last glimpse of the flush of Apollo's ears.

Often, Winnie dreamed she was at her old house. *Before* the fire. With all of her clothes and toys and pastel decorations that she remembered, with Marcel chasing her through the hall to accuse her of something she swore she didn't do. The pranks and screams and laughter and love.

Her father stood in the kitchen, leaning against the counter with a deep grimace. He kept watching the back hall as if he was waiting for something, for someone to emerge. The house shuddered in a sigh.

His nose wrinkled at a bitter, acrid stench.

Winnie sniffed the air too—it smelled of smoke. Of something burning.

This was a vision with the soft edges of a dream.

Jacob Bray darted for the hall and down the stairs, taking the flight in one nimble leap. He landed with a *thud* in the basement, where a blaze was underway. It roared, having already eaten through the things on the shelves, the animal pelts hung up to dry. It climbed the walls and licked at his skin as he weaved among the racks.

"Mr. Rathbun?" he shouted before doubling over in coughs. Between gasps, he peeked around the corners, still looking for something. Someone. "Theodore?"

On his workbench sat a luminous white box that he didn't recognize, and then there, on the ground, was a body, unmoving and already devoured by flame.

He turned through the wall of smoke and ran.

Unwilling to see more, Winnie squeezed her eyes shut, and when she opened them, she found herself in a new house.

It wasn't a place she'd been before, with someone else's coats hanging in the entrance. Old brown leather and long tan coats. The couch in the living room looked impossibly old too, the retro pattern that was kind of ugly, long before Winnie's time. A toddler darted around a corner.

"Daniella, stop running through the house. You'll get hurt."

Daniella.

That was her mother's name.

A younger version of Winnie's grandmother, still wearing that uniform, rushed through the hall and into the bathroom, clutching laundry detergent to her chest. She shut and locked the door behind her and took a moment to breathe. There was panic in her expression, an urgent fear that Winnie had never seen before; she hadn't ever known her to be afraid.

"I did a good thing," Catherine told to herself, in the same voice she'd sometimes used for praying. "I did a good thing."

She was talking about *stealing*.

And after she'd said it enough times to console herself, when her hands stopped shaking, she reached into the detergent and retrieved the carved box. The heirloom that Cyrus wanted so badly, that Winnie had found in her basement, that for certain had killed her father.

Catherine contemplated it, holding it up to the low bathroom light and reaching for the latch. Then she insisted to the box itself, "I know that I'm doing a good thing."

She raised the lid just a fraction of an inch, for a fraction of a second. Light tore through the bathroom, blazing and sharp. The house rumbled, medicine bottles and toothbrushes in the cabinet falling into the sink. She winced and stumbled back, clamping the lid shut. Her breaths sounded pained and slow . . . but she was alive.

How?

Something pulled Winnie away, shook her awake, and she stirred in her body on the cushions.

"Winnie?" Apollo sounded nervous. "Can you hear me?"

She rubbed her eyes until the grogginess cleared.

They sat close, right in front of her, with panic on their face, mouth agape. Clutched to their chest was the box, and when her gaze fell to it, they moved it out of reach. "Can you see me?"

Outside, wind chimes jingled lightly.

"What . . . ?" Her brows knit in confusion.

"You almost opened it." Their voice was somber, trying not

to sound accusatory but failing. The way they looked at her was reproachful and a little afraid. "I stopped you, but you—"

She climbed to her feet and patted herself down. She felt fine, alive, in one piece instead of vomiting blood and bleeding from the eyes. *They* were still in one piece. "But I didn't! I couldn't have. I would never—"

Apollo pouted. Like they wanted to believe her, but whatever they'd witnessed made it too hard to take that leap. Their dark brows sagged in pity. "Did you see something? When you were dreaming?"

Winnie pushed the hair from her face and nodded. Her throat was dry. Somehow in a dream, she'd reached deep into the filaments that comprised her relationship to the box and found her father and grandmother. Something else she'd never done before she'd touched it.

"I guess we solved that mystery," said Apollo with a grimace. They climbed to their feet. "Your power isn't broken then. Something's wrong with *me*." They didn't move away, and they didn't sound happy with that idea either. "So what was it?"

"My grandmother opened the box. After she took it."

Woo-woo stuff.

Y'all are a lot alike.

It made sense in a perverse kind of way.

And then Winnie added, "I think she was psychic."

If Winnie wasn't the only psychic in her family, the connection between her, her grandmother, the box, and Apollo's grandfather was stronger than ever. How else could Winnie find the box in that house, hear its whisperings? Then loneliness settled deeper and hardened in her, when she realized what could have been if her grandmother was still alive. How much Winnie had lost, having to do this whole psychic thing by herself. She was grieving a *what if.*

"Is that how *you* got your sight?" Apollo set the box aside and stepped toward her, eager.

"I think I'd know if I saw this before." Her voice was hard, angry. The box had tried to trick her, almost *did* trick her into opening it, but they had stopped her. Which she might have been prepared for if her grandmother had said something, written something down like Apollo's grandfather and his notebooks.

"Not if you opened it really young," Apollo countered. Their eyes brightened. "Maybe it changes people. It changed her, and changed you before you even knew it." They held up their fingers, barely scabbed over, and looked at hers. "And I don't know—I've been having all these nightmares and headaches, the sun's been feeling *extra bright.* Maybe it changed me too."

Hesitant at first, hovering over their skin for just a moment, Winnie pressed her hand into theirs. Skin to skin, warm and real just because she could. Just because she couldn't read them anymore, and she wanted some comfort in that.

If their theory was right, Apollo had bled on the box, and now she couldn't read them. They were marked by it, now a little more like her than anybody else. And she would have to keep awake from now on if she wanted any of this to stay that way.

CHAPTER 18

It's Raining Maggots

Apollo stumbled into their bathroom, bleary-eyed. Their limbs still weighed heavy with sleep, and the cool tile beneath their feet sent jolts of pain up their spine. They were exhausted.

It had been a long night, full of tossing and turning, stops and starts, as dreams bled into nightmares that made them lurch awake.

First it was Winnie, standing in that dark, secret corridor with the box in her hand, her gaze burning into them, daring them to move, willing them to say, *Destroy me*, so that she could.

And Apollo felt on the verge of saying yes. Saying, *Please turn me to dust.*

And they'd blinked, and they were standing on the rocky shores of Lake Erie on a gray, cloudy day, holding the box in their own hands this time, extending it out over the churning waters and up to the sun. A solar eclipse moved through the sky, darkening the waters, and Apollo opened their mouth to scream as loud and as hard and for as long as they could, only what came out wasn't their voice at all, but the screams of millions. Billions of voices that couldn't be but were, sounding up in protests. In horror. In ecstasy. Blood dribbled from Apollo's mouth like saliva.

It was doomsday.

They didn't understand what any of it meant, and perhaps Winnie did, but it nonetheless succeeded in rendering them afraid and distracted. The cipher key was still incomplete, so many letters remained unaccounted for, and they didn't know how they were supposed to finish it, save Winnie, stop Cyrus, if they couldn't even *think*.

In the bathroom mirror, with all the blinds down, they bore dark circles under their eyes. The bags were deep purple bruises, and the whites of their eyes were colored a sleepless pink.

"Today's the day," they told their reflection.

Today they'd finish the key. Decipher the seal, the notes, the *box*. It had been long enough.

Then Apollo pulled the shirt over their head, stripped down, and climbed into the shower. They turned the water as hot as they could stand it.

Water slid down their scalp, lime green from the dye they desperately needed to refresh, running down their arms and shoulders. It burned away their exhaustion, the uneasy dreams that had settled under their skin.

And as they blinked droplets from their lashes, the water changed to blood.

Deep, violent red spattered over the white shower tile. Thicker than water, it fell on Apollo and coated their skin, their upturned palms, slipping into their gaping mouth and tasting coppery. It fell straight from the showerhead, against the glass door, pooling at their feet, circling the drain.

Every drop was a loud *crash* against their ears.

And in a blink—it was water again. Clear, flavorless, thin, washing them clean. No red marred the shower at all, and it had only been Apollo's imagination. Their exhaustion battling with the box's influence, in the same way it had manipulated Winnie in her sleep.

Like a disease, something had seeped out from the cracks of that strange box and infected them. Made them invincible to

Winnie's power and plagued them with dreams. What did it want with them?

"It's just a dream," muttered Apollo under the water. "A waking dream and a stupid box and nothing more."

Their eyes drifted shut as they raised their face to the water, to the heat, to the cleansing, restorative power of a good shower. Apollo would spend forever in its cocoon if they could, wait here until the end of the world and then die here in its warmth. Its comfort. Taking shelter in the stream when the apocalypse came.

It was far better than trying to do the impossible, to kill a thing that couldn't die, destroy a thing that couldn't break, outsmart a thing that could make them hallucinate. But hiding here meant leaving Winnie to do it alone, and Apollo wouldn't do that to her.

She'd saved their life.

There was something in the flush of her cheeks, her hand on their throat, that warmed Apollo from the inside and rewired their brain so that they looked *forward* to helping her. To seeing the mystery written on her face, breathing in the wind as it fluttered through her hair.

Apollo was remaking themself into a hero just for her, and they couldn't stop now.

Raising their face to the shower spout, they felt the water change again. The droplets grew heavier, bigger as they rained down and coated their shoulders. One moment, they felt determined, felt a smile creeping on their face, and the next, the beads were beating against their eyelids.

Maybe Cyrus was taking a shower too, and the water pressure couldn't handle it.

Water crashed onto their scalp and cheeks and writhed around. Crawling at their feet, almost like—

The showerhead was raining maggots.

Maggots.

Thick white insects: Tiny legs and round white bodies writhed along their arms, slithering across their collarbones, where Winnie had touched them, through their toes.

Apollo flung the door open and stumbled out of the shower. They slipped and crashed into the towel rack, body folding over the sink and gripping desperately onto the marble countertop to avoid cracking their head open. Still, their skull knocked into the door pane a little, sending stars blooming in their vision.

Darkness flickered as their gaze swam again, and in waiting for the returning light, for the room to stop spinning, the maggots disappeared.

Gone.

Just like the blood, there was no trace of them. Nothing in the shower, on the wet and slippery floor. Nothing between Apollo's toes, on their arms or the crook of their neck.

Heart hammering in their throat, they grabbed their towel and wrapped it tight around their body. Tight enough to protect from the crawling sensation still working its way down their spine. From the box that was definitely messing with them.

They shivered.

"Just dreams and waking visions, hallucinations and tricks of light. It can't—" The reassurance died in their throat. Apollo's heart seemed to stutter to a stop as they turned around.

Sitting there on the counter, right next to the toothpaste and the detangling brush they stole from Artemisia, was Morning Star. The carved box that Winnie had locked in the Red Hourglass when they left last night.

It was sitting here, when it shouldn't have been, when it wasn't before. Just like the trail in the park. It *couldn't* be here, just like it couldn't, shouldn't, be able to conjure an apocalypse. Manifest blood and maggots in showers and hijack Winnie's dreams.

"It's *not* here," Apollo told themself, squeezing their eyes shut.

If they could disappear the blood, disappear the maggots, then they could disappear this too. Back to where it was supposed to be.

"It's at the Red Hourglass, sitting at the bottom of the stock closet. Winnie left it there, covered in a bunch of herbs, a bunch of juniper and bay leaves and black sage. It's. Not. Here."

But when they opened their eyes, it was. It hadn't moved—although, perhaps in Apollo's panic, it seemed even closer to them now. Like it wanted Apollo to hold it, like it wanted Apollo now to *open* it.

Wind fluttered through the room with its closed door. "*U guwij qsi qehqi yl oya, lbuizj yl hiib.*"

It sounded like insects were crawling down their spine, like fat beads of blood from the faucet. They tightened their towel again and took a step back, shaking their head and unsure of what to do. Take it to Winnie, to the Red Hourglass, to Lake Erie and pitch it in for the fish to contend with, weld the damn thing shut—

"Yfiz ci af ezj hii vseq ighi U dez jy."

Back in their bedroom, on the other side of the door, they heard a *bang*.

Cyrus's voice bellowed after, "Apollo? You up?"

Apollo's pulse spiked.

Their cousin was loud and uncomfortably close to the bathroom door, close to seeing the box he sought, was hinging his whole future on, sitting right on Apollo's bathroom counter. Cyrus would think it was right under his nose the whole time, while they'd refused to help look for it.

Apollo lunged for Morning Star, holding it between their hands, just like in their dream. But instead of standing over the lake and raising it to the sun, they opened a cabinet door and shoved the carved box under the sink. It wedged precariously between stacks of toilet paper and spare towels, and they managed to shut the cabinet just in time for their bathroom door to lurch open.

Cyrus barged in and ground to a halt.

They straightened. "Do they not knock in California?" They did their best to sound exasperated, annoyed, although he didn't seem to notice.

Or care.

Cyrus looked perfectly polished, his hair combed neatly back, his shirt pressed and pants free of wrinkles. He arched a brow and stared at Apollo, in their towel, although it had the effect of making them feel like he was staring at everything *except* them somehow.

Could he see the blood? Could he hear the box?

"Are you avoiding me?" Cyrus asked casually, leaning against the doorway with his arms crossed.

It had been days since they'd talked to each other, really *seen* each other, since Apollo was surviving off takeout and microwavable meals and hurrying out of the room whenever they heard Cyrus coming. They didn't want to move things anymore, carrying reams of paper and assembling furniture for weeks on end for *his* big break. Some nights, they intentionally went into the dungeon to break things: unplug this machine, snip the cable to this sensor with a pair of scissors. All of it worked great to frustrate their cousin, but it didn't slow him down.

And they also didn't want to look at him and see Winnie, imagine how he might one day kill her, remember how they'd pressed her hand to their throat.

How's this?

Apollo had wanted to leap out of their skin and surrender it to her right there. It had taken everything not to kiss her again, and now here was Cyrus, a bloodhound on the scent of betrayal, looming like he could sense what they were thinking about, instead.

"I—"

"Don't care," he interrupted with a shrug. "Get dressed. I just hooked up the last of my equipment, and I need your help testing it."

Apollo didn't know what to do with their hands as they listened. Cross them? On their hip? They leaned awkwardly against the counter, feigning casual. Their voice pitched high as they asked, "Test? Have you found it? Morning Star?"

"No, but I'm getting closer. And if this doesn't get calibrated, things go boom. So." He clapped his hands.

Apollo grimaced. They didn't like being rushed, pushed into helping, even if it meant that Cyrus didn't suspect them, even if they were trying to convince him to give up. "Sounds dangerous—maybe we should just let it go. Try something else—"

"Don't tell me to let it go. It's *mine*, and I could change the world with it. Get rich with it. Keep paying off your problems with it—" Cyrus pulled his teeth back and sneered, but then something caught his attention before he could say more. His gaze drifted up to Apollo's hair and narrowed, and he wrinkled his nose. "But maybe you should shower first."

Confused, Apollo raised a hand to the wet, green bangs dangling in their face. Fingers closed around a round, soft body. A thing that squirmed when they squeezed.

There was a maggot clinging to their curls.

With unnerving calm, they replied, "Will do."

CHAPTER 19

Pants on Fire

Winnie didn't want to think about dying today. She didn't want to feel like the clock was counting down, which it was, and like she still didn't have a plan, which she didn't. The solar eclipse was only days away, and she didn't want to be reminded that they were failing. She wanted to look like the Winnie who smiled in her clients' faces before she lied, telling them that they'd escape the city when she knew they wouldn't. The Winnie who was smug about getting out, who rolled her uniform skirt up two inches the moment she left Kavanaugh's gates and added an extra wing to her eyeliner to feel like an angel.

So she would.

The box didn't visit her at home after she'd locked it in the closet earlier this week, giving her some nights of . . . *Peace* wasn't exactly correct, and *sleep* was out of the question, but *rest* was close. She had enough energy to don her favorite lip oil that smelled like cherries and put on a nice dress and cozy sweater instead of the same sweatshirt she'd been wearing for days now. She tied her faux locs into a little bow and smiled in the mirror like she would have before. She tied a gold chain around her neck and a bracelet at her wrist, and then she convinced herself that it had nothing to do with Apollo Rathbun or how they might react.

How their eyes might catch on the highlighter on her nose, for example.

Winnie didn't think about them at all, just as she hadn't thought about the corridor kiss or Apollo pressing her hand to their collarbone.

And if her energy waned and she started to doze, she had a backup, a tin in her pocket with a sewing needle to shove under her fingernail to keep awake. Easy.

It was a slow Saturday at the Red Hourglass, a very boring shift of arranging candles dressed with dried herbs and berries and oils and then taking photos and filming videos for the shop's burgeoning social media accounts. There were a couple of online orders to be filled, and even as Winnie worked her slowest, she finished that within twenty minutes and found herself pacing around the floor. Waiting for the bell to ring.

Apollo would come today, and they'd talk about the cipher. They'd finally crack the code on the box and find a way to subdue it. Destroy it. Whatever was needed so that they'd both finally be free.

She focused harder on photographing the jars of scorpions. The lighting was perfect when the sun sank in late afternoon, and with the newly dressed candles and handcrafted leather-bound journals lining the shelves in the background, the images seemed to work. Arcane, mystical—

But when the bell chimed over the door, Winnie turned too quickly. Too sharply. She had to remind herself that this was nothing. *It won't happen again.* After all, Apollo's hair was an ugly shade and unkempt, and their flowy all-black fashion was trying too hard, and she was bound for Cambridge. Apollo was *soft*—betraying their cousin all because she batted her eyelashes, kissing her even after she'd introduced a box that burned and almost killed them. They didn't fit.

She turned coolly. "Hey, Apoll—oh." Her voice turned flat,

and she glowered. It wasn't who she expected at all gracing the Red Hourglass's narrow aisles. "What are *you* doing here?"

Cyrus Rathbun took one calm step inside and looked around. He was dressed like he was headed to a convention, in pressed slacks and a nice sweater, and his hair was parted and combed back and neat. *Pretentious*, it said. *Well-to-do*. His watch glowed red from the window light. His mouth was curved into a frown.

"You were expecting my cousin?" he asked, a little clipped. "Why? Have they . . . been around?"

All alone with him, she felt the shop begin to darken. Her arm ached in its cast. Winnie set down her phone on the counter and picked up the folded lavender knife that she'd used earlier to open a package. It fit perfectly in her palm, hidden by her sleeve.

"I don't think that's any of your business, Cyrus."

"You know they're a *felon*, right?"

Then she turned to him. "What do you want?"

He didn't immediately answer. Instead he sauntered slowly through the walkway, pretending to skim items on the shelves though he hardly gave them a glance. It was unsettling for him to be here, to see him working up to something and not know *what*. The only way Winnie would know was to touch him. Which she wouldn't.

"I know you have the carved box."

She straightened. "What—?"

"You don't have to deny it," he said quickly, with a smile that gave her a chill. "Let me guess: You found it in that burned house, right? I couldn't figure out why my grandfather's journals pointed to it being there, but it wasn't. I went all through the city, checked every box in storage, every pawnshop. And then I considered you, and Apollo sneaking around and breaking things, and your reaction just now was as good as a confession.

"Now I don't really care why you didn't tell me. I don't even care what my peon of a cousin has to do with it—I'm simply offering you a chance to help me now. If you want partial credit, you can have it. I . . ." His gaze took an indulgent trip down the length of her body. "I play well with others."

Winnie balked. "You broke my arm."

He tilted his head. "I *did* apologize and let you extort me though."

She laughed, baffled. At why he was here, how he finally figured out she had the box, and what he thought she'd do with it. He had the confidence to just walk into the shop and offer her *partial credit* for the thing that'd kill her, and think she'd seize the opportunity. Throw herself at his arrogant feet. She had half a mind to deny it. *"Get out."*

Her answer seemed to surprise him.

Cyrus stopped walking and faced her head-on, his brow furrowed. "This is exactly the kind of thing Cambridge looks for. Don't be arrogant—I'm trying to help you, Winona."

Winnie shrugged. "I'm not interested."

Silence drew out long between them, with him glaring at her, anger brewing in his eyes, and her standing with as much coldness as she could muster. There was a twinge of fear when he looked at her like that, as if he might break her other arm—she was no stranger to his temper. Or her own.

She tightened the grip on her knife. Just in case.

"Look, I'm sorry that we got off on the wrong foot. Truly." He ran a frustrated hand through his hair, ruffling the smooth arrangement of it. "I'm not . . . that guy, usually. I just really need this, and you're . . . clever, cutthroat, ambitious, intriguing. I want you."

He took a step.

"To help me."

And then another.

"Please."

Despite the honeyed words, he looked at her with loathing. Like it was *her fault* that he had to beg, and begging was beneath him. There was power in this, taking in the darkness in his expression, the hunger and hope and aversion held within his eyes. Winnie felt it when she'd pushed him for money, when she made her clients tip extra and lied, and she felt it now: perverse and rousing, holding someone moneyed in the palm of her hand. She liked that feeling, drawing out their discomfort.

"What will you give me? For my help?" she asked calmly.

Cyrus inched closer. "Ten grand."

She shook her head. She didn't know what she wanted, only that he could offer her the world, and she'd still refuse after what she'd seen. After how he treated Apollo, calling them a *peon*, the blood that would pour from her body. She wanted him to beg and then watch his despair when he realized it wasn't enough.

"It's all I have." When she refused again, he charged toward her. "Whatever you think you're using it for—"

Winnie drew the blade and held it up for him to see. Poised right about where his liver would be if he kept coming at her. It wasn't so large, but it was enough to do damage.

Cyrus lifted his gaze from the metal to resume staring at her. With the glint in his eye, she could have laughed then, at still finding herself in this position. Here with him, with his greed. He took another step. "Do it."

Somehow he knew that Winnie wouldn't stab him. She wasn't at all sure, because even though she'd seen this all before, her frustration at her own powerlessness was mounting. But he looked sure because . . . Because, what? He knew her? How could he, when they weren't anything alike?

Cyrus closed the gap between them, until the tip of the blade was pressing into his cashmere sweater exactly like she knew it would. "*Do it.*"

Up close, he wasn't anything like Apollo. His face was sharp, from the cut of his jaw to the angles of his cheekbones, his nose, his brow. They both had hazel eyes, but his felt remarkably cold—where Apollo's had the sweetness of toffee, his had the edge of rust. He was taller, and wider, and older, muscular and so very *petulant*. Apollo might have been the delinquent, but Cyrus was self-destruction itself. Half the girls at Kavanaugh would have fallen over themselves to have Cyrus look at them, even like this, while Winnie squeezed the knife until it hurt.

And his attraction to her obstinacy was clear as day. Why she didn't stab him was . . . harder to understand.

She wanted to, and she didn't.

Winnie raised her head to him and watched his gaze lock onto her lips. He wanted her to kiss him. It made her feel warm all over, knowing that someone like Cyrus could despise her and want her both, and for a moment, she wasn't sure which direction she'd take. "If you come near me again, I will." Then she stepped away and pointed at the door. "Get out."

Every second he lingered before he turned back was a second she didn't breathe. She didn't move until the bell over the door chimed, until the autumn breeze trickled in, and he was really truly gone.

And she stayed like that for minutes, for what felt like hours, waiting for her pulse to slow, her skin to cool, until the bell chimed again.

Apollo looked awful. There was an almost gaunt quality to the lines of their face as they walked inside. Even with the sunglasses and all that eye shadow to cover it up, they seemed worn thin, and it didn't help the way that cropped, boxy shirt hung off their form, the way the layered apron and wide pants seemed to weigh them down.

"Feeling okay?"

They nodded absently, stifling a yawn. "I'm pretty sure Cyrus is torturing me on purpose." They drifted through the narrow walkways of the shop until they reached the register and flopped in the chair. "He's calibrating his machines. Made me move one back and forth for an hour."

Winnie stared at the knife still in her hand. She wouldn't tell them about Cyrus, add to their worry, but now she wished she *had* used it.

"Plus I feel like I'm losing my mind. Like it's bad enough I'm forgetting things, but then I started seeing stuff."

Winnie pivoted. "Seeing stuff? Like the future?"

She chewed her lip, trying her hardest not to feel excited. Thrilled at the idea that maybe Apollo was psychic too, because if they could see the future, if they had the same thing that she did, then she wasn't alone. Then she had something to tether to.

But they shook their head. "I thought I saw blood in the shower, and then it started raining maggots. I can't *focus*."

Was this the box's doing? Wearing her down and then moving on to the next? The way Apollo was downing the frothy matcha in their hand, they wouldn't be much use breaking the cipher.

"What if we take the day off?"

Winnie used her sweetest tone, the voice she'd cultivated over the years to get people to swallow her lies. Unless they'd changed everything just by keeping Apollo alive, avoiding their accident,

Cyrus might still somehow get the box and open it. He knew she had it, but didn't know that it was here, and they had the box, the key, and knowledge on their side. For today, that had to be enough. And with the solar eclipse getting closer, she was feeling reckless. Itching to do anything but stay here.

Apollo raised their brows and looked up at her. Their surprise transformed to a glimmer as they took her in, the gloss and the hair bow and the dainty gold chain. As if they finally noticed that they had pre-doomed Winnie and hadn't expected it, hadn't built up their defenses against it. "Take the day off?"

She approached the register and nodded. "You've been at the cipher for a week, and I found a box of my grandmother's stuff that might lend a new perspective on the psychic thing. Or we can just . . . recharge. The box is here and—"

"About that."

Winnie stopped pacing. The fine hairs on her arm stood on end, hearing their unease.

"The box was in my bathroom when I got out of the shower this morning," admitted Apollo, scratching the back of their neck.

In a heartbeat, Winnie crossed the floor and wrenched open the supply closet. Impossibly, only dried herbs and wood bundles littered the floor. There was knotted twine where it had all been held in place, but the box itself was gone. It had jumped locations *again*.

Her hand tightened on the doorknob. Instead of fear came a spike of envy—that it was choosing *them* now. She'd failed to open the box, failed to solve its mystery, so it hitched its ride with some more willing mark.

"I won't open it," said Apollo glumly, into the silence, so close that she felt their breath tickling her shoulder.

Like you did were the words she heard at the end. They wouldn't be like her, so weak that she let the box wield her instead of wielding it the way Cyrus wanted to. He'd come to her when he should have looked at the cousin he thought so lowly of.

"But you're right about the whispers. I hear them now."

Winnie was too dismayed to appreciate how close they were, how she had to step around them. She didn't want to be envious of the box's attention—she wanted it gone. Away from her and Apollo *and* Cyrus. That they heard the whispers meant that it was changing them like it had her, but on the other hand, it meant she wasn't so special or chosen or even important like she'd come to accept.

She needed fresh air.

"So let's go." Apollo set the latte cup on the counter and tucked their lip between their teeth. There, leaning against the register, it was such a striking image, the way their jaw shifted, their gaze faraway, their brows knit in thought. The dark of their roots was beginning to grow in, adding dimension to their hair that Winnie found herself appreciating.

She tried to suppress her relief. "Go where?"

"Does it matter?"

She supposed it didn't. Against the rising panic, anywhere was better than here, than standing in place, thinking about how futile it might all be. How she might die soon. This was why Apollo was dangerous, her inner voice warned her, because they could sway her so quickly, dispel her dark thoughts and rouse her impulsiveness with the flip of their hair.

Could Winnie be so irresponsible as to just close the shop early and take off? Run away?

She shouldn't, but she could. And with Apollo raising their keys, waiting for her reply, Winnie knew that she would. If she was going to die, then she might as well live.

With an unencumbered smile, she slid her bag onto her shoulder and grabbed her phone. "No. Not at all."

The sun was beginning to dip in the sky, racing toward the horizon, yet the van kept cruising down the highway. Apollo had driven for an hour, and when they stopped for drinks, they asked if she wanted to turn around. And Winnie said no.

Another hour, far past the outer towns, both ignoring their phones that kept lighting up, and Winnie still said no.

The farther they ventured through the southern wilderness of New York, the more Winnie felt her chest opening up. Her lungs filled out for the first time in weeks. Her fear had been shed somewhere along US Route 219. She rolled the window all the way down until the air battered her ears and drowned out the ticking clock of her thoughts. Apollo didn't seem to mind.

After a drive-through when she ordered the sweetest thing on the menu with extra caramel sauce, they pulled away and asked, "What if I don't ever want to go back?"

The sign announcing an exit for Allegany State Park grabbed Winnie's attention as they whizzed through. She sank deep into her seat and drank. She didn't want to go back either, and they were so far into the country now, nothing around but trees and streams for miles, that it all seemed so much more appealing than a cursed box that followed them wherever they went. In fact, she sometimes looked back into the van to make sure it hadn't followed them here too.

Apollo snuck a nervous glance at her and waited. She knew they were bracing themself, for her to tell them to stop, to pull over and head back.

But she didn't. She wouldn't.

"Don't."

It took only a few minutes to get the van settled into the park's camping grounds. They'd already grabbed an assortment of foods at a rest stop, and once the van was parked, bricks wedged behind the tires, Apollo opened the back so they could watch the last dregs of sunlight slip beneath the horizon.

Winnie sat with her legs dangling over the edge, listening to the rustle of the darkening tree canopy. Better than the whisper of the box.

"So what's all this?" Apollo asked, picking up the old filing box that she'd brought with her.

It held a stack of Polaroids, some of her grandmother's letters, cards, and papers. Everything that was her grandmother condensed into this, minus the dead roses. And whatever allusions to her psychic ability that they might find.

Winnie started with the photos. "Bray-Casey archives. I figured that if my grandmother opening the box started all this, maybe she'll help us find a way to end it."

They pulled out a stack of greeting cards and said, "You really didn't know that she was psychic?"

"Not until my brother said something." In her hand was a candid photo of young Winnie, asleep on the couch with her head resting in her grandmother's lap. "I kind of wonder how much would've changed if I did. I've just been making it all up as I go along."

"You said my camping idea sounded lonely, but I can't imagine being the only psychic you know. I'm sorry."

For some reason, her eyes stung, and she looked around the van to keep from crying.

Between the cooking pot shoved into a corner, the cushioned floor, and the array of blankets and pillows, it was certainly on its way with the necessities. Winnie didn't see anything that would really stop them—if she were Apollo, she would've just driven off the moment she'd been told she would die. So why didn't they?

"I'm not afraid of being alone," she lied. "You don't have to spend so much time convincing people if you're by yourself. No one around to call you a liar."

"Is that why you lie so much?" countered Apollo as they leaned back on their elbows. "Because there's no point in telling the truth?"

Winnie didn't answer.

"Being alone scares me. People think I'm so self-sufficient and that I can take care of myself, but I don't know if that's true. I like my freedom, but I also like feeling needed. Being seen for who I really am, whoever that is."

She considered Apollo with their pout and begrudging forwardness, the way they pretended not to care about anything, to not be fazed by anything. It gave the illusion of being older, more mature, self-assured, and fearless than they were. But she knew better, probably the same way they could see through her.

"It's okay to want company, you know," Apollo mumbled. "This van has room for two."

"Thanks." She glanced up to find them looking right at her, struck by the intensity in Apollo's eyes, and then moved away. "For being here. And believing me."

She flicked absently through the photos: her mother, Daniella; her aunt and Yasmine's mother, Daphne; her grandfather Ernest, who'd died before she was even born; her and Marcel and Yasmine; her grandmother Catherine.

None of them with any premonitions she could glean.

Winnie was still caught up on Apollo's total read on her loneliness. She was simultaneously disregarded by her family as foolish, a child who couldn't know anything, and also an adult who should know better, be wiser, and always say the right thing. Apollo understood it. They too had been on their own, while people made up all the facts about them whether they were true or not.

"I suppose I should finally explain the fight, right? What you saw? Why I'm not close to my family anymore?"

Winnie raised her brows.

Then they finally told her about Patrick Barnes. Some of it she knew, and the rest she'd guessed: the harassment, violence, and powerlessness that preceded the fight. Bright scarlet bloomed on their cheeks and throat as they avoided her gaze now, like they were waiting for Winnie's judgment. Like this was the cost of knowing someone. To reward her for opening up, Apollo had bowed down at the guillotine and was waiting for the blade to fall.

Only Winnie refused to drop the rope.

Of all people, she knew what it meant when no one listened, having to fight to be heard, to save yourself. And maybe that was why Apollo had stayed with her.

An hour later, surrounded by piles of Winnie's grandmother's things, the search so far fruitless, Apollo checked their watch and smothered a yawn. "It's getting late. You need to get back?"

Winnie shook her head emphatically. Going back now meant dealing with the box sooner. Facing reality and returning to that place that didn't fit her. No, she'd rather stay with them, here, in this van that wasn't *that bad*, she supposed. "You have to consecrate this camper some time, so why not today?"

They blinked incredulously and then grinned back at her.

But she'd have to be smart about it.

She fired off two quick texts: one to her mother, saying that she was with Kristina and it was getting late so she'd sleep over; and another to Kristina, informing her that she was Winnie's cover. It was the weekend at least—the worst she'd get was her mother's ire when she returned in the morning. Unless Kristina told Yas, who'd tell Marcel.

Her mother might actually kill her if she knew the truth. There was only a rug, crowded by blankets and pillows, one space for the two of them to share, and a dark, quiet forest surrounding. With the skylight open, they could lie back and gaze up at the stars and just fall asleep here, in this van that wasn't really all that big, though she swore it wasn't even a big deal, sleeping right next to Apollo.

"You sure?" they asked, avoiding her eye. After locking the doors and killing the lights, they seemed fixated on a particular pillow, as if they knew she was overthinking it and didn't want to point out the same exact thing.

It won't happen again.

Winnie wrapped a blanket around her shoulders and turned her focus to the stars. This far from the city, they were so bright it almost scared her. "I'm sorry you couldn't camp under better circumstances."

Every time Winnie told the truth, she ruined something. She hurt someone. Even in trying to prove that her ability could be worth something, she'd still landed casualties. Even if Apollo wouldn't say as much, because they were the only one to be spared.

"It could be worse."

They lay close, their voice low, and somehow the van felt more cramped than the secret corridor. In the corner of her eye, she studied Apollo. Under the constellations, their lashes seemed darker, face delicate. Even in the face of death, blood, serpents, and chasms, Apollo looked impossibly vibrant. Real. Warmth radiated from their skin, within reach, that she could *touch* now, though she didn't.

Their lips twitched though they didn't look at her. They kept their eyes on the stars and asked, "Do you like me, Winnie?"

There was no innocence to this question: It was a challenge. Just as she knew they didn't mean *as an accomplice*. And even though, from the first day they met, they could sense the lies on her, read falsehoods on her face like she used to read them, Winnie scoffed. "No."

Apollo just chuckled, because of course they knew it was a lie, and rolled onto their side, bringing them face-to-face. She wished she could read them right now, know what came next.

Calmly, slowly, they ran a finger down the length of her nose, skating across her lips and chin, as if to confirm that she really couldn't. And perhaps it was her imagination, but she felt herself lean into their touch. Revel in it.

"Do you want me to kiss you again, Winona?" Apollo whispered next.

Her full name in their voice induced a shiver. She couldn't help but glance down to their lips for a second. The combination of her name, the contact, of cinnamon and mint from their skin, was hypnotizing.

Slowly, softly, she said, "Do *you* want to k—?"

"Yes. I have no problem admitting this." They lifted her chin, raising her gaze to theirs, and added, "But I want to hear you say it."

Apollo was trying to kill her.

She clenched her jaw but didn't dare look away. Didn't retreat even though her heart was rioting in her chest. She begrudgingly bit out, "Yes."

"Yes, what?"

Prying that truth from her chest would kill her before the box did. Her vision swam from just the strain of staying still, present, sane. She gritted her teeth. "*Yes*, Apollo. I. Want. Y—"

Apollo grinned wide, beaming like a puppy, and then kissed her again. The warmth of their mouth captured Winnie's, and she thought she might dissolve on the spot. Even if they didn't know it, even if they couldn't feel it, Winnie clung desperately to their touch, which was a buoy in deep waters.

How long would they have to run before Cyrus blew their world apart?

"I need you," she corrected herself, in a whisper.

"Finally."

She pressed her hips to theirs, savoring every point of contact, just in case tomorrow was the end. This was too messily perfect not to—she didn't know the last time she'd been touched, kissed, or wanted like *this*, if it would ever happen again, but she knew she didn't want to stop.

January 1976

Theodore Rathbun paused outside of his father's bedroom to take a breath and center his thoughts.

"Prepare yourself," he warned the new servant girl standing close behind him.

In his last days, Charles was a taxing man to care for. Lying constantly in his bed in the master suite, he was prone to fits of yelling, and the smell of sick was difficult to tolerate. Distracted thoughts made it easier to lose one's temper. It would have been bearable at least if he was in a smaller room, but the old man wanted to die in his own bed.

Utterly grotesque.

Theodore was the only Rathbun in name left, Charles's only heir, so it made sense for him, his wife, and their children to stay in Rathbun Manor, caring for the old man rather than his aunts or cousins. Then again, it *also* made sense that Theodore, as the head of the clan, should have the master suite too, but well . . . He and his wife remained confined to his childhood room, and his sons each had one of the same size. His father had even tried to keep control of the study, all the way up from his bed, but Theodore had eventually won that battle.

He turned the knob and dragged himself over the threshold. "Dad, it's time for your medicine."

Immediately, Charles moaned.

The new girl that Theodore had hired to tend to the house remained by the door. Her skin shone like polished wood, and her dark hair, kinky, was brushed and pinned back from her face in a very neat bun. She was attractive, not too curved but not too thin either, petite, though his gaze had lingered in annoyance when they met on the simple silver wedding band on her finger.

He couldn't be bothered to remember her name—there were just so many, when the manor was like a revolving door.

"Caroline? Is it Caroline?" Theodore offered the handful of pills and a glass of water to his father.

"Sofia," Charles corrected despite having never met her.

She took a step inside, her dark eyes alert. Clever. She was only part-time from what he *did* remember; she was taking night classes at the community college, one of the housekeepers mentioned. "Catherine, sir."

"*Sofia,*" Charles seethed.

Theodore cleared his throat. "Don't mind him—please sort through all of his clothes, shoes, anything that might work as a donation. He's not using them anymore anyway."

The young woman hesitated for a moment, glancing at Charles, who stared at her, before nodding curtly.

Theodore glanced around the room. Twice a week, the servants came to clean everything; the linens were always fresh, and all the corners appeared swept and dusted. It looked spotless, like it was all ready for them to move in, except for the book on the bedside table and the eyesore currently swatting his hand away.

"*Weak* man with *weak* morals," said Charles as he nestled back under his blanket. "I see you with your bottle. You'll die just like men before you."

When his father finally died—which doctors assured him would be soon—all of this would be Theodore's responsibility to oversee, to have packed up or thrown away. Did he want the bed his father died in, the bedside table he died beside? Would the cleaning staff reuse the linens, the pillow where Charles laid his mortal head?

"Sofia!" Charles turned his attention to the girl, whose name was most definitely *not* Sofia. "It was the alcohol, I told you, but it's gone in the end. I called a priest to stop the whispers."

The girl did not turn, did not stop cataloging his shirts.

The doorbell rang below.

Charles Rathbun wasn't a sentimental or expressive man. He'd kept to himself all of Theodore's life and rarely shared any of his past; in fact, Theodore hardly learned anything about his father's upbringing, and his aunts never said much either. What Charles had been like as a child, or a young man before the war, was anyone's guess. As for Theodore's *grand*father, Charles refused to say if he ever even met him.

"And any jewelry and personal effects, we'll store in the attic," Theodore added casually.

He was curious what mementos the old man kept hidden in this room; were there photos in the drawers, letters from a lost love in the closet? When Theodore's mother, Charles's wife, had died only a year before, the old man had hardly shed a tear. He seemed fond enough of the boys, Edward and Richard, but Theodore's wife, Jean, said his detachment was just like a lot of the men of his generation.

Jean sauntered down the hall and waved to him. "The electrician's here."

So Theodore excused himself from watching the room and the girl—*Charlotte?*—and descended to handle more pressing affairs. He'd called an electrician to examine and update some of the wiring. Rathbun Manor was old and falling apart; the wood panels on the first floor were prone to rot, the vents had a constant draft and rattle, the walls hissed and creaked, fuses in the cellar seemed to short frequently, and the new washing machine lost power often. It was the curse of houses like these: their constant need for upkeep.

Theodore was looping through the study when someone called after him.

"Sir?" It was the girl again. Courtney—no, Clara. She held a thick iron key in her hand and offered it to him like a boon. "I found this buried in his shirts. I shouldn't put it with the mementos, should I?"

He stared at it, waiting for some recollection of what it might belong to. Why would the old man keep an old key in his *shirts*? Did it have something to do with the war? Was it an old factory key from when Rathbun Steelworks was still in business? He had no idea. There weren't any doors in the manor with locks that big; he'd been born here, he'd know.

So he snatched the key from the girl and tossed it onto his desk. The electrician waited in the entrance, rocking back on his heels patiently.

"Basement?"

The man was Polish, with a thick accent, and Theodore led him below. He was uninterested in whatever the man had to say, whatever game show he was fond of watching and using to make conversation. There was a lot of work to do this coming week, where Theodore was close to making partner at the law firm—he had no time for idle chitchat or silly keys among his dying father's things.

Eventually the electrician took the hint from his nonanswers.

Theodore couldn't remember the last time he walked around the cellar. He came and went only to the wine rack, which his father, annoyingly sober, had often commented on when he saw it. He felt embarrassed now looking at the mess, the accumulation of furniture and racks of moth-eaten clothes. Had it always been so cluttered? Or was this the reality of living in a house with children? Edward and Richard seemed to fill up all the space they could, and they shed clothes like snakes shed skin, all down the hallways and on the stairs and even, bafflingly, at the dining table. There was always something lost, another thing to replace, and when it came to toys and furniture, he supposed this was the graveyard for broken things.

"I apologize for such a mess," Theodore mumbled as he shoved aside a box topped with a musty pile of blankets. Dust rose into the air and forced him to double over with coughs.

The transformer that the electrician needed to reach was wedged between the stairwell and an old armoire. He wheeled away a rusted bicycle.

"What's that behind there?" the journeyman asked, shining his flashlight at the wall. More specifically, at the *gap* between the armoire and the wall.

The furniture wasn't flush with the wall or even close, and it looked as though the placement was intentional, as though the armoire had been shoved here to cover it up. Theodore thought that perhaps rats had gotten into the wall and chewed through the wiring behind this spot. Neglect here on top of all the house's other problems, his father hiding this infestation like he hid his life, past, and family history.

Theodore rolled up his shirtsleeves. "Give me a hand, will you, please?"

Together, he and the electrician pushed against the armoire with all their might. Its curved feet scraped loudly against the floor, and the wood swayed uneasily from the pressure, like it might collapse any moment. However, they managed to move it enough to reveal more of the wall, which held a padlock. And a door handle.

A *door*.

There was a secret door hidden behind this old armoire, one that had been here for as long as Theodore had been alive, probably longer. Did his father know it was here, or was that the work of *his* father, whom he hardly knew? Theodore felt like a detective in a film, one that was ready to uncover a gangster's hideout.

The padlock on the door was large, industrial. Whatever was inside, it seemed no one wanted them to get in. Or, as he considered the armoire again, know it was even there. There were tunnels like these all over the country, dug for bomb shelters but poorly structured, poorly maintained. For all Theodore knew, two steps inside and the whole house might collapse on top of him.

"Houses like these always have secret rooms," said the electrician before he turned to the transformer, to doing his job. "Tunnels from the Prohibition Era."

"Mm-hmm."

Theodore glanced at his watch. It would only be a matter of minutes to fetch the key from upstairs and see if it went to this lock; he had some time to spare before he had to be at the office. If it was a defunct smuggler's tunnel, then he'd know immediately. And if it was an empty bomb shelter from his father's paranoid imagination, then the mystery would solve itself either way.

"I'll be right back," he said to the electrician, who didn't care, before darting up the stairs.

This room might finally help him to come to know his father, the stoic man who was Charles Rathbun, the stranger who had raised him and doted as best he could on his sons. If not him, then his grandfather Joseph, who founded the Steelworks, or the others who came before who existed only as name plaques around the city. After all, was Rathbun such a great name if it had no staying power? If the ones who came before weren't even specks of dust worth remembering?

A line of once great men, decrypted at last.

CHAPTER 20

Well, Hello

Qsi Beqsxaz xyo vsy sej dyzkuzdij suchigl qy xi e cez veh ziebxo ezj ucfequizq. Si sigj e jikudi qseq icuqqij e xyqsibhyci zyuhi epeuz ezj epeuz, ezj uq byhi uz lbimaizdo vsiz si deci dgyhib.

Dgudw, uq heuj. Dgudw dgudw.

Qsibi veh dgeqqib uz qsi byyc xihuji ci, qsi hcehs yl qsuzph ezj qsi hdbiec yl lbahqbequyz.

Si vezqij qy xi e pbieq cez, xaq suh qicfib vyagj xi suh azjyuzp. (U ziij zyq jy ezoqsuzp xaq veqds.) Beqsxaz ciz vibi zyq pbieq; qsio juj zyq azjibhqezj vseq "pbieq" ciezq.

Dobah ezj qsi cedsuzi deci dgyhib. Dgudw dgudw dgudw.

"I know you have it," *si heuj, lyggyvij xo qsi sups-fuqdsij hseqqib yl pgehh.* "I know it's here somewhere."

Si vezqij qy sabq suh dyahuz, ezj zyq tahq xideahi yl ci. Xideahi yl qsi guqqgi hiib. Pubgh guwi sib vsiqqij effiquqih, hsebfizij qiiqs.

(U xbiew qiiqs, hazjib ciz ezj qsiub effiquqih.)

"Just like I know you're with *her* right now."

Dgudw dgudw dgudw dgudw.

Si veh uz qsi byyc vuqs ci, byyquzp qsbyaps jbevib elqib jbevib. Suh juhjeuz veh fegfexgi. Suh azvybqsuzihh, suh ebbypezdi, fibcieqij qsi eub. Si veh Egirezjib Beqsxazh siub, vuqsyaq e jyaxq.

Gupsq luggibij qsbyaps qsi hsigl eh si yfizij qsi jyyb ezj hev ci.

"Well, hel*lo*."

Suh hcugi veh e vyglh hcugi. (U jikyab vygkih.)

Si sej zy bupsq qy qyads ci, xaq si juj hy ezoveo. Si juj zyq iebz qsi fbukugipi qy debbo ci, xaq si ehhacij hy ezoveo. Suh guqqgi jikudi veugij eq co luzjuzp epeuz ezj epeuz, hy U wuggij uq. (Qyy cezo febqudgih, ezj ikiboqsuzp dez xi wuggij.)

"Good thing I have spares," *si heuj qy suchigl eh si dgucxij qy suh liiq.*

Dobah qadwij ci azjib suh ebc ezj debbuij ci eveo. U giq suc. (U jujzq guwi uq, xaq U guwij laz. U vezqij qy hii vseq qsi guqqgi hiib vyagj jy.) Hqugg, si feahij xihuji e fgezq qseq veh befujgo jouzp lbyc qsi lybdi yl ci ezj kycuqij.

Ul si habkukij gyzp izyaps uz co fbihizdi, si vyagj vugq qyy; sacez xyjuih ebi view. Pbiij, syvikib, wuggh cads lehqib qsez U debi qy.

CHAPTER 21

A Warning

Winnie was having a nightmare. Apollo was too—a snake careening through the dark sky while the ground crumbled to cataclysm—but then she flinched in her sleep, which jolted them awake.

The pair lay swaddled in fleece, so close that it was effortless to reach out and find her through the fog. The moment they blinked and looked around, the first thing they caught was her face, round and somehow *more* innocent-looking without her glasses. It was uncanny.

And watching her sleep, glimpsing her bare shoulder sticking out from under the blanket, made the night come back to them. Every exquisite second of it.

"Hey." Apollo picked the locs away from her face one by one and then nudged her awake.

Despite the both of them tossing and turning, Apollo had slept a little better here. They couldn't tell if it was the quiet and dark of the woods and stars, or if it was Winnie, but for the first time in weeks, they felt rested. At ease. And it seemed that went for Winnie too.

She propped herself up on an elbow and mumbled, "Good morning."

Quiet settled. They lingered. Birdsong filled the air, and though Apollo knew they should probably get her home, they didn't move. If neither of them moved, if Apollo kept twirling their fingers around her locs, if she kept rubbing her eyes, they might be able to stay in this moment, this peace a little longer. They could ask her whatever they wanted, say whatever came to mind in this van, in this park, because time had stopped. The threat of *later* ceased to exist right now.

"Was this your first time . . . camping?" They didn't know if they should say it or retreat. Give Winnie the space to recoil, realizing what a mistake they were in the light of a new day.

Winnie cocked her head, uncomprehending.

"In a van," Apollo said slowly, willing her to understand, because it was more than *the beat-up, rickety, uncomfortable van in the middle of nowhere* that they were asking about—it was the fumbling, achingly sweet, *other* thing. They gently wiped away the smear of makeup from her cheek and nodded to the pile of clothes nearby.

It was hard not to fold in on themself just now. They sounded weak. Desperate and pathetic and weird, giving her yet another reason to keep her distance, stay the perfect prep school girl, and excise them from her life on her way to Cambridge. Discard them like their family had. Sometimes they didn't get why she didn't.

Winnie sidled close and traced their collarbones with her fingertips. "Yes, I'd never . . ." She met their eyes and then pressed her mouth into the crook of their neck. "*Camped* before. You?"

"First-time camper," Apollo rasped under her touch.

She whispered against their skin, so soft they almost thought they'd imagined it, "Well, I liked . . . camping . . . with you."

As if to stop the blood rushing from Apollo's head before they could reach for her, their phone lit up. It caught her attention too, and they weighed the choice of holding off the outside just a little longer. Let them remain like this, pretending the box wasn't hidden in their bathroom, ignoring that they still hadn't figured out how to stop the box from destroying her.

"We can't stay here forever," she said, beating them to it.

With a sigh, Apollo wiped the lust from their eyes and grabbed the phone. It seemed too early for Artemisia, but it could have been their mom, finally ready to talk and make up—

CYRUS: You're fired.

The text wasn't followed by anything—no explanation, apology, or emoji that might indicate a joke. It was all they had to go off, that Cyrus finally got the hint from them dodging and cutting cables and had to let it be known in the most obnoxious way possible.

They scowled and turned to Winnie, who sat up, very still, and stared at her own phone. Running a hand down the length of her exposed back, they asked cautiously, "Everything all right?"

"I think my mom knows something's up." She pulled her dress over her head and began to gather the photos and letters spread across the floor. "She seems pissed."

Guilt gripped Apollo like a vise, an accusation poisoning every interaction, every time they looked at her. All they made were bad decisions; trouble followed them wherever they went, and now their bad luck was glomming onto her.

"I'm s—"

"Don't," Winnie snapped, cupping their cheek. Her voice was sharp, but her eyes were . . . unusually tender. "I'm glad I'm here. Besides, it could be about anything—a pay stub from the Hourglass, even."

Not letting go of their face, she reached out to smooth a photo with her other hand. The corner had been bent, but the moment she picked it up, her muscles seized. She gasped. And then *Apollo* felt it—sudden pinpricks traveling from her fingertips into them, commandeering their nerves, burning out their eyes.

Before Apollo understood what was happening, they were staring at Rathbun Manor. A Black woman stood on the front step, a small child beside her, and knocked on the door. The woman's expression was troubled, nervous, and she fidgeted by massaging scar tissue on her wrist. *Burn* scars, specifically.

Then the door opened, and a white boy in a high-collared sweater stared at her. He couldn't have been older than his early teens, with his fair hair unruly, his eyes cold with scorn. Apollo was sure that they'd seen his photo before, that it was their great-grandfather Charles, if they had to guess.

"Who are you?" the boy snapped.

The woman tried to smile. "My name is Sofia. I used to know your father."

Charles blinked slowly. "My father is dead."

Before he could slam the door, she caught it in her grip. "I read about the tunnels. I wanted to give my condolences—"

"Thank you—"

"But it's not over," the woman insisted. The child stared on blankly, but she pressed forward, until the door was wide open, and the boy was red in the cheeks.

"I already had a priest, lady—"

"No, you have to return it to the—"

He slammed the door in her face.

Winnie dropped the photo, and slowly, with a sting, the vision faded from Apollo's eyes. The portrait sat before them on the shaggy rug, faded and sepia-washed, showing the same woman unsmiling, hands folded in her lap.

"Did you see—did I just . . . ?" Apollo couldn't find the

words. Pressing the heels of their palms deep into their eye sockets, they waited for the pain to recede. Was this how she always felt? It was awful.

She balked. "You saw it too?"

It traveled through her fingers. She made *me see.*

Immediately, she turned over the photo, and written on the back was a name: *Sofia, maiden name unknown. Catherine's great-grandmother.* A woman long since dead, but a lead nonetheless. Another generation of their families embroiled over this thing.

"What do you think she was gonna say? Return it where?"

Winnie kept staring at the photo, chewing her lip in thought. "Not a clue. How's the cipher coming along? Can we use it today? Maybe it'll tell us?"

Itching for the chance to be of use, to be more than a nuisance, they fetched the key from their shirt pocket and nodded eagerly.

A	B	C	D	E	F	G	H	I	J	K	L	M
E				I				U			G	C

N	O	P	Q	R	S	T	U	V	W	X	Y	Z
				B	H	Q	A	K	V	R	O	

There were plenty of gaps, sure, but with the two of them, they could drive back and fill it in today. Maybe they didn't even *need* all the letters to make a guess; Apollo had already added the most important ones, vowels and some consonants, the ones that took the longest.

"We need to go back to the house where this all started."

The grim determination in Winnie's voice, on her face, made Apollo dress faster. They didn't bother to remove the tangles from their hair as they pulled on their boots and stumbled from the back of the van. "Your old house? Don't you have to get home?"

She raised a defiant brow. "So my mom can kill me before Cyrus does?"

Any fog they might have lost themself in had quickly vanished—here was the call to finally prove themself a hero, and they wouldn't miss it. They wouldn't let her down.

"Okay." They pulled the bricks from beneath the tires and started for the driver's seat. Winnie was already fastening her seat belt beside them.

"What do you think Cyrus is doing?"

Their brow furrowed. "Don't know, but he fired me. That's not a good sign."

With their hands wrapped tight around the steering wheel, Apollo headed back to the city, and it felt like driving right off a cliff.

Apollo parked in front of 483 Heritage and waited patiently for her to move. After years of only dreaming of this place, Winnie had now visited twice in a month, and she couldn't remember what it used to look like anymore.

Before the disaster.

How had it looked in her dreams? What color had the paint been long ago, and how did it gleam in the summers?

Now all Winnie could see when she stared at this house was death. Her father's, her own, her innocence—everything she had and was had been taken from her in this very house, and now they were sitting outside and getting ready to go back in.

"Maybe we don't have to—" Apollo started to say, but she shoved the door open before they could finish.

"No, I have to."

It wasn't that they were out of options, that she didn't have faith in the cipher; everything *started* in this place. The solution had to be with her, her family. Winnie had found the box here, and there had to be some reason hidden in its walls for why her grandmother had stolen it in the first place. Was it originally theirs, an act of reclamation, and the Rathbuns had stolen it first? Would Catherine really keep her family around something so dangerous? If she'd coveted it, then why had she looked so afraid? And why did Sofia try to warn the Rathbuns?

On the long drive from the woods, it occurred to her that perhaps her grandmother and Sofia had been thrust into this position, just as Winnie had: a never-ending loop of girls fighting to survive the ambitions of men like Cyrus. Perhaps the Rathbuns were always chasing after this thing, convinced of their destiny to wield the power it held, and girls like her were the obstacles, and one day, if Winnie survived and ever had a daughter, she'd be next.

"Do you want me to wait here?"

Apollo stood awkwardly by the van, and she couldn't help but think about the night. This morning. She didn't know how to do things like this, the mornings after where desire warred with duty. She'd expected to feel changed when she woke up, like she'd *lost* something or was missing a piece of herself, less whole, but no. And then she expected to regret it, or think better of her impulsiveness, but instead found that if she had her way, she'd drag them back into the van and onto the road, have them discover new ways to make each other shiver. Or see a movie, go swim in the creek, get ice cream on the waterfront and watch sunsets on the lake—*date* things before the end of the world.

This would have to do.

And besides, she *definitely* didn't want to go alone.

Winnie grabbed their hand and dragged them through the busted front door of her old, condemned house. It still smelled like smoke and burnt things. She still feared the door closing shut behind them, being trapped in this nightmare.

"I saw the fire, you know," she said softly, to fill the silence. It felt like the house was watching her. And it didn't help her unease that every step through the hall, down the stairs to the basement, was a step her father had taken.

Apollo craned their head to look around. "When it happened or in a premonition?"

"Both. No one listened to me then, of course."

In the dark, cluttered basement, Winnie tried to guess which footsteps in the soot belonged to her father, to Theodore Rathbun, to herself. All of the destroyed furniture, partially melted garbage resembled the meltdown of a nuclear reactor. A place still radioactive, a place she shouldn't have been that day, curious and looking for a payday. And right across from the big metal table was a large black smudge where she'd seen Theodore's body lying.

She pointed to it. "Your grandfather must've opened the box in the basement. The fire started here, on the table, and his body was found there, against the wall."

Apollo squinted at it like there might be something to recognize.

There were no bones or discernible remains of clothing or skin to make out; instead, they could only see where the wood panels were darkest and eaten through. Perhaps once there had been a little number for evidence like in other crime scenes, but this was forgotten in time. The metal table guarded its pristine rectangle where the box had sat.

First, Winnie pressed her hand to the ash on the table. It

was cold and silent, not a trace of anything to see. And then she dropped to the body-shaped dark spot on the ground, which was warmer under her fingertips but hardly a flame to coax. Like a game of hot and cold, she could feel that she was onto some discovery, close to figuring *it* out.

Squatting beside her, rubbing ash between their fingertips, Apollo glanced up. "How do you feel about your . . . ability now? You *did* save my life, after all."

"I . . ." She chewed her lip and shrugged. The last time she was here with Yas, she'd been careful *not* to touch everything. The last thing she'd wanted was to use her power, see something she didn't want to. "Now it's not so much the taboo it used to be."

It was a part of her, like her dark eyes and sweet tooth.

Giving up on the basement, Winnie climbed the stairs. She held on to Apollo with one hand and dragged the other along the walls, the railing, the door handles, the windows—hoping to not only see something, but let them see it too. She didn't know if they were slowly becoming psychic like she was, if that was how she'd become psychic in the first place, but it was a thing that she could share. That they didn't seem to mind partaking in.

She wished she could share something *good*.

Through the kitchen windows, Winnie pointed to the backyard. "My grandmother used to be famous for her rose garden."

The bushes had no trace of flowers now, and probably hadn't for years, but she remembered being proud of them. Talking about them, itching for the excuse to show them off and how she'd had a hand in their growth. Her family didn't have much like the Rathbuns, but the garden was supposed to be something she'd inherit. In a way, that too died with the fire.

"It used to be so important to her to teach me how to take care of them—"

Her eyes went wide.

Before Apollo could follow her train of thought, or ask why she'd stopped, she was dragging them away, back down the stairs and crashing out the side door. The roses might be dead with nothing to salvage, but her grandmother didn't leave her *nothing*. The garden shed was still standing tall. There might have been something inside, a message for Winnie to find, all these years later.

"I don't understand," said Apollo, scrambling to keep up.

"If my grandma was psychic, and *I'm* psychic, then maybe it wasn't the roses she was preparing me for."

When she'd first touched the box, it had shown her the roses. Now her heart raced just standing before them, at the memory of some being brighter, stronger, at the feeling of being on the edge of something important. There was a little divot in the ground where something had been dug up, the hole never filled.

Memories didn't feel like premonitions; they weren't picture-perfect. They blurred on the edges and fragmented. After so much time, there was only a *feeling* that the hole in the ground had once been bigger, that her grandmother was trying to tell her without telling her, rather than the fire of certainty. And it was Apollo's idea after all that she had been young and would hardly remember it—so why not?

The walls of the little garden shed were sagging inward, in danger of collapsing. The wood rot was evidence, but it didn't stop Winnie from throwing the door open and dropping to her knees. Everything was rusted, wooden handles cracked and disintegrating just as she'd expected. There was an unopened bag of fertilizer, the plastic faded and broken through. A small hoe sat beside an old spade and, out of place, a little plastic bottle had faded to yellow.

This is it.

Excited, Winnie grabbed the spade, and it was as hot as fire. It seared through her palm and wrist, and she felt herself spasm back before the vision took over. Before she wasn't herself at all.

Her grandmother, wearing her favorite yellow hat and overalls, was kneeling in the dirt. She leaned over a hole, humming an old church song to herself, while she buried the box. The white lid seemed to glow under the summer sun, but she piled the dirt on quickly. One scoop after another, and then she topped it off with a sprinkling of seeds and misting water to dampen the soil.

She was planting her roses on top of the box. The box had been here, right in front of Winnie's face, the whole time.

"Here's that sacred oil you wanted," a woman called as she approached—skin the color of walnut, wearing loose purple fabrics. Winnie recognized her instantly, of course; it was Hortense. She pressed a small plastic bottle into her grandmother's hand, smiled, and turned away.

And when the rose seeds were covered in a fine layer of dirt, Winnie's grandmother opened the bottle. She'd called it fertilizer once, Winnie remembered, but there was a bag of actual fertilizer right *next* to her.

Catherine leaned forward and gave the bottle a shake. Then, with a stern voice, she said over the dirt, "Just a little something to keep you in there."

That should have been Winnie's cue to let go, but the fire wasn't done. Her fingers wouldn't release their hold on the spade, wouldn't reach for Apollo to share what she was seeing, and her eyes wouldn't return to herself. There was only fire, her grandmother trying to show her more, flaring brighter in her sight.

She squinted at the pain, her eyes watering.

The flash of light receded to a dark room, and inside, Apollo was breathing heavy through gritted teeth. Blood caked in their swollen brow and sweat slicked hair to their neck, and beside them was the box, its mouth pried wide open, their hand deep inside. Deeper than the box appeared to *go*.

With a scream, amid the violent shaking of the walls, they pulled something free from the box and held tight. It looked like a star, glowing so bright that Winnie winced. A star, calamitous and light, snatched from its hiding place.

By Apollo.

The star flared in their grip, and then Winnie found herself lying on the ground, coughing up blood. All around her, the ground was crumbling, fissures swallowing up cars and sundering buildings, roads cracking like spiderweb fractures before they fell down like sand. It was loud, the destruction widespread, and it showed no sign of slowing. She didn't push herself up; she only rolled over to look at the sky.

The solar eclipse was over, because the moon was gone from the sky. In its place was a cloud of dust, a rupture that sent asteroids raining down on them. Colossal rocks ablaze were rapidly chasing away the darkness for one long, gorgeous moment before they promised the end. Something had *shattered* the moon, and what was left of it was falling on them. Would crush them, or conjure heat so fierce it reduced them all to nothing.

Slithering in its place in the sky was the serpent. It surrounded the sun, large and swirling again and again on itself as it stretched its jaw. Reaching, swallowing, *devouring* the light—

Only then did the fire spit Winnie out, and she went skittering backward, away from the spade. A pair of shovels and a garden hoe fell away from their hooks from her kicking, clattering loudly as they crashed onto the overgrown, weedy grass. In an instant, Apollo reached for her, but she couldn't stop skittering, fighting to catch her breath, blinking until the taste of blood went away.

"It's not just me," she heard herself mumble.

Her mind was trying to piece together all it'd seen while her pulse kept racing. And since she'd forgotten to grab Apollo, here they were, on their knees, holding her face still in their warm hands, hazel eyes beseeching an explanation. For her to share that burden.

"Tell me."

It should have calmed her—*they* should have calmed her. But they didn't.

Winnie shook her head and tried again. "It's not just me who dies. That was apocalyptic, and it's . . ."

It's your fault.

What the spade had shown her was clear: Apollo would remove the star from the box. It might be Cyrus who unleashed its light, sickening and killing Winnie, but it was *Apollo* who'd be her undoing. Welcoming the beast that would kill them all. She'd saved them, only for them to betray her.

Of its own accord, her fist closed around something while Winnie fought to meet their eyes. Hearing whatever they were saying beyond the blood pounding in her head was an effort.

"—don't worry. We'll stop it." Apollo insisted in that soothing tone that used to work so well. However they hadn't seen what they'd do when the time came, the destruction they'd wreak, what the box had chosen them for. "I believe you."

The one who believed her would be the one who crushed everything. Not only would Winnie have to save herself, she'd have to stop them and save a world that didn't believe in her too.

With white knuckles, Winnie held on to a pair of garden shears. Rusted though they may be, they were still sharp enough to kill and poised right next to Apollo's stomach.

One thrust, and they'll be stopped. Shove it up, and it'll all be over—

"Winnie?" called Apollo, oblivious. "Did you hear me?"

She threw the tool aside, hating herself for thinking it, if only for a fraction of a second, and nodded.

The box had chosen Apollo over Winnie, but that didn't change who she was. She was a lot of things—a psychic, a liar, one of Kavanaugh's best—but not a killer. She wouldn't do that unless she was sure, unless she had to. Just as she'd stopped Apollo's accident, she could stop this. Stop them from reaching for the star, from starting an apocalypse.

Lying in the grass, dislodged by the falling shovel, lay the little plastic bottle she'd seen her grandmother use: the *fertilizer* that wasn't fertilizer. The moment her hand closed around it, she understood what had to follow, what her grandmother wanted of her, and it started with getting the box away from Apollo.

I won't open it, Apollo had told her when they confessed to it following them home, appearing in their bathroom. Was that the truth? Did Winnie have any reason not to believe them now?

"Let's go get the box," she said, following them hand in hand to the van. "My mom can wait a little longer—I know how to end this."

CHAPTER 22

One Expensive Temper Tantrum

Winnie had been skittish ever since they left the old Bray house: staring off into the distance and distracted when Apollo spoke to her. They tried to dismiss it only as the trouble with her mother, maybe nerves at going back to the place her father died, but with her, they could never be sure.

Though she was the psychic, she was easy to read—*something* was bothering her, and she didn't want to let it show. The stoic way she kept her back straight, tried to mask her face, was as good as flashing signs. The only problem was knowing *what*. She'd grabbed the garden tools before Apollo had a chance to latch on too, so whatever she'd seen, they could only take her at her word. That her grandmother had buried the box among her roses didn't explain the fidgeting, the small plastic bottle in her grip, *or* her sudden assurance of what came next.

"Are you sure we don't need the cipher key anymore?"

She smiled blandly. "It could still be useful if we fail—wait, Cyrus is home?"

Apollo pulled into the circular driveway behind two cars. The manor wasn't empty—parked behind Cyrus was a sedan they didn't recognize, and something about it sent a nervous chill down their spine.

For three weeks, they'd been so distracted with Winnie, with learning about ciphers, with their nightmares, with *Winnie*, that they hadn't really bothered to pay attention to their cousin's movements. What equipment he had them carrying piecemeal into the cellar was for, how they fit in a plan with the box, the confidence with which he calibrated a small-scale reactor with no fuel.

You're fired. The car probably belonged to the new lackey tasked with following Cyrus around, writing down his every inane thought, carting his things, pretending he was actually *onto* something. There was a reason people generally didn't hire family.

"He's probably busy with his new assistant," said Apollo as they climbed out of the van and headed for the front door.

Nervous, Winnie was glued to their side. "But won't he retaliate? Seeing us together?"

They stopped in the doorway and considered. It wasn't until the drive over that they had even *thought* about their cousin—what he'd think if he discovered them with Winnie, if he knew how they felt. They didn't know if he was competitive, but it was obvious that Cyrus didn't have a chance, even if Apollo wasn't in the picture—he was rotten, and Winnie had more discernment than that.

Cyrus was definitely the kind of guy who pitched fits if he didn't get his way—so how would he retaliate against Apollo? Shout and kick them out? He'd already fired them. They toyed with the idea of letting slip that the skin of her throat tasted as good as she smelled, just to push his buttons. After all, he deserved it.

"I'm not afraid if you aren't," Apollo replied cautiously, sliding their hand into hers.

For a moment, the Winnie from this morning returned, marveling at their hands entwined as if she'd never done it before . . . Probably because, like everything *else* they'd done, she hadn't had the opportunity.

"No, I'm not." Her candied smile helped to assuage the last

of Apollo's nerves from the drive over, from any retaliation they might face now.

The foyer of Rathbun Manor smelled sour when they stepped through the entrance. From somewhere inside, there came the sound of movement and conversation, but it was hardly the bustle of a party. A few people to keep Cyrus distracted while they ran up to Apollo's room and back out; hardly enough activity to shake the memoriam feel of this once-great family that now amounted to only an accidental thug and their spoiled cousin.

Just as with the first time she came to Rathbun Manor, Winnie looked all around as they led her to their grand staircase. The chandelier twinkled in the early daylight from the windows, sending a rainbow of colors across the perfect white walls. Portraits lining the second-floor corridor held her attention, and she halted her footsteps at times to study them with recognition—she'd probably seen more Rathbun patriarchs in her visions than Apollo could name.

Then halfway down the hall, they ground to a halt.

Apollo's bedroom door was wide open. The floor was littered with their things. Someone had come and shoved the iron bed frame aside, and then overturned and slashed the mattress open, exposing old springs. Perfect white down feathers from all the pillows coated the clothes and shoes and upside-down drawers like freshly fallen snow.

"Oh my god." Winnie's breath stopped as she stepped inside and crouched. Broken glass shifted under her sneakers.

"*Cyrus.*" They growled his name.

There wasn't a burglar in the world who'd invade Rathbun Manor and leave all the art and crystal decorations, the fancy rugs and Fabergé eggs, leave all the other rooms untouched. The person who'd come here was looking for something specific, or trying to *fuck* with them, just like he'd gone to Winnie's old house and broken her arm over something specific.

Apollo bolted for the bathroom. They leapt gracefully over the debris and rounded the corner to find towels and toiletries scattered on tile. The cabinet doors were pulled wide open, and Morning Star was gone.

"It's not . . ."

Either it was smart enough to transport itself to the Red Hourglass again, waiting them out in hiding, or Cyrus had found it. Maybe it *wanted* Cyrus to find it next, thinking he'd be arrogant enough to open it where Apollo had refused. Even as they hoped and prayed to a higher power they didn't believe in that it was the former, it probably wasn't the case.

"It's gone." Apollo righted the overturned chair to the vanity and dropped into it. Now it was their turn to feel shaken.

Winnie was still in the entrance, running her fingers along the broken frame of a mirror. It was sitting on top of a pile, so clearly an act of rage rather than a desperate search. She was trying to find a premonition in it, though they didn't need to touch her to know the culprit.

"This is one expensive temper tantrum," she mumbled, gently pushing aside shards of glass. One of them made her hiss, made her eyes flicker back with strain, and then she nodded resolutely. "He definitely has it."

Apollo chewed their tongue, hands trembling in their lap no matter how much they tried wringing them to stillness. To steady the rolling boil in their blood. It was the same feeling they'd had right before assailing Patrick Barnes—a fury that wouldn't be quelled, their heart ramping up and up and up until something gave.

"Not for long." They vaulted to their feet and marched out of the room.

Winnie was right behind. "What are you—Apollo!"

It wasn't just that Cyrus had the box; it was that he didn't even bother to ask Apollo honestly, *really* share what was going on, that he had so little respect that he'd inserted himself into their life and then smashed up their things when he couldn't buy their gratitude. It was the flagrant disregard as he lied about them being equals, eyeing their every move with suspicion and then pretending that he was gracious.

He didn't need to smash the mirror. He didn't need to snatch all the photos Apollo had hung with string on the walls.

Their boots rumbled like thunder down the staircase, through the hall, and into the cellar. They wanted to sound like a warhorse, to send fear through their cousin.

Cyrus wasn't afraid of Apollo, but he should be.

There were two other men in the dungeon with him, and they all quieted when they heard Apollo's approach. They looked somewhat familiar from photos, Cyrus's adviser and the department head, perhaps. Older white men, both standing around and chatting in the vestibule, while Cyrus lounged casually against the wall.

Apollo charged into the room. "You went through my stuff?"

"Do you mind? We're in the middle of something," Cyrus said coldly, rolling his eyes. Then to the two men, he said, "Can you call the police and ask them to send a car? I tried to take my cousin in, but they're known to get violent."

"What? You wrecked my room, violated my privacy, and stole from me!"

His eyes blazed to life, and he raised his voice, ready to deny it. "*I* stole—?"

Then Winnie caught up, crossing into their grandfather's creepy dungeon, breathing heavy. When he noticed her, he seethed. The fire in his expression sharpened to deadly ice.

“Considering I pay the bills and invited you here, you don’t have a right to privacy and neither do your guests. Now, go away. The adults are talking.”

She stepped forward. “Cyrus, you can’t do this—”

He pushed off the wall. “Why is *she* here?”

Apollo could hardly think with all the adrenaline coursing through them. They wanted to hit him, smash his face in, bring him to the ground, break teeth. But even if he deserved it, their family would look at them like they were a rabid dog that needed to be put down. Their anger was a weapon, where Cyrus’s was an asset.

“She came over to help me study for the GED.”

“Studying? In yesterday’s clothes?” Cyrus arched a severe brow, his tone acidic and mocking. Stepping close, he adjusted the rumpled collar of Apollo’s shirt. “And since when are hickeys on the exam?”

Apollo’s fist tightened. Their mind went blank—

Cyrus was stumbling back before they could even strike. Winnie had thrown a punch and moved in front of them, guarding Apollo from Cyrus the way they should have been guarding her from him. Their cousin crashed back into a cabinet and struck his head with a sickening *crack*.

Blood dotted his mouth where she’d hit him and was beginning to run from a gash at his scalp, and though she was shaking out her good hand, she took a step forward, ready to do it again.

“No—” Apollo caught her before she launched, teeth bared.

It took all their strength to haul her back, the softness and warmth from last night and this morning transformed to a feral creature. A devil, beautiful and poised to defend them, that in another instant, they would have bowed down before.

Winnie was screaming. "You arrogant *prick*, I should've stabbed you when I had the chance! *Where is it?*"

Only when they were halfway through the cellar did she calm and stop fighting them. The fight seemed to leave her body, and she dropped onto the steps. Her shoulders were heaving, her head pressed against the cool stone wall though her eyes were still shooting daggers.

Cyrus yelled after them, "Hey, Apollo? Take your shit with you and get out. You're not welcome here anymore. Find a new place to stay."

His words hardly registered.

Climbing to her feet before them was a girl who'd thrown a punch to spare them the trouble. She took their hand roughly and pulled them upstairs and outside, her grip tight enough to make their bones twinge, but they didn't care. She was their savior twice over—they'd follow her anywhere, to any end, to the pit of hell if she wanted.

Absolutely stricken by her, Apollo let her lead them past their van and down the sidewalk. The instant she turned around to say something, they captured her mouth in a kiss. Her eyes dancing, nostrils flared with spite, the rapid rise and fall of her chest—it drew them in like a moth to a flame.

One furious kiss in thanks, in devotion.

That seemed to dull her rage, a little.

She kissed them back, and they could feel her begin to pout. When, finally, the energy completely petered out, she said, "My hand really hurts."

Apollo started to laugh when a shadow fell over their shoulder. A police car parked right by the hedges, ready and waiting for them, thanks to Cyrus's instructions to call from an Upper Bryant address. Behind them stood an officer in a too-tight uniform, his hand resting on the bulky black thing attached to his belt.

Winnie's eyes went wide, and they took a step to shield her from view. "Is there a problem, sir?"

"I'm here to make sure you stop trespassing. This is private property." The officer reached past them to pinch Winnie's shoulder, smirking when she winced.

She twisted out of his grip, her lashes fluttering. "But they live here! This is Apollo *Rathbun*, they have just as much right to be here as Cyrus does."

Her protests didn't seem to matter. He didn't care to listen, not when his mind was made up, and there was more authority on the other end, making the calls. The both of them were deemed a nuisance, and it needed no proof. He resumed his grip on her and squeezed hard enough that Apollo saw her grit her teeth and stumble, even with the sweater fabric blocking his touch.

"Let's go, in the car," he commanded, and Winnie let him lead her back up the street. "Both of you."

Apollo sneered. "You don't have to grab her like that."

"Shut it," the cop sneered back, "*boy*."

It sounded like a jab, like he wanted Apollo to feel inferior, to remind them of their place beneath him. And what could they do to fight it that wouldn't land them in more trouble? How could they ever resist anything if everything landed them in more trouble?

"Don't call them that—" Winnie started, though she didn't get to finish.

Apollo lashed out, sticking their flexed foot ahead of the policeman right before they reached the car. He tripped, his weight pitching Winnie forward as he stumbled. She had just enough time to turn around and watch him crash into the car door, to see the hatred burning in Apollo's eyes.

"That is not my name," Apollo snarled, feeling brave, and wild, and dangerous. They stepped around the man and took Winnie's hand. "Come on, we're going—"

The cop scrambled to his feet and seized Apollo's arm, wrenching it behind their back. Pain spiked through their shoulder. Then he kicked at the back of Apollo's knees for added measure, bringing them down hard, onto the ground, on their stomach in retaliation. Their chin bit into the driveway asphalt.

"How about this, *punk*? You just assaulted an officer of the law. Let's go."

Apollo clenched their jaw but said nothing. Handcuffs curled around their wrists.

"Wait!" Winnie's voice sounded soft, pleading.

Another officer, who'd been on the lawn, talking with Cyrus, seized her from behind by the elbow. "With me."

As they were both steered away, the officer taking a handful of Apollo's hair with glee just to shove them into the back seat, they caught Cyrus in the doorway. Watching. He winked, his bloodied mouth curving to a smile before he went back inside.

Neither Apollo nor Winnie was actually under arrest. They could have been, they very well *might* have been, if it weren't for *Judge* Elizabeth Rathbun and her husband, Richard, who were already on their way. They sat in cheap plastic chairs among the crowded desks, Apollo still in handcuffs solely for the humiliation of it. However, they refused to feel embarrassed—it didn't matter that they'd scraped their knees and chin, could feel the fabric of their pants sticking to the blood underneath. It didn't matter that Cyrus's university colleagues had watched them be shoved to the ground, forced to kneel for a petulant man who didn't like being shown up.

He'd grabbed Winnie when it wasn't necessary. Apollo had watched the man salivate over the pain he caused, liked how she'd tensed up. Just like Patrick Barnes, who didn't regret the trouble he'd caused, so why should Apollo?

When a police officer finally stopped watching them, she turned her head and whispered, "I'm sorry."

"You shouldn't be here," was all Apollo could think to say back. "And you shouldn't be apologizing to me."

"If I hadn't *hit* him, maybe he wouldn't have—"

And then their mother rounded the corner, tall and lean, dark hair long and sleek and tossed over her shoulder. It bounced with every step, her nice coat swaying around her ankles, heels clicking on the cheap floor. Her skin was perfectly smooth, not a wrinkle in sight even as she glared at Apollo, her russet brown skin glowing against the gold jewelry.

They shrank back in their seat.

Richard Rathbun followed his wife, a federal judge, as she strolled across the floor to talk to the chief. Recognition colored Winnie's expression immediately, her head whizzing back and forth between their mother, their father, and Apollo. It was also hard to miss their mother's glare, but her cheekbones, Richard's sharp chin—there was no mistake. And the flush in their cheeks at being here, having to be rescued by their parents again, only made it more apparent. Their mother spent only a moment in the chief's office, uttering a few quick words, before she turned around.

"This ought to be fun," Apollo muttered, bracing themself.

"Your classmates weren't enough? You had to go pick a fight with a police officer?"

They kept their head down. "I didn't pick a fight. He grabbed Winnie, and she wasn't even doing anything wrong—"

"We don't want to hear it, Apollo," their father interjected. "You *hit* Cyrus. We don't want any more excuses. We don't want to know anymore."

We don't want to know you *anymore.* That was what Apollo knew he'd meant to say but didn't. That was what Apollo understood anyway. They didn't want to know an Apollo who stood up for people, who defended themself and the people who mattered to them, because that was inconvenient. It shattered appearances. They wanted an obedient, spineless people pleaser. Someone who licked their blood off the boot before it came down to stomp them again.

And in front of Winnie now, Apollo couldn't hide how much that hurt.

Winnie twisted in her seat and cleared her throat. "You're not being fair. Apollo didn't pick a fight, *I* hit Cyrus, and he did this to be malicious, which you'd know if you bothered listening to them for once."

She punctuated her reproach with a scowl, though their parents merely regarded her with pity. As if she was as naïve and innocent and helpless as she looked, as if she couldn't possibly understand what their troubled brood was really like.

Apollo's heart swelled.

"If you're smart, you'll keep your distance," their mother said instead, while an officer pried away the handcuffs. Then she turned and strolled out of the station, her husband on her heels, leaving Winnie with her condescension and expecting Apollo to follow.

"Thank you," they whispered.

Winnie only inhaled calmly and said, "We'll stop him."

She kept glaring at their mother's back as they retreated, passing by a woman with Winnie's same doe eyes.

July 1978

If anyone were to ask Catherine Casey, she'd tell them that Rathbun Manor was haunted. Some of the other staff around the house seemed to implicitly agree with her; they wouldn't necessarily say it *out loud*, they wouldn't say ghosts, but they knew something unusual was going on, especially after Charles Rathbun died.

Something dangerous if you didn't follow the rules.

Which Catherine did. Mostly.

When she felt like it.

As she carried folded laundry back up the servants' staircase, she steeled herself against the whispers that lived in the walls. The whispers were gradual at first, but now they were steady, reliable alongside the strange sounds coming from the thinner walls and the vents, from which the Rathbun family was mostly insulated. They never took the rickety stairs with paper-thin walls, so they never had to listen to the ghosts hissing and asking for things inside.

They spoke in some language she couldn't discern, which was exactly how her mother said it would go; the dead weren't human anymore, they didn't speak a language you might understand. Then again, Catherine's father disagreed, and said that the dead were still human, but it was *demons* who spoke no human language you might understand. It had been a rowdy debate at the dinner table the first night Catherine described what she heard, and her husband, Ernest, ended it by questioning how the devil could tempt you if you couldn't understand him.

A full day later and Catherine still wasn't sure she knew.

Whatever it was and what it was saying was none of her business; she had no interest in answering.

She scurried up the stairs, grateful that she was only part-time. She cleaned to help out around the house while she was in night school, studying to become a librarian. It was her mother's friend at the church who helped her get a place at Rathbun, where the work was mostly tedious, harsh on the hands if you didn't use gloves, but it wasn't so bad. The Rathbuns didn't treat you as poorly as some other employers in the city and were often flexible with hours. Mrs. Mabel promised that no one would put their hands on her either, and that held true though occasionally she caught the eldest Mr. Rathbun lingering with his eyes.

For a moment, Catherine thought herself special from the other staff; when she started, she'd made sure to remind everyone that she wasn't like them. She was only here *temporarily* because she was going to be a librarian. She loved books, she loved walking among the stacks, she loved guiding people in the place of knowledge—that was her *true* calling . . . And they disabused her of that notion quickly; Willie was a talented musician, and Nora was working on a novel in the rest of her waking moments. And librarian or not, Catherine still scrubbed toilets and linens, she cleaned the windows and polished the silver, and she was paid just the same, ignored just the same.

Her high horse got swept out from under her quickly, but the others, like Mrs. Mabel's daughter Jessie, didn't hold it against her at all. They then became her friends.

Catherine tucked the boys' clothes away in their respective dressers. She was getting better at folding them to be perfectly crisp, and it helped that she now had a baby of her own, little Daniella, whose clothes she could practice on.

After the boys' things, she tended to Theodore's wardrobe. His clothing was growing harder and harder to handle; often his things would arrive in his basket covered in stains that took extra effort and cycles to wash out, stains that looked conspicuously like blood and offal. Or sometimes it wasn't blood-colored, but still smelled foul and bodily, human, and other times it was dark and didn't smell human at all.

It wasn't her job to ask questions. She didn't answer the ghosts, and she didn't ask what Theodore Rathbun did in his spare time to be smelling like that.

Nora in the kitchen swore Rathbun Manor hadn't always been like this; the problem was Theodore, she insisted, and the old man's death had changed him.

The rules came soon after. There were only certain times that the staff—that *anyone*, including Jean and the boys—were allowed in the cellar. They weren't allowed when Theodore was working, for example, which meant the staff had to schedule their work around his own whims. And when he was down there was when the whispers were the loudest; once, while she was mopping the floors, Catherine swore she heard him chanting. Nora sometimes heard chanting too when she vacuumed the rugs.

It wasn't just strange noises; the electricity was inconsistent around the house. The laundry room over the basement didn't have reliable power like everywhere else. And sometimes Catherine and the others would find themselves losing time; Catherine might begin folding a shirt and when she tucked it away, the sun had long since set. Sometimes she found Willie standing at the bottom of the cellar stairs, just staring. Jessie had conversations with herself.

Once, Catherine went down into the cellar to find a bottle of wine for Nora, and everything among the shelves had fallen to the floor. Or been thrown. The shelves were still standing, all in perfect condition, but the things on them, every single one, lay on the floor and rolling in the direction of Theodore's private room. The only door they weren't allowed behind and didn't have to clean. It looked as if one of the big earthquakes did it—after decades of stillness, they were back—although nobody could remember if there'd been one recently, or if they'd *heard* the things fall.

And it took her hours to put it all back in place.

"Coincidence," Ernest had told her one night.

Weird was more like it. All of it was weird.

Theodore retired early for the night, yawning to himself and skipping dinner. She watched him drift up the stairs with his eyes closed.

"Can you go get some detergent?" asked Nora, flickering her gaze to the cellar door, which was propped open. She avoided ever going down there, or going down there alone, and Catherine understood why: The cellar was where the ghosts spoke the loudest.

But Catherine, always eager to help someone in need, preparing for her life as a librarian, nodded. She didn't fear the ghosts simply because she refused to acknowledge them. So she descended the steps quickly and turned on the light, only to find Theodore's private room open too.

Normally he shut the black door, but today it was ajar and the room beyond it dark. A draft whirled around the cellar though the small windows were closed. The whispers were loud tonight; it felt as if the ghosts were perched on Catherine's shoulders and talking directly in her ears.

She drifted deeper inside, toward the noise, toward the dark room. And all she could think about was how there used to be five of them working at Rathbun Manor.

They were overseen by Alfonso, an older Black man who would hand out the assignments, make sure they were all on the same page, that they did them right. The Rathbuns loved him because he anticipated what they needed, could guess before they ever had to ask; he knew them better than they ever bothered to know themselves. One day Alfonso went into the basement, into the private room, and walked out blind.

The skin of his cheeks was burned and raw, and Nora, ever the storyteller, said there was nothing in the sockets. He had stumbled his way out of the room, wailing, and only Nora was still there to hear something crash below. She said she found him panicked and blaming "the box," though she hardly understood what it meant.

He never returned to work here. Catherine even went to visit him, and all he said was, "Don't open the box! It's evil."

Now, with the box of detergent tucked under her arm, when she stepped into the doorway of Theodore Rathbun's private little room, she finally, *finally* understood.

Set atop a lone cabinet was a box more luminescent than pearl. It shone strangely, wrongly, and the room seemed to spin and twist when she looked at it. The whispers on her shoulders went silent. She didn't recognize it, but it recognized something in her.

Here she saw the thing that Alfonso had cried about, his fear so strong that she remembered his trembling in his hospital bed. She could feel it as if he were still here, holding on to her hand and whimpering from the pain.

The private room was dark, but Catherine discerned some of the kinds of things she saw in the late-night news. This was the kind of place her mother would refuse to enter, would kill her if word ever got out that she *did* enter. Strange carvings on the floor and ceiling, the kind of darkness where the ghosts weren't ghosts at all but forces that humanity wasn't supposed to play with.

Exactly the kind of thing that might snatch a person's sight and never give it back.

"*Jyzq oya vezq qy hii vseq uh uzhuji?*" a voice whispered to her from the dark.

Catherine stilled.

She was raised to take care of other people; if this stayed here, and Willie or Nora or Jessie weren't careful, if one of the little boys got curious about their daddy's hobbies—someone would be hurt. Again. Theodore Rathbun was reckless to play with it, reckless to leave it out, and he wouldn't learn until it killed somebody he really cared about. And how many of the staff would he go through until then?

She thought of Charles Rathbun, old and sick and wailing in his bed, what he'd yelled at her, thinking she was someone else. *I called a priest to stop the whispers!*

Was this what he was talking about? Then what Sofia was he talking about?

Catherine grabbed the box anyway, stashed it inside the empty laundry detergent box that she'd come to dispose of. She'd take it home with her tonight and get rid of it.

Her mother had the pastor's number memorized; she was sure he'd know what to do.

As far as Theodore Rathbun was concerned, she was doing him a favor.

CHAPTER 23

Sweet Suffering

Winnie hardly spoke on the drive home; her mother did most of the talking. Not yelling, but this low seething tone that seemed designed to cut much deeper. It wasn't the rage of a broken window or the annoyance of a forgotten chore—it was the sting of a parent's disappointment.

"*Police*, Winona," her mom had griped, using her full name to really make it hurt. As if there were anyone else in the car, in the world, to evoke such a response. "You got arrested! What about Kavanaugh?"

"Not arrested, they just wanted to scare me—"

The daggers in her mother's eyes silenced Winnie, and she stared into her lap. There was no point in saying that she *wasn't* scared. If anything, she was determined to try harder. Even the fist she'd used to punch Cyrus was fine. It ached from the impact, but Marcel's playground lessons long ago had finally proved useful: not broken, no swelling or sprain. However, the excitement she might have felt at telling him this was replaced only by a sense of indignation.

"But Cyrus stole from Apollo. We were just trying to get it back—"

"I don't want to hear it. I don't care what you have to say, and you won't be around your little friend ever again."

Winnie didn't feel guilty either. Unlike when she'd broken

her arm and sent her mother racing to urgent care in a panic, this time she knew she didn't do anything wrong. Cyrus had sicced his power on them just to put them in their place, to be vindictive. No one cared about him abusing his power, about the cop manhandling her, so why should she feel guilty?

"Getting arrested for *any reason*, right after I caught you *lying* to me about where you were going? School and work, nowhere else for the rest of the school year. Your room, no visits, not even Yasmine. Do you understand me?"

The authority in her mother's voice said there was no room to object, no room to argue. It was law.

"Yes, ma'am."

Even though the law was sometimes wrong. Some laws were meant to be broken.

"Whatever you thought you were about to get into, I want an attitude change *stat*."

"Yes, ma'am."

Winnie stared straight ahead. It was easier this way, to just agree and grin and bear the punishment so it would be done with. There was no use in pointing out her mother's anger about the lying alongside her disinterest in the truth. That Daniella Bray, like everybody else in the world, didn't want *honesty* or *morality*; she wanted obedience.

When they finally arrived at home, Winnie silently trudged inside. She caught Marcel hovering at the top of the stairs out of the corner of her eye, trying to eavesdrop on such a rare occasion of Winnie getting into trouble, but she didn't linger.

"I don't even want to see your face right now," her mom called out after her, which was all fine and well, because Winnie didn't want to see *her* either.

Winnie had other plans.

After a shower and proper change of clothes, she made a show of taking out her homework and putting on her headphones. When Marcel crept slowly by her room, she shut the door in his face, so that her bad attitude was palpable. So that she became a ticking time bomb that everyone tried to avoid. It was easy—since he was yet another person who'd told her to shove it all back down, to let the world kick the stuffing out of her and do it with a smile. She wouldn't keep explaining herself to him either.

Then when the night fell, when her mother retired to bed, and Marcel locked himself in his room, Winnie did something else that was once unthinkable: She snuck out. On a school night, no less.

She used to consider herself a well-behaved girl, mostly. She got good grades and stayed focused in school. She worked a job that wasn't the most honest, or legal, but it wasn't robbery either. Telling Apollo they might die was the first crack in that image. Lying to stay out all night, punching Cyrus Rathbun in the face—those were just par for the course now. Perhaps because she couldn't remember the last time she had a full night's sleep, the unthinkable had become tangible. Reasonable. Her body had pushed past exhaustion right into madness: The rational part of her brain that cared what others thought, what was good and *acceptable* behavior, had shut down.

And until this box problem was solved, it would just have to stay that way.

Winnie slipped through the back window, tiptoed around the side of the house, and darted up the dark street without a second of hesitation.

If anything, she felt a little more honest now: with herself, with Apollo. She didn't change her mind about *camping*, and she certainly didn't regret hitting Cyrus in the face for teasing them about it.

On the bus, she knew exactly where to go, who she was looking for, and tried to prepare herself on what to say, how he might refuse and how to convince him otherwise. She dug a sewing needle under her thumbnail to keep herself awake, to keep her adrenaline high. The moment police escorted them both away from Rathbun Manor made her determined to return.

To talk to Cyrus. One-on-one.

The streets of the Bryant neighborhood felt ghostly quiet. Perhaps a little haunted. There were no other people on the sidewalks, no cars zooming down the streets. It was like the city was fast asleep long before nine P.M., except she knew now that it never really awoke during the day either. All these great houses of Buffalo's past were husks, and now *she* guarded the future.

She marched through dark hedges, her conviction rising. The porch light was on as if he was waiting for Apollo to come back. Or expecting her.

Winnie rang the doorbell and waited for her racing pulse to slow. If there was a police car patrolling by, if Cyrus called the police on her again, then she'd be dead. Worse than dead. Her mother might let her rot in jail. Kavanaugh, with their arbitrary code of conduct, might find some reason to expel her.

"Yes?" The large door opened, and Cyrus appeared.

Winnie's racing thoughts stilled.

His cut lip was a little swollen. His neat pressed shirt was unbuttoned at the top, blood dotting his collar; his hair was unkempt, as if he'd been running his hands through it, and peeking through the mess, she saw butterfly closures holding his scalp together. The dark circles under his eyes were particularly brutal against his pale skin.

"What do you want?" he asked suspiciously, keeping most of his body behind the door as if she'd strike him again.

Rather than guilt, she felt proud and resisted the urge to smile. "I just want to talk. I'm offering a truce."

Cyrus glanced over her shoulder as if she had reinforcements. As if *he* wasn't the one who'd called the cops. But then, he nodded curtly and drew the door wide for her to enter.

Each time Winnie crossed the threshold of Rathbun Manor, she felt more and more like she was traveling back in time. Like she was Sofia and Catherine and all the women in between combined and needed to watch her step in this place, because people like her were marring the floor and its white walls, sullying the chandelier just by being in the way of its light.

"Follow me."

He shut the door and headed through to the study. The wall covered in books made her feet hesitate briefly. This room was where she'd eventually bleed out if her gamble failed. However, the solar eclipse was in a couple of days. For tonight, she told herself, she was safe.

There was a little scratch on the floor where the bookcase had swung open from the secret corridor, but Cyrus merely sat on the edge of the large, dark wood desk with an amber-colored drink in hand, not noticing. "Well?"

"I . . ." Winnie searched for the words. Of all the ways she'd run through this in her head, him letting her walk right in and speak wasn't even an option. "I mean it, a truce. You leave Apollo out of whatever you're doing—drop it with the police, going through their stuff, and stay away from them. I'll keep them away from you."

She didn't know what Apollo would think of her being here, bargaining on their behalf, but they deserved better than him, than a cousin turned enemy who seemed to enjoy watching them suffer. They didn't need to be a part of this anymore, and if Cyrus kept his distance, maybe they'd never reach inside the box, pull the star out, and bring the world to an end.

It was for their sake and everyone else's that Winnie brought herself here. And Cyrus had called her clever, asked her to join him, so maybe he'd listen.

He just stared now, showing no sign of either accepting or refusing.

She added, "I'll give you whatever you want. *I'll* help you with the box if that's what it takes."

This was her second, secret purpose. If Apollo could no longer use their proximity to watch Cyrus, then Winnie would offer herself. She had something Apollo didn't—her ability—and with this "truce," Cyrus would shake her hand. He didn't know that she was really, truly psychic, that she'd read him like she'd gone groping around the cellar. Intentionally mining a person for information was a first, but if there was ever a time, it was now. She needed to know where he kept the box.

"Whatever I want?" asked Cyrus, arching a brow.

Winnie started toward him and held out her hand. "That's what I said. If you want me to help you, I'll help you. Scrub your floors, fold your laundry, fetch your coffee—"

"I already have an assistant. What I want is out of reach, so go away." He finished his drink and rose to his feet.

"But—"

Then came his frown as he scanned her over and then glanced away, like he didn't want his look to be scrutinized. But it was too late—it was the same expression Cyrus had when he'd visited the Red Hourglass, when he'd stood close even while she was brandishing a knife. He'd looked at her lips as something starved. It wasn't the tender want of Apollo; Cyrus was hollow.

"You want . . ." Winnie faltered.

Cyrus inclined his head. His eyes glimmered in the low light. "Apollo and I apparently have more in common than just our taste in family heirlooms. I have the box, but well . . ."

He gave her another once-over and started for the door.

She scoffed. "I'm trying to help you. You don't know what you're dealing with—"

"And you do?" He raised his voice. "Where's your degree, Winona? Where's your experience? Please enlighten me on what could be stronger, better than *uranium fuel.* Otherwise, please just go away."

She clamped her mouth shut. This wasn't going anything like she'd planned. "So what? I seal it with a kiss, just so you can run bragging to them?"

"You think I'm that cruel?"

"*Yes!*"

As if pained, Cyrus dropped back to sitting on his desk and scowled. He looked unbearably childish. "I'm not a monster, you know."

She doubted it.

But if it was only a kiss to save Apollo, and herself, and everyone else, she could manage. It wasn't a handshake, but she'd still touch him, still read him, picking the threads of him apart until she found the box, something she could use.

And besides, Cyrus wasn't *not* attractive.

Winnie took a step closer, noting how his grimace seemed to elongate his face. How palpable his fear of her felt, and how delicious it was. The shadows of the room and the contrast between his dark hair and brows and the ghostly white of his skin made his features look severe and carved out, like an emaciated dog.

And *she* was food.

"You're pathetic, you know that?"

His temper flared. "Yes, I'm well aware."

It was dangerous, explosive, playing with fire, but he didn't bother denying it. The glimmer in his eyes was rife with hatred;

he despised her, and he wanted her, and he hated himself for it. Still here he sat, hoping she'd put him out of his misery.

She liked how pitiful he was before her and how it made her feel powerful.

The perfect Rathbun, begging for a lowly psychic.

She grabbed his jaw between her fingers and leaned to kiss him, and Cyrus opened his mouth to receive her. Even the fire from touching him was weak; it didn't lance through her the way Apollo's touch had. She had to press close enough to the source of his warmth and coax the flame from him. Stepping into his head at the same time his body started to unwind.

The premonition was of Apollo, kneeling on the floor. A violent gash marred their forehead, blood running and crusting around their eye, in the collar of their shirt. Eye makeup was smeared and faded from sweat and tears, and spots of blood and glass shards dotted their cheeks. They gritted their teeth and tried to squeeze their eyes shut, to reel away from light opening up before them.

"*Give it to me*," Cyrus hissed right in Apollo's ear, sharp enough to make them wince.

He set the box on the dark wood floor and watched as Apollo forced their hand inside. Their face scrunched as they reeled away, weak. Heat seared them both, peeling away skin at the palm and fingers.

Then, pried away from its shelter, freed from its prison, Morning Star blinked before them. Cyrus threw the box aside to lunge for the star, ignoring the tears welling in Apollo's eyes as they staggered away.

A tilt of her head, and she found what she wanted: Cyrus shutting the box in the dungeon, behind the heavy black door.

Then Winnie pulled herself back to her body, back to kissing him and being ready to let go.

It wasn't like kissing Apollo. He smelled of men's cologne, and she tasted smoke on his tongue. There was a ruggedness to his body and an eagerness to his hands as they floated up to her waist. Cradling his neck and with her fingers rooting through his hair, she found him very square cut and sharp. All-American and very certain and *man*.

Everything about him repulsed her, and yet she found she enjoyed this, that it was made sweeter by knowing how he'd suffer when it was over.

Winnie had a fistful of Cyrus's hair. It was thick, and soft, and her tight grip seemed to make him hungrier. His teeth scraped her lip. She wanted to make him whimper.

"Cyrus? I have a question about the cadmium rods—" A girl's voice sounded behind them, and Winnie took the excuse to shove him away.

Standing in the doorway to the study was a girl a little older than her, sporting a university sweatshirt and a dark, messy bun. Her eyes were wide, and she startled at the sight of them, Cyrus's swollen lips, the split that was starting to bleed again, the indecent mess of his hair and top button undone.

Winnie savored the thirst in his gaze and turned for the door. "Truce it is."

LBII QSI HQEB, HACCYZ QSI HIBFIZQ.	UZ QSI EXOHH U XIGYZP, QY QSI EXOHH U BIQABZ.
?REE T?E STAR, SU??O? T?E SER?E?T.	I? T?E A?YSS I ?E?O??, TO T?E A?YSS I RETUR?

Apollo paused their high-stakes game of cipher hangman to fidget with the bunching ends of their sister's sweatpants again.

Artemisia was shorter than them, so even though they shared the same eyes and nose and hair, her borrowed pants crowded around the midcalf on them, and it was annoying. Despite Cyrus's "no trespassing" thing, they would have no choice but to return to Rathbun Manor—aside from the fact that it was their inheritance too, all their clothes and boots and things were still lodged in that bedroom. And they couldn't very well be expected to wear their sister's clothes in perpetuity—they were too bright.

Apollo looked like a *marshmallow Peep*.

They were folded over their notebook and pen, working on the cipher key. It was still only partial, not enough to reconstruct the full phrase, or for them to be any use to Winnie besides getting her into legal trouble, but maybe in a few sleepless hours, they'd have the rest.

Artemisia strolled into their shared bedroom with a loud yawn. When her eyes locked on Apollo, her yellow sweatsuit, the notebook in their lap, she ground to a halt, dropping her backpack on the floor of the doorway. Her eyes went wide.

"You . . ." Their sister cocked her head and blinked rapidly. "You're back?"

Apollo set the notebook aside and grimaced. "Why do you think?"

"Oh no." She pulled off her coat and sank onto her bed facing theirs. Lying on the floor between them were all of her clothes and books that they'd had to remove from the mattress just to reclaim their side again. "Cyrus?"

"He trashed my room and then called the cops to say I was trespassing." Apollo wasn't eager to rehash it. It was quite embarrassing to explain that the cousin who took you in also called the police because you kissed the girl he liked and kept a family heirloom from him. It sounded so petty it had to be a lie. They understood exactly why Winnie lied so much.

Their sister shook her head in disbelief. "How did Mom and Dad take it?"

"They took his side, wouldn't even let me explain. Winnie even tried to tell them . . ." Apollo's voice trailed off as they lay back, hands laced behind their head, and stared at the ceiling. It had stunned them in place when she'd spoken up for them, even as their parents' expressions shuttered to block her out.

They didn't want to fight alone anymore, and for one glorious second, maybe the only time in their life, they didn't have to. *She* was *their* knight instead of the other way around.

"Hey, why didn't you ever take my side?"

Artemisia shifted. "What are you talking about? I always do."

"No," said Apollo, keeping their eyes on a thin crack. "You didn't say anything about Patrick Barnes. And you don't have to; I still would have done it, but I got in trouble defending us both, and even though you said I did the right thing, you didn't even try to tell our parents. Or the school. Or Patrick's parents."

"That's not fair—"

"In fact, you never said anything to our parents at all about them being too hard on me. You could've told them that I was going to stay, demanded it. They may have chased me out, but you didn't stop them."

A weight was lifting from Apollo's chest as they spoke, even as their gaze stayed locked on the fracture in the ceiling, and they imagined it widening. Impassible ceiling breaking open. They had been marooned on this island, carrying shame all because every-one else was afraid of stepping up. Not anymore. Artemisia was their first friend, and though she'd promised to stand with them through anything, she bolted the first chance she got. It was her betrayal that hurt most.

"What?" Artemisia snapped, her voice tight. "So I was supposed to let them chase me out too?"

As if.

She was always going to be the favorite—their parents would have never risked it. And Apollo didn't know if she'd truly never understood that or if she was pretending right now just to save herself. To make herself feel better for always staying safe.

They shook their head. "You were afraid to risk your place, so you just watched me lose mine."

"Says Apollo, on their high horse again." She climbed to her feet. "Always so sure of yourself and wanting everybody to do the same, no matter the cost. Must be *so easy*. Next time, don't come back."

And then she stormed out.

Some part of Apollo wanted to feel bad for saying all this, but they didn't. It didn't hurt anymore, feeling unprotected, indefensible, *alone*, because now they knew they weren't. Winnie Bray, a psychic with a truth-telling problem, had punched Cyrus in the face to shield them, defend them, stand by them—why couldn't Artemisia?

They picked up the notebook again and resumed cracking the cipher. They wouldn't fail Winnie the way everyone else had failed them.

October 1996

On her off days from the library, Catherine liked to just knit. She sat cozily on the couch, soap operas playing on the TV in the background while she knit her daughter a sweater that she'd probably never wear.

Daniella was headstrong just like her, and adolescent girls these days enjoyed showing skin and boxy, asymmetric, and unflattering silhouettes that Catherine wasn't sure she'd ever understand. Everything was baggy and misshapen, and since the sweater Catherine was knitting *wasn't* baggy and misshapen, it might very well collect dust in the closet or end up at Goodwill. But she liked the routine anyway, the repetition, the art of caring, even if it was hard to hear the TV over Daniella's out-of-tune singing upstairs, the low thump of her radio as she jammed to some boy band and tried to study.

"How can that girl even hear herself think with that music?" Catherine muttered to herself, stitching and looping and pulling more orange yarn from its bundle at her side.

Her younger daughter, Daphne, who lounged on the couch and watched the medical drama unfold with an unblinking gape, shrugged absently.

Then came the rumble of Daniella's footsteps, the sound of her socked feet sliding across the floor, the snap of her fingers as she entered the hall. A laundry bag hung on her shoulder while she flipped through flash cards, *snap*, flip, *snap*, humming loud enough for the neighbors to hear.

It was silly—*Daniella* was silly—but the coordination was mesmerizing to watch.

Daphne stirred at the noise of her sister and groaned. "Dani, would you shut up? We're trying to watch something here."

To that, Daniella only hummed louder.

Catherine was grateful for the interruption of the doorbell, which stopped Daphne before she could launch something across the room or, worse, throw a barb sharp enough to require defusing. That was more of a thing for Ernest to do because the girls listened to him better, but her husband was out fishing on the lake. In fact, he was such a pacifist inside the home and out that they didn't even *eat* the fish he caught—he tossed them back.

Her eldest set down her laundry bag and the cards and bounced and slid her way to the entrance. The music was still blasting from upstairs when she opened the door and immediately said in her most formal tone, "Sorry, we're not interested in subscriptions—"

"No, you misunderstand!" came the voice of a man before she could shut the door. It was a voice that Catherine recognized, though it was hard for her to place. A distant memory, some nagging voice that would bother her for days if she didn't figure it out, perhaps an old visitor to the library, a patron who no longer came around. There was authority and a sharpness to the way he spoke. "I'm not selling anything. I'm looking for someone—does Catherine Casey live here?"

Daphne turned her head curiously toward the door.

Catherine's knitting needles paused, so that she could listen. A library patron wouldn't know where she lived. Any church member knew to call her *Mrs.* Catherine, instead of tacking on her last name, and an old classmate would know her as Catherine

Bishop. Did something happen to Ernest? If the man was police, wouldn't he say?

Daniella didn't move, though her voice dropped to suspicion. "Who are you?"

"I'm an old coworker of hers," the man continued, undeterred. "Is she home now? I just want to speak to her."

If it was someone who worked at the library, another librarian or an administrator, city staff that handled cleaning or maintenance, Catherine would have noticed. She was good with faces, voices, everyone had a distinct place in her mind, especially since she saw them every day. Yet something about the voice burrowed inside her and refused to settle. She *did* know it from somewhere.

So she set down her needles and rose to her feet, aware of Daphne's raised brow, how her daughter watched her every step.

Daniella maintained her grip on the door handle. "No, she's not. Do you have a card—?"

"It's all right," said Catherine calmly, though she didn't feel calm. She felt unmoored and anxious. Something about the man's voice, his unwillingness to really identify himself, carried foreboding. "Hi, I'm Catherine. I didn't catch your name, Mr. . . ."

The words died right on her tongue when she saw him.

Theodore Rathbun waited on her front porch, still a tall, proud man in one of his nice pinstripe ties. His blue eyes were watery, the whites turned red and bleary with fatigue, and though he stood straight and with the same blank expression, Catherine could not miss the lines on his face, the age that had turned his dark hair silver. He had never been one to smile, but the severe creases at his mouth had deepened, like he was permanently relegated to grimacing.

"Hello, Catherine."

Oh, so *now* he knew her name.

Catherine hadn't seen him since the day after she stole the glowing box. After she'd disguised it as an empty box of laundry detergent and taken it home, she returned for one more day to throw off his suspicion. There was no way she could ever seriously work for him after seeing that room, after knowing that he was engaged in something dangerous. She'd held that darkness right in her hands and knew what it could do, the thing that haunted her colleagues and had blinded another. The day she quit, Theodore had lined her and all the others up and made them watch as he threw a fit, smashing a vase, stomping on the flowers, throwing a portrait of old Alexander Rathbun from the wall. He'd yelled at his sons and his wife and then come for the staff, accusing everyone of taking it. Empty threats that never came to bloom.

Who was it?

Who'd sabotaged their future?

No one knew the answer except Catherine, and she'd stayed quiet. Afterward, she told Nora that she wasn't coming back, that she didn't care to leave a forwarding address, right after she'd collected her final pay.

It was almost twenty years ago, but it felt like a century. Daniella hadn't learned to walk yet when Catherine quit; Daphne wasn't even an idea in her mind. All this time, Theodore kept looking, and now he'd found her.

"You look familiar," she pretended, scratching her head and leaning against the door frame. "Have we met before? How did you find this address? Do you need help, sir?"

Theodore was not convinced in the slightest. The pleasant expression—as much as he was capable—had turned to a glower as he took a menacing step forward. "You're very hard to track down, Catherine, but I think you know exactly why I'm here."

She shook her head. She wouldn't admit anything, not to him, not with what he was into. That room, the strange stains and smells, the whispers, Alfonso's eyes and the bone cancer that claimed him only months later, all spoke of a dark hubris that sacrificed many for the gains of one; it was godless. She didn't used to consider herself superstitious or religious—she'd thought her mother and grandmother were exaggerating, anxious women—but the earthquakes stopped when she left Rathbun Manor with that box. Losing time, her forgetfulness, the sounds, things moving—all of it stopped when she called the pastor like old Charles Rathbun suggested, and together they buried the box at the church next door. On hallowed ground.

"I'm sorry, I'm not sure I do."

He pointed a finger in her direction, jutting like a dagger. "You took something that doesn't belong to you."

"Is that so?" She arched a brow and dared him to say it. He was bold, coming to her house and calling her a thief, even if she technically was. But why was it okay for people like him to pillage the world for their gold and diamonds, but trying to save lives made *her* the problem? "And what was it exactly?"

"That box was an heirloom."

That may be so, but she didn't care. There were other things to pass down to his children.

Theodore bared his teeth like a threat, but to Catherine, he reminded her of a small dog, like the one Ernest's mother had—it would growl and raise its hackles, but it was only posturing. Just posturing. The kind of men worth fearing didn't have a need for threats.

And without his box, what did Theodore have? That family had been hemorrhaging money when she was there; they were on the brink of ruin, of being *regular* people like her, not that they had much of the work ethic and fortitude to bear it. His threats? His power? She leveled her gaze.

Then there was a *creak* behind her, and his eyes flicked over Catherine's shoulder. She was sure that both her daughters were eavesdropping; of course they were. But that seemed to bother Theodore more than it bothered her. It was just two nosy teenage girls, yet his suspicion of them made him blanch, because he didn't want to talk about this in front of anyone. Because he knew he was wrong.

This heirloom he wanted, this box and whatever evil was inside, he didn't want to name in front of them. His secrecy was as strong as the arrogance that would get him killed one day, she was sure.

Catherine sighed and grabbed the door handle. "Well, I'm sorry I couldn't be any more help. Best of luck, have a nice Sunday."

She shut the door on him and his glaring. He'd likely return, she suspected, now that he knew where she lived. Perhaps he'd arrive again with police behind him and a warrant, although that seemed excessive for a haunted jewelry box. Who was to say she still had it after all these years?

He had no proof.

He didn't know that the night she took it home, she'd opened it for just a fraction of a second. Just to see what was inside, to get an idea of *why* Theodore might have let it hurt Alfonso, why he didn't want people in the cellar while he was there, why that room was off-limits to cleaning when the disgusting smells seemed to come from within. Opening the box was like peeking into hell. Everything her mother had told her about suffering, it was inside—screaming, tearing, walls shaking, fire, glimpses of a small girl crushed, another burning her hand just to hold it in her palm—and this was what Theodore was playing with. What he expected her to let him continue playing with.

She wouldn't.

When Ernest came home, she would talk about moving. Catherine would find a new house in a new neighborhood, a new township even, and then she'd retrieve that box from the border with the church and find new hallowed ground, just in case, and then Theodore would have to start his search all over again.

CHAPTER 24

Succubus, Vulture, Urchin

Cyrus cracked the window of his new Rivian despite the cool autumn temperature and closed his eyes. The fresh air helped to hold his nausea back, keep his lunch down as it threatened to rise in him, as everything else did and had been for a week now.

He was undeniably ill.

It was slowly building through the days, the nausea and headaches, the dizziness, and though doctors chalked it up to a concussion from being hit, he wasn't so sure. For one, he was hit by *a teenage girl*, and she was half his size. And for two, the doctors didn't know about Morning Star. How just holding the box after he'd found it had made him sick in the fake houseplant by the front door.

"Are you positive you don't want to postpone a little longer?" asked one of his new assistants, a freshman at the university named Sadie, eager for experience and sucking up to whoever she could, unpaid be damned. She was in the driver's seat while the other, Hugo, was in the back. The car behind them honked because she was staring at Cyrus rather than watching the road. "I think we should."

He shook his head and turned his face back to the window. Breathing in that perfectly scentless, clean air. He would keep his lunch down. He would make it back to Rathbun Manor without asking her to pull over *again*.

There was nothing in the world that would make Cyrus postpone. His adviser and the department chair both had invited some of their contacts in defense and aerospace to visit Cyrus's makeshift lab, see Morning Star in action as he ran preliminary tests on its output, tracking the particles, their velocity. Why would he postpone a demonstration that would change his life?

When he was done, Cyrus wouldn't have to cower behind his parents anymore, asking them for money to buy his way through obstacles. With Morning Star, he wouldn't have to snivel up to his classmates, trying to align himself with greatness. No, *he* would be the greatness and prove his father wrong, surpassing his grandfather along the way.

That was the world Cyrus was trying to build.

He cradled the heirloom box to his chest like an infant. When he'd retrieved it from Apollo's bathroom, it had looked in disrepair, like it was ready to fall apart at any moment. Sometimes he was afraid it might vanish from his grip. So he kept it close.

"No, we proceed as normal."

A little sickness, some bad dreams, wouldn't matter when his face was printed in textbooks, when all the world was scrambling for a piece of something he created. His face on a flag, planted on some asteroid that he'd gotten to first.

It wasn't just the world Cyrus was pioneering, but a *future*.

He could hold out until then, recover after.

"Where are the painkillers?" he asked, and began riffling through Sadie's bag.

His mouth and head were killing him, and he spent the last couple days wondering why he had to be the enemy in all of this. It wasn't a complete surprise that unprincipled Apollo would betray him, but why was the box punishing him too? It was breaking him down, when Apollo kept it hidden in their bathroom just fine.

What was it about Apollo that was so great, that everyone, every*thing* chose them first?

Well, now he had turned Winnie to his side at least. The way she'd kissed him last week, there was no way she could ever settle for Apollo again. He had the box and the girl—Cyrus had won.

Time for a victory lap.

He tossed back the pill and swallowed it dry. "Swing by Elmwood before we go home, I need a pick-me-up."

There was a curse in this world where people who amounted to nothing hated others with success. Apollo, with their record, had already messed up their own life, and even though Cyrus tried to help them, they seemed determined to drag him and Winnie down too. The girl was naïve, but in the end, she saw reason and made the right choice. Put herself and her future first. That was the effect Cyrus had on people; it couldn't be denied.

"This street," he said as they turned onto the main avenue lined with boutiques. Of specialty candy and cheap boho jewelry. "The Red Hourglass."

Cyrus had no doubt that she was working now. The first time he had visited, it had been easy to call the owner of the shop and ask for Winnie's working hours. The very sight confirmed his expectations then: Red lights in the window were gaudy, the display of roadkill macabre and desperate. And there she'd stood in its center, a gleaming black pearl.

But not in a racist way, of course.

"Wait here," he commanded Hugo when he climbed out. "And watch this."

Cyrus set the box on the seat behind him and shut the door.

The chime over the door of the Red Hourglass was tacky. The shop was overcrowded with *things*, ugly knickknacks that were as disgusting as they were base—animal skeletons that had been scavenged from the dirt and cleaned, little insects frozen in resin like talismans. All of it was a little pathetic, Cyrus thought, but he hadn't been surprised to find this was where Winnie made her money. She would be used to lowly things until she knew better.

Then his gaze snagged on her. Them. Together.

"One second!"

Winnie sat behind the register up ahead, staring at bottles of oil. At her side was Apollo, their arm draped comfortably around her waist, and they were watching her face, nearly cross-eyed and pathetic with desire. Cyrus didn't believe in witchcraft, but if he did, it would've been because Winnie had somehow bewitched Apollo into selling him out, had almost bewitched him too.

He balled his fists and seethed.

When they noticed him, the couple broke apart. Winnie's eyes went big and innocent like the liar she was. Cyrus had seen the look before; he knew girls like her.

"Still haven't learned your lesson, huh, Winona?"

Winnie stepped around the counter. "You got what you wanted. What more is there, Cyrus?"

You're pathetic.

He didn't know how she could still spew these things after she'd kissed him, after she'd put her hands through his hair and drained the energy and desire right out of him like a succubus. He had lost himself right in her grasp, and now she was pretending that was all imagined.

"How long after you were finished with me did you run on over to them?" he asked, and cursed himself for how much his voice wavered. Over her of all people. And her gaze, the little vulture, studied him for weaknesses and made him feel armorless. Sweat beaded his temple.

Apollo came around the register and pressed a hand into her lower back, as if they wanted to show it off, throw it in his face. "Cyrus, are you okay? You look sick—"

When his cousin stepped close, Cyrus lurched back. "Don't you pretend to care now, traitor. I'm not stupid—you left the manor, but you aren't leaving *this* alone. You're going to try to steal it from me."

Caught red-handed, Apollo shook their head, tried to deny it. "I—"

"Your own flesh and blood, yet you tried to sabotage me for a *girl*? A known liar and thief? She's playing you, and you're the one too clueless to see it."

They scowled. "Don't say that."

Behind them, Winnie glared. "Reckless and vindictive, and now we can add *delusional* to the list—"

Cyrus ignored the urchin. Everything out of her mouth was poison. *She* was poison; and it was probably her presence that was making him feel so poorly. He swayed on his feet and caught himself on the table. "Did she tell you about the money?" He wanted to goad Apollo, make them hurt as much as he was hurting, and it thrilled him to see Winnie freeze. "How she blackmailed me for money?"

"You broke my arm—"

Apollo was ready to mount a defense, but Cyrus wouldn't let them finish.

"Or what about the kiss? After you left the other day, she came over and kissed me and told me not to tell you."

She balked. "That was on *you*, Cyrus—"

"You kissed me back, Winona," he said, giving her a withering stare. "We don't like liars. I didn't make you."

Winnie's jaw dropped. She didn't have much in the way of denial, so her silence was damning. It was enough to let the doubt weasel its way into Apollo's understanding. Their mouth closed, and they slowed to a stop.

He continued, "She's been playing you since the day you met. For the box, for my plans, for our *money*, so she can make it big herself and get into Cambridge. And you fell for it."

All she had to do was bat her eyes in Apollo's direction and they'd crumbled immediately. It made sense, in a way, why she'd choose them over Cyrus, how little she considered him, when she was just looking for a means to an end. She couldn't manipulate him the same way; Apollo, on the other hand, was too weak to resist a little sugary perfume and a breathy whisper.

Apollo shook their head, their gaze flickering between Winnie and Cyrus, a choice to be made, and they were waiting for her to give a good counter. Which she didn't have.

Her voice was small as she tried to make it go away. "He asked, and I—I was trying to read him . . ."

Cyrus kept talking, refused to give her the space. "I've known you my whole life, and you think this girl who's only looking out for herself has your interest in mind? You could buy her loyalty and a kiss for less than a grand in cash. Ask my assistant, she walked in on us."

"Calling the cops wasn't enough?" Winnie glared at him.

Apollo now turned their full attention to studying Winnie, the way she glowered at Cyrus, how rigid she stood. There wasn't a true word to ever come out of her mouth, and now they were starting to realize. It wasn't *completely* too late, but late enough. "You didn't take his money, did you? And *don't* lie."

Her mouth opened to spout some nonsense, but then closed firm. She blinked rapidly like she might cry, and her voice trembled as she said, "He's twisting everything. You're supposed to believe me."

This was so easy. Apollo kept shaking their head and backed away from her. Cyrus was still winning, and they didn't even realize.

"And then you kissed *him*? Of all people?" Apollo's voice broke. Their upset was almost hard for Cyrus to watch.

Almost.

"*Ouch*," Cyrus griped. He wasn't *that* bad; it was all her.

"Because that's what he—I'm trying to save you," was all she could say. Her well of lies had run dry. "All of us."

"You tried to take it from the fire, you were afraid of it being destroyed . . ." Apollo frowned. "All along, you wanted to keep it and know what he had planned, so you used me? You are unbelievable, Win."

Fire danced in her eyes. It made her more attractive, Cyrus was ashamed to admit, and when this Morning Star business was over, he might come back just for this, to feel her loathing on him again. She'd kissed him so hard the other night that she tore his lip right open, and he'd relished every second of it—he couldn't fault his cousin for falling for the same.

Winnie pointed to the door. "Is that so? Then get out. And don't ask for my help when he tries to *kill you*."

"Let's go, cousin," said Cyrus, trying hard not to sound *too* victorious as he retreated to the door, as Apollo trailed slowly behind him. He needed the pair apart, and cleaving was like child's play. Over his shoulder, he glimpsed Winnie one last time, the alluring flush to her cheeks, and warned, "Know your place, little lamb."

She punctuated her hatred by slamming the door to the Red Hourglass, the jingle sounding down the street. It thrilled Cyrus while Apollo flinched at it, their head hanging low. He kept his head high, because now he had it all: Morning Star, *Apollo*, while Winona Bray, the thief and grifter, was left with neither.

Apollo betraying their whole family for a snake oil saleswoman was just typical. They'd have to earn Cyrus's trust back, but Cyrus knew just the way.

CHAPTER 25

A Swell of Sound

Apollo stumbled out into the evening in a daze. The lush trees of Elmwood were beginning to turn colors, the leaves golden in the darkening sky. It would have been a marvelous view, a sweet place to go on a walk down the road, arm in arm, before slipping into a cozy coffee shop when the rain came unexpectedly. However, imagining that instead made their chest ache.

They felt sick.

Standing beside them, Cyrus pushed his phone into his pocket and nodded toward his futuristic black truck parked across the street, the person sitting in the driver's seat—he didn't even *drive* himself. "You want a ride? I'm headed home, and you can . . . stay if you want."

In the flood of red light from the Red Hourglass, he looked especially pale. Bloodless and clammy. The sway in his posture was more obvious now, and Apollo felt they should be ready to catch him at a moment's notice. *How hard did Winnie hit him?* "No, I drove—are you sure you're okay?"

Cyrus gave them a thumbs-up. "Flu. Will you help me with this Morning Star thing now? I could really use another hand."

"No," replied Apollo glumly, shaking their head. Winnie had betrayed them in the end, so they found they wanted nothing to do with any of it. "Not interested."

And they could tell that something was *really* wrong with

Cyrus, that he had changed in a way that didn't feel right. Good. If it was the box doing this to him, it was far different from what it had done to Apollo, different from Winnie and her sight. *If* it was doing anything at all. It could just be another of Winnie's manipulations, making them think this way.

If she was a traitor, then that meant the one thing Apollo had chosen for themself wasn't much of a choice at all. Everything they thought about themself, a hero, lovable, *worthy*, was all her orchestration. A means to an end. They thought of everything she'd predicted—a car accident that didn't happen, Cyrus killing her, a star engulfing everything, earthquakes, a snake—and how they saw none of it but some glimpse from the past. Nothing more than a tap on the brakes one late night. The bad dreams could have just been *stress,* and Apollo was so easy to deceive.

They could hear their mother's voice, severe and certain, as clear as that day in the principal's office. Maybe she was right, and this was just a ruse they'd imagined, let themself believe, crafted for attention to prove Apollo was more than they really were.

Maybe they didn't need Winnie's protection because there was nothing to protect them from.

"I don't want anything to do with it," they said finally, turning on their way.

They wanted to be alone. To have time away from Winnie, time to think, to see what they were really made of rather than giving whatever it was that she wanted. Every moment Apollo felt that she was seeing them, the real them, she wasn't. *Camping* was just her creation of them, shaping a weapon she could use.

Apollo moved languidly up the side street to where their van was parked, an eyesore in a sweet little neighborhood where an old woman glared from her window. She watched them closely as she always did when they visited Winnie, no doubt seconds away from calling the police, so they waved at her this time, and she closed her curtain. *Message received*, more than enough to let them know this was yet another place where they weren't welcome. The closed curtain was better than the note she stuck to the windshield, saying Apollo couldn't park here even though it was perfectly legal—they'd checked.

"Fuck." They snatched the newest note away. "*Fuck.*"

They didn't want to do this anymore. They didn't want to be here in this city anymore, be this person, trapped and aimless and always waiting for someone's guiding hand, to be someone else's hope. Where was *their* hope?

"Where to now?" Apollo asked, throwing the van in drive. There was no one around to say the answer, which was: *anywhere but here*.

They set off and hoped that Cyrus would find something more important to do with his life, that Winnie was lying about the box killing her to manipulate them, and they would all be okay. The foreboding of his request for their help, letting them return, knotted in Apollo's stomach and refused to soothe itself as they drove out of the neighborhood and onto Main Street, waiting for their light to turn green.

The only place they really had left was home, back to the house they shared with their parents, that room where even Artemisia wasn't speaking to them anymore—a house that wasn't really Apollo's anymore. There was an implicitness in their silence that they all wanted Apollo gone.

Well, you and me both.

So from here, they'd head straight to the highway, *any* highway, do them all a favor, and disappear.

At the switch of the light, Apollo accelerated in a daze.

And it was only after they'd applied the gas, crossed into the intersection, that they saw it. That they felt the wall of shining black metal as it passed by. Crashed into. Tore *through*.

A swell of sound and then the world fell silent.

They were thrown into a tailspin. Their head whipped left, smacking against the van window, and then righted rapidly. The shatter of glass sent shards at them. With a *whoosh*, the airbag threw them back in their seat. As suddenly as it all began, it swiftly stopped.

A high-pitched ring permeated their ears as they sat there, limp. Curling white smoke came up from the engine, the front of their van folding tight around a light pole. All they saw was, at once, darkness and flares of light.

They'd been hit.

Be careful at the intersection of Main and Bryant. Winnie's voice echoed through Apollo's head as their gaze flickered again to their rearview mirror, which dangled uselessly, as boneless as they felt. Their heart sank as they read the cross street: Bryant.

They'd been *hit*.

Blood ran from their forehead into their eyes, stinging, eliciting tears.

The van was years of saving, of bagging groceries and mowing lawns and painting their neighbors' walls for spare change. Years of dreaming, of studying manuals and watching tutorials just to get the thing running. Hunting down parts from across the country—it was theirs, the one thing they had that their parents and Cyrus and Winnie and Patrick Barnes couldn't take, and now it was crumpled. A worse heap of ruin with them trapped inside.

Some asshole runs a red and . . .

Apollo sniffled, wondering when anything might finally go *right* for them and stay that way. They thought they'd avoided her premonition, that she'd saved them, but they were wrong. They were marooned again, alone, in blinding pain and bleeding out in this wreck of a van.

"Hurry up," someone snarled from somewhere up the street. The voice was muffled.

Apollo lolled there, unmoving, unsure if the wet running down their face now was blood from hitting their head or tears from the pain in their side, behind their eyes, their legs and spine. From Winnie stabbing them in the back but still being right about *this*. Maybe it was some other trauma that they hadn't registered quite yet.

The passenger door lurched loudly, and gloved hands reached inside to pull Apollo out. She didn't look the way Apollo expected a paramedic to look—young, not wearing a uniform. The stranger unbuckled their seat belt and dragged them away by the armpits. Another pair of hands grabbed their dangling ankles. The hurt in their joints swelled with the motion, everywhere they were held, where they dangled, was pain, and they had no energy to right themself.

The collision had stripped the fight right out of Apollo, or perhaps Apollo was tired long before this from all the fighting. With Patrick Barnes, with their parents and Artemisia, with Winnie, fighting to stay alive, fighting for the space to exist.

"Leave me alone," they mumbled as their lids drooped.

The figures were hauling them into the back seat of a truck instead of onto the bed of an ambulance. The smell of hot, twisted metal and oil thickened the air. Maybe Apollo's blood too. Was the other driver okay?

"I'm sorry, but I have to do this."

This voice belonged to Cyrus, but Apollo didn't have the energy to pursue it. To find where it came from, why Cyrus was here when they'd been hit, what he was referring to. Their head already hurt too much to think about anything more.

"Are *you* taking me to the hospital?" Each word was laced in sharp pain.

"No. We have work to do."

Then came the rattle of a car door slamming shut, and Apollo was moving. The truck was moving with them in it, perhaps. They imagined this was what it felt like to be in the womb, the hum of background noise and being moved around somewhere when you couldn't see or do anything about it. What would happen to their van? The light pole?

Would anyone look for them?

They reasoned that it'd be better just to sleep and wait, wait and sleep. So they closed their eyes and dreamed once again of fire.

August 2011

483 Heritage Street was known for its roses. People walked by the front of the house, saying hello to Mrs. Catherine just to smell the sweet and earthy fragrance. They asked after her eldest daughter, the nurse, and her new husband, Jacob, who was a chef; when Daphne would finally finish her degree; and if she was eating well. Kids stroked the soft pink petals and, when caught, went wide-eyed and stuttered out, "Is Marcel home?"

And Catherine would just smile and call after her grandson before she stepped off of the porch.

She was known as the Rose Lady in the area because she often gifted rose water and rose oils to friends on the street and at the church, when a family needed to know that she was thinking of them in hard times as well as when new bundles of joy moved onto Heritage. She was known more for her roses than she was for her books, though the rumors that she knew the perfect book gift for any occasion persisted long after she left the library.

"Mama!" a high-pitched voice called after her as she headed around back.

The rosebushes in front of 483 Heritage were famous, yes, but those lucky enough to enter the backyard would see her favorites. The pinks and reds were more vibrant, the blossoms blooming in greater abundance, the thorns sharper and more vicious, and they somehow lasted longer into winter. It had baffled Jacob when he first started coming around to see Daniella, how even in the deep January mounds of snow, he could still see rose petals like drops of blood poking out, and Catherine had only shrugged and said, "Thank the lord."

Privately, she suspected it was something else, the thing buried beneath them. Was it the sacred oil or the box that fed the roses?

Little Winnie tottered over to the roses, to Catherine, as she watered the bushes. She liked to do it in the evening, when the sun was close to setting, which allowed her to enjoy droplets glistening on the thorns in the dying rays of light and against such brilliant color.

Her secret had blossomed into something great; she had sown a great deed, she was sure, when she buried the box here.

"Are you ready to help?" Catherine asked as she offered the watering can. "Do you remember the instructions?"

Winnie, with her small hands, took it gladly and nodded. She seemed to think the roses belonged to *her* as much as they were Catherine's work, the only one to take an interest in their color, their watering. Some days, she insisted on helping Catherine fertilize the soil, watching her every step with those big doe eyes while Yas's only concern was taking the earthworms underneath as pets. Marcel, like his mother, found all of it boring.

When Winnie was a baby, Catherine would lay out a little blanket for her curious granddaughter to watch her work, and she'd watched indeed.

"We gotta get this spot the most," repeated Winnie, her tiny feet standing directly over where the box was buried. Where the roses were the hardiest, where the sacred oil was needed most. "These roses like the extra water, they told me so."

And Catherine nodded, though her smile had stiffened. She

knew it was just a manner of speaking, but it was impossible not to think of all those days at Rathbun Manor, the whispers over her shoulder and at her back. The only times she'd heard them after she left was when she buried the box at the old church and again the day she buried it here, as if it was begging her not to go, not to leave it alone.

Tricks.

The first scrape of hallowed dirt had silenced it again and again. When she occasionally spoke to the others who used to work at Rathbun, they sounded lighter, freer, and she felt it too. However, now Catherine wondered if it might try soliciting her family next. Not Daniella or Daphne—they were too old—but the children. Did she bury it deep enough? Did she add enough of the oil? Did she need to call that herbalist Hortense that her friend recommended and ask for something stronger?

"What else do the roses tell you?" she asked nervously, afraid for the answer.

Children were always a little unnerving, she knew, *hearing* things and *seeing* things that nobody else did. Was it Winnie's burgeoning imagination or the box? What would she do if it was the latter?

Winnie only glanced up at her and grinned. "That Mr. Johnson cuts one every day to give to his wife. I saw him leaning over the backyard fence yesterday through the window when he thought no one was looking."

Catherine laughed.

So her precious granddaughter didn't know about the box, then. She didn't see what it could do, the hell it made Catherine see, the hell it put Alfonso through, and Catherine was pleased to consider that Winnie never would. Her granddaughter would never know that Catherine was a prison guard, that beneath these roses was a prisoner, and this was a secret Catherine would take to her grave. Catherine smoothed down Winnie's hair, content to know that the little girl would tend well to the roses as she grew, when Catherine passed, an oblivious warden. It was peace of mind to never know what the box wanted to summon, how it could sunder a planet and yawn through the sky, a serpent ready to devour the sun.

Catherine didn't have much to pass on to her children, her grandchildren, but the roses—she could at least give them this.

CHAPTER 26

The Lamb Sharpens Its Teeth

A*pollo actually left.*

Winnie gripped the edge of the counter tight and stared into the distance, unseeing, trying to stop herself from shaking. From wrecking everything in the shop. From screaming. Disbelief, anger, and hurt stormed within her, replaying over and over again how they actually believed the garbage Cyrus spewed without question, turned around, and left her here to stop this apocalypse by herself.

An apocalypse they'd start if she didn't stop *them.*

And today was the solar eclipse.

She'd been delirious enough to believe the false truce would hold and Cyrus wouldn't tell, as if his vendetta against Apollo didn't run so deep that he'd do anything to hurt them. Apollo only pretended to be a wolf, but in the end, they were as fragile as glass and had shattered just as easily. If she wasn't so tired, wasn't running on fumes and espresso and sugar, she would've seen it coming.

She would've seen *all of this* coming.

Unable to bottle it up, she took to pacing. Exhaustion had long since fled her body in place of frenzied desperation; her pulse was hummingbird fast, her heart threatening to give out if she didn't wrap this up soon. Yet her glare locked on the door, still envisioning the way they wouldn't even meet her eyes while Cyrus ranted about the kiss, as if he hadn't smashed their room to pieces and then called the cops. As if he hadn't been lying about her and her family for weeks. It was so easy to make Apollo fold, make them default back to thinking Winnie was a liar, and they just couldn't pretend anymore to tolerate her, to like her, to believe her.

You are unbelievable, Win. They couldn't have picked a worse word.

"Well, good riddance," she muttered bitterly to no one but herself and the shop full of dead animals. Then alone and trying not to feel defeated, she turned back to the sacred oil.

That was what Hortense and her grandmother had called the infusion in the white bottle, what she'd sprinkled over the soil after she buried the box. Perhaps this was what kept it dormant for so long, why their burial in the park hadn't worked.

Winnie had no choice but to believe she'd seen that premonition for a reason.

She'd been about to make her own when Cyrus stumbled his way inside. Now she held the bottle and just wished that she'd listened more closely when Hortense spoke of herbs that carried intentions, that acted as magnets for good and evil. She didn't want to call and worry Hortense, or make it known that she hadn't been paying attention; and now she ached for the chance to remember her grandmother's instructions, trying to coax a premonition from old, hard plastic to no avail. Instead, all Winnie had was her intuition.

Her hands.

So much time wasted treating this like a parlor trick, dreaming of running away instead of considering it a part of her. Not a curse but just . . . *her*. Her grandmother's gift to her, her inheritance in place of roses.

Groping around Hortense's altar in another game of hot and cold, Winnie tried to re-create the steps by following her gut. Hot enough to sting her fingertips like a fresh mug of tea was a carrier oil, to be added first. She closed around a tub of turmeric and felt nothing, but the little bag of dried hawthorn berries somehow felt alive. A jar full of rue clippings heated all the way up to her arm, and rosemary oil made her sweat.

"I don't need Apollo," she told herself as she shook the final infusion, running through the plan one last time. "I can stop it on my own."

But in the back of her mind, she wasn't so sure. Cyrus thought his heirloom was a thing of science, measured by its potential as fuel, while her grandmother treated it like a creature to be caged, through oil and herbs. *Tradition.* And maybe it was both, but Winnie only had access to one.

Cyrus had everything, but she only had herself. She'd been on her own for so long. No surprise that it was now up to her to stop Cyrus. To save a world that didn't care whether she lived or died.

Or even to listen to her.

Then vertigo struck, and she swayed on her feet. The room seemed to spin around her, and for a long moment, her body was made of lead, and she couldn't summon the strength to take a step. Leaning against the altar, she fished the tin from her pocket, the sewing needle from within, and pressed it under her fingernail.

She didn't have *time* to slow down—what if something went wrong?

Blood beaded on her skin as she tucked the needle and tin away, and in the seconds that followed, she was back. Alert. Standing upright and wide-eyed again.

Only a few more hours.

She tucked the sacred oil into her bag and swung it over her shoulder. Three big bottles of booze jostled inside with the motion, and the weight almost sent her careening to the side. She'd swiped them from the back of Marcel's closet this morning while he was in class, while she was skipping her own because she couldn't be half-assed to waste hours in another classroom with people who thought just like Cyrus. And now they carried her hope that this would work, and that by the time he noticed they were gone, by the time her mother got word of her absence, the worst would be over.

Or they'd all be dead.

Winnie wasn't an expert in Molotov cocktails any more than she was an expert in sacred oil, but they seemed good enough for this. The alcohol certainly *smelled* strong enough. And she'd already taken a shirt and cut it to strips for preparation; combined with the pack of matches Apollo had set aside from their back pocket, she was all set.

She really, truly didn't need them. Or anybody. If Cyrus thought she was a lamb, well, she had sharpened her teeth.

"And if I screw up, the whole world deserves to burn anyway."

Winnie marched past the counter. There was a nearly finished energy drink sitting there, and with a trembling hand, she tipped the can back to pour the last fizzy drops to settle on her tongue. It tasted like citrus and battery acid, but it would have to do.

Just a few more hours. She willed her pulse to calm.

Her gaze lingered on the cipher pages still sitting at the register. Apollo had barged eagerly into the shop earlier, but then hadn't even looked at it in their rush to get away from her. Hadn't even finished.

LBII QSI HQEB, HACCYZ QSI HIBFIZQ.	UZ QSI EXOHH U XIGYZP, QY QSI EXOHH U BIQABZ.
?REE T?E STAR, SU??O? T?E SER?E?T	I? T?E A?YSS I ?E?O??, TO T?E A?YSS I RETUR?

Like a twisted puzzle she couldn't pry herself away from just yet, she let it suck her in for a second and tried piecing it together. Just in case it confirmed what she was going to do. Just in case the world was ending anyway, and she didn't want to die not knowing what it said.

T?E could only be *THE*, which meant that *S* was really *H*; Z was probably *N*. And in the second line, *A?YSS* was probably *ABYSS*. She rewrote the translation again:

FREE THE STAR, SU??ON THE SER?ENT
IN THE ABYSS I BE?ON?, TO THE ABYSS I RETURN.

None of it made any sense to her now, not when she was on her way to do something reckless, so she tucked the sheet into her pocket and locked down the Red Hourglass. Hortense wouldn't mind her closing early, would understand, considering the world was barreling toward its end. Like her mother, like Marcel, perhaps the old woman would either be angry tomorrow or there *was* no tomorrow.

Winnie made it only halfway down the block before she tottered on her feet again. She braced herself against an elm tree and scrambled for the tin and sewing needle, breathless. "I need a *car*."

That was the part of the plan she really hadn't considered, had taken for granted: Apollo driving her places, saving her energy, saving time, instead of having to walk so many blocks with weeks of sleepless nights under her belt. The city continued to punish her, even on the day of her death.

One step, and the blood rushing to her head seemed to recede. Another, and her body turned to lead again, collapsing into the black. Eyelids heavy, fighting against the current, unsure how much time had passed, Winnie felt someone touch her shoulder. A flashlight darted over her face.

"Are you okay? Do you need us to call someone?"

Temple pressed to the concrete, gravel embedded in her cheek, she forced herself to nod. To push herself up on her elbows.

"Do you need some help?"

She wouldn't make it far like this, not in her condition. Just because she was used to going it alone didn't mean she *wanted* to. That it was fair, or she even had to.

"Yes, I do."

CHAPTER 27

Bones Aren't Supposed to Do That

When Apollo came to, the engine had stopped. They were still folded somewhere they shouldn't have been, with pain blaring in every inch of their body, but at least they weren't moving anymore.

It was hard for them to keep track of anything, much less time, when they were drifting in and out of consciousness, of being here and then somewhere else, in a plane torn between awake and sleeping.

They were alive, they knew, but beyond that, they couldn't tell much of anything. And even this fact felt tenuous.

Apollo tried to push themself up but groaned and flopped back down. Their voice felt like it was full of shards as they demanded, "I need to go to a hospital. *Please.*"

They couldn't tell if anything was broken; there wasn't one big hurt, but rather, they felt composed of a million little ones. Like glass had broken and been embedded inside of Apollo, replacing all their bones and organs and blood, until they were only jagged, awful shards now.

No one answered them.

Instead, they heard the sounds of bustling, commands and footsteps so far away, and then the gloved hands returned to grab them. They made a feeble effort to break free, but their arms had no strength to them, their legs no real fight. It felt almost effortless for them to be subdued and seized; a man they'd never seen before picked them up beneath their armpits like a baby. Bodies and doorways sloshed into them as they were carried, body bag–style, to another location.

"Where are you taking me?"

Apollo's eyes stung. The light was bright when they crossed an archway and moved indoors, and then came more jostling to their aching spine as their captors hauled them down a flight of stairs. The smell of cold, wet stone and metal was distantly familiar, but the headache raging through them wouldn't make the connection.

Then finally they were dropped into a chair, sitting upright with their head lolling to the side.

It took all Apollo's strength to stay awake and focus, take in their surroundings and what was happening. The room had a sterile kind of light from above that cast the corners in shadow; some familiar machinery was pushed against the wall, full of piping and water, and rounded steel basins they didn't understand. Candles lined the perimeter still. Apollo slowly recognized Rathbun Manor's cellar beyond the door.

"Why did you bring me here?" they asked roughly.

They needed water—no, they needed medical attention.

Cyrus stood at the cabinet, Morning Star in hand. People in white coats fidgeted around him with the equipment, talking quickly to each other about readings, adjusting the position of thin rods. None of them paid any attention to Apollo, or showed signs of hearing the scratching, scraping noise that seemed to coat the walls. That brushed against the back of their neck and ruffled their hair.

It was otherworldly, something that shouldn't be forced into existence, into this space. Something not from here, that would rend their reality in two.

"Lbuizj yl qsi hiib, cebwij xo qsi izj, ebi oya biejo?"

"Oh no."

Apollo squirmed in their chair, managing to rise briefly before getting dropped back down. Was this what Winnie meant by Cyrus killing them? She'd been right, and they wouldn't live to apologize.

"You know," Cyrus said calmly, "going through all the notebooks, the manuscripts, and research logs, I couldn't quite figure out the *randomness* of the box's effects, the timing. It doesn't just seem to be energy output."

The girl who'd grabbed Apollo from their car, now with a gash on her brow, donned a white coat and set two small items on the cabinet by the box. It was too far to make them out, Apollo's eyes refusing to settle. Instead, they glanced at the door, which might as well have been an ocean away.

"What are you talking about? *Why am I here?*"

Cyrus ignored Apollo's questions. "It isn't just light and heat. Dr. Dalloway, my adviser, suggested we get a Geiger counter, then a dosimeter. Do you know what those are?"

Despite the grinding, gnashing headache that felt like it'd split them in two, Apollo did their best to glare at Cyrus. If their cousin wouldn't answer their questions, then they wouldn't entertain his either. No one seemed to even register that they were trapped here, concussed and broken and bleeding.

"See, we've been talking, and he has a theory: He thinks that this box is the fuel, emitting ionizing radiation—a lot when it's opened, but still a passive amount when it's closed. All these particles race through the air, most we know about but some we don't, and it can change us depending on the particles, their amounts, the duration. That's his theory for the variation, why I'm sick. He thinks it's from carrying that thing around, suddenly and nonstop."

Cyrus grabbed Apollo's face and lifted their gaze painfully to meet his.

"But I disagree. It doesn't explain why you aren't sick. That much passive radiation, and you'd be shedding all that green hair of yours. You'd be rotting from the inside out. *I* think the radiation is some kind of fail-safe to protect the thing inside, and only some people who know the key can get to it safely. You're going to help me."

He dropped their head abruptly and returned to the cabinet to flick on the two small devices. One immediately came to life. Slow *tick*s with a lot of space between them, drawn out and chilling. Apollo stiffened, waiting for something to happen.

Tick.

Tick.

Tick.

They didn't know what Cyrus was talking about, what radiation, what *key*, whatever was inside. All they knew was that the box could trigger cataclysm upon opening, and they and Winnie fought so hard to keep it out of his hands. They fought, and lost, and ended up right back here.

The last thing they'd said was that they didn't believe her.

"Sensors at the ready!" From behind the cabinet, Cyrus reached for the box lid. "Now, let's see if we can confirm my theory, shall we?"

The moment he pulled it back, the small device erupted. Grating and dissonant, the *tick*s swelled, so fast they were nearly indistinguishable from each before and after. It was a warning, an alarm sounding at Apollo to get up. Flee. And they couldn't even muster up the strength to turn away.

"Turn it off!" someone shouted.

Apollo squeezed their eyes shut against the flood of light,

feeling it sting against their lids. A wall of heat came with it, and the smell of something burning filled the air. The manor shook, rattling the legs of their chair, dislodging dust that trickled down on them. A low rumble tore through the place as the walls trembled and the equipment quaked. A high-pitched whine pierced Apollo's ears and grew louder, higher, sharper. The single dangling light bulb overhead burst. There came the sound of papers scattering, the murmurs of nervous people.

And then followed the squelch of flesh and a scream. Something dropped to the floor with a wet *thud.* Wind whipped through Apollo's hair.

Suddenly the light was gone.

The excess heat retreated immediately after, followed by the dying down of wind, and then the rumbling came to a stop. The frantic *tick* of the device, however, didn't slow a beat, remaining loud and furious. Apollo kept their eyes squeezed shut, listening to the swinging spotlight overhead as it creaked in the aftermath. It smelled of smoke. Of fire, burnt wood, and flesh. Blood and burnt hair.

And when everything finally settled around them, when the room went quiet, the box's scratching, skittering, whispers eked out and climbed all over Apollo's skin. "*Juj oya guwi qseq?*"

They shuddered.

From somewhere in the dungeon, there came a choked gasp. Apollo peeked, opening their raw eyelids slowly to take it all in. Their face stung.

The air was still several degrees warmer, and the room was . . . changed. The paint on the black walls was singed and no longer shiny. Some of the sensors had dislodged or fallen, and water was leaking from one of the larger machines. Cyrus crouched beside the cabinet, a hand pressed to his chest. The gasp, the strangled cry of fear, had come from *him*, but Apollo couldn't take their eyes away from the piles of bone scattered across the floor to ask.

The remains sat in some kind of liquid. Something wet and sticky and thick, not dark enough to be blood, not that it mattered. They belonged to multiple people, more bones than one human body could hold.

Cyrus staggered forward to the nearest bundle, to what soiled the singed remains of a white coat. Scraps of long dark hair clung to a piece of scalp, and the scalp was stuck to the floor with some macabre adhesive. Their cousin shifted it aside to pick up a single bone, long and thick enough to be a femur perhaps, his hand shaking.

The bone didn't *behave* like bone, however. Apollo watched it sag in Cyrus's grip, limp and soft like gelatin.

"Bones aren't supposed to do that," Apollo heard themself whisper, suddenly hit with a wave of nausea.

It was only then that their cousin looked up at them, as if he'd forgotten that they were still in the room. Stuck in that chair, because he'd put them at risk.

Cyrus grabbed the closed box and clambered over to them. "See? You—you're fine. You're not . . . You have some resistance to it. It was pointed right at you."

Apollo smacked the box out of his hand. "Get that thing away from me."

Their skin hurt all over. Even if the box may not have killed them *yet*, they didn't want to stick around to give it another chance. Or die here, in their grandfather's freak dungeon, with a cousin who'd just tried to kill them. The moment they pushed up to their feet, the room dipped and spun. Cyrus just watched as they caught themself on the wall and had to sink down.

If he opened the box again, they wouldn't be able to stop him or run.

"There's something inside," said Cyrus feverishly. His voice was unsteady, breath racing. "Apollo, you could just reach in and pull it out. If you'd just do this for me—"

Apollo shook their head and gritted their teeth. "I won't."

They tried not to look at the wet mess, the bones, the crispy skin and strips of fabric. *Mess* that used to be people, and Cyrus had only stepped over them and kept pushing. Winnie was right about everything, and they had let doubt infect them.

"*Do it*, or I find that cute little psychic and put her to the test instead."

"*No.*"

Cyrus grabbed the box's carved lid and sneered. "Rathbuns don't take no for an answer."

Light shot out from the crack, and Apollo screamed.

March 2013

There was a strange man lurking around the house when Winnie and her family came home from her grandmother's funeral.

Her father had wanted to pick up some things for the wake at Auntie Daphne's house—he was a chef, after all, so everyone counted on him to bring the good stuff—and though he insisted it was only supposed to be a minute, her mom hopped out of the car to change into more comfortable shoes, and Marcel had to pee, so it turned out to be more than just a minute.

While they all rushed inside, Winnie decided to collect a couple more of her grandmother's roses. She'd already taken a whole bundle, thorns and all, to tuck into the casket, but the wake was for the living, her mother had explained, and the living deserved to smell the roses too. Maybe more so.

Specifically the *good* ones in the back.

She strolled into the backyard, pulling a pair of garden shears from the shed as she went, and that was when she noticed him.

The man didn't look like anyone from the neighborhood—not Mr. Johnson who snuck roses over the fence, or Ms. Adele who sometimes came to talk with her grandmother in the afternoons. No, this man was white and skeletal, wearing a crisp, blue suit, and unlike everybody else who came into their yard, he wasn't smelling the roses or marveling at the blooms. Instead, she found him on his knees, digging around in the dirt with his bare hands instead of wearing gloves like her grandmother had, and muttering to himself.

"I know it's here, Catherine," he grumbled between pants as Winnie got closer. "I know you have it."

Winnie tightened her grip on the shears. "Who are you? And who said you could touch my roses?"

When her grandmother died in her sleep, those roses became Winnie's responsibility. Hers to care for and love like nobody else.

The side door shuddered behind her.

The old man went rigid and glanced over his shoulder. He was ready to dismiss her, fixing his small mouth to say something snide, but then his eyes went a little wider. Winnie followed his gaze and found her dad towering right over her. And her dad was tall. *Good.*

Jacob Bray smoothed back Winnie's hair and stepped around her. "Hello, can I help you? I don't think we've met."

Though she could see the wide smile on his face, the dimples and crinkles around his eyes, it wasn't his normal smile. This was his scary smile, the one that said he wasn't really happy at all and you had to beware. He'd never used it with her or Marcel before, saving it only for other grown-ups who he revealed he didn't like afterward.

And he was using it now.

The old man seemed to register it, because he stood calmly and brushed the soil from his hands. The moment drew out long before he finally reached into his pocket and showed her dad a letter. Nobody bothered to show it to her.

He said, "I'm Theodore Rathbun. I knocked around front, but nobody answered. The previous owner owed back taxes to the city, so I bought this property and finalized the paperwork about a month ago. I'm here to inspect it in case any work is needed before I get an appraisal."

The conversation sounded serious. Winnie didn't move from her spot, didn't release the shears that were pointed right at the man's stomach. Just in case.

"'Appraisal'?" her father asked.

The old man nodded. "Consider this a heads-up. I'll be poking around, and you might want to start looking for a new place."

Winnie's dad was quiet for a long time. His fists fidgeted at his sides. The two men seemed to be talking to each other through the silence, staring into each other's eyes, while she was left out. Then finally her dad pointed toward the house. "My wife is inside; can we do this with her?"

The two men stepped around Winnie and left the backyard, her father doing his best to give her a reassuring smile that didn't reach his eyes. It looked just like when they told her and Marcel that their grandmother had died, that sometimes these things happened, and it was okay to be sad. She'd thought then that he was saying all of this for himself and not really for her at all, because her grandmother was old and that's what happened to old people.

Nonplussed, she marched forward with her shears to inspect the strange man's work. Originally she'd figured it would be fine to take just two blossoms from the brightest bunch, trim the thorns, and stick them in her pigtails, to match her red beads.

Her grandmother would have liked that if she could see.

However, this was where the old man had been digging. Right in the center of the bushes. Something strange, thick, and white was exposed by the gaping hole he left in the soil, encased by thin, spindly roots.

Winnie rushed back to the tools, grabbed a spade, and resumed the man's digging. There was something *buried* here—she crossed her toes, hoping that it was a T. rex fossil—and she had to uncover it fast before the strange man came back. What if he knew it was here?

How did he know her grandmother's name?

She heard a faint voice as she cleared out the dirt, chucking spadefuls over her shoulder, soiling the knees of her tights. Not that she cared—would her mother still be angry when Winnie was the youngest person ever to dig up a *fossil*?

"Oya, U wzyv oya."

The whisper grew louder, though she hardly registered it. It could have been the conversation between the old man and her parents, muffled shouting from the house, or maybe someone on the other side of the fence whispering to her.

"Gotta hurry, gotta hurry," she mumbled to herself instead.

Then finally Winnie wriggled her treasure free from the roses' root system . . . and frowned. It wasn't the skull of a T. rex, nor part of *any* dinosaur, and neither was it a pirate's gold chest. No gold at all, in fact, aside from a latch.

Buried under the precious roses of Heritage Street was a white box with all of these drawings on the sides, though they were hard to see through all the caked-in dirt. She didn't know how it got here, if her grandmother had known it was here or not since she'd never mentioned it, but it was under the roses that she had left for Winnie. And therefore it belonged to Winnie, by default.

So Winnie unstuck the latch and grabbed the lid. A bright light cut through the seams, piercing her eyes. There was fire, hot and moving fast, and her father was running—

Then someone snatched her hand away roughly.

She dropped the box and stumbled away. Her eyes hurt, like that time she'd tried staring into the sun, and the world seemed to be spinning around her. It took a moment for her to see anything, to register that it was her mother pulling her away, to glance over her shoulder and catch where the box had fallen shut, back into the dirt hole where she'd found it.

"Winnie, let's go!"

What was that thing?

Rubbing her eyes furiously, Winnie pointed. "Mommy, that man was digging in the roses, and I saw Daddy—"

"I know, but we're gonna be late."

"But there was a fire—"

"Everybody's waiting," her mother snapped in a way that meant it wasn't a conversation. She sounded angry.

And so Winnie followed her out of the backyard without another glimpse of that strange white box. She passed the old man who waited at the gate for them to leave and then reentered without a word. Without her *permission*, which she felt was particularly rude considering the roses were hers.

Her dad stood at the side door and stared after the man, grimacing. "I don't want to leave him alone here, so go on ahead of me, and when he's done, I'll walk over."

"But, Daddy, I saw you running—"

"*Enough*, Winona." Her mother glared now.

Her parents kissed while Winnie climbed into the car. Marcel was already waiting, a pile of food trays in his lap, and he twisted in his seat, squinting at the backyard.

"Who was that?"

She shrugged and blinked again and again, waiting for the white light to fade from her vision, knowing that something was wrong though she didn't understand how, or what. Looking around now was like peering through the condensation that gathered on the inside of the windows in winter, where she could draw pictures, except on her *eyes*. And as they finally drove away, she remembered that she'd forgotten her roses.

CHAPTER 28

I Need You

Marcel's car was parked in the driveway when Winnie reached home. Her fingertips tingled with nerves as she veered around it, as she hauled herself all the way along the side of the house and through the small metal gate. Her mother wouldn't be home from work to rage about truancy for another few hours, completely unaware that the world was ending, and Winnie was going to save it or not come home at all.

No, she *would*, even if she had doubts that this would work. Even if it started with saving Apollo from Cyrus, though they didn't deserve it, or killing them and their devious cousin just to keep the star contained, the serpent from hatching, the sun in the sky.

To keep all the blood in her body.

The gate latch was undone, and just around the corner of the house came the shuffling of footsteps in the grass. For the flash of a moment, she saw two creatures made of bone, the size of a human and gaping at her. Jawbones framed accusatory eyes like brows. But then they were gone in another flash.

She was starting to dream while awake now.

"What's taking so long?" Yas muttered in a low voice as she paced the length of the backyard. Her white sneakers were so clean they glowed like the box.

Winnie rubbed her eyes.

Farther inside, she found Marcel lounging in one of the old wooden lawn chairs, watching their cousin pace. He only nodded impatiently, ignoring her words, but when they noticed her, Yas threw her arms wide. Her agitation seemed to warm the cool autumn air.

On the way here, Winnie had drifted off on the bus twice, lulled into the rolling dark to hear the crashing waves on Lake Erie and Apollo's scream from that vision with the star. Her breaths were thin and racing. She felt weak, and tired, and wired. But she needed to keep moving, not to slow down too much lest the exhaustion take her where she stood, to get to Apollo before it was too late. And for that, she needed Yas and Marcel.

She stifled a yawn and took another sip of coffee. "Hey."

"Okay, what's this about?" Yas asked, rubbing her arms.

Winnie only gestured to the other lawn chair for her to sit and stood before them.

I NEED YOU.

The text seemed alien when Winnie read it back on the ride over, even though she'd typed the words herself.

Winnie Bray didn't need people. She lied in order to *avoid* needing people. When people didn't listen, when they only let her down, she'd had to fashion herself into someone who needed nothing. No one. There wasn't anyone on this earth who could possibly be reliable when they also couldn't be bothered to stay still long enough to heed the words coming out of her mouth. It was the lesson instilled in her from years of trying.

She'd thought Apollo was the exception, but she was wrong.

"I know this is gonna be hard to hear, but—"

"What's wrong with you?" Yas grimaced and peered into Winnie's face. "Are you drunk?"

“Staying out all night, getting arrested, *and* day drinking?” Marcel prodded, leaning forward in his seat with a grin. “I don’t know whether to be worried or offended you didn’t invite me—”

Winnie forced herself back a step and put up her hands to silence them. “*No*, I’m exhausted. I haven’t slept in days, barely slept at all in weeks, but we need to—”

This only made them stray further from the topic at hand, further from Apollo, the box.

“Is that why you look dead?” The skepticism in Marcel’s voice made her shrink beneath her collar.

“I knew something was off.” Yas pulled out her phone and started searching symptoms of sleep deprivation. “Impulsive or reckless behavior? Check. Impaired judgment? Check. Poor balance—”

She smothered another yawn while they examined her, talking over each other about her. Not to her. Not listening. Winnie rushed forward and snatched the phone from her cousin’s hand. With her hands shaking as they were, she dropped it down the front of her pants to prevent Yas from wrestling it back.

“I need you to listen to me.”

Her cousin and brother stopped moving. The backyard went quiet at those words. Still. Something in Winnie’s chest began to crack open, a chick hatching in its nest after waiting so long for the right time. They kept gaping.

“I need you to listen,” said Winnie softly, again, just for herself. She wanted it to sink in, to give herself courage to do the rest. She was needed. Her voice was needed. “Apollo is in trouble, and then we’re *all* gonna be in trouble, and I can’t do this alone.”

Her tone was sobering enough that Yas didn’t seem to mind her phone sliding down Winnie’s wide pant leg. Where would she even begin? At the beginning? With her grandmother's roses? She didn't know how much to share to keep them listening and hated that even now, *even now*, that was something that mattered.

Winnie raised her arm to show off her cast. "I found a box at the old house. I didn't know what it was, or what it was for, but I planned to pawn it until . . . something happened."

It suddenly seemed so much harder to recount it than it was for her to live through it. She didn't know how to describe the carvings on all the sides, the cipher and how the box spoke on the wind every time she tried to close her eyes. But she needed their help, which meant they needed to know something.

"It's not just a box. It's not *normal.* It whispers, and it fucks with your mind, makes you start seeing and hearing things, and bad things happen when it's opened. It caused the fire. Mama had it buried in her roses, but someone dug it up and opened it in the house."

Marcel's gaze sharpened as he straightened in his seat. "I don't like this—"

"And some other things! When I touched it, I saw . . . A lot of people dying because of it. First Dad, then me, Apollo, the whole world cracking apart. Apollo is the only one who believed me, and now they're in danger. I think saving them will help stop Cyrus and prevent everything else from happening. I stopped their accident, so we can stop this too."

Yas twisted back to see Marcel's reaction. The pair shared a long glance, saying nothing but with their eyes, where Winnie was just waiting for their judgment, waiting for their disbelief. Neither looked convinced, and she knew she wasn't doing that great a job of presenting her case. She was tired and couldn't mount it any other way; the eclipse was coming.

"You shouldn't be playing with this, Win," Marcel started.

"So, you're definitely a thing?" Yas wriggled her brows. "Were you with Apollo when you lied—?"

Pacing the length of the backyard, Winnie turned and glowered. "Earth cracking like an egg, and that's what you wanna ask?"

Her cousin snickered and dropped into the other lawn chair beside Marcel. "It's just . . . how would *you* handle all this? It sounds a little woo-woo—"

"How *else* do you think—?"

"We all know you make stuff up when you're bored." Her cousin's voice was sharp then, final. Like she didn't want to do this argument again even though it was always a lot of people telling Winnie about herself and not actually making room for her to tell them who she was.

Marcel joined in. "And you can convince yourself of anything when you're nervous. I get it, you and Apollo got in trouble, so you came up with this whole story—"

Winnie shut her eyes and let her head drop again, sucking in cool breaths to keep upright. She didn't have time to convince them the way she had Apollo, and it wouldn't work even if she tried—she'd already played this game with them. She knew them too well for the psychic thing to sink in with patience and kindness and curious questions. She was going to have to get ugly.

"I'm telling you to listen to what I'm *saying*," she insisted, "and not what you think I mean. Don't tell me what you think I'm feeling."

Her brother only scoffed. "The words you're saying don't make any sense, Win."

"Yeah, a talking box and the end of the world is not your most convincing lie," Yas added, trying to punctuate it with a smile that fell apart.

"And if *this box* caused the fire, why didn't anybody find or report it? Why didn't it burn with everything else?"

Yas added onto Marcel's doubt with another. "*And*, if it's something that can end the world, how come you're the only one who knows? Not Homeland Security, not FBI, it's just you?"

"If Apollo's really in trouble," said Marcel, "then what are we supposed to do? Why don't you call the police?"

Winnie bared her teeth. "If I could find somebody powerful enough who actually listened to me, why would I resort to begging for *your* help? Since y'all are so accepting."

Yas gave a withering glare but said nothing. Marcel continued to smooth a hand over his waves before finally, languidly, climbing to his feet. His disinterest was cold and sharp, every step toward the gate like a door repeatedly shutting in her face. Her big brother who had only told her not to look it in the eye. After several steps, Yas followed with an apologetic grimace.

An expression that said *I'm sorry, but you're hopeless.*

"Even if you're both too afraid to admit it, you know I can see stuff," said Winnie in a low voice. "That sometimes I just know stuff."

It was enough to make Yas slow down.

"Like all the stuff you do when Mom's not around, when you think no one's watching. Like that time we went to Cradle Beach, and I refused to go in the water because I wanted to stay on shore to get help when Yas almost drowned."

With one hand resting on the gate, Marcel glared over his shoulder. "I thought we said you wouldn't—"

"No, *you* decided, and guess what! I did anyway!" Winnie threw her hands in the air and shrugged. "And if I'd listened to you, I wouldn't know that there's a guy out there with a weapon that's gonna eat the sun if you don't stop being a jackass and help me."

Neither of them acquiesced, but they didn't leave either. They weren't convinced to help her, or even entertain what Winnie was saying, but they didn't have enough conviction to walk away. To turn their backs on her. Light that burned the skin from Apollo's hand, a torrential rain of blood from Winnie, the chasms that birthed the end—she didn't have every detail, but she knew in the same way that they'd happen, that it was all connected. Like dominoes.

And the solar eclipse was an hour away.

So she blew out a breath and said, "If you really loved me, you'd listen to what I'm saying: We're in danger, I'm tired, and a rich white boy's hubris is gonna kill us all if you waste any more time."

Yas rolled her eyes and sauntered back into the backyard. She dropped into the chair ceremoniously, with all the begrudging support that Winnie had hoped from her. And more. It would get weird if Winnie launched herself into her cousin's lap to hug her, and with her coordination, she'd probably miss and hurt herself, but if they survived this, she just might.

"That's all you had to say," Yasmine grumbled.

Marcel, however, didn't move. "How do we know you're not just doing this for attention?"

This boy—

Before Winnie could open her mouth to yell at him, Yas interceded. "She said she needs us and that's that." Marcel let go of the gate but continued to glare hard, this time directed at Yas instead. "And when have you ever known Winnie to *want* attention? How could she when you're always yapping your mouth?"

Winnie snorted.

Her brother softened enough to turn to her fully, and some degree of embarrassment filled his narrowed eyes. His jaw worked as he tried to think of some comeback but drew up short. He had always been the star athlete, the genius, the charismatic hero, and now his little sister was coming to him for help, and she could see him evaluating her. Assessing just how much he really knew her. Understood her.

Winnie wouldn't accept an apology until he said it. So she crossed her arms and waited.

Marcel blew out a big sigh and said the next best thing. "Fine. What's the plan?" He reached into his pocket and withdrew his car key. "You *do* have a plan, right?"

She sagged with relief.

CHAPTER 29

World's Worst Criminals

The ground rumbled incessantly when they arrived, like the earth was bereft and couldn't be consoled.

Winnie braced herself against the hood of her brother's car and sucked in full, cold breaths until her lungs felt like they might burst. The box was definitely here, and Cyrus was up to something. The whole drive, she'd been calling Apollo, texting, trying to explain Cyrus's cruelty and what he wanted, always taking, taking, taking, but there'd been no answer. Hoping they were still alive, in one piece, with the star in its place, had kept her awake at least.

She shielded her eyes and craned her head toward the sky. A couple sparse clouds were gathering, but there was no sign of the moon. *Yet.*

"You sure about this?" asked Marcel.

With knuckles pressed to her teeth to stifle another yawn, she nodded.

Although the latest cup of coffee was enough to keep her going, her pulse hadn't slowed. Her hands wouldn't stay still, and it felt like someone had tied weights around her wrists, ankles, and throat. She needed sleep. She needed pain medicine for the dull ache pounding the inside of her skull. She needed . . . Apollo. To look at her and just know what to do.

Winnie nodded again, more convincingly this time. "They're here, I'm sure."

Yas shoved her hands into her pockets and rocked back on her heels. "So then what's the *real* plan?"

They stood on the street corner, and all looked at Rathbun Manor, rising behind its hedges as normal. No sign that the world was on its last moments, that someone dangerous lurked inside. And then in broad daylight, Winnie unzipped her bag to reveal the bottles of liquor and strips of cotton to prove she was serious. That the plan she'd said in the car *was* the real plan. They glanced between her face and the bag, the bag and her face, still waiting for the punch line to land.

"I wasn't joking."

"What *happened* to you?" Yas furrowed her brow and inched away.

Marcel ran a hand down his face and turned away. "Man, if we get caught, I'm snitching."

Still neither left. Neither of them climbed into the car, turned the engine, and tried to drive away. They were here and wouldn't leave Winnie to fight alone.

A cold sweat slicked her throat, and she fought the urge to shiver. "I promise, Apollo and the box are in there, and we just need to draw Cyrus out long enough to get to them."

Her brother was nodding again and again, like he was trying to convince himself that this was a good idea. Like he was trying to convince himself that he believed Winnie deeply enough to go along with what was clearly a half-baked plan by a delirious girl who could be outrun by a turtle.

"How about we start with this?" Yas asked diplomatically, proffering a chunk of concrete from the crumbling sidewalk. "And I can keep those as a backup if you need it." She tried to give Winnie a smile as she took the backpack, but Winnie was too busy suppressing the urge to rub her eyes. "Maybe you should stay in the car—"

Winnie shook her head and started down the street. "No, you need me. I've already been in the house. I know the way." Then she fetched the matches from her coat pocket. Something fell with the motion. "By the way, you'll need this."

Her brother grabbed a crumpled scrap of paper from the sidewalk. The partially translated inscription. "'Free the star . . . summon the serpent. In the abyss I belong, to the abyss I return'? What's this?"

"You . . . how'd you get it?"

"For one, I sleep."

Another quake rippled through the street, rattling the bottles in the bag and shaking the cars on their axles. Winnie trudged forward, stumbling left and right, even if she didn't know what was unfolding inside just yet, where they were in time. The eclipse wasn't here yet, even if the earth was angry with Cyrus and his greed.

Marcel scurried to catch up. "Let's say we distract Cyrus long enough—how do we even get inside?"

Winnie shrugged. "Worst case, the front door. They never lock it."

"Well, of course," grumbled Marcel.

Just a little longer, Winnie told herself. A little longer, and Apollo would be safe, and the box would be back in her care. A little longer, and she could bury it in a cemetery, or underneath the dead roses, now that she'd made the sacred oil. A little longer, and Winnie could crawl into her own bed, cocooned in her blankets, once again a normal girl who wasn't on a runaway train barreling toward death and destruction.

A senior with her winter formal fast approaching, and maybe, finally, having someone to ask instead of getting set up on a pity date. If they ever forgave her for kissing their cousin.

Just a little longer.

Lights in Rathbun Manor flickered like a warning, and the ivy on the side of the house shivered with the shake of the ground. The cars from last time were in the driveway again—a nice sedan, and the black truck now with the front smashed in. The sight slicked her stomach with a greasy feeling.

Winnie crouched down for a glimpse through the basement window, to see the strange dungeon Apollo had taken her to and get a feel for where they might be inside, how many. The last thing she wanted was to hurl herself through the front door and walk right into Cyrus's twisted experiment.

And her instinct was right.

"Oh shit." Yas fell back in the grass.

Marcel peered around Winnie's head and covered his mouth.

The door to the dark chamber was open wide, and the light was on. Apollo sat against the wall, fighting against a blood-spotted gag on their mouth and dirty, haphazard restraints that kept their hands and feet bound. Their nervous gaze was fixed on something else in the room.

Lying across the doorway was a mass of something, though Winnie couldn't discern much. There was blood and flesh collecting beneath a tangle of bones. Not quite in the shape of a person, but something *after*, as if the skin and most of the muscle and organs had liquefied. It made her vision swim just to look at, and she had to lean against the side of the house to avoid falling over.

Winnie gagged.

It was so much worse than she'd seen, or could have imagined.

"If you're right about this, then . . ."

She squeezed her eyes shut and pictured kicking her brother. Instead, she settled for an "I told you so."

When Winnie opened her eyes, she saw her cousin waving

right in front of the window. There seemed to be no one else but Apollo in there, no one *alive* at least, and soon her motions captured their attention. When they recognized her face, and Winnie's, their eyes went wide with panic and relief both.

Winnie pushed against the basement window, but it didn't budge. Locked. At that, Marcel pointed to the trellis, which rose to the second floor, where a window was cracked open like an invitation. The very thought of more strain made her lids grow heavy, and her heart sank—it'd be hell if her legs gave out when she climbed in.

Just a little longer.

"So I smash the front window, run around to this window, and wait for you to let me in?" asked Yas as she pulled the hood over her head and stretched the neck of her shirt to cover her nose and mouth. "Y'all got five minutes. Don't get caught."

Winnie started her climb without another word. The wood swayed beneath her with every step, making it hard to keep her footholds. But she didn't have any more time to think about falling, to remember that horrible sound of her arm breaking from somewhere inside her; in a matter of minutes, she crested the top and threw her leg over, keeping her grip tight on the wood.

After sliding up the bedroom window, she waved for Marcel to follow. The side of the house sloped, the roof gabled, and she hooked a hand on the ledge for the leverage to haul herself inside.

Then her sneaker slipped.

In the span of a gasp, Winnie's ribs cracked into the ledge, the angle digging in close. The sudden impact snatched the breath from her lungs, and for a moment she had a flash of herself sliding backward, onto the trellis that would crumble with the crash of her weight. Taking her and her brother to the ground.

Alerting Cyrus that she was here.

Another desperate lunge pitched her over, dropping her onto the floor with a loud *thud*.

"Dude, are you good?" she heard Marcel whisper from beneath the window. Before she could bring herself to stand up and offer her help, he was already hauling his way inside, far more gracefully.

Then a loud *crash* sounded from below. The walls shook with the shattering of glass. Marcel and Winnie looked at each other as they listened to distant footsteps racing through the house to the damage. Nothing on their floor though.

Marcel poked his head into the hall and nodded to confirm. They moved quickly, Winnie ushering her brother to the grand staircase to peer over the railing. Cyrus stood at the entrance to the study, talking with a young man about Marcel's age, with cropped hair and a broken nose. He shook his head and charged through the front door to investigate, leaving it wide open. Cyrus left.

Did Yas get away? What would they do to her if she didn't?

Like the first time she'd come to Rathbun Manor with Apollo, the house was eerily silent. Despite the cars in the driveway, there were no more voices, no more footsteps other than Cyrus's—nothing to cover their descent. Each stair creaked and groaned, and when the rumble of the house paused, the wood was practically screaming.

Winnie darted to shut the front door and lock Cyrus's accomplice outside before he came back. One less person to deal with. The rush of energy made her lean against it for a moment, her breathing fast and so very shallow. Under her fingertips, the wood felt soft and warm as flesh, wet and with a pulse—and then the hallucination faded to cool, dusty wood again.

"You're making me nervous," whispered Marcel, but she was already flitting to the cellar door as fast as she could manage.

A little longer.

She pulled him after her and leapt down the stairs, two at a time, as quietly as the wood would allow. She didn't know if Cyrus moved down here, or if there was someone she hadn't seen guarding Apollo, but perhaps the speed would help catch them unprepared. Perhaps the search for a vandal masked her steps.

Marcel parked himself at the bottom of the stairs on lookout. "We've got to be the world's worst criminals."

The basement light was still on, and the air smelled rank. It was damp and wet and sour, like old meat at a butcher shop, and the air mostly still except for Apollo's panicked breaths. On the floor of the vestibule, lying atop the inscriptions on the ground, beneath the inscriptions on the ceiling, were bodies. Three of them in different states of destruction. One was mostly bone, bowed, the fat and flesh rendered off. The others were somewhat intact, an upper torso where sinew and tendon clung furiously here, a puddle of blood and discolored legs there. Layers of skin and muscle had been peeled away, layer by layer.

Winnie pressed her sleeve to her mouth to block out the stench, the bile that slicked her mouth. She swayed on her feet and caught herself on the wall.

And then she found Apollo, contorting on the floor beside the bodies to undo their ties. Winnie drew her pocket knife from the small of her back at the same time they muffled a scream. Apollo's eyes widened at the sight of it, the gag wet with sweat and tears. But then they softened and stopped fighting when they rolled and saw it was her, when she ducked down to free their mouth.

Apollo sucked in panicked breaths. "He killed them, and he's gonna kill us if we don't go now!"

They threw a glance toward the dark corridor of the dungeon. She didn't have to guess who *he* was.

Rather than waste time trying to saw through the strips of fabric used as restraints, Winnie pulled Apollo to their feet and started for the door. They needed to get as far away from the bodies, from Cyrus, as possible.

One of the lumps of remains had long, dark hair, and her gaze caught on it. It belonged to the girl who'd interrupted her kiss with Cyrus. She had no face to look surprised now, all of it having slopped off on the floor, and the upper part of her body was misshapen; only clumps of scalp remained. Nausea climbed in Winnie's throat.

Then the doorbell rang above.

From deep within the dark hall, Cyrus growled. "No—*Apollo!*"

His footsteps thundered after them.

Winnie scrambled faster, trying to hand Apollo off to her brother before Cyrus caught up. Before he opened that box and killed her here, now. They could hardly move with their ankles tied together, so they resorted to jumping, to throwing themself over the threshold. Her shoe slipped on a gelatinous *something* as she followed. Then she felt Cyrus's fingertips grasp at and lose her coat, and a sharp twinge lanced through her scalp when he caught onto a loc of hair instead.

Her heart skipped a beat.

"Come on!" Marcel seized her elbow and jerked her free.

Through the pain, she only just glimpsed that brown loc in Cyrus's hand before Marcel threw his full weight against the heavy black door, trapping Cyrus inside.

"The lock, get the lock!" Apollo shouted, gesturing toward a nearby shelf, where a massive, rusted padlock sat discarded.

Winnie grabbed it, swaying breathless with its heft. On the

other side of the door, she could hear Cyrus's fists pounding against the wood, his ferocious screams, as she pulled the padlock through the latch and shoved it closed.

Marcel took a cautious step back, but the door seemed to hold.

Upstairs, the doorbell rang again and again.

"Where's the box?" asked Winnie as she began sawing through Apollo's restraints. The skin at their ankles was red, raw beneath, but it wasn't as bad as the side of their face, inflamed with minor burns. Just like in her vision, blood was sticky and crusted at their brow and scalp, and their cheeks and chin were speckled with tiny cuts from broken glass. Glass from a *van*.

Which meant that they hadn't avoided the accident in the end. Dread settled in her stomach. They might not avoid what was coming either.

The contusion beneath their right eye was swollen and discolored.

Apollo massaged their wrists. "It's in there with him, but he needs us. He—"

Then came a *crash* from above. The clatter of more glass, larger, closer, definitely a second broken window, followed by a shout.

"Fire!" Cyrus's assistant shouted from outside. A smoke alarm blared in the hall, and Winnie turned to her brother in a moment of shock. His mouth hung open.

"She actually used it," said Winnie, unable to hide her incredulousness, her admiration. Yas actually threw—no, she *believed* Winnie enough, trusted Winnie enough to throw—a Molotov cocktail, to give her and Marcel the cover to get what they came for. She swayed on her feet again.

"Come on, I don't think he knows about the—" Apollo eyed Winnie warily. "Are you okay?"

She nodded and hauled herself up the first few steps before remembering Yas, the window. And then her body felt heavy again before she could turn around.

The sudden motion, pulled up and forward, sloshing into Apollo, the smell of sweat and mint and fear and all the blood and offal—blood rushed to her head. Her legs gave out, and her vision tunneled until she was weightless.

CHAPTER 30

Now Is Not the Time

Apollo had only barely managed to catch Winnie before her head struck the railing. They watched her slow and then careen to the left, and then her legs buckled, and despite the aching exhaustion in their bones, they launched forward to wrap their arms around her middle and pull her back. The sudden exertion sent shock waves through their nerves.

The boy that they assumed to be her brother—for they shared a complexion and the same soft, innocent features—grabbed her legs and sighed.

"I told her this was a bad idea," he grumbled, and together they laid her out on the basement's cold, concrete floor. Just feet away from the dungeon where they could still hear Cyrus raging. Something shattered and fell to pieces against the wood, making the door shudder.

Upstairs, the smoke alarm continued blaring in the aftermath of whatever chaos Winnie and her party seemed to have wreaked on Rathbun Manor. It was a rescue mission for the box *and them*, Apollo reminded themself, and hoped that they would be enough. That their refusal to help Cyrus would be enough to stop him. However, their cousin still had the box, and he was after whatever was inside, so while they were out here, he might still wreck the world trying to retrieve it in there.

"We still need to get the box from him," said Apollo, and

beneath them, with her head in their lap, Winnie moaned. When they pressed a hand to her forehead, the skin felt clammy, and she sluggishly tried to slap them away.

Now she wants to put up a fight.

She pushed herself out of Apollo's arms. "Let go of me. You smell terrible."

There was an impatient knock on the basement window overhead. Crisp white sneakers paced in the grass.

"You *look* terrible," they retorted, unable to stop themself from trying to spot her again when she climbed to her feet and tottered ever so slightly to the side. "What's gotten into you?"

She was already making her way to the window. "Coffee's not working anymore," she said in a disaffected tone, not looking back as she unlocked it and pulled her cousin inside.

There wasn't enough time for Apollo to ask everything they wanted—how much coffee did she have? Her heart might give out before this was over if she'd been drinking coffee like this for weeks just to stay upright, if it was *that* bad. Then again, if she'd fainted on the way over like she did just now, Cyrus might have already killed them. They understood the stakes, even if they didn't like it.

Still, despite their muscles screaming with every step, Apollo pressed close to catch her again, just in case.

Yasmine passed a backpack over to Marcel, and its contents clinked when he slung it over his shoulder. Nobody bothered to tell them what was inside, but judging by the alarm blaring above, it was nothing good. Then she looked at Apollo, took in their bruised and bloodied face, the weariness in their eyes, and grimaced. With the way their day had progressed, from borrowing their brother's shapeless clothes to their accident and the *light*, they were sure they looked as bad as they felt.

"What's taking so long?" Yasmine asked, drawing them forward in a huddle at the base of the stairs.

Cyrus had finally moved away from the door, but he could still be heard smashing things farther inside. Her brows knit with concern that she didn't bother voicing. Were there any words to explain it anyway?

Smoke, acrid and sharp, drifted through the foyer, down the steps, and curled in Apollo's nostrils. Marcel wrinkled his nose and took the words out of their mouth. "Well, great timing on the fire, but we still need to go in there since he has the box."

As if to accentuate his point, Cyrus toppled something large enough for its crash to reverberate through the floor. Eventually he'd run out of things to smash and turn back to the door, to breaking it down.

Yasmine scowled. "I gave you five minutes, and there was a guy outside chasing me. Next time, instead of *arson*, I'll just leave your ass." Then she turned to Winnie and Apollo. "We obviously can't just walk through the door with him like that, so what's the plan?"

"No," said Winnie, and her eyes fell to Apollo, sparkling with mischief. It was the look that had drawn them to kiss her last time. Then, in a whisper, she added, "Good thing we know another way in."

Apollo couldn't help but match her smile.

"How many more people are here?" asked Marcel nervously. "Winnie locked someone outside, there's Cyrus in the freaky room—anybody else?"

They shook their head and shrugged. "I don't know, I was a little too banged up to notice. I think most of the people were in there with us when he opened the box, and you saw what was left of them on the floor."

He shuddered. "Well, let's be careful just in case."

Yasmine gave a resolute nod, just as another *crash* hit the door. This time, it was so loud and forceful that the latch jostled on its hinges. Many more of these, and the door might fall away. Winnie eyed it warily.

"Maybe we should reinforce this first."

Nods passed around the circle, and then Marcel and Yasmine got to it, shuffling an old armoire across the concrete ground to block the door. Feeling worn out and a bit faint, *bloodless*, Apollo dropped onto an old stack of milk crates to gather themself. Their body throbbed all over from the pain of the accident, reminding them that it was only hours ago, and no one had looked at them.

Winnie, fussing with blood under her fingernails, hung back as well.

"How'd you find me?"

She tapped a finger to her temple. "Psychic, remember? How are you still alive?"

They looked down at their hands, where the hair on their knuckles had been singed away. Their face stung. They had indeed survived, though, and that fact made them consider that perhaps Cyrus had some idea of what he was ranting about. About resistance, about being *changed* to survive the thing inside, to wield it like a weapon.

"Cyrus had a theory that you can build up a tolerance to the box," they explained, "or that the box changes you. A little bit over time, to make you able to withstand its light."

"Like poison?"

"Like poison," Apollo echoed. "He thought that maybe it was a fail-safe to make sure only some people can reach what's inside. He needs us to get it." They watched her pace and bite, noticing the hair around her temples frizzing. In another time, it would have been nice to be here with her, in Rathbun Manor, just talking. If they could have started over, if they weren't tangled with apocalyptic visions and dangerous heirlooms. "So what exactly was your plan?"

Marcel paused dragging the armoire to say snidely, "She didn't have one. Otherwise, we wouldn't be in the basement of a *burning* house."

"Yas was supposed to smash a window while we snuck inside, and then throw a Molotov cocktail to get us out." Winnie smoothed her hand against the basement's cement wall for effect, to make it clear that they weren't, in fact, out as intended.

Still Apollo couldn't stop themself from grinning. It felt so easy talking to her, being next to her, being warmed by her. "So the plan was to die in a house fire before the apocalypse could start?"

It brought a smile to her face too, and they took her hand. The nail beds were indeed bloody, and her knuckles were scraped with gravel, skin broken where she'd hit Cyrus in the mouth. Even tired, weak, and bloody, she was pretty.

Uncharacteristically soft and hard to draw away from.

She didn't hesitate to tighten her grip, her cold hand in theirs, and then meet their eyes for a long, languid moment. The frankness from her was just as startling, considering what happened the last time they saw each other. What Cyrus had said. It was too easy to forget she'd kissed him, regardless of the reason.

With a huff, Yasmine headed for the stairs. "Okay, we really need to get moving."

Apollo climbed painfully to their feet but didn't let go of Winnie. Were it another day, another time, were they someone else, they might have refused to forgive her. They wanted to keep grudges more; they wanted to preserve their anger, not let everyone walk on and abandon them. She was a liar when they met, had sat on a pile of secrets when she asked for their help, and then she had the poor judgment to kiss their rotten, *killer* cousin. For their benefit or not, Apollo shouldn't have cared, and it should have made them burn with hatred.

Yet she was here for them, even as it wore her down.

Marcel pushed past them and tried not to notice how close they stood, how low they talked, how Winnie worried her bottom lip.

"You were right," they said, loud enough for him to hear, "about the accident."

When she craned her face up at Apollo, they felt powerless to resist. She had a magnetism that drew them down to her, even as the world was ending, and they were no longer convinced they could be this hero that would do all the fighting for her.

But she did all the fighting to get to you.

Maybe it was too late.

Maybe it wasn't.

"I wish I wasn't." Her thumb smoothed the tender skin just beneath the gash on their cheek, the reason their eye felt puffy and head full. The room was half blurred around them.

"Now is *not* the time," Marcel snapped from the top of the stairs in a hushed whisper, peering out from behind the door in case there were others.

Apollo knew as much, yet their brow grazed Winnie's anyway. Even through the pain, their noses touched, their mouths only a hair's breadth apart. They easily recalled the softness of her lips, of her body pressed against theirs in the van, how the heat of bare skin had seared itself into their memory. The same girl who'd punched Cyrus and looked at Apollo as more than a problem—she was pulling their want from right between their teeth.

Winnie almost kissed them.

But then Apollo jerked and turned to the cellar door. It had stopped shuddering. There was no more smashing glass, no crashing of furniture, no screams of frustration, or angry footsteps. Cyrus had stopped throwing things and stomping through the halls.

He'd gone strangely, suspiciously quiet.

"I can't hear Cyrus anymore."

They tried not to look at the disappointment on Winnie's face, how she blinked at them and then nodded slowly in agreement. There was a reluctance in her face as she admitted, "Yeah, weird."

She thought the world was ending. She wanted one last kiss before they all died, but Apollo couldn't. Wouldn't. If they didn't kiss her, they'd have to do everything to ensure the world *didn't* end. Then later, when this was all over, *truly* done with, they would explain as much. Even if she didn't put her hope in them, they would prove themself worth it.

That all of this had been worth it.

For now, Apollo pulled her after them and darted up the stairs. "Come on, let's end this."

The main hallway of Rathbun Manor was filled with smoke. There was the soft crackle and hum of a fire somewhere in the back of the house, no doubt eating its way through their grandmother's lace-trimmed solarium, but Apollo figured that it was far enough away to not be a problem right away.

It would only take a minute or two to slip through the hidden door in the study, surprise Cyrus, and snatch the box. Down there, they'd get a couple of hits in too, for the accident, for the police and burns and *carnage* that seemed to stem from his fingertips. If Apollo brought trouble everywhere they went, Cyrus was walking destruction.

“So what’s inside the box exactly?” Yasmine asked behind them. “What, um, did it do to those people?”

“A star,” was all Apollo said before they turned the corner.

Winnie gasped beside them and tightened her grip on their hand. Her brother and cousin drew up short at her side, gaping at Apollo’s grandfather’s study and the sight before them. The secret door built into the bookcase was wide open, exposing light into the dark and dusty corridor behind. Cyrus and the box were free to roam.

Winnie turned to the front door, which was closed and locked. A smoky haze was beginning to fill the foyer, but still they saw the dread coloring her features as she explained, “He’s out. Somewhere in the house.”

CHAPTER 31

A Deranged Tech Bro on the Loose

Winnie squeezed her eyes shut and leaned against the doorframe to the study. Nausea rolled through her, and she didn't know if it was the coffee and energy drinks, the gore from below, or the panic of Cyrus's escape that unsettled her most in the pit of her stomach, but all of it made her shiver nonetheless.

"Your house has a hidden door?" Yasmine paced the length of the study, shaking her head. "And now we have a deranged tech bro hiding in it? Are there others?"

"I don't know, I just found out about this one." The irritation in Apollo's voice was evident. That their cousin was once again one step ahead of them was a sore spot.

Winnie tried not to think about how they almost kissed her. They almost forgave her, but they were *here* of all places, in this wicked house, trying to stop their wicked cousin. It wasn't the time for forgiveness or kisses, but they didn't *have* time for anything else. The accident hadn't been avoided; they were going to fail. Die fighting, but dying nonetheless.

She staggered to the broad windows of the study and drew back the lacy curtains just to confirm. The solar eclipse was here. The sky was darkening, and if she squinted through the ache in her skull, she could see the moon inching closer. These things lasted for only a matter of minutes at *most*.

"The eclipse is starting," she said in a shaky voice. Something was trying to climb its way out of her throat. Panic, fear, *blood.*

She folded over a trash can and hurled. The vomit was citrusy and bitter, tasting exactly like the combination of energy drink and espresso that she'd had—*all* she'd had in hours, now that she thought about it. The cramp of her stomach as she retched kept her there for longer than she wanted, though she tried to keep it quiet in case Cyrus was listening.

Apollo's apocalypse-appropriate boots came to stand beside her, and then a hand smoothed across her back.

A tremor rolled through Rathbun Manor again as she stood. Storm clouds gathered on the dark horizon, and wind continued to whip through the hedges, sending leaves aflutter as if to remind her what was coming. Threaten her into straightening up and *going*. Impress upon her what would rise from the depths and what would fall from the sky if they didn't somehow hurry to do what she suspected couldn't be done. When would the earthquake sunder the building and swallow her bones in all of this?

She didn't know.

She pulled one of the remaining bottles of liquor from her bag on Marcel's shoulder, took a swig, sloshing the burning liquid around in her mouth, and then spat. Right in the middle of the wood floors out of spite. Her mouth still held the residue of sour bile, but at least now it felt cleaner. Her head felt a little clearer.

Her heart was still fluttering fast, but the room wasn't spinning.

Marcel snatched the neck from her and took a *proper* swig and swallowed. "For courage," he replied when the others looked at him, "and because it's mine anyway."

Apollo cleared their throat and leaned against the desk, exactly the way Cyrus had when Winnie was here last. When she'd kissed him, partially to stop him and partially out of her own vile curiosity. "He could still be somewhere in the house."

"He could be listening," Winnie noted, looking sorely away from how they sat, from how much like and unlike their cousin they were.

"So we split up?"

Yasmine shook her head. "That's how you *die*—"

"The house is too big to find him if we're all together," Winnie countered, "and it's *burning*. We go in pairs."

Then she fetched the sacred oil from the bottom of the bag and pressed the cool bottle into Apollo's warm palm, wrapped their fingers tight around it. "He makes *you* try to take it. Don't, no matter what he says. This will keep it buried."

Stonily, Apollo replied, "We don't have to die." But they didn't let go, and they didn't make her take it back.

Marcel tapped her shoulder and turned to the dark corridor beyond the bookcase. "All right, since you both look like you're about to drop dead, Winnie, you're with me. Yas, you take Apollo."

There wasn't much of a guarantee that they would win this, that they'd even *survive* it, but Winnie felt a hell of a lot safer with the oil in Apollo's hands. Having told them to resist their cousin at all costs. Her future was with them, and she trusted them, and that had to be enough.

Let it be enough.

Her brother grabbed an antique brass paperweight in the shape of an apple from the desk and started down the stairs. Winnie was right on his heels with her phone light.

The walls felt somehow quieter than usual, and down below, the dungeon was still. The hairs on her arms stood on end with the feeling of being watched; did Cyrus find this corridor after them, or had he known all along where they were? When she and

Apollo had escaped him that night, did he know exactly where this would spit them out? When she kissed him, did he know that she'd been here before?

The very thought of Cyrus watching their steps made her skin crawl, just as much as seeking him out now did.

"You know what to do, right?" asked Marcel as they reached the landing. The door on the other side was wide open, showing where Cyrus seemed to have escaped, and low light from the decorative sconce trickled in. "I get him, and you take it and run? Don't look back?"

There was a fierce determination to his expression, which struck Winnie silent because, for all her life, Marcel hadn't believed her. He said she'd caused trouble with her ability, had been cursed and brought curses upon their family, yet he was here anyway, helping her break into Rathbun Manor, helping her track Cyrus down to get back this box.

She didn't feel nearly as confident as he looked, but she nodded nonetheless.

He nudged her with his shoulder. "Thanks for coming to me, Win."

Then they moved on. Her vision danced as they crossed into the room, where the walls flickered between faded yellow paint and the pulsing of flesh. There was a cardboard box on the desk, and a small quake made its contents rattle inside. Even if they stopped Cyrus, it could be days before the city was free from the aftershocks he'd started, weeks before *she* was free of the havoc it wreaked on her mind and body.

A breeze carried through the room, tickling her scalp. This far down, it wasn't natural.

She turned to her brother. "He's down here."

Then Winnie held out her hands and groped around again. The bookcase door was lukewarm with the residue of Cyrus's touch; it didn't show her anything, but he'd definitely been the one to open it, considering everyone else down here was dead.

It was easier than simply looking, trying to get her eyes to focus. Her sight was unsteady, the exhaustion unbearable on her nerves, and the walls were flickering back and forth between hallucination and reality. One moment, there was a wall sconce and faint light, and the next, the walls were coated in pink flesh lined with arteries that twitched to her heartbeat.

Thud.

Thud.

Thud.

She knew it wasn't real but caught herself wondering if maybe it was.

Marcel headed for the dark hall. "How far does this place go? Do you know?"

The moment his foot crossed the threshold, Cyrus lurched.

He charged from the hall at Marcel, the box raised in one fist like a weapon. He brought it down on her brother before he could raise the paperweight, and then Marcel was sprawled in the doorway, and it was just them two standing.

Winnie and Cyrus.

"You just don't know when to quit," Cyrus seethed, his voice raw and scraping at the back of his throat. He stepped over her brother, face contorted with rage.

Winnie ditched her phone in favor of her pocket knife, the blade pulled free. She should have stabbed him in the Red Hourglass, or later in the study. Instead of kissing him, she should have shoved the thing right in his callous heart.

In a shaking voice, she asked, “Marcel, are you okay?”

Her brother groaned in response. Behind Cyrus, he was scrambling to get to his feet.

“People have already lost their lives,” she tried to reason, with the knife visible for Cyrus to see. “If you just give up the box, no one else has to get hurt. It doesn’t have to be the end of the world.”

If he thought she wouldn’t use the blade now, he was sorely mistaken.

Instead, Cyrus shook his head like *she* was the pitiful one between them and then laughed. Edged and dry. “You aren’t smarter than me, Winona. I’m—”

The brass apple struck him on the back of the head, and he stumbled forward. Winnie raced to pull the box from his hold. Her grip was weak, hardly putting up a fight that he couldn’t resist, even in a daze, but then Marcel landed on his back, and the pair went spiraling as Cyrus struggled to stand.

“Win, what are you waiting for?”

Marcel and Cyrus crashed into the desk behind them, spilling books and cloths and cups from the cardboard box across the floor. They both collapsed onto it, where her brother immediately lashed out a strong kick to Cyrus’s head.

This was her chance.

Winnie lunged for the box and snatched it from Cyrus’s distracted hands. Her knife slipped from her grasp, but she was already retreating. Marcel could buy her a new one when this was over.

“Go, go, go!” Marcel was up and behind her, and they were running back through the dark corridor, back up the narrow, dusty, cobweb-ridden staircase.

She had the box.

“I got it!”

They were free—

Then came a rush of wind, and her brother made a choked gasp close to her ear. The stairs shook behind her a moment later. Winnie stumbled out into the study, catching a glimpse of Yasmine sprinting toward her, Apollo hobbling quickly after. She shouldn't have turned around; she knew she had to keep moving no matter what . . .

But she did turn.

Marcel sprawled across the stairs with her lavender knife sticking out of his throat, and his eyes on her. He kept a hand pressed flat to his neck as if to keep it there, as if there wasn't a rush of blood running down his shoulder and into the wood.

"Marcel?" Her voice sounded far away.

Then Cyrus stepped over him carelessly and ripped the blade out. Feebly, Marcel reached for the Rathbun's pant leg to stop him, as if he wasn't bleeding out of his neck, and saving his little sister was more important.

"Run," he tried to say, but it only came out as a whistle.

Winnie backed away. Her hands were shaking, she wasn't breathing. She couldn't do this. Marcel was never supposed to die; she didn't see him here, and he wasn't supposed to be anywhere near this until she—

In a wicked scream, Cyrus launched at her, closing the gap before she could turn, before she could run. His body crashed into hers, and they dropped to the floor. Holding the box out of reach was no use, for his long arms subsumed hers, and then he had a knee digging into her ribs.

Into her chest.

His full weight pressing into her.

Winnie let out a pathetic gasp, tears welling in her eyes.

"Stop!" Cyrus shouted, and then she felt the press of a blade to her skin. Her head was a balloon that was going to burst. "You so much as move and I will kill her, Apollo."

"Where's Marcel? What did you do?" Yasmine shouted.

Pressed against the wood, feeling her pulse in her ears, Winnie struggled to gasp again. She couldn't breathe.

Darkness crowded around her vision, while the blade began to dig in. The blade that was still wet with her brother's blood, now hungering for hers. From somewhere nearby followed the sounds of a scuffle, and then Cyrus's body weight fell away. Winnie gulped for air and tried to skitter away from him.

He caught her ankle and struck her across the face with the box. Its sharp corners dug in and sent her vision spiraling.

The young man that she'd locked out was back inside now, and he held Yasmine by her hair, a broad hand planted on her shoulder to force her to kneel. Apollo's gaze flashed between her and Winnie and the bookcase corridor where Marcel wasn't emerging.

Wouldn't emerge, unless by some miracle Cyrus had missed the artery. The one time he'd listened to her had cost her brother his life.

Clutching her face, Winnie glared at him. And then he pressed her knife back to her throat.

"Here's the deal," said Cyrus with cold fury in his eyes. "I want what's in this box, and you're going to give it to me, my dear cousin. And if you *don't* stick your hand inside and pull it out, I am going to shove this knife into her very pretty neck just like I did that guy."

Winnie tried to lash out, to kick him, but he shoved her foot away feebly. She was tired, and weak, and dizzy, and her heart was rent in two. She'd been fighting all day, all week, for *weeks* only for it all to come to this.

Apollo stared at her for a long moment, their eyes shiny with apology. Then they said, "I won't, Cyrus."

Swiftly, Cyrus rammed the blade through the back of Winnie's good hand, and she shouted. The pain was sharp and bright, her fingers spasming against the floor, and then he wrenched it out, pulling another scream from her mouth. She jerked the hand to her chest, pressing as if she could stop the blood from pouring out. It was only a flesh wound, but that was enough for Apollo's resolve to crack.

"Don't test me," he growled.

She shook her head. "Don't do it—"

Cyrus set the box down on the floor and pried back the lid with one hand, returning the blade to her throat. The edge was biting in again with his impatience.

Light poured into the room, so bright that Apollo turned and threw up a hand to shield their face. Wind whipped through Cyrus's hair, and the light from the box made his eyes glow dangerously. His teeth seemed to sharpen in his sneering.

"Don't make me wait!" Cyrus shouted over the rumble in the ground. The crystal chandelier jingled over them, and the windows clattered.

Though she tried to put on a brave face, Winnie couldn't help but wince at the pain in her palm. Her sniffling made Apollo come forward, pressing against the heat as if it and its pressure were a solid thing to overcome. Her skin felt flushed, just watching them grit their teeth and drop desperately to their knees.

"Give it to me!" Cyrus snarled, pressing hard enough with the knife to make Winnie gasp.

With their eyes squeezed shut, body reeling away from the light, Apollo shoved their hand inside the box and screamed.

CHAPTER 32

Morning Star

Heat flooded the room, but inside the box was cold. Apollo could feel the heat stripping skin away from their wrist, the back of their hand, their fingertips, but once inside, there was a new kind of burning sensation.

One that soothed as much as hurt.

Apollo closed their hand around something round and palm-size. It stung the same way it did in winter, when they grabbed a massive icicle that had gathered and fallen from a rooftop, the impressive spears that lined the driveway. Here, now, stinging in their bare hand.

They didn't want to give it to him.

But they wanted her. Alive. Even at the end of the world, they wanted to spend their last moments with her.

Morning Star quivered under their touch. Like it was a living thing that was reacting to them. Like it was a mouse that wanted to escape, or Winnie, excited to finally be held.

It pulsed impatiently as they pulled back.

Rathbun Manor roared around them. The floors shook harder than anything Apollo had ever experienced. Books clattered from the shelves. The great crystal chandelier fell to the floor with a loud *crash*. A car alarm outside triggered, and then another down the street. Blaring.

The star crested the box lid.

A loud *crack* ran through the floor, the wall, the ceiling, the house.

And as Apollo pulled it free, Rathbun Manor shook and shuddered and split in two. The ground opened up beneath the house in a yawn, tearing the ceiling apart and taking half the second floor and stairs with it, planks of wood trickling down like hail, until they saw clouds. Until they were squinting up at the dark sky, a total solar eclipse overhead.

Until the end.

CHAPTER 33

The Call of the Abyss

The instant Apollo pulled the star from the box, Winnie used Cyrus's distraction to kick away from him. She struck him in his side and skittered toward Yasmine, and her cousin bucked her captor to reunite with her. Neither really noticed, because Apollo was holding a *star* the size of a crystal ball in the palm of their raw fingers, breathing heavily to hold back another scream.

"They . . . ," she found herself mumbling, while Apollo stared right into the thing, as if they couldn't believe what they held either.

If they didn't put it back, they might not have any fingers left.

Blood lined their gritted teeth.

"*Give it to me!*" Cyrus snarled, rising to his feet to take Morning Star from his cousin. His eyes were wide with desperation, with excitement. Wind made a mess of his hair. "It's mine!"

The house shook fiercely. Wooden floor panels were falling away one by one, sinking into the stretching abyss, and Winnie grabbed on to the desk leg to keep from falling in. She had to squint to find Apollo.

Over the light, they looked her square in the eye, gaze drifting briefly to the cuts at her throat, the blood running down her clenched fist.

And then they punched Cyrus in the face with the fist that held Morning Star. Once and then twice, the blows came, and then the two Rathbuns fell to the floor in a grapple, a storm of fists and grunts. The swing of Apollo's arm, the force behind every hit, was a ferocious rage that had been building for weeks, and Cyrus wasn't prepared. He'd underestimated what Apollo was capable of, even as he teased them. Now he struggled, for only a moment, until they flipped.

Then he hovered over Apollo, wild-eyed and blistered, slamming their wrist into the floor to shake the star free.

Their fingers spasmed, and Morning Star fell easily from their hold. It rolled across the floor, and Cyrus clambered greedily after it.

Winnie scooped it up first and stumbled away.

It was like holding ice, so hot it was cold again. It was too big to have somehow fit into the box, like it was growing, and yet it was still smaller than she expected, for something that could cause so much destruction. That had put her through hell.

"Winnie! The box!" shouted Apollo, and they threw the bottle of sacred oil at her feet before taking a blow to the face. Their already-battered face was bleeding, and the strike made their head whip back.

Yasmine hurried forward to grab the oil, to help.

Yet Winnie . . . hesitated.

The light from Morning Star was so overwhelming that the moment she looked at it, she couldn't see anything else but white. And black. Light and darkness. Everything and . . . nothing. So loud that she could no longer hear the world breaking apart at her feet. Couldn't feel the burning in her palm, the bleeding beneath it, the exhaustion in her bones. The throbbing of the stab wound through the back of her hand and the cuts on her neck, the pitter-patter of her heart all ceased.

She stared at this star, this unlimited power, the fate of the *world* resting squarely in her hand, and she felt . . . nothing at all.

"Oya dez izj uq egg."

Winnie and her grandmother and grandmother's great-grandmother had been fighting with Cyrus and his grandfather and his grandfather's great-grandfather over *this little thing.* Morning Star. A ball of light. Something so far beyond them that it seemed to bend reality as she held it now.

If she put this star back in the box, what did she have to return to? Her brother was dead. Marcel was gone, and she'd have to return to that house without him and explain to her mother why yet another of their losses was her fault. Why should she have to go home to that? Why would she want to *live* through her mother's anger?

Was she supposed to go on living her life without her big brother, get married, and pop out some kids just for Cyrus's entitled bastard to come along and ruin their lives all over again? To do this again in twenty, forty, sixty years? Was she supposed to prepare another generation of psychics who nobody listened to, nobody cared for, and try to convince them that this all was worth it?

"Zy, xaq oya dez jy hyciqsuzp exyaq uq."

"I can't . . . ," she tried to say, but she wasn't sure who she was talking to, what she was talking about. Tears were running down her face, and she was fighting sharp and shallow breaths she could hardly take.

If she put the star back in the box, she might save the world.

But nobody deserved to be saved. It was her grandmother's fault that she was in this mess for stealing the box in the first place, for burying it where Winnie might one day find it, for bringing the Rathbuns into her wretched life.

It was Apollo's fault for being a coward. For talking all about justice and doing the right thing and being honest and speaking up and trying to convince her that she *could* save them all when she couldn't.

It was Marcel's fault for telling her to ignore it, for following her, for listening to her, for *listening* after so many years of doing the opposite. If he hadn't died, she could have gotten away and Cyrus wouldn't have it, and she wouldn't have had to make this choice at all.

It was her mother's fault for pushing Winnie into this dark hole of doubt and isolation, alone in this madness until she wasn't. Her father's fault for dying, for giving them a reason to doubt and blame Winnie in the first place, for leaving her alone with people who doubted and blamed her. For giving Cyrus something to gripe about instead of letting Theodore Rathbun burn on his own.

And it was Winnie's fault too. For getting cursed in the first place.

If she put this star in the box, Cyrus would still live. He'd walk around free, having killed her brother. Having kissed her and played the pathetic, lonely heir just to lure her here. His greed so deep that nothing but the end of the world could fill it, even while his cousin had sat bleeding on a cold, disgusting floor. His arrogance brought this star into her hands, and Winnie alone could punish him.

"Winnie, put it in the box!" someone shouted, but she couldn't see who. Could hardly hear them over the light, the heat, the call of the abyss it promised.

She only shook her head and said more firmly, "I can't."

Winnie didn't understand why it had to be her who saw the world ending. Why it couldn't have been someone that people cared about, that people listened to. Someone with the actual power to do something. Someone who hadn't been forced to don the cloak of a lamb.

In avoiding her fate, she'd just dragged them all right into it—it was her fault for not fighting the stream hard enough, for laying her head unwillingly on the chopping block, for leading herself kicking and screaming nonetheless to the slaughter.

She was supposed to save a world that didn't give a damn about her, a world that didn't listen to or believe her, but still expected her to deliver salvation—they didn't deserve it.

They all deserved to perish, to hurt like she hurt, like Marcel had been hurt, and when she was done, there would be no more of anything.

And Winnie was so. Damn. Tired. Of trying to save everyone while no one spared her. Of being their mule.

She could put it all to an end now.

Morning Star was growing in her hands, feeding off of her hate, her pain. And staring into it, she saw now that it would grow until the serpent found it, and ate it, and then the serpent, once free, appetite whetted, would look for another star, another light. The stars would both die, and everyone would die, and this rotten place would be no more.

She could do them all a favor.

We don't have to die.

Apollo was wrong for saying that—they did. They would, because the star had rolled into her hand instead of Yasmine's. Because they grabbed it instead of telling Cyrus no and letting her die with her brother.

They were so optimistic, had so much sickening, wasteful *hope* in her that they truly believed they would make it through this. That Marcel would get to walk away. That Winnie wouldn't be at a knife's edge.

They had hope.

They hoped that she would tell them the truth, that she would like them as much as they liked her, that she would save their life. They hoped she wouldn't kiss Cyrus or take his money or lie to them. And they were trying now to win her over with that hope.

"Ahi ci. Giq ci pbyv."

The star was growing bigger and bigger, and Winnie had to cup it with both hands. It was the size of a heart, her heart, and it was going to end them all.

Apollo pressed their hands over hers. Trying to help her bear that weight. Here when they should have been running, praying, calling Artemisia to say their last goodbyes.

"Winona," they whispered, soft, as if they knew why she didn't let go, why she didn't put it away.

Apollo and their soft hands.

Apollo and their soft lips.

Apollo and their soft words.

What was at the bottom of Pandora's box? Apollo and their stupid, dogged *hope*.

That belief that she was better than she was. That she wanted better than they'd ever get. That she could be good, honest, righteous, and do good. That she would protect them at the end of the world.

Apollo.

The star quivered and started to grow again. Something came crashing down around them. It was almost here.

"Wzyv oyab fgedi, guqqgi gecx."

But she wasn't.

Winnie Bray was *not* a fucking lamb.

She clenched her fists instead of letting the star free and told it, "*No.*"

CHAPTER 34

The Call of the Abyss (Remix)

Tightening her fist on the star made some of the light recede. Winnie blinked and watched as the world came back to her, as Rathbun Manor was a trembling, collapsing ruin, as the chasm that cleaved through it was growing wider and wider, destroying the neighboring houses, the street, the city.

And kneeling beside her, holding the box like a proposal, was Apollo, waiting.

Just in case she decided to change her mind and stop this.

"I can't—" she tried to explain now, that the star was fighting her, but she couldn't get it out.

It wanted to expand as she wanted it to compress, and the light and heat of it was searing away her fingers, the blood. Something startled in Apollo as they understood the choice she'd made, that she was here and lucid and fighting back, and they lurched up to try to help. Their hand closed around hers and squeezed until her knuckles cracked. Until she couldn't tell where the pain was coming from, where her hand began and theirs ended.

Light speared through her from the effort. Twinges of pain spiked in her head, her chest, her stomach, but Winnie wouldn't let go. Even if her breaths were frantic now, panting. Even if the noise was so loud, she couldn't hear herself scream.

"Now! Now!"

Apollo took her hand and plunged it into the box, and then

she pried her fingers away. Hesitated only a moment before she pulled back and let them close the lid.

They were hit with sudden darkness. The light's retreat was immediate along with most of its heat, and then she was stumbling back, blinking, struggling to see. The wind stopped, plunging the world into only the quiet rumble of the house.

"Yasmine? Apollo?"

Hands closed around both her arms as Yasmine said in a shaky voice, "I'm here," and Apollo whispered, "I got you."

She stifled a cough. "We have to mark the box with oil and throw it into the abyss. Then it won't come back."

Debris was falling around them, blanketing them in violent snow. The rumble of the earth had calmed a little, but still shook her bones, what was left of the house's foundation. The windows had shattered, littering the broken floor in glass and wood chips and shreds of newspaper used for insulation.

Cyrus was doubled over and sobbing. "What did you *do*?"

A fissure had split the room in two, and they all reared away, fighting against the shakes that might bring the last of Rathbun Manor down on top of them. Apollo propped her against a beam as another cough racked her body.

"Okay, I—where's the oil?" they said, their voice as shaky as she felt.

Yasmine fished around in her pocket for the bottle. "I have it."

They worked fast, shaking the bottle all over the lid, coating it until it was slippery in Winnie's hands, while a bloodied Cyrus, trembling, tried to draw himself to standing. His clothes were grafted to his skin, and the flesh of his face was raw and burned through and smoking in places.

Holding the box, Apollo helped Winnie approach the fissure, and then she chucked it over. It fell silently out of sight. The earthquake was slowing a little, but around them, furniture continued to crash down into the chasm. The floor was still falling away piece by piece, because the earth had been cracking, the foundations of Rathbun Manor carved away, and the fissure still needed to settle.

"No!" Cyrus screamed, lunging for Morning Star and crashing at their feet. His voice was full of anguish, madness, and Winnie turned to see the outline of his shape. The cliff was unsteady, still crumbling, and the sudden force of his fall was enough for the flooring to shift beneath him. Then he was slipping, reaching out for anything. He grabbed Apollo's ankle. "Why would you—!"

Winnie and Yasmine lurched forward to pull Apollo free. They tried to kick out, as Cyrus clung to the fabric of their pants. He who killed her brother for this box. His greed, like his grandfather's greed, had marred her family again with irreparable scars that would forever ache.

"*Know your place, little lamb.*" Winnie bared her teeth.

She lashed out and struck him in the temple, and his fingers faltered for just a moment. He loosened, and Apollo followed up with another kick to break free. And although he'd reached again, wooden planks were sliding away, sweeping out from under Cyrus, taking him over the edge. His scream was piercing and long.

Winnie inched away, Apollo in her grasp, and waited until Cyrus stopped screaming, until she was sure Cyrus wouldn't come back. Then she turned to the collapsed bookcase. "I need to get my brother."

Carefully, they helped her carry Marcel from the rapidly collapsing staircase, out onto the lawn of Rathbun Manor. Sirens wailed some blocks away, and with all the lampposts out, the city was the darkest it had ever been. People stumbled out to fill the streets, calling for help and looking to lend a hand.

Another cough made Winnie double over until it left her gasping for breath. It was hard to right herself, especially when she couldn't stop the scratching feeling in her throat, as if the star was now inside her and scraping to get out. Folded over, she heaved.

Blood spattered the cobblestone walkway.

She tasted iron and tried to sniffle, tried to wipe her nose, but her fingers came back wet with something thin and red. "I don't feel so—"

Her body spasmed again as something forced its way up her throat. More blood, trickling down her chin and slicking the grass. It came in waves, one after another after another, more violent than the last, even as the earthquakes had settled to quiet aftershocks.

"Win?" Yasmine darted from flagging down help in the street.

Winnie was bleeding out, exactly as she'd seen it. Saving everyone else's fate just to fall prey to her own. She lay on the ground, beside her brother's corpse, and pressed her face into the soft grass. It felt like lightning was darting around her insides. Just like in her vision, she rolled onto her back to watch the sky, to know for sure that she'd done it correctly. That at least, if she died, her death wasn't *wasted.* That she died doing something that mattered.

The moon was shifting through the clouds, but there was no serpent undulating behind them. It was whole instead of raining down on them in fiery pieces. Nothing was there to knock it down and chase the sun afterward. Despite the fire raging through her, she felt relieved.

Apollo's face blocked the sight. Sweat slicked green curls to their forehead. "You're going to be okay. Help's coming."

She nodded and squeezed their hand as hard as she could, which wasn't very hard at all. "We did it?"

"We did it."

"We don't have to die," she repeated to herself, aloud, because she didn't want to. She wouldn't—she *refused*. She willed her body to stitch itself together on hope alone.

Winnie wasn't a lamb, and still she'd outsmarted the butcher. She was free.

CHAPTER 35

The Earth Didn't Stitch Itself Shut

The earth didn't stitch itself shut.

At the hospital, doctors and nurses whisked Winnie away, and Yasmine followed, leaving Apollo alone in their bed. Nobody else had followed them here, was waiting and watching over *them*, because there wasn't really anyone to call, even fewer who would pick up. So they sat back against the pillow and stared at the ceiling and tried to rest.

Whatever that meant now.

Between dozing fits, they heard terrified murmurs and footsteps, probably the panic of someone else's loved ones, but then someone called *their* name.

"Apollo!"

Artemisia was the first through the curtain, and she launched herself into their bed. Careless of their injuries, or perhaps she simply couldn't help herself, their other half crawled into their lap, wrapped her arms painfully around their neck, and then squeezed them in the middle. As if she could sense everywhere they hurt and wanted to suffuse it with aching affection.

They shifted uncomfortably. "I'm fine . . ."

"We thought you were dead," she whispered into their hair, her voice shaking, while their younger brother, Orion, who resembled Cyrus even more than Apollo did, sat at the foot of the bed and nodded, eyes wet. "They called and said they found your van destroyed, and then there was the earthquake and . . ."

The rest was unintelligible, but they hazarded a guess.

Apollo didn't tell everyone that Cyrus tried to kill them, because they didn't see the point. It was better to leave him and Morning Star buried, and they weren't good at holding grudges anyway.

Their parents, the great judge and her indomitable husband, remained standing until finally their mother forced Artemisia off of Apollo. Then she located some administrator to annoy, insisting that she was Apollo's mother, their guardian, and she needed to speak to a doctor immediately about their care.

Even if none of them called it what it was, it was plain relief on everyone's faces. On Apollo's, because their family needed them alive. The relief of them being alive, Cyrus be damned, was stronger than any disapproval, misunderstanding, or frustration their family had at what Apollo might have done. Nobody understood the box, the war with Cyrus that involved police, but they were in one piece at least, and that was enough for their parents to work with. Painfully imperfect, but it showed that their parents *did* plan to work through it at some point.

So the relief was bittersweet, to have family, knowing Apollo would keep them at arm's length.

After their discharge, Apollo picked up Winnie's shifts at the Red Hourglass for something to do. They didn't pretend to be psychic, but they knew their way around the shop, and the old woman who owned it—Hortense—was grateful for the help. She didn't ask *how* Apollo knew, instead only offering a knowing glance the way old ladies did. So they spent their mornings lounging on Winnie's hospital bed, pretending to study for their GED exam when they were really studying her, and then they went to work to feel less . . . aimless.

For something to do, another apocalypse to avert.

Winnie said that she wasn't going back to the shop anyway. She didn't want to tell fortunes to strangers, even if she didn't know *where* she'd go next. She'd confessed it one day while Apollo was watching her face for changes—any sign of paleness, dizziness, unfocused eyes that said she might start coughing blood again.

Acute radiation sickness, they were told, but she would be fine. They caught it early, and the exposure was low.

And so Apollo watched for that now just like they watched her smiles and her frowns, watched her sleep and mumble as she dreamed.

Winnie awoke in a hospital, surrounded by beeping machines, even though she didn't remember falling asleep. The first thing she saw was light, and she had flinched in fear that Morning Star was back, that none of it was over, but then she'd started retching: There was a breathing tube down her throat.

Her body had felt like it had been smashed to fine pieces with a hammer and then reconstructed shard by painstaking shard. However, it was undeniable that she *was* whole. And in too much pain to not be alive. She followed the penlight that was put in front of her face, she recited her name and her address. She didn't know the date, but it turned out that she'd been asleep for days. The last thing she remembered was stumbling out of the ruins of Rathbun Manor. Lying down to rest beside Marcel.

Afraid to face her mother.

Her mother passed long hours at her bedside, reading or sleeping. Sometimes she went to fetch *good* food so that Winnie would eat and get her strength back. She brought books to read and homework from Kavanaugh and pretended to be stern about Winnie getting it all done, even though Winnie spent most of her time sleeping.

She forgot how much she loved to sleep.

Throughout her recovery, however, her mother's eyes didn't lose their haunted look. Even as she smoothed down Winnie's hair and scolded her about her impatience in wanting to get out, even when Yasmine came to visit, and they just sat and talked. Even when the doctor came and finally told Winnie that she'd be getting discharged soon if she kept progressing—

Marcel was a ghost that hung around Winnie.

She'd tried to explain the box to her mother after she woke up. That there was a star inside, that it summoned the earthquakes that the city was trying to grapple with, and there was something trying to escape the earth. She tried to explain that Cyrus Rathbun was greedy, greedier than they expected, and that people weren't worth anything if he couldn't have his power. It was Winnie's knife he used, because Winnie brought Marcel there to help.

Her brother made her run first with the box, hoping she'd be safe, as big brothers did.

Hoping.

If it wasn't for Marcel, they would all be dead. Everything would be ruined. His death saved people; also, he should be alive.

And her mother nodded through it all, though it seemed that she left her body toward the end, like it was too much to handle. She didn't call Winnie a liar, which Winnie had braced for, probably because the star was as preposterous as losing Marcel. Or maybe her mother finally believed her. Either way he was gone, so why couldn't the devouring light and its serpent be any more real? They each pretended not to notice the other looking at the door as if Marcel would walk in at any second.

Still, Winnie felt her mother crawling into her hospital bed one night, an arm wrapped around her, and whispering into her pillow, "It's not your fault, Winnie. It's okay."

The earth didn't stitch itself shut, but Winnie was starting to. Her family, without Marcel, was a mess of sutures, but it was together. So she'd stay in Buffalo, her home, to keep it that way.

Then one day, Apollo strolled into her room, sunglasses and a big, sugary, *decaffeinated* drink in hand, while she was in the middle of doing math proofs. Pretending to do math proofs even though her eyes were glazing over. They'd told her she might have trouble concentrating, and indeed she did, or perhaps a hospital room with codes and visitors and a paper gown for clothing wasn't the best circumstances *for* concentration.

Even in their brother's shapeless sportswear, Apollo still looked cool, back to their old self. The scar under their cheek had healed nicely. Their eyebrows danced as they approached, swishing the drink for her to take.

"I hear you're getting discharged tomorrow," they said casually, calmly, as if they weren't hanging around her every day anyway.

Winnie nodded and claimed her treat. "I heard that too."

"That's good, because I *also* heard that Kavanaugh has a senior winter formal coming up. Just in time." They sat on the edge of her bed, and the way that the words *senior winter formal* rolled off their tongue made her heart stutter.

Her eyes narrowed. "Who told you that?"

Apollo grinned. Which obviously meant that it was Yasmine.

She shook her head. "Well, I told that very same person long ago that I wasn't going. I don't have any interest in hanging out in some sweaty ballroom with a bunch of people in formal wear."

"Not even if I were to go?" They raised a dark brow in challenge, and her insides did a flip in response.

Her jaw trembled with the effort to betray her. It *didn't* sound appealing, she reminded herself, no matter how sweet they tried to make it sound. She was too busy for formals, too different. She shook her head again, slow and very rigid. "Nope."

This only made Apollo's grin widen. They leaned in close, enough that she could smell the cinnamon and mint of their toothpaste, see the specks of toffee and forest green in their eyes, which inevitably drew her gaze to their lips and thoughts of how little she could kiss them in this wretched place.

If she couldn't focus enough to do math proofs, they certainly didn't have the privacy for anything else.

"So, if I asked you to Kavanaugh's Senior Winter Formal, which would surely annoy the school administrators who expelled me, you'd refuse?" Their thumb brushed her bare calf, and Winnie tried not to melt. To break into a million particles in the air. She still couldn't read them, so the contact burned in a carnal way, a heady sensation that raced through her as she tried to hold her ground.

She could feel her brother's ghost hovering, grinning, urging her to go.

Winnie stared at Apollo, at their hideous, awful, obscene green hair, which would look offensive among the Kavanaugh crowd, and said in a low voice, "Why don't you ask me for real, and I'll tell you?"

Apollo's eyes glittered at that. "Will you take me to your formal, Winona?"

Was this the game they were playing? If so, she'd play it every day until the world ended.

"Yes, I think I saw it in your future."

CHAPTER 36

Uq Veuqh

Uz qsi bauzh vsibi Vuzyze Xbeo gilq ci, uq uh jebw ezj mauiq ezj icfqo

guwi hfedi.

Egyzi U veuq

ezj veuq

ezj veuq

azqug hyciyzi ziv luzjh qsiub veo qy ci, ezj yzi jeo U ceo epeuz qbo qy liehq.

Qy dyzmaib.

Qy jihqbyo.

Qsi guqqgi hiib ceo seki gilq ci sibi, egyzi, xaq qsibi uh egveoh hyciyzi ziv.

QSI IZJ (THE END)

Acknowledgments

The threads of fate that tie Winnie and Apollo took a city's worth of people to untangle. As always, I thank my partner G, my agent Jennifer March Soloway, my editor Jess Harold, and Luna the cat for trusting my (at times incoherent) vision.

This book would not be where it is without friends like Sabrina Estudillo Butler and Thais Carreira Afonso, and I would not be writing these acknowledgments at all without my Helsinki gang for getting me away from my desk and keeping me sane.

Of course, I owe all of this to people like JXJ and Karín, Bethany and so many more who helped make fond memories of my city; my mother and grandmother, both of my aunts, and all my cousins who make Buffalo a place worth returning to and family a frustrating but rewarding centerpiece; whoever at Spot Coffee invented cinco shakes, because you singlehandedly got me through high school; and the City of Good Neighbors for the rich and colorful history that I got to embellish but also grow up in.

About the Author

Jamison Shea (they/them) is an Ignyte Award–winning author of dark fantasy and horror novels. Their first book, *I Feed Her to the Beast and the Beast Is Me,* was called "relentlessly gory and almost euphoric in its embrace of the horrific" by NPR. Hailing from Buffalo, New York, and now dwelling in the dark forests of Finland, they drink milk tea and search for eldritch horrors in uncanny places when they are not writing.